SIGNATURE WOUNDS

ALSO BY KIRK RUSSELL

Ben Raveneau Mysteries

A Killing in China Basin

Counterfeit Road

One Through the Heart

The John Marquez Mysteries

Shell Games

Night Game

Dead Game

Redback

Die-Off

SIGNATURE WOUNDS

KIRK RUSSELL

THOMAS & MERCER

Text copyright © 2017 by Kirk Russell
All rights reserved.

Published by Thomas & Mercer, Seattle

www.apub.com

Amazon, the Amazon logo, and Thomas & Mercer are trademarks of Amazon.com, Inc., or its affiliates.

ISBN-13: 9781503942714
ISBN-10: 1503942716

Cover design by Cyanotype Book Architects

Printed in the United States of America

For Susan Berry

Saturday, June 17th

The plane was a well-cared-for Cessna 182T owned by a retired American couple. Their bodies lay on the airstrip at their ranch in Mexico as their plane flew west toward an orange sunset. The pilot had done other work for the cartel and was reliable, though disturbed by the casual execution he'd just watched. His passenger seemed unaffected. As they entered US airspace, the pilot made the planned emergency call, reported engine trouble, and landed at a private airfield in the Imperial Valley.

Two vehicles were waiting. Two said the passenger was important. The pilot got another look at him as the man climbed out, but knew not to look too long or hard. He turned the plane and took off again, skimming dark fields, then circling and climbing ahead of the mountains. The plane was his. That was the agreement, and he already had a buyer. He needed to forget about the old man shielding his wife before they were shot. *Deliver the plane,* he thought, *get a clean hotel room, and then go down to the bar and drink.* He liked the hotel bar and they knew him. At the bar he would forget what he had seen today.

On the ground, there was no waiting. The cars pulled away, and only the passenger looked back. He watched for a flash of white light. It came as the plane reached four thousand feet, crossing mountains at the edge of the valley. Like heat lightning, it was there only a moment, then gone, but in his head he saw more. He saw the plane shatter and the pieces falling, twisting and turning, tumbling in darkness.

1

Jeremy Beatty hesitated when he opened his trailer door and saw me, then stepped outside and pulled the door shut, keeping the cool air inside. He was dressed for the heat, wearing sandals, shorts, and a gray T-shirt with blue letters reading *United States Air Force* arced across the chest. In sunlight, his face looked older than thirty-one years. His clothes looked slept in. But the gunfighter eyes were there, and that's what I was looking for. I didn't need or want an apology.

"I sent that text last night, then crashed," Beatty said. "I was drinking. Sorry I didn't get back to you today, Grale."

"I thought you were done with late-night drinking."

"I am."

"Okay, so what happened last night?"

"Some bad news, and I kind of lost it."

In truth, it was none of my business what he did with his nights, yet I had something of a mentoring role with Beatty.

"When I got home yesterday, two Air Force Office of Special Investigations officers were waiting here. They're working with the Department of Defense on a joint investigation. Supposedly, the drones I test-flew in Taiwan last February were built from stolen plans. They told me I should have known and reported it. Grale, I had no friggin' clue. They want me to wear a wire and set up a meeting with the guy who hired us."

Air Force OSI working with DOD to scare Beatty into wearing a wire sounded like an idea cooked up in a joint meeting. I could make a call or two and find out, but for the moment I was just relieved he was okay.

I didn't see Beatty often anymore; I took in the changes, but also what hadn't changed. His hair was still cut high and tight, as if he'd never left the air force. Lines etching the corners of his eyes were deeper. Beatty had gone from a go-to drone pilot in the Creech Air Force Base flight trailers to living alone and struggling with PTSD while kickstarting a drone consulting business.

"Did the Taiwan work come through that job broker Eddie Bahn?" I asked.

"It all still comes through Eddie. He rips me off, but he gets me work. For now, it's what I've got."

He moved farther out on the deck and said, "When I got on the plane to go to Taiwan, I swear, Grale, I thought, 'This is made up. This can't be.' They sent me first-class tickets. I've never sat in first class in my life. I kept thinking, 'This isn't for you, dude, something is wrong here.'"

"What did you think when you got there?"

He smiled and said, "It was pretty cool to fly halfway across the world and get paid to fly drones. It made me feel like everything was going to turn out fine after all. The drones in some ways were like the Predators I used to fly, but that's just the way it is. Everyone is stealing from us. Everyone wants a drone program. Anyway, that's what happened last night. That's where that text came from, but I'm not suicidal. No bullshit, Grale. I don't have those thoughts anymore. Hey, you must be on your way to the party. Sorry about the text, and I owe you for stopping by. Have fun tonight."

That was my cue to leave for my sister and brother-in-law's Fourth of July party. I was ready to kick back and have a cold beer and hang with my sister, Melissa, and brother-in-law, Jim, but I wasn't leaving yet. Black plastic was taped over the windows of Beatty's trailer. A militaresque *BLDG J* was stenciled in red paint to the right of the front door. The plastic could be about blocking sunlight. The *BLDG J* was troubling. Beatty saw me looking at it.

"I'll clean it off today," he said. "I was drunk."

"What's it about?"

"Honestly, I don't even fucking remember."

Jim and Melissa were my connection to Beatty. Jim is an air force drone pilot stationed at Creech and an old friend of mine. He married my sister twenty years ago and went from a B-52 squadron in Idaho to the drone flight trailers at Creech. Melissa, Jim, and their two kids, Nate and Julia, are all I have left for family. We're close. Melissa and I laugh a lot. We try to get together once a week, and every year Melissa and Jim throw a Fourth of July party for Creech drone pilots and friends. That list of friends includes Jeremy Beatty. Always will, Jim says. It was Jim who'd asked me to help Beatty when he was spiraling down after his discharge. Jim knew how I'd fought my way back to active duty at the FBI.

"Hey, I might have gone to the party tonight," Beatty said. "But I can't, because I've got a new job starting tomorrow. I'm moving out to the airfield tonight. I'd just finished packing when you knocked."

"Good about the job. Where is it?"

"In bumfuck nowhere, dude. Way out in the desert, north of Indian Wells and off to the west on Bureau of Land Management land leased from the government. I'll text you directions. The company that hired us does mining-assay work and is switching over to drones. They put an airfield out there and some trailers. I'll be teaching drone pilots, probably guys good at Xbox who've never flown a plane. If it goes well, it could become a long-term thing. I'm hoping for that."

He drifted back toward his door and again waited for me to say good-bye. Instead, I asked, "Got anything cold to drink inside?"

"I drank all the beer last night, so no, unless you count Diet Coke."

"Coke is fine."

"Naw, dude, take off, go have fun."

"I'm here. I haven't seen you in a while. Let's talk some more."

"Okay, come on in, but don't go all FBI on me."

"Meaning what?"

"I did some remodeling."

I followed him into the shadowed cool and looked around at the gutted interior of the trailer. I didn't get it. The trailer was leased. It would cost some serious money to restore.

"I was trying to get the feel of a Creech flight trailer. I want to be in that space in my head as I teach."

"You ripped out your kitchen and half of everything else to make a flight trailer?"

He didn't answer, and I let it be. Whatever it cost him in repairs was his problem. I looked at a small drone in the corner. Quadrocopter. Like the thing the Florida mailman landed on the White House lawn.

"What do you do with that drone?"

"Lately I'm taking videos. I'm under surveillance. They've got four people on me, maybe more. I thought it was the CIA watching me before the OSI officers showed up last night."

"The CIA here in Wunderland Trailer Park?"

"I know it sounds batshit crazy."

It did.

"It's about a drone strike we made before they booted me out. Talk to Jim, he'll know exactly what I'm talking about." He looked over. "Our orders were to never talk about it."

His face fell as he said that. It was emotional for him and discouraging for me. I felt a weary sadness that after all his struggles with post-traumatic stress disorder and getting a new career and life going again, Beatty imagined the CIA watching him. The intensity and focus in his face conjured memories of him after his fiancée, Laura, finally gave up. At that time, he wasn't getting any help from the VA either. His first Veterans Administration appointment had still been nine months away when his fellow pilots stepped in. But by then he was down to where he was questioning even his close friends. He was restless, angry, and drinking hard, his thoughts twisted by paranoia. No, it was worse than that. He'd lost interest in the future. He didn't care anymore.

That's when Jim had approached me and said, "He might listen to you, Paul. His friends are burned out on his relapses."

I said I'd try. I could feel for ex-Lieutenant Jeremy Beatty. He'd signed up with the air force at twenty-one, became a drone pilot, and the air force became his family. After his discharge and after Laura left, he was alone with little to look forward to. I liked to think I'd helped him see a way through, but looking around here, I saw what vanity that idea was. Maybe it was just a way of covering my guilt at not having seen him much in the last year.

I remembered a night when he'd pulled a Glock 17 out of a drawer and stuck the barrel in his mouth before I could move. And all the middle-of-the-night text messages and alcohol-fogged despondency had worn me down, same as his friends. I tried, but I hadn't really made any difference. That was more like the truth, or what it felt like, looking at what he'd done here.

Two bedsheets hanging from the ceiling separated his "flight trailer" from his bedroom and bath. In here, the only place left to sit was a worn tan Barcalounger, similar to what drone pilots sat in when Beatty worked in a Creech Air Force Base flight trailer. In front of the Barcalounger was a table with three computer screens. Beneath the table was a stack of white Styrofoam fast-food containers. A chair, a table, three computer screens, and a rat's ass swamp-cooler air conditioner rattling away.

"This your work station now?"

"This is it."

"Does it give you the feel you were after?"

He wouldn't answer that, but he said, "Try out a program while I get the Cokes. A friend modified some software for me. Use the push pedals to fly the drone, but don't freak out over the targeting. It's a simulation. It's chill. Don't worry. We had to pick places to aim at, and with the GPS settings, these are easiest."

"I'm not sure what you mean by that, but okay."

I sat down on the Barcalounger and reached for the mouse as Beatty went for the Cokes. A map of the US lit up, and I clicked on DC. Drone flight time to get there registered in the upper-right corner of the screen. So did distance to target. I changed the city to Las Vegas and heard a refrigerator door shut. Distance to Vegas was ninety-two miles. Not a long flight at all. Inside of an hour. Completely doable.

The bedsheets fluttered as Beatty returned and asked, "Where's the Fourth of July party this year?"

"At Alagara, but you must know that."

"Oh, yeah, right, the Alagara, I forgot. I like that place. Their fish tacos are killer."

"The tacos are gone. The guy that started Alagara was going under and sold it. The new owner uses the building for party rentals."

Beatty handed me a cold can of Diet Coke and took a long drink from his before saying, "Hard to picture Captain Kern celebrating the Fourth inside a building."

"Two of the kids in the group had trouble with the heat last year, so they're trying this out. And they got a great price."

"Your sister probably negotiated that."

"She did."

I picked Seattle as my next target while Beatty worked around to telling me about this secret drone strike that Jim allegedly knew about and the air force had hushed up.

"Since you're hanging around, Grale, I'll show you some video I shot with the drone in the corner. It'll be quick, and you can walk out the door anytime you want."

"Okay, show me, and then tell me about this drone strike no one can talk about."

"It made national news. It got talked about plenty for about two minutes. It's the officers who were there who are not supposed to talk."

I leaned back in the creaky Barcalounger as Beatty slid a flash drive into his laptop. He spun the laptop around and slid it to me. I tapped the arrow and played a three-minute black-and-white video the little drone took from three hundred feet above Wunderland Trailer Park.

The lens zoomed in on two cars sitting around the backside of the pink laundry building, a man in one car, a woman in the other. They might have been unmarked police vehicles, but it was hard to tell. The woman got into the passenger seat of the man's car and was there a couple of minutes before she got out and drove away. There wasn't enough there to draw any conclusions.

"I can't tell who they are," I said. "Maybe they were there to repair the slot machines in the laundry."

"Those got fixed. I won twenty bucks yesterday."

"Show me more video. Show me time stamps. Show me the same people on different days."

"You got it."

I watched two more, and Beatty looked expectant, but I couldn't draw any conclusions.

After a silence, Beatty said, "I met this therapist in a bar last year. We were drinking and talking for a couple of hours. She told me the only way to get rid of things is to talk about them. If the air force wants to come down on me, they can, but I'm through being quiet. Do you remember a twenty-four-year-old schoolteacher from New York named Hakim Salter, who was killed in one of our drone strikes in Pakistan in 2013? He made it into the news, but as a bad guy."

"Sure, I remember."

I also remembered talking with other agents about it. The official version made you wonder what had really happened.

9

"I launched the missile that killed Salter. In Afghanistan the drone strikes were military, but in Pakistan they were CIA. The CIA had their own drones, but they used us to fly them. They wouldn't tell us shit, but they always thanked us for killing their targets. Very polite that way."

Salter's mother was a Pakistani who had married an American decades ago and moved to New York. Her twenty-four-year-old son, Hakim, got it in his head to go teach school in the village where she was born. Taliban came through, but did so without killing or kidnapping Salter, and that got the CIA wondering what was up with that. Allegedly, Salter conspired or aided Taliban soldiers, but as far as I knew, no evidence was ever offered. That was the game nowadays. If you lack evidence, you make allusions and let imagination and fear go to work. Innuendo stands in for truth.

Officially, Hakim Salter was unlucky collateral damage in a drone strike on Taliban terrorists. Off the record, a different story was leaked to quiet the media. That version said Salter's pilgrimage to his mother's birthplace was far from innocent. Those whispers inflamed the family. They went to the *New York Times* and found an ambitious reporter who was interested enough, and for a news cycle or two, the *NYT* reporter's article on Salter's death was national news.

"I was on trigger, ready to go, but they made us wait until the kid came back into the courtyard."

"They wanted you to wait for Salter?"

"You got it. We circled and waited. I saw his mom crying on CNN. She said he was over there staying with her relatives and was friendly to Taliban fighters so they wouldn't kill him. Maybe they would have or kidnapped him, but I'm pretty sure he was there trying to do good. I took him out with a badass missile called Special K. That's what fucked me up, Grale. No, that's not what did me, but it was the one that put me over. Those Taliban were my last recorded kills. Up the chain they would have counted Salter, too, if they could have."

"Salter was in the wrong place at the wrong time."

"I know you, G-man, you don't believe that shit. Bottom line is, we took out an American without any real proof of anything, and I compromised myself."

"Come on, you lived with collateral damage for a long time."

"Hakim Salter wasn't collateral damage. He got wasted because it was convenient. They had questions about him, and taking him out was easier than keeping track of him. Check it out with Phil Ramer if you don't believe me."

"I don't know a Phil Ramer. Who is he?"

"An Aussie pilot we were training. He was on sensor, meaning he was operating the laser targeting. It's how a launch works. Ask Captain Kern tonight what really happened."

Beatty pulled the flash drive out of the laptop and handed it to me.

"There's more tape of surveillance here on this."

"I'll watch it."

I slipped the memory stick into my pocket and walked out to my car. From the deck railing, Beatty called, "Happy Fourth of July, G-man! I'm buying dinner at that steak place next time I see you. I'll call you."

When I turned onto North Las Vegas Boulevard I was less than fifteen minutes from the Alagara. I could easily have waited until the party to talk with Jim about Hakim Salter, or taken it up another day and left the holiday a holiday, but I brought up Jim's number and called.

2

"Where are you, bud? Melissa just asked me to find you."

Jim laughed. He liked the idea of my older sister locking in on me. He probably visualized a target.

"She's saying you promised to make it on time this year."

"I'm ten minutes from you. I had to make a stop. Save me a beer."

"What stop could be more important than this party?"

Jim sounded upbeat. I heard laughter and voices in the background, the party well under way.

"I checked on Beatty. He sent me a suicide text last night."

"And you texted back and left him messages and didn't hear from him today, so you stopped by."

"That's about right. I just left Wunderland."

"You're his backstop. He knows you'll check on him. It's time to break the cycle. I hear his business is working, and he's making good money." After a beat he added, "You know he's invited to this party."

"Yeah, he said he would have come this year but has a new job starting in the morning."

"That's bullshit."

"It's pride. He doesn't want to stand around with pilots he flew with and chat about teaching farmers how to fly agricultural drones."

"Whatever. He needs to get over it. They're still his friends. It's time to leave that refugee camp he lives in."

Wunderland was home to indigent workers living five and six to a trailer. It also housed parolees and aging retirees whose monthly checks often came up short. The retirees made do by skipping meals and leaving the heat and air conditioning off. You could move into Wunderland and just about disappear, which was Jim's real point.

But Jeremy had once told me something simple and different about why he lived there. He said Wunderland was the only place he could afford where he could walk outside and be looking at nothing but blue sky and mountains. He loved the desert sky. I thought about that a moment then pushed forward.

"Jeremy told me a story tonight about his discharge that I hadn't heard."

"Oh, no, here we go."

"Do you remember a twenty-four-year-old American schoolteacher named Hakim Salter who was killed in a Pakistani village in a drone strike?"

"Beatty talked to you about Salter?"

"He just did, but also said his orders were never talk to anyone."

Jim was quiet, then said, "They were and it didn't happen the way Beatty says it did."

"I haven't told you what he said yet."

"You don't have to. I've talked enough with him about it. There were much worse drone strikes. Beatty had almost a thousand kills. I don't know why he had so much trouble with that one. The Salter kid shouldn't have been there to begin with. He was told not to go. Hell, the State Department contacted the family and warned them the area was too dangerous."

"Beatty told me the strike was delayed until Salter walked back outside into the courtyard."

When Jim spoke again his voice was slower, and the upbeat note he'd answered the phone with was gone.

"The targets were in a courtyard and Salter walked *into* the house and *then* and *only then* was the go given. Not before. There was no long delay, and as you know, pilots don't make the call. It's made above us. We know it's not always right. Like everything else in life, mistakes get made. With drone strikes, the order comes and you execute. You don't second-guess. It's not our decision. In fact, some of the officers giving the orders think they should get the kill, not the pilot. The pompous fucks really believe that, but nothing is like pressing the trigger. What happened to Jeremy wasn't about Hakim Salter. It was about being on trigger one time too many."

"He said that tonight. The Salter strike was the one that put him over the top."

"Well, there you go, from the man himself in his own words. He's starting to see it."

"Were you there for the strike that killed Hakim Salter?"

"Was I in the same flight trailer? No, I wasn't in the trailer, but after Jeremy had his breakdown I was briefed. When Salter came back out into the courtyard of the house, the missile was already in the air. It was too late."

"So he was in the courtyard and went inside, and they thought he'd stay inside?"

Jim sighed. This was the absolute last thing he wanted to do right now, but I'd spent a year and a half trying to help Beatty without ever hearing about this. Why was that?

"They had followed and tracked these Taliban guys for months, Grale. Finally all of them were together in the courtyard. That's when the go was given."

"That's what you got from your briefing?"

"Yes."

"Beatty tells a different version."

"No kidding, but what I just told you actually happened. Look, I'll see you when you get here."

"All right, and I'm not far away. Sorry to do this to you—one last question and it's a quick one. Do you know a Phil Ramer? Beatty told me Ramer was an Aussie pilot on sensor and that I should talk to him."

"You should talk to him?"

"That's what he said."

"Why should you talk to Ramer? You're not investigating. The launch was investigated and it's done. I don't know why Beatty is back on this."

"Maybe he never left it."

"Ramer was on sensor. He shipped home right after, so if you want to find him, look in Australia. But why are you digging into this? That strike has already been analyzed every which way, and nothing is going to change."

I didn't answer fast enough, and Jim said, "Hey, your sister is helping the Hullabaloo driver carry the cake in and she's waving at me. I need to go take over for her. There are five or six kids here waiting for it, and then we're going to boogie over to the casinos to watch fireworks. I'll throw a burger on the grill for you."

He broke the connection, and I turned onto Lake Mead Boulevard with more questions than answers about the Salter strike. What followed was a string of red lights that delayed me even more, but the Alagara was only about a mile away. I'd be there soon.

In the distance the higher glass on buildings reflected orange-red, and looking at that last light and the Fourth of July evening coming on, I started to unwind. I had promised Melissa I'd be on time this year, but she of all people would understand about Beatty. My sister had great patience for those with wounds to the psyche.

Truth was, I also thought Beatty needed to get on with life. He wasn't the first soldier diagnosed with PTSD. People figure it out and deal with it, right? You don't hole up in a run-down trailer park, complain about the air force, and drink yourself to sleep at night while you circle the same spot over and over.

At the next red light, a tricolor Hullabaloo party van heading in the opposite direction was stopped, waiting for the light to change. I looked across the intersection at the van and the driver, probably the guy who'd delivered the cake to the party. He was on his cell talking, but glanced over when he felt me watching.

When the light changed and I pulled forward, a hard, deep sound paralyzed me. It was distant, not close, and yet I felt the blast pressure wave pass through as a voice in me screamed, *Take cover!* My foot slipped off the accelerator. I drifted into the intersection, and the guy behind me was patient until he saw me looking up at the sky. He honked, swerved past, and in that moment I was everything an FBI agent shouldn't be. But I found the smoke. I saw a black column rising and hit the gas pedal hard.

I drove toward it, but why were my hands trembling? Wasn't I over all that? Shouldn't I be? Was I weak? As I oriented on the smoke, I called Jim. The explosion must have been close to the Alagara. Jim would be outside figuring it out. He'd have a better view.

"Come on, Jim, pick up. I'm not calling about Beatty."

Acrid smoke was drawn into my car as I closed in. A quarter mile ahead, a brown Toyota Camry was stopped in the road near the Alagara, its male driver standing outside with his door open and a cell phone pressed against his ear as he looked toward the Alagara. I drove around him, looked over, and my gut wrenched. Smoke streamed from the Alagara roof. The big lot between the bar and street was carpeted with blast debris. Doors and windows were blown out. The front door had cartwheeled into the lot. I knew what I was looking at and called 911 as my car crunched through glass. I popped the trunk lid as a 911 operator came on.

"This is FBI Special Agent Paul Grale. There's been an explosion." I gave her the intersection just to my left. I didn't have the Alagara address, but they couldn't miss the smoke. "We need a full response."

"Special Agent Grale, we have another report of this as a fireworks cache explosion. Can you confirm that? Can you tell me how many are injured, and if there are burn injuries? Is there a fire?"

"I don't see fire. I don't have a count yet. There's a great deal of blast debris surrounding the building, and there may be twenty-five or more people inside. I was on my way to a Fourth of July party here and think those numbers are close. Anyone inside is injured. We need a full response. I'm going in. Stay with me. Stay on the phone."

I pulled gear from the trunk and yelled at two young guys getting out of a car. "FBI. Over here, I need your help."

They started toward me as I said to the 911 operator, "About a dozen inside are military drone pilots stationed at Creech Air Force Base. Notify the air force but stay with me, okay? I'm on my way in."

I had two gas masks and gave those to the two guys. "Put them on. One of you bring the second flashlight, one of you carry the first aid kit. Follow me! Let's go. Right now, come on!"

We stepped over a twisted metal window frame and entered the smoke. The hole in the roof was venting it, but visibility was still poor. I coughed, wiped my eyes, and then saw how bad it really was. Bomb debris was pushed up against all exterior walls. I stepped over a torn bleeding torso coated in dust.

One of the young guys said something I couldn't hear through his mask, and I answered, "We're looking for anyone alive."

The 911 operator heard that. Her voice deepened and softened as she said, "Give me your best estimate of the number of injured and types of wounds, Agent Grale. Make a rough count. With fireworks, there are almost always burn victims."

I heard her but from a distance. My training saved me. It brought me back. It kept what I feared just far enough away.

"I work bomb makers," I said. "I'm a special agent bomb tech. I work with the Critical Incident Response Group at headquarters in DC. I'm on the FBI Domestic Terrorism Squad. I'm telling you a bomb exploded in here. There are at least fifteen dead. We're moving in deeper."

"Sir, did you say bomb?"

I was several moments before answering yes, and sent one of the two with me back outside after he vomited in his mask. Then I lay my phone down and knelt in a pool of blood and moved debris off a body I recognized. I couldn't talk, couldn't find words, or even accept what I was seeing. I touched Melissa's still-warm face. I cradled my sister's lifeless head and wept.

3

In the men's room was a boy with a compound fracture of the right arm so severe I was afraid moving him would do more harm than good. The bone had torn through his shirt. He was trapped by debris and, with whatever other wounds he had, was slipping into shock. We freed him as the air filled with sirens. Outside the restrooms were two more children. The first was a young girl with a broken neck who was dead. The other was my fifteen-year-old niece, Julia, alive and injured. I talked to Julia and reassured her, but she didn't recognize me. I took her hand.

"Julia, it's Uncle Paul. Hold on. Fight with everything you have. Hold on, Julia! Ambulances are here. We're getting you to a hospital. Fight, Julia, fight, I'm right here with you. You can do this. Can you hear me?"

I thought for a moment she realized it was me, but I wasn't sure. "Julia?"

A first responder yelled, "Agent Grale!"

"Back here!"

A fire captain in fluorescent suit and helmet and carrying a bright light came toward me.

"We've got it in here. You need to call in. Your office is looking for you. What happened here?"

"A bombing."

I waited until Julia and the boy in the men's restroom were on backboards and had paramedics over them. First responders worked the bar area looking for survivors, but there weren't any. Among the dead was my nephew, Nate, a gangling teenager who'd been closing in on his dad in height. I knelt and touched his face.

Outside was chaotic with sirens and lights. I called my supervisor, Dan Venuti, who heads the Las Vegas Field Office Domestic Terrorism Squad. It was very hard to hear, so I got in my car where it was quieter. Moments later, Venuti patched me into a conference call with the counterterrorism desk in Washington.

Someone there asked, "How confident are you that it was a bomb, Agent Grale? Gas explosion, fireworks, can you rule those out?"

"They're out. It was a bomb and a large one."

"Air force drone pilots are among the dead?"

"Yes."

"Are you certain of that?"

This was difficult to answer. I hesitated, and the question was repeated: "Are you certain?"

"My sister and brother-in-law throw the party every year. He's air force. He was a drone pilot. He manages drone pilots now, or did. I recognized several other dead pilots. My sister, brother-in-law, and nephew are dead. I was on my way here to the party. I was late or would have been inside."

I tried to be clear and accurate, though it felt as if I were speaking from somewhere very distant. I felt separated and torn inside, yet was trying to focus. I felt both terrible grief and something bordering on hate. I would find who had done this.

Venuti broke in saying, "Creech has officers inbound. They're twenty minutes away."

The voice from Washington came back with another question. "What about secondary explosives?"

"There's a line of For Sale vehicles along the front of the lot, so yes, there's a real risk," I said.

Four minutes later, the conference call ended. Venuti called me within seconds and said, "Las Vegas Metro has a bomb squad on the way. Ours is just leaving. Domestic Terrorism and two evidence-recovery squads leave the field office in the next fifteen minutes. ATF says they have a team en route. Tell me where this should go, Grale."

"To a focus on secondary explosives," I said.

"Las Vegas PD is talking fireworks explosion. You're certain it was a bomb."

I paused, wondering why I wasn't getting through. "Are you asking if I'm thinking clearly?"

"Your family—"

"Dan, we're not looking at Fourth of July fireworks. This was a bomb placed under the bar. It was in something, possibly an appliance. There are metal shards. The explosive may have been C-4." I took a steadying breath. "A dozen or more drone pilots were in there. These are guys flying in the Mideast. Get everything up, fusion center, everyone. Everybody. Every agency in Washington."

I looked through the windshield at the destroyed face of the building as I remembered Jim many years ago, smiling when he said Melissa was pregnant. I continued with Venuti.

"We need a bomb squad checking out the For Sale vehicles at the end of the lot," I said. "That's my highest priority here, and I need agents. Send everyone you can. We need the first responder vehicles out of here. We need to establish a perimeter. Let's coordinate with Las Vegas Metro and cordon off ten blocks and search.

"There are apartment or condo buildings across and down the street with a good view. I'm looking at them right now. Whoever detonated this could be there. I was a mile away on Lake Mead when it went off. Could have been someone on a balcony there watching. A cake arrived when I was on the phone with my brother-in-law, Captain Jim Kern. The driver that dropped the cake may have passed by me going the other way. I saw a Hullabaloo van. That driver may have been the last one inside." I paused, gathered myself, then said, "Text me as our bomb squad rolls."

"You're not staying."

"The fuck I'm not. I'm not leaving here. I'm a material witness and the best we have for bombings."

"You're leaving."

"My sister and brother-in-law and nephew are dead in there. There's no way I'm leaving."

"I'm ordering you to come in."

"I'm telling you, I'm not leaving."

"There are other issues I'll explain in here."

"Explain now or come here. I can't leave."

"Jane Stone is on her way. Brief her, and she'll take charge of the scene. Then come in, and we'll get you back out there as fast as we can."

"I'm not leaving."

"Grale, listen, we've got a problem we can only solve in here. We've just been contacted by the Department of Defense. This is non-negotiable."

"Talk to me. What's the problem?"

"I can't stay on the phone. I've got calls stacked up. You're getting pulled temporarily because of a former drone pilot you were with tonight."

"Jeremy Beatty?"

"Correct. Department of Defense investigators just contacted us. A pair from their Criminal Investigation Division are on their way here. They believe he's involved. The rest you'll have to get from them. We'll get you back out there as fast as we can."

Venuti broke the connection. When I called back, I got Venuti's voice mail. I tried twice more, and then watched Julia being carried out on a backboard.

4

My niece was eased from a backboard to a gurney, and then strapped and lifted into an ambulance. As the doors closed, a first responder described a wound in the middle of her back near her spine and multiple shrapnel wounds on her legs. She had an arm wound and a torn ear. I thought of Melissa's call yesterday, ostensibly about the party, though really about her kids. She was cheerful about Julia getting her learner's permit, and told a funny story about Julia parallel parking. I'd felt her happiness with how her kids were growing up. Intense grief swept through me again as the ambulance carrying Julia pulled away.

I turned and saw a radio pole rising just beyond some For Sale vehicles at the edge of the Alagara lot. It looked like a police mobile command station setting up on Lake Mead Boulevard, too close to be safe. The line of For Sale vehicles there were yet to be cleared by a bomb squad, so I headed that way to get them to move.

The vehicles included two panel vans, two pickups, an older Cadillac, a dusty Jeep, and a tired Toyota sedan. All faced the street. I passed between a pickup with tricked-out wheels and custom gray fleck paint and the vintage Caddy, and then stepped over a heavy link chain bordering the lot. My focus was on the deputy commander overseeing the setup of the mobile command station. I recognized his drill sergeant posture. His name was André Dubrious, or "Dubious," as he was called behind his back at Las Vegas PD Metro.

"You want to back your officers away until these vehicles for sale are cleared," I said as I reached him.

"Our bomb squad will clear them."

"Then let them do that first." I pointed at the Las Vegas Metro bomb squad vehicle arriving. "Give them time, or set up farther away."

He didn't like that at all.

"Aren't you the agent who got blown up playing soldier in Iraq that the *Las Vegas Sun* wrote up as a hero? I heard they bent the rules to let you back onto active duty."

"We're not talking about me. At least back your officers away. You stay. Only you. How about that?"

Dubrious pointed a finger at the Alagara where smoke still seeped from the roof and blast debris had sprayed across the lot.

"What happened here happens every Fourth of July," he said. "When this is over, it's going to be a fireworks explosion. Checking these vehicles is just practice for the bomb squad."

"You've seen all this before?"

"I've seen enough."

"What in the fuck does that mean?"

I don't know where the anger that enveloped my grief came from, but it was bright and intense. Maybe it was because Dubrious had primped his hair in anticipation of a TV interview with the destroyed Alagara in the background. I took a step toward him, then had to get a grip.

"I'm going to report you," he said. "Count on it."

Without another word, he turned his back. I almost grabbed him, but saw an officer I recognized on the Las Vegas Metro bomb squad and walked over to him. We work together often. I know them. They're top-notch and it was good to see they were close to moving onto the lot.

Then I saw Jane Stone coming toward me. She wrapped her arms around me and said, "I'm so sorry, Paul."

"Why is Venuti pulling me? What's going on with the Department of Defense investigators? Venuti said we got a call from DOD and two investigators from their criminal investigative division are on their way to our office. They think a former drone pilot I know should be questioned in connection with the bombing. The rest he'll explain when I get to the office. When did we get this tip? I was just at Beatty's place."

"Maybe fifteen minutes after the bombing. How well do you know him?"

"Fairly well. He said a pair of air force OSI came out to question him last night about a drone pilot training job he did in Taiwan. But what's this about?"

"He's part of a joint OSI-DOD investigation. They've been tapped into his communications for six months. You'll get it from Dan. Where do you know him from?"

"From my brother-in-law, who died here. I met Beatty at Melissa and Jim's house years ago."

I had to look past her after I said that.

"Beatty was a top pilot in the Creech flight trailers until he developed what's called 'kill inhibition,' meaning he didn't want to press the trigger anymore. The air force tried to bring him around, gave up, and discharged him with a PTSD diagnosis a couple of years ago. He had trouble adjusting to civilian life. A lot of trouble. I'd gotten to know him from barbecues at Jim and Melissa's house, so Jim asked me to try to help him."

"You've mentored him."

"That's too big a word. All I've done is try to help him. He had a tough first year—suicide was possible—then things started getting better. Last fall he connected with a job broker who's been getting him drone consulting projects."

My voice trailed off. I couldn't stand here and explain Beatty's drone consulting business or my friendship with him any longer.

"Paul, you're going to have to go in and get briefed."

I shook my head and said, "That's not right, I belong here."

"Would this Jeremy Beatty know about the party here?" She asked.

"He was invited. He's always invited."

"Invited? Oh, through your brother-in-law."

Her cell rang and she showed me the screen.

"That's Dan wondering how long ago you left. I've got to talk to him."

She was still on the phone as my headlights caught the white Tyvek of the FBI ERT—Evidence Response Team—suiting up. But I didn't drive to the office. Twelve minutes later, after passing under the rusted iron arch of the Wunderland Trailer Park sign, I came up behind a black SUV blocking the thin asphalt road leading to Beatty's trailer out at the end of Wunderland. It wasn't one of ours; I drove around it and arrived in time to see Beatty's computers being carried out of the trailer. A young Department of Defense investigator flashed a badge and moved to stop me as I started up the trailer-deck steps.

"That's as far as you go," he said.

I pulled my FBI creds and said, "It's a terrorism investigation that brought me here, so I could ask you to leave. What are you doing here? Who are you? Identify yourself."

He looked around for help. What he told me without saying anything is that he knew my name and he didn't want to give me information. I stepped around him and looked in the trailer. The computers and the small drone were gone. A scan of the trailer walls was underway. I walked back out to the young investigator.

"When did you get a search warrant?"

"This morning."

"Does it reference possible bomb-making equipment?"

"I can't talk about it."

"You can't talk about the search warrant to an FBI agent?"

"I can't discuss this with you."

"Why is it you can't talk to an FBI agent?"

"My orders are not to talk to you, sir."

"Your orders?"

"My boss."

"Is your boss waiting for me at the field office?"

"Yes, sir."

"Give me the person's name."

"Sarah Warner."

"Is Sarah in the Department of Defense Criminal Investigative Division like you?"

"Yes, sir."

"Why are you looking at Jeremy Beatty?"

"I can't talk about that."

"Did Sarah tell you not to talk to any FBI agents or just me?"

"Just you."

I pulled out my phone.

"What's her phone number?"

Fireworks popped, popped, popped from the direction of the casinos, and I kept pushing the young investigator for the reasons why they were there. But then came a deep, hollow boom that froze and frightened me. The young investigator also heard it, but it didn't mean the same thing to him. He saw my reaction though and went quiet. I asked again for Sarah Warner's number, and to get free of me he gave it up.

I called Sarah Warner from my car, but not until after trying to reach Jane Stone and starting back to the Alagara. My call to Jane rolled over to voice mail. I called Sarah Warner next. I was going to call Venuti but wanted to be back on-site at the Alagara before talking to him. Caller ID wouldn't give Warner my name, but I had guessed right. She assumed I was law enforcement and answered on the second ring.

"Sarah Warner here."

"This is Special Agent Paul Grale."

"I'm waiting in your field office. We'll talk here."

"I have a question first. Do you have any evidence tying Beatty to a bomb plot?"

"I'm not doing this over the phone."

"It's a yes or no question."

"I'll see you here."

"You and I are going to have a problem."

"Guess what, we already have one."

She hung up, which annoyed and angered me, but didn't matter anymore after Venuti called.

"Secondary explosion," Venuti said. "A bomb in a pickup, at least seven dead, and we can't find . . ."

His voice failed him.

"I heard the blast. I'm on my way back," I said. "I'm almost there."

"It's locked down. You'd be standing around. Come in. Let's get this cleared up with the Department of Defense investigators and get you back out."

I didn't answer.

"Grale."

"I'm here."

"Come in."

I put the flashers on top and raced to the field office. En route I took a call from Jo Segovia—Dr. Segovia, Jo to me. I hadn't heard her voice in six months, though we'd been together for a year before that.

"I'm calling as a doctor, Paul, and I'm outside the bounds here. You should be getting this directly from her doctor. How much do you know about Julia's wounds?"

"I was there. I found her. Her ear looked bad, but her back was the worry. What do you know? How is she? A first responder said her legs and back took shrapnel. One piece was close to the spine."

"Dangerously close. She's on her way into emergency surgery. I've seen the X-rays. Most of the other shrapnel is embedded in muscle in her hamstrings and will come out. After those wounds are cleaned up, they should be fine. The fragment near a vertebra may cause bruising or swelling at the spinal column. That can lead to paralysis."

"That can't happen. Too much has happened to her already."

"She's with a top surgeon, and I'll watch after her, Paul. I'm here. I'm calling to let you know and to say I'm devastated and sorry."

"Please call me as soon as she's out of surgery, Jo."

"I'll do more than call you."

5

The agents standing near a TV in a conference room shifted so I could see the screen better. A Las Vegas TV affiliate of CNN with a helicopter up to catch casino fireworks had veered toward the column of black smoke soon after the blast. The TV crew filmed the initial response and caught the secondary bomb explosion before the FAA excluded unauthorized aircraft from the area. Their helicopter was low and close when the pickup exploded with a brilliant flash of white light. It was horrific to watch and was played over and over. In the upper right corner of the TV, a timer ran down the seconds to detonation.

I watched it yet again and saw the LVPD mobile command unit topple over, its radio pole bending and twisting across the median. In the fraction of a second it took for the blast cloud to swallow them, you could see other small figures. Seven law enforcement officers were known dead. They reported an FBI special agent missing but didn't have Jane Stone's name yet.

In an interview room the two Department of Defense investigators waited, a man and a woman, both on their phones when I walked in. They ended their calls and stood to shake hands. Sarah Warner was square shouldered and sober. Her partner Jon Griswold was older and deferential to her. He was mild mannered, balding, and loosening around the middle. As he cleaned his glasses, his myopic stare locked on me and only accentuated how wrong it was to be here rather than at the Alagara. It was wrong, but what did they know that put a smug look in the old boy's eyes?

After adjusting his glasses, he gave me his name again, pronouncing *Griswold* like a puzzle answer on a TV game show. We traded phone numbers as Warner talked.

"After you left Jeremy Beatty tonight, he was out of his trailer carrying a gear bag within minutes." She made that sound extraordinary, but Beatty had told me he was going out to the airfield tonight. "You weren't half a mile away when he rode his motorcycle up a ramp onto the truck bed and strapped it down."

"You were tracking me?"

"I'm saying it wasn't long. It was planned. He was out of Wunderland eight minutes after you left. Are you hearing me?"

"I'm hearing you, but waiting for your point. Beatty didn't know I was stopping by. He was packing, getting ready to go out to an airfield and a new job."

"That's hard for us to believe."

I tried to make sense of that then skipped over it. "Tell me what you have on Beatty. Tell me why you're here."

"Special Agent Grale, I want to ask you something. You're a SABT, special agent bomb tech, and highly trained. You've got quite a reputation. Could you build bombs like the two used tonight?"

"Probably." I stared at her. "I left the bomb scene because my supervisor said you had something urgent. What have you got?"

When she stalled, I slid my chair back and got ready to stand.

"Please don't leave yet," she said. "How would Beatty get to this airfield?"

"It's north of Indian Wells, approximately two miles beyond the Mercury cutoff. I can forward the directions he texted me."

"So he would take 95 North?"

"Yes."

"That's not what he did."

"Okay, tell me. I can't do the rest of this game. I'm going to ask again, what have you got?"

"He drove toward Bar Alagara and we followed but lost him. He made a series of evasive moves, ran stop signs, reversed course, raced through yellow lights—my squad isn't trained for that."

"What are they trained for?"

That came out harsh. That was my anger again at the bombings and being pulled into the office.

"Criminal investigation," she said.

"With a computer and a mouse, right? They're all good at driving a mouse, just not so good with vehicles. I was driving slowly along Lake Mead Boulevard. If Beatty was following me, he was driving slowly."

"You were driving slowly. We saw that. Does that mean you were waiting for him?"

"Excuse me? You're telling me you were following me and then followed Beatty as well. That's what I'm hearing. Is that what you're saying?"

"Were you always going to the party? Were you invited?"

"You've got to be kidding me. Was I invited?"

"Were you?"

It hit me, and it was unbelievable. I answered slowly. It was possible the DOD had nothing connecting me to the party. But if they had questions about me, why didn't they tell Venuti? He would have cleared it up.

"It was my sister and brother-in-law's annual party. I try to get there every year."

She looked at Griswold then back at me.

"Your sister is Melissa Kern?"

I shook my head. "My sister is dead."

She must have read the emotion crossing my face. She bowed her head. She looked at Griswold then back at me.

"We've made a terrible mistake, and I apologize."

"My brother-in-law, Jim Kern, was one of the pilots killed tonight. Melissa was my sister and only sibling. I found her body and the body of my nephew. My niece is in emergency surgery right now. After his discharge, Beatty had a hard time and Jim got me involved, trying to help him. Beatty used to regularly send texts that sounded suicidal, like one I got last night. I hadn't seen one like it in over a year, and since he didn't return my calls or texts, I stopped by before going to the party."

She shook her head, then found the grace to look me in the eye.

"I'm so sorry," she said. "I'm an idiot."

"Just bring me in. If I'm wrong about Jeremy, I need to know what I've missed seeing."

I pulled the memory stick Beatty gave me and slid it across to her.

"That's video Beatty took of you with a small drone he owns. He didn't know the surveillance was DOD until last night when OSI told him he was being investigated over drones he flew in Taiwan. Until they knocked on his door, he thought you were CIA."

She looked at the memory stick and then at me with kindness in her eyes. Her voice softened and slowed.

"We have wiretaps of an angry Jeremy Beatty talking about the US Air Force. Read the transcripts we'll send you tonight and come to your own conclusions. He harbors extreme anger over his discharge. The last thing in the world I wanted to do was turn over a year's worth of investigation, but I didn't see how we could ignore it. He knew the victims. He knew the party location. He was invited and declined to attend. He has knowledge of explosives."

"Jeremy doesn't know anything about explosives."

"He was trained in the air force."

"Only about the ordnance the drones delivered, so you're really stretching it." I paused, took her in again, then said, "Are you saying you were worried about his state of mind before there was a bombing?"

"That's right, and we're turning everything over tonight." She did something I didn't see coming. She reached across the table and touched my fingers, then pulled her hand back. "I'm so sorry, so truly sorry for your loss."

"Is there any hard evidence on Beatty?"

She didn't answer.

"Is there any hard evidence?"

"Not yet."

Desperation mixed with grief crept into my voice. "You should have told my supervisor that you had questions about me. I should be out there."

"I see that now." She glanced at Griswold, who was cleaning his glasses again and wouldn't look at me. "Any questions about you are my doing, not my team's," she said.

I didn't care if it was her or her team or whatever. I needed to be at the Alagara right now and wasn't. She was still talking, and I wasn't hearing her.

"But not about Beatty," she said. "He needs to be questioned. Everything we have, transcripts, everything—the Joint Terrorism Task Force will have it all before dawn. I should tell you that he canceled his phone tonight."

I pulled out my cell, called Beatty, and got a recording saying the phone number was no longer in service.

"When you saw him earlier, did he tell you that he was cutting his phone off?"

"No."

"Yet you were kind enough to drive out and check on him after you had left several messages for him. Don't you think it would be basic human decency to tell you the number you've been calling all these years will stop working in a couple of hours?"

I nodded at her. I agreed. I was surprised.

"That's all I have, all we have. We've been working a stolen blueprint investigation with OSI, and we're swamped with cybertheft. That's been my whole life the past six months. Beatty's not implicated in our Taiwan problem, but his job broker could be. That broker, Edward Bahn, is a scuzzbag, and the man who paid Bahn is a black-market heavyweight. I hate to turn everything over before we've moved on our investigation, but there seemed to be too much to ignore."

"Maybe he disconnected his phone due to your surveillance and after OSI officers questioned him last night."

"Maybe he did, and it just happened to coincide with the hour of a terrorist attack."

I registered that and stared as my phone rang.

"That's my supervisor. We'll go through everything you turn over as soon as we get it. For what it's worth, Beatty misses the air force and thinks of those days as the best in his life. Check out his haircut."

"You don't have an answer for him canceling his phone, do you?"

"Only that he's trying to shake your surveillance."

"Ahead of an attack."

I didn't touch that, walked out, and talked to Venuti only long enough to tell him I was on my way upstairs to his office.

6

"Send me back to the bomb scene."

"I can't."

"Yes, you can."

"Not yet, headquarters is . . ."

"Screw headquarters, Dan. I belong out there and you know it. I just dealt with the DOD farce. Send me back now."

My anger was intense, and I interrupted as soon as I understood what he was planning.

"You're going to shuffle me off to look at a van two detectives have already looked at that's about to get hauled to our yard. You've got to be kidding."

"Grale, listen to me. I'm sorry. I'm very sorry for you. I don't know how you're doing it right now, but I can't send you back yet. Headquarters doesn't want you at the Alagara."

"Headquarters doesn't want me there? Why would that be? Did someone here say what the DOD brought in needs to be looked at closely? You're the only one they've talked to, right? So what did you say? That you'd backwater me somewhere while I get looked at for some asinine reason?"

"The Hullabaloo driver has been identified as a twenty-seven-year-old Hispanic named Juan Menderes. Presumably fled. I'll text you the address for the van. The Las Vegas PD detectives there will wait for you. Go there. That's an order. You're on Menderes until we get this sorted out."

"It's already sorted out."

"There's no other way, Grale. You need to go."

"I don't get it, Dan. I don't get any of this. I'm needed at Alagara, not tracking this guy down."

"This is not a debate."

"What this is, is wrong." I pointed a finger at him. "I never belonged at a crime scene more than this one."

"I'm trying to get you back there."

Twenty minutes later I said hello to the Las Vegas Metro detectives, then I circled the lime, orange, and red Hullabaloo van while they watched. I had a hard time concentrating, but they had already done their search of the van. They had other information after talking with Hullabaloo. The driver, Juan Menderes, had texted the Hullabaloo bakery office after making the cake delivery to Bar Alagara. That was confirmed. That was Hullabaloo's protocol. You deliver then communicate the delivery was made.

Menderes had made two more deliveries after Alagara yet in the van was a lone red, white, and blue Fourth of July cake with the address of one of the last scheduled deliveries taped to it. Las Vegas detectives and FBI agents were at the Hullabaloo bakery building and had verified that the recipients of the final two deliveries had received their cakes. One was at home and the other out watching fireworks but could be reached on her cell phone. So either the cake still there was an extra that got mistakenly made or something else was going on.

I called the woman whose name was on the tag and identified myself. She confirmed her cake had been delivered and asked what anyone would ask: Why was the FBI interested in her Fourth of July cake? I heard nervousness in her voice and leaned through the van door and looked at the address on the cake in the van again. It was her address. So there was that to figure out. I thanked her and said good-bye.

The LVPD detectives also had witnesses who could put the Hullabaloo van in the neighborhoods of the final two delivery locations, one on Bonanza and the other a mile and a half from Bar Alagara on North Torrey Pines. It was the North Torrey Pines cake that was still in the van. I could read the address on that one but didn't climb in to avoid contaminating evidence should there be any. The van would go from here to the FBI yard, and a bomb dog would get in first. I looked at the Metro detectives, and one asked me, "What do you think?"

"I think somebody has a side business."

"That's what we're guessing too."

Menderes's girlfriend lived on the third floor of the apartment building over a parking garage and was home when the detectives and Metro officers had knocked on her fourth floor door. She was in a Metro detective's car on her way to a station to be interviewed, but so far she was claiming she'd had no contact with Menderes tonight.

After the van was loaded onto a tow truck, I followed the detectives to where Menderes lived. As I drove, the office texted me a photo of Menderes's driver's license. Looking at it, I confirmed that Menderes was the Hullabaloo driver I had seen talking on his phone at the stoplight just before the bomb exploded. Who was he talking to then? I wanted that answer tonight.

7

Menderes lived with two roommates in a drab three-bedroom house with tan paint and a concrete tile roof, same as all the houses on the block. Four Metro patrol cars and an unmarked sat nose-to-tail on the street in front of the house. I skirted those but paused at a Ford Taurus with bald tires and flecked paint dying in the driveway.

Inside, Menderes's two roommates, Enrique Vasco and Jaime Cordova, worked hard to separate themselves from Juan. Yes, he was their roommate. No, they didn't know him well. Cordova hadn't met him until after he'd moved in. Vasco had once worked at the same casino as Menderes but barely knew him then. When they were looking for a roommate, his name had come up and now they lived with him, but everybody had different schedules so nobody ever talked or hung out together. I had heard it all before.

"It's not that big of a deal we don't know him that well," Vasco said.

"Maybe not," I answered. "Which of you heard he needed a room?"

Vasco looked puzzled. Hadn't he just explained this? He tapped his chest.

"I did."

"Where did you hear it?"

"From this chica. I don't know how she knew."

"What's her name?"

"Rosamar something."

"Rosamar what?"

"Don't know, dude."

"My name is Paul Grale."

I got out my FBI cards and gave one to each of them. I expected Venuti to redirect me to the bomb scene, but I'd follow this until Menderes was found.

"None of this is going away until we find Juan."

Vasco shrugged and said, "Juan is a quiet dude and always wearing headphones. He's into soccer and music."

"You know his hobbies, but you don't know him."

"I didn't say I don't know him. Just when he's here he's got his headphones on."

Neither roommate knew anything about his family. Vasco thought Juan might have a relative living in Vegas, but he wasn't sure. We did this some more, then I asked to see Juan's bedroom and the Vegas detectives who'd arrived before me stepped outside. They'd already seen the bedroom.

Clothes were lying around, but there was little else. Menderes slept in there, little more. One window was shut tight, the other unlocked and opened an inch, enough to bleed air conditioning into the hot night. The window frame was warped and Vasco volunteered that you need someone on the outside pushing to get it locked.

"Is it usually locked?" I asked.

"I'm never in here."

"Why is it open now?"

"I don't know."

"Make a guess."

"I don't know."

"Does Juan ever come by the bar where you work?"

"No. Where I work is a big deal. They wouldn't let Juan in. It's like a club bar. Why are you coming down so hard, man? We're freaked out and trying to help you guys. We were watching it on TV when you got here."

"Three roommates living together usually know something about each other. I'm trying to get my head around you knowing next to nothing."

"Why do you need him so badly? Juan didn't blow anybody up. The dude is not political."

"Why would he run?"

"Probably got scared."

"Scared of what?"

"Police."

"Why?"

"Seriously?"

"Why run? What does that get him, other than us looking for him?"

"I'm not saying I know what he did, but he comes from a place in Mexico where if the police are looking for you, it's always bad."

"Where in Mexico?"

"Some village. I don't remember. He said it was bad, and he was never going back there."

"Could he have come home and you didn't see him?"

I pulled on the window handle again.

"You're really on that window."

"Does your landlord pay for your air conditioning?"

"Yeah, and he buys all our food and beer too. The landlord is an old asshole. We asked him to fix the window. He told me to fix it myself."

I looked around at the room again. The carpet hadn't been changed in thirty years. The paint might have been older.

"If later it turns out you covered up for him, that could pull you into a terrorist investigation. You don't want a jury at a terrorism trial thinking you withheld evidence. You really don't want that."

"Sounds scary."

Sarcasm, and early for it after what had happened tonight. I took that in, along with Vasco's features: high forehead, jet-black hair razor-cut with clean lines, a handsome face, sensitive mouth and eyes. Everything about his look was a look, but maybe that just came with a high-end bartending job in Vegas.

I returned to the warped window and pictured Juan coming home for what he needed, then climbing out the window. Twenty steps from the rear of the house was a six-foot-high fence bordering the backyard.

"What did he do?" I asked. "Come home, get money, a different ID, an unused burner phone, and then hop out the window and climb over the fence. Let's walk around back."

We looked over the back fence in the moonlight together, Vasco and me—Vasco tired of repeated questions and going dark like the other roommate, Cordova. His answers got shorter and shorter. Waiting me out and not overly affected by the bombing. He was in a far different space than I was.

I looked at moonlight reflecting off a gravel road running through pale desert. Beyond the road and across an open area of scrub were the lights of another subdivision. I knew this road. It led to six abandoned concrete slab foundations that teenagers used for parties. Neighbors had complained about the noise and the drinking. Six years ago there had been a murder out here later linked to two other unsolved killings in Tucson and Kansas City. I shined a flashlight beam on dry, crumbly soil at the base of the fence and held the beam on a heel print.

"You know we'll find him, right?"

"I'm not covering for him."

"You're not being straight either."

"Why would I lie?"

Juan Menderes had a green card. He was documented. He had a job that sounded better than his previous stints as dishwasher, bellhop, busboy, casino worker. I stared hard at Vasco, and he finally gave me something. He also convinced me he was still holding back.

"Juan did stonework in Mexico and now he gets to drive, listen to music, deliver cakes, and makes good tip money. Maybe he doesn't want to lose that. Maybe he thinks if he goes away for a while everything will be okay."

"Hides while we catch the bad guys, then pops back up."

"I guess that's stupid, but that's my only idea."

I moved the flashlight beam to the next footstep; the one where whoever jumped had regained his balance after landing.

"Let's go back inside," I said.

I talked to the Metro detectives, then drove the gravel road alone out to the abandoned foundation slabs and walked back along the road with a flashlight looking for footprints intersecting the road. I'd have to call about getting a dog out here in the dawn. I got back in my car, grief coming in waves as I crossed town to the Summerlin address of the owner of Hullabaloo and the Alagara, Omar Smith aka "The Turk."

A dozen Bureau and LV Metro PD cars were in the driveway of Smith's house and on the street when I arrived. If you lived in Vegas and listened to AM radio, you'd heard Smith's ads. He called himself The Turk, but legally his last name was Smith, a change he made after becoming a US citizen in 2003. In his ads, he said Omar was his Turkish name and Smith his American. He had comic timing and made both names sound funny.

Tonight, he was anything but funny. He looked stunned, anxious, and deeply worried. He looked shocked. He'd granted us full access to his business records and computers as soon as he was contacted following the bombing, said he wanted to help in any way. He didn't know of any enemies, hadn't had any threats personally and didn't know of any disgruntled employees. He had debts, sure, but didn't every true entrepreneur? He was current with his debts.

He gave a large discount to the drone pilots for their party and said he very much liked Melissa Kern, the woman he'd negotiated with. He volunteered that he loved America and that he was Muslim, and the drone pilots fighting against radical Islam was a very good thing.

"Of course, many hate the drones," he added. "Many want the pilots dead. You must know this."

This brought more questions about his views, and he clarified, saying, "I am a Muslim but I am never at the mosque. This does not mean I don't have faith. But I am not an active religious man. The Muslims who kill are like the Christians and Jews who kill. They are not really of any faith."

At the FBI we never turn down free information. He talked more about himself, speaking as he sat on a white leather couch in a large, comfortable room with tile floors, rugs, high white-painted walls, and art. A housekeeper offered tea and coffee. No one accepted. I saw a big man emotional over the bombing, answering questions without a lawyer present. Offhand, I liked him, but doubted he ever did anything without a reason.

For five hours he answered questions about how the party-rental business worked and his other businesses, and how the drone pilots ended up renting the Alagara. He talked with his hands as he explained the constant breaking down and moving of party equipment and the running of his bakery, which made signature bread and cakes. None of that work happened with his long elegant fingers. His hands were far too smooth.

On his own he returned to religion, saying, "It is impossible in America for these pilots to be killed in a business owned by a Muslim and not have this become a question. This is another reason I opened my home and offices to you tonight."

"Why do you say that?" an agent asked. "The country was founded on freedom of religion."

"You're an FBI agent so maybe you are right that America is for all religions. I was not aware of that." He stared at the agent and added, "I have only been in seventeen states. Maybe it's different in the others."

This led to more philosophical talk, and I left the room. I toured the house. I doubted it would be open to us the next day.

In a media room, a large TV screen was tuned to reports on the bombings. The sound was down low. The first agents here told me that a housekeeper had let them in and led them to Smith, who was sitting in front of this TV, weeping. I went upstairs and walked through the bedrooms and lingered in the master to see how he lived and then came back down.

Across a garden path lined with low landscaping lights and curving around a pool and a fountain was his home office. I found Bill Murtha, an agent I've known forever, with three other tech types downloading everything on Smith's computers. Murtha said, "Smith wants to cooperate fully." He said that like it was righteous and smart. It was probably the opposite, and the vibe in here was urgency. Like a team of hackers who knew the police were already on their way.

Two hours later, I talked to a fatigued Omar Smith about Juan Menderes, my reason for having come. Not my only reason. I had needed to see in person the man who had rented to my sister.

"I like your ads," I said. "Always have. I'm fine sitting at a red light when I'm listening to one of them."

He absorbed that, then said, "My father heard them on his one trip to America when he came to stop me from changing my name to an American name. The ads disgusted him."

"I want to talk with you about Juan Menderes."

"I already showed the agents the text he sent when he delivered the cake. It is a requirement for the drivers. I cannot say why he ran. If they get a speeding ticket, they cannot drive for me ever again. They are responsible for their vans. They drive the same one every day."

He held up two fingers. "Twice a year is a party for the employees. I talked with him at the holiday party at the end of last year, and he convinced me he should be a driver."

"Do you videotape your parties?"

"Yes."

"I'd like to see him in a party video."

Full disclosure on my part: after the Patriot Act, there were really no rules left with a terrorism investigation. If Omar Smith had said no to anything this night, we would have found a reason to seize his computers and phones. But maybe he knew that and beat us to it, opening his house and records. We watched the party video together and he made me a copy. I said I'd talk to him again soon and left him with something else.

"My sister was Melissa Kern. Her husband, Captain James Kern, also died, as did their son, my nephew, Nate. My niece is in emergency surgery right now."

"You were the FBI agent who was first inside my building?"

"I was. If you remember more about Juan Menderes or anything else, call me. I don't care how insignificant it seems. Call me at any time of day or night."

"I am very sorry for you, and I will call if I remember anything."

He heard what I was saying, and I knew he would call me. In that moment we connected. How or why we did I couldn't say yet.

8

At four thirty that morning I was driving when my cell rang with an unidentified number. Didn't recognize the phone number and in my grief and worry over Julia's surgery I almost didn't answer. But it turned out to be Beatty on a burner phone.

"On the radio they're saying a teenage girl survived. I was hoping it was Julia."

"It is Julia."

"Is she okay?"

"She's in the hospital."

"Will she be okay?"

"The doctors don't know yet. What happened to your phone? Why are you on a burner phone? Are you at the airfield you texted me directions to?"

"Yeah."

"I can't talk long right now, Jeremy."

I started to tell him that Melissa, Jim, and Nate were dead along with pilots he knew, but I couldn't do it. Plus, I could tell he'd been online. His name was out there and he knew. It could have come from someone in our office. It could have come from the DOD investigators or a whole lot of others.

"Why didn't you tell me you were shutting your phone down?" I asked.

"I don't know, paranoid, I guess, and I read an article saying the FBI wants to question an ex–drone pilot who was in the vicinity when the blast occurred. The headline says, 'Vegas Terrorist Attack Has Possible Local Link—Ex–Drone Pilot Sought.' Is that me?"

"It is, but don't take it personally. We're questioning everyone. You were in the area and were invited. You didn't show up. You knew pilots, and like you said, you were under surveillance, even if for something completely different. We're looking at every angle, anything, and everything."

"So it came from you?"

"No."

He was quiet long enough for me to wonder if we had lost our connection. Then he said, "I'm really sorry, Grale. You lost a lot tonight. I'll deal with whatever questions there are about me."

I wished that were true. I wanted it to be that way, but didn't think it would work out like that.

"Tell me about the airfield," I said.

"I'm in a flight trailer that's two double-wides combined. There's an asphalt runway for the drones and light aircraft. They graded miles of road wide and smooth enough for trucks, but went cheap on the runway. There are other trailers for living and a commissary. There's a temporary hangar for the drones that looks like a circus tent and a whole lot of desert and mountains behind here. From the air it's going to be a black strip of asphalt in a flat desert valley. We're not that far from the atomic testing area. Is the FBI coming here?"

"How soon after I saw you did you head out there?"

"Right away, and I almost followed you to the party. I chickened out for the same old reasons and went to that Carl's Jr. you and I used to go to. I had a burger and fries, watching for anyone following me. Everything I told you about Hakim Salter was true."

"It's not about Hakim Salter tonight."

"Captain Kern always said the war would come to us. He said we couldn't fly drones indefinitely without getting pushback."

Jim did say that.

"I see all kinds of bad things coming, G-man. My mind is messing with me tonight. I see arches in a courtyard with cinder-block walls and dirt raked and watered. They don't fill the cells of the cinder block with concrete and steel in Pakistan like we do here. They just stack them up. Cinder-block chunks tear the shit out of a house after a missile goes off. I see Laura when I close my eyes. I try to take back everything bad I said to her. I hear Melissa offering me a room in their house for as long as it takes me to get back to normal. Why is it the best people get killed?"

"I don't know why."

"What I told you earlier was true. I asked Ramer what we were waiting on. All the Taliban dudes were there, and I was ready to go when command said make another loop. I did, and Salter came out, and command told Ramer to sparkle the target. Ramer adjusted the infrared marking laser. The speed was right, the range was right, my thumb was there, and then Salter steps back toward the shadows as if he'd forgotten something inside the house, and one of the Taliban dudes looks up. He fucking looks up. Salter also looked up, both he and the Taliban dude. They heard it coming. I've done a lot of research on Salter. Did I ever tell you that? I know all about his life."

"Jeremy, I can't do this, but don't run."

"Grale, I'm sorry. I'm so sorry."

A moment later I ended the call and pulled into an empty shopping mall lot, then stood outside breathing deep, trying to calm myself. I must have stood there forty minutes pushing grief back. I wanted the bombers. I wanted the vengeance of justice. I wanted back what was forever gone. The hard truth of that came with the dawn.

9

Dr. Latik, the orthopedic surgeon who had operated on Julia, held a small piece of twisted metal between his fingers.

"Let me show you what we're dealing with."

He put up an X-ray of the thoracic vertebrae near which the metal had lodged.

"It corkscrewed in."

He handed the piece of metal to me.

"Rub your finger along the tip and feel the little hook. That's how it dug into the bone."

"What happens now?"

"Now we hope the surgery doesn't cause new swelling and that the initial swelling has peaked. That can take up to seventy-two hours." As if anticipating a question I might have had, he added, "We couldn't delay the surgery, and we're debating whether to chill her to impede swelling. We'll decide on that this morning."

Worst case was paralysis. Best case was the swelling subsides and Julia retains full movement and sensation. Melissa and Jim's trust named me as executor. Separately, I became custodian of their children until adulthood.

In the post-op room, Julia looked at me through half-closed eyes. Other shrapnel fragments were pulled from the backs of her thighs. Her torn left ear was bandaged, and the surgeon who did the work said it wouldn't look the same as the other ear, but it would be close. She did not yet know about her family, but that changed as I stood alongside her bed.

She asked in a faint voice, "Where's Mom?"

I didn't know how else to say it, and I'd already resolved never to treat her as less than an adult. Anyone who would be going through what was ahead for her was owed that.

"Your mother was killed."

Her look was disbelief, but when I didn't correct what I'd said, her face crumpled. It broke my heart when I saw she knew I was telling her the truth. But I also understood the reflexive denial that came next.

"That's not true."

I knew she didn't remember anything beyond going into the back of Bar Alagara with another girl, so it was possible she didn't believe me.

"A bomb exploded in the bar area when you were in the bathroom. You and another boy are the only survivors."

Her voice rose. "My dad and Natty?"

I could only nod and take her hand.

"That can't be."

Her eyes brightened with tears then closed tight, and I wiped tears from mine. She brought her hands to her face and sobbed. Less than ten minutes later, she asked again what had happened. I took her through it very slowly, and her body wracked and shook. From deep in her throat came a low keening cry that drew a nurse. It was a very hard way to find out that you were an orphan. There was no other family on our side. On Jim's, just his mother, who was in a retirement home with no short-term memory left, and beyond her, only very distant relatives.

I left Julia with the nurses, and in the early light I unlatched the garden gate of the house Jim and Melissa had bought fifteen years ago to raise the kids in. The squeaking hinges started the Kerns' young black Lab, Coal, barking. I had their house key at home, but they kept one under a porcelain tortoise near the pool. When I opened the kitchen door, Coal jumped on me and then ran out to look for his family. I found the dog food. I cleaned the pee off the kitchen floor and was rinsing my hands when Venuti called.

"JTTF wants you on a call in twenty minutes. So does headquarters. Why aren't you here?"

As in, why in the fuck aren't you here?

"My niece just came out of surgery. I checked on her. I'll be on the Joint Terrorism call."

"Where are you?"

"At my sister's house feeding the dog."

There was a long pause before Venuti asked, "How did the surgery go?"

"Well, but she's not out of the woods."

"We're all pulling for your niece. I want you to know that."

"Thank you."

Another long pause, Venuti working around to something else and trying to be sensitive before asking, "Who authorized you to question Omar Smith?"

"I did."

"Say that again."

"I'm working Juan Menderes, the missing driver. Omar Smith was his employer. I had questions for him."

"Make sure you're on the call and find me when you get in. I want to hear what you got from Smith."

I got the call-in number from Venuti, then hung up and walked the house before leaving. I stood at the door of each kid's bedroom. I remembered their births and the joy. Seventeen-year-old Nate had looked like his dad. Julia had a string of soccer trophies on her dresser and two dolls from younger days leaning against the second pillow on her bed. I turned off her computer, then walked back down the hallway to the study and faced a wall of photos.

One was of Jim beneath a B-52 wing in Idaho before the move here, another of the family in Bryce Canyon National Park, and then Jim with drone pilots at Creech, and one of Jim and me along the Green River in Wyoming in a different world in a different time. Could we have ever imagined Jim would someday become something called a drone pilot and die in a bombing on the Fourth of July? I don't know how we could have.

Jim once said, "I'm a legitimate enemy target. I'm on the battlefield here. Think about it, bud. It's the asymmetry of modern warfare."

I had thought about it many times and sat in meetings in the field office where the risk was evaluated. For several quiet minutes I stood in front of a picture of Jim and Melissa, then I walked out and sat with Coal, who closed his eyes as I held and talked to him. It calmed him. It helped me a little too.

"You hang in here, Coal, and we'll make a plan you'll like. But you've got to be tough right now."

The Joint Terrorism Task Force call went down as I drove to the office. I answered questions about my first minutes in Alagara and about Melissa's party planning and Facebook interaction, neither of which I knew anything about. Melissa didn't talk with me about the party planning, and though I have a Facebook account, I'm never on it. I answered a stream of questions about Jeremy Beatty. The call ended just as I reached the field office garage.

Venuti was upstairs at the Domestic Terrorism Squad, and as I came up we walked together to the ASAC's office.

Our ASAC, the assistant special agent in charge, was Mark Thorpe, a large man light on his feet and careful with his words. He could be acerbic. He could be hard and offended some, but never me, because he was always forthright. I liked it that Thorpe knew who he was. The prior ASAC lacked self-awareness, and working with Venuti was like riding in a rodeo.

Thorpe offered condolences. He said, "You're very strong. I don't know if I could be working." But of course he would, so I went on alert. Venuti and Thorpe must have something in mind.

"How's your niece?" Thorpe asked, then added, "The whole country is pulling for her."

I saw he meant it and told him the details of what the surgeon had said. We talked about that for several minutes. Thorpe asked, "What do you want to do? Given the magnitude of what's happened to your family, where do you fit in the investigation?"

At the Bureau you don't get to decide what you're going to do next, so I paused on that. It was a critical moment, Thorpe assessing me. Venuti no doubt was arguing for a passive role that would confine me to the office, where he'd assign me work and give me time for my niece and the memorials for Melissa, Jim, and Nate. I needed to be very clear with Thorpe.

"I belonged at the Alagara, but I understand the decision last night." I gave it a beat and said, "Put me on finding the bomb maker."

Thorpe responded with, "You're one of the top special agent bomb techs in the country, not just here. That's not the issue. You lost family. You were first in. You know a possible suspect. If we put you out there, will you be able to focus?"

"I'm already focused."

He heard something in that and said, "We're not after revenge. We're after justice and stopping anything else that's been planned. What about this ex–drone pilot Beatty?"

"I don't think there's anything there. I know people disagree with that, but we know where to find him, and we can look closely at him. He called me earlier this morning, distraught over headlines saying we're looking to question him. He expects to get fired today. He's very disturbed. I don't think he understands why this is happening."

"Why did you stop and see him before going to the party?"

"Didn't anyone tell you?"

"I want to hear it from you."

"Late in the night of July 3, he sent me a text message that was similar to suicide texts he would send during the worst days after his discharge. He didn't respond to the messages I left on the Fourth, so I stopped by on my way to the party."

Thorpe mulled that over and said, "That may have saved your life."

It had, but I didn't want to talk about it. I agreed the timing of Beatty reaching out to me raised questions, so did ditching his phone for burner phone—until you factored in a surprise visit from Air Force Office of Special Investigations officers. Then Beatty's actions made more sense.

"How did Beatty spot the Department of Defense surveillance?" Thorpe asked.

"I don't know exactly. He saw the same people too many times and got suspicious, then got a little drone up for a look and took video."

"I hate those goddamned drones," Thorpe said.

Thorpe glanced at Venuti then looked back at me and in a harder voice asked, "What does it mean to target US cities with drone instruction software?"

"It doesn't mean anything. A friend of his modified a video game so he can use it as a teaching tool. He's a drone flight instructor. That's his business. Corporations are his primary clients. Look, he flew the real deal for seven years. Nine-hundred-ninety-nine kills were attributed to him."

Venuti shook his head. "Quit one short of a thousand. Why doesn't that surprise me?"

I looked at Venuti. "What do you know about Jeremy Beatty, Dan?"

Thorpe cut that off before it went anywhere. He asked, "Is his drone consulting work legitimate?"

"Seems to be. He works primarily through a job broker who has gotten him business with farmers, mining companies, utilities, and others. He worked on a movie. He gets referrals. I think it's legitimate and growing, but I don't know much about drone consultants."

"Did he tell you he was canceling his phone?"

"No, Sarah Warner, the DOD investigator, told me. I believe she also thinks I'm an apologist for Beatty. But like I said, when I saw Beatty last night, he showed me videotape of their surveillance. He made a copy that I gave to Warner. He thought they were CIA coming back to check on him about a drone strike he was the trigger on and is not supposed to talk about." I looked at their faces and added, "Jeremy knew my sister, Jim, and the kids. Melissa was fond of him. Jim is who got me involved trying to help him. Dan knows this."

"Show me the text he sent you July 3."

I pulled out my phone and brought it up.

Thorpe turned to Venuti and asked, "Is anyone reading what DOD gave us?"

"I don't have anyone available yet."

"Have you looked at them?"

Venuti shook his head and I looked at him, debating, and then I said, "The DOD investigators told me the Bureau has been aware of their investigation of Beatty for months."

"This office?" Thorpe asked.

"Yes."

I'd been sitting on that one. I knew from the way Sarah Warner had said it that it was probably true, and, if so, probably tracked back through the Domestic Terrorism Squad.

Thorpe turned to Venuti.

"Were we aware OSI and the DOD were investigating a civilian former drone pilot and Special Agent Grale?"

"Something was communicated, but it didn't make much of an impact on me. Obviously, if they were genuinely investigating a special agent we would have heard a lot more about it. If I'd known it was a chance to get Grale suspended, I would have been all over it."

Venuti meant that to be funny. Had to admire him for even trying, but it repulsed Thorpe this morning. The Venuti I knew might let them investigate me, just to see if they could come up with anything. He was that way, and it didn't offend or surprise me.

Thorpe asked Venuti, "Were you aware Agent Grale has tried for a couple of years to help Beatty adjust to civilian life and figure out his PTSD?"

With me here, Venuti couldn't dodge it. "I was aware," he said. "And I'm sorry for the bad joke. Grale is beyond question, so I didn't worry about whatever thread DOD was following."

"Did you alert the DOD investigators to Grale's mentoring of Jeremy Beatty?"

"I'm not sure. I think so. I hope so. I should have, but this was right after the bombing and I didn't talk with them very long. It was understood that Grale would come in, answer questions, and go back out to the Alagara." He looked at me. "That's what we talked about."

I nodded, but he never told the DOD that Beatty and I were friends. He knew it. I knew it. DOD said they had wiretaps, and he got curious.

Thorpe returned to me.

"You get a suicidal text the night of July 3. That's Beatty reaching out to you before he kills the pilots in an act of revenge against the air force. Then he goes somewhere to take his own life."

He turned to Venuti again. "Isn't that what we're getting from DOD?"

"More or less."

"More, I think," Thorpe said, "but almost anyone in America will tell you the ones responsible for this are the people we're hammering with drone attacks. So I guess DOD's idea is that Beatty is allied with our enemies."

Neither Venuti nor I touched that, and Thorpe asked me, "What do you know about Jeremy Beatty's discharge?"

"Only what my brother-in-law and Beatty have told me, and they had differing accounts. Jim said Beatty developed what's called 'kill inhibition,' which is not the same as PTSD. But he exhibited symptoms of post-traumatic stress disorder, so they went with that on the discharge."

"After that many kills, Beatty developed kill inhibition?"

"Drone pilots get familiar with their targets, and the air force has learned the collateral kills work on them. It builds up. With Beatty they tried for a year to bring him around before medically discharging him. Think of what they had invested in him. You can bet they didn't give up on him easily." After a beat I added, "The air force has an ongoing retention problem with drone pilots."

I paused and when no one said anything, I continued.

"A few times in the past two years Jeremy has alluded to an air strike that put him over the top. But last night was the first time I heard he was part of the Hakim Salter strike. Do you remember the controversy around that one?"

Thorpe nodded.

"Beatty also told me they were all under orders not to talk about Salter. My brother-in-law, Jim, confirmed that. I called him as I left Beatty's trailer. A therapist Beatty met in a bar somewhere has convinced him to do otherwise. I don't know whom all he's told, but he's talking. He wants the air force to apologize to Salter's family."

"Good luck with that," Thorpe said and stared hard at me. I knew the look. I knew what was coming.

"For a couple of years, he alludes to a drone strike that put him over the top but doesn't give you a name until last night. And that doesn't raise red flags after the bombing?"

"I can't make the jump DOD did."

Thorpe turned to Venuti. "Can you get me a copy of those transcripts?"

"Sure."

"I mean now."

"I'll have to go to my office."

"We'll still be here."

As Venuti left, Thorpe said, "We've got a little bit of a situation with you, and this is my proposal to your supervisor. You'll still report to Dan, of course, but if you're up to it, I don't want to lose your skills in this investigation. No one would fault you if you're not able right now."

"I don't want to be anywhere else."

"You'll have full autonomy to choose where you put your investigative energies, as long as they're within an area a terrorist sleeper cell or a homegrown bomber would work from."

"Terrorist sleeper cell."

"Washington is waiting to see if anyone claims it."

So was everyone else. I nodded and asked, "I can follow a lead wherever it goes?"

"I want you to pick up the orphan leads and focus on the bomb material, and as you said, the bomb maker."

"Dan won't go for autonomy."

"Well, you know what I mean by autonomy, and you know how to make it work your way better than anyone around here. I don't see you chasing what the task force is swarming over. Play to your strengths. No one in this office is better on the street, but as you know, your supervisor doesn't like street agents. You'll need timely results."

"Have you talked to Dan about this?"

"He's against it, but he'll do it. He's actually worried about you. He said you were very close with your sister, and Captain Kern was your best friend."

"That's all true."

Thorpe studied me before continuing. "If Beatty is as innocent as the baby Jesus, it still won't matter to some of the officers on the task force. They're going to hold you at a distance just to be safe. You and I know that. But I want you to do what you're good at, so we're going to try this."

"I get to choose my leads, and I'll have support."

"As long as they're of the character we just talked about."

"What about the JTTF?"

"You'll have full access to the Joint Terrorism Task Force and every file in the fusion center. You're not getting shut out in any way at all. I don't mean to say that. I think a mistake was made last night not leaving you out there. We need you."

"I'll need someone in the office working with me who can write FISA requests and—"

"Work out who writes the requests for surveillance against foreign spies with your supervisor. This starts now but before you go, tell me what you think Beatty's root problem with the air force is, and I know what you just said, but put it in one sentence. I've got a meeting coming up and he's on the list of subjects."

"Beatty believes he was ordered to do something that was morally wrong and compromised the values of the US Air Force, and as a consequence compromised him. He's still angry over it."

I reached across Thorpe's desk and tapped the photo of Beatty being circulated.

"Take a look at his haircut. He'd still be an air force pilot if he could be."

Thorpe glanced at the photo then back at me.

"You don't need to wait for Dan to come back. Go find them, Grale. Let's get these bastards."

"I'm going to focus on the bomb maker."

"It's your call."

"And you're going to back me?"

"I'm backing your track record. You've got more bomb-tech experience than the rest of the office combined and no one in this office is a better investigator on the street. You're cleared to start right now, this second. Go."

10

The conversation with Thorpe helped. I was thankful he'd thrown his umbrella over me and would keep Venuti in check as I found my investigative footing. Venuti and I usually got on pretty well together. We didn't have an ongoing supervisor-agent tension, but he did like control, and he'd almost sidelined me. No, more than that, Dan burned me last night. He should have left me out there. His reason for pulling me wasn't good enough. He knew it. I knew it. Thorpe knew it and stepped in. I was thinking about that when my cell rang.

"Sarah Warner, DOD, here. There's something I forgot to tell you. Do you know the toilet called the Headwaters Casino out near the California border?"

"Sure, I like the place."

"Ex-USAF Lieutenant Jeremy Beatty met there with a black-market arms dealer named Lucian Hayworth. That's where all of this came from. At the time, Hayworth was attempting to buy blueprints from hackers for a small, older drone called a Raven used by our combat troops. How much do you know about drones, Grale?"

"Not enough."

"I believe that."

"How about you back down a little?"

She sighed and her voice slowed. "I'm sorry, I didn't intend to be that way. I mean that."

"What happened at the Headwaters Casino?"

"It's where we first came across Jeremy Beatty. He rode up on an old motorcycle, not the expensive new Italian Ducati he bought with the money Hayworth paid him, but a beat-up Harley. We had no idea who he was until he sat down with Hayworth and we ran the plates on the motorcycle. We got his name and went from there. This was on a cloudy, cold afternoon in January with wind sweeping in off the Mojave. I'm painting the scene because it was seriously cold and your friend was in jeans and a light jacket, which is behavior I associate with people high on drugs or Alzheimer's victims."

I remembered the cold at the end of January and into the first days of February and knew about Beatty's disregard for his body. I could also picture the Headwaters Casino and Bar. Too many tables, bad light, watered-down drinks, but not a bad place if you wanted to meet unnoticed.

"It was obvious to us they knew each other," she said. "Long handshake, general friendliness, ease, male crap that wouldn't be there if they weren't already acquainted."

"Familiarity."

"The waitress who served them was one of our agents. She was both wired and eavesdropping. Beatty downed three vodkas in thirteen minutes, and they talked about flying drones in Taiwan and what the similarities would be with drones Beatty had already flown."

"Was that taped?"

"There were some problems with the taping, so it's not clear what got said from the recording, but our agent heard enough to tie things together."

"Who set up the meeting with Lucian Hayworth and Jeremy Beatty?"

"Edward Bahn."

"I know Eddie Bahn. Jeremy wanted my take on Bahn when he started working with him, so we all met at a bar."

"He's a blowhard and a crook."

"I wasn't that impressed either, but he's gotten Jeremy work. He takes a fifteen percent cut, maybe more, but it's helped get Beatty on his feet and working again. Send me what you have on Bahn that makes him a crook. I got the blowhard part when I met him."

I heard keys tapping. She was sending it. She continued on about this "aha" moment in the bar with Beatty and Hayworth meeting, but I wasn't seeing it. I wanted evidence, not just association.

"I doubt Jeremy had any idea who he was meeting. Bahn probably told him where to be and to talk drones with the man they signed a contract with."

"You make him sound naïve."

"About business he is. He signed up with the air force at twenty-one. Eight of the last ten years he spent in the service and two since trying to get his life back together."

"In ten days in Taiwan he made enough to buy that bike."

"I'd bet Bahn negotiated the payment terms."

"When I called you an apologist for him, maybe I was too soft. Do you know what a Ducati bike sells for? Beatty could have upgraded his life if he hadn't bought the bike. But that would have meant depositing a large cash payment into a bank, and you know the rule. Banks have to notify the IRS of any deposit ten thousand dollars or bigger. Did he tell you he got paid in cash on the Taiwan outing?"

"No."

"Of course not. Your shining example for postmilitary entrepreneurship is in the cash economy and knows not to talk too much about it."

My phone buzzed and I looked down at the caller ID.

"I've got a call coming. Let's pick this up later."

She hung up, and I took Beatty's call.

"I'm coming in to your office this morning to get interviewed," Beatty said. "Any chance I can meet with you first?"

"Sure. Where are you?"

"How about Willie McCool Park in an hour?"

"See you there."

11

I sat on top of a picnic table in the shade at Willie McCool Park and watched two white-haired seniors in shorts, sandals, and T-shirts fly remote-controlled World War II–era model airplanes. They looked very into it but were aware of me and probably thought I was there to watch them refight the war. The buzzing planes were loud. The park was otherwise empty and hot.

I cleaned my sunglasses and thought about Jeremy flying remotes here. After his discharge and after his ex-fiancée, Laura Cotter, moved out, he would sometimes call from here, his voice tight with anxiety. This place was a refuge for him, an emotional touchstone named for a hero of his, so it wasn't surprising this was where he wanted to meet before a long day of interrogation.

As a child, Willie McCool flew remote-controlled model airplanes with his father on the airfield at Ann Road and Fifth. Later as a pilot, he flew from the USS *Coral Sea* and the *Enterprise*. He learned to fly twenty-four different types of aircraft and was forty-one years old and captain of the space shuttle *Columbia* when it broke up over the southern United States sixteen minutes before landing.

Beatty was a next generation pilot, certified by the US Air Force as an "external pilot." He learned at the unmanned aerial vehicle school, usually called the UAV school, in Fort Huachuca, Arizona. He loved video games and, like Willie McCool, he was avid about remote-controlled aircraft. Beatty never made carrier landings or flew a space shuttle, but he flew in the early coming-of-age years of the drones. It wouldn't be long before they were everywhere.

I turned at the smooth sound of Beatty's motorcycle then watched him park and walk through the gate. I wanted to reassure him he was doing the right thing, coming in to answer questions, but I was too roiled by sadness. I didn't have it in me. He'd have to sail his own ship. He walked up and embraced me.

"If you need me to do anything for Julia or at Jim and Melissa's house, just tell me," Beatty said.

I nodded but said, "Let's talk about you."

"There's not much to say. I want to get my name cleared, so I'm coming in to answer questions. They can ask me whatever they want to."

"They will, don't worry. Are you bringing a lawyer with you?"

"I don't need a lawyer."

"No one ever does, I guess."

But I was glad he was going in alone. I sat on that several seconds and watched that WWII Japanese Zero attack again.

"I'm pretty fucking keyed up," Beatty said. "When I told you about the Hakim Salter strike, I said I'd thought the surveillance watching me was CIA. I saw your face when I said that. You thought that was insane. But is it more insane than what I'm going to do this morning? I'm going to your office to try to convince the FBI I didn't have anything to do with my friends getting murdered. It makes me think the FBI has no clue where to look."

"It's true. When you said CIA, I didn't get it. You took out some bad dudes, Jeremy, a lot of them, but more than a few bed down locations get wiped out with everyone included, families and all, right?"

"Sure."

"The CIA knows the public is inured to collateral damage. And to be blunt, Salter is probably old news to them. They'd probably have to look him up to remember him, and most likely they'd look you up first. You've had psychological issues. That gives them a big door to walk through if they want to discredit you. They don't need to watch you. Forget the CIA. You'll probably never see another CIA employee in your lifetime. How angry are you still at the air force? That's a question I'd be asking myself if I were you."

"Does it mean anything that I'm coming in on my own?"

"It doesn't change the questions, but it says something about your character."

"And you'd bring a lawyer, that's what you're telling me. But you're good with me not having one. You're FBI to the core, you know that."

Beatty stood, glanced up at the air war, then back at me.

"I'm like you, Grale. I want whoever did this found and killed. I want them dead. I know you do too. You just won't say it."

"Are you ready to go in? If you are, I'll follow you."

Beatty flinched and looked out through the gate at his bike then back at me.

"I'm angry about what happened. I'm angry I have to do this, but I'll do it."

"I'd be angry too."

"What would you do if you were me?"

"I can't answer that this morning. You'll have to go in there and solve it on your own. You know what's true, and that's all they're really after."

"You're right, and I'm sorry, Grale. You don't need to think about it at all, but thank you for meeting me."

Beatty fired up his bike and left. Half a dozen agents would trail him to the field office, and four or five more would burn a day questioning him. There was nothing I could do about that, and it didn't really matter that I sat awhile longer before heading to the Alagara.

12

I walked around outside first. No vehicles were left in the lot, which was wrapped with crime tape. Las Vegas Metro patrol units sat on the street. I crunched through tiny fragments of broken glass and debris. From memory of the CNN video, I found the spot where I thought Jane Stone was when the pickup bomb detonated. Then I moved to where the For Sale vehicles had been parked. The paving was gone and the desert soil underneath churned. A four-foot-deep crater was under where the pickup had sat. I saw flowers on the sidewalk, a lone desert rose and two or three bouquets of roses and yellow chrysanthemums. It meant something to me that people had already reached out.

When I turned back, I realized the hole the smoke poured out of last night was where a skylight had been. The balled-up black aluminum frame of the skylight was somehow still attached to the roof. A Metro officer standing guard opened a padlock for me on a temporary one-inch-thick plywood door and let me in. First smells were char, blood, and dust. A darkening trail of blood mixed with grit marked the path of first responders and everyone who'd followed. I stared at the blood trail with no sense of investigative detachment, only sorrow and anger. I felt incapable of focus.

Overhead, sunlight filtered through a blue tarp draped across the roof hole. Blood spatter stained the white-painted walls and the ceiling seventeen feet above. Just before leaving to meet Beatty, I'd read that the bomb was likely in a new wine refrigerator swapped out with an existing one that had failed several weeks ago. The swap-out occurred during several hours of minor construction work yesterday afternoon. That much was already known. Fragments of a detonator were found last night. I stood over the scarified patch of concrete at the bar where the bomb had detonated and visualized the unmarked van arriving, the man installing the new refrigerator, rolling it in here on a dolly, his movements and look telegraphing normal, the refrigerator wrapped in plastic.

After steady thefts of liquor and a bartender who made a habit of undercharging friends, Omar Smith told agents last night he'd made the decision to install video cameras that operated 24/7. The cameras filmed the wine refrigerator swap-out, but the face of the man who did the changing was largely hidden. Nonetheless, this morning, segments of that video were running through every facial-recognition program available.

Toward the back, temporary lights had been strung in the corridor leading to the restrooms, the food-prep area, kitchen, and Omar Smith's office. I stood for several minutes in each room before returning to the ruined bar. A long, thick thread of ropy dried blood tracked along a wall. I looked at it and remembered the first Fourth of July parties.

They were outside and uncomplicated. The kids usually had a pool or a park to play in, and there was no Facebook chatter leading up to it, just a few calls and a "see you there." Then a stop at the store for hot dogs and beer and whatever else was needed. Maybe it wasn't as connected and efficient, but it had been simpler.

I stood near the destroyed bar and patch of scoured concrete that was ground zero. The shattered pieces of the bar were hauled to the airplane hangar where we were storing all debris, but I could picture the former bar. Like Beatty, I'd eaten tacos here several times. The face had been plywood. The owner once told me he'd stained and lacquered it himself. He was proud of his work and had put his heart into making his restaurant-bar work. I heard he had lost everything, including his house.

He'd also stained and waxed the concrete floor where his customers were, and it was easy to see where that line of stained and waxed floor ended at the bar. I looked at the line of the color difference of the concrete and pictured a table out in front of it, one about ten feet long, sitting directly before the bar but not blocking people from getting drinks. The table was for the children and would have a red, white, and blue paper tablecloth. It was a thing Melissa always did at the Fourth of July party. She liked the kids front and center. They made her happy. She didn't care if they screamed and made a lot of noise.

So the kids there and excited as the cake arrived and adults nearby watching as Jim and the Hullabaloo driver, Juan Menderes, carried the cake over to the table. "Happy Birthday" was sung, not for the country, but for two of the kids, one born on the Fourth, one today. Menderes sends a text while still on the lot and passes by me in the intersection, going in the opposite direction, about a mile away.

Omar Smith has owned the Alagara for two years. He holds the keys. He determines who gets in and when. There are regular cleanings. There's upkeep and in recent weeks, repairs in the bar and bathrooms. A scrutinizing of the subcontractors here yesterday was well under way. The tile setter who spoke only Spanish didn't see anybody. A plumber did. The plumber was here when the wine refrigerator swap-out was made. He'd talked to the man changing the refrigerator and said the guy wasn't happy about working the holiday. Described him as a normal dude.

The plumber had answered most questions straightforwardly but had danced around others. I'd watched that interview video this morning. Thought about how the plumber had gotten squirrelly, then my thoughts flickered through my impression of Omar Smith the night before. Smith claimed that he didn't return in time to meet with the tile setter and plumber and sign off on their work because of a business trip to Houston. Did that mean anything? Did it matter?

Smith was a media artist. Opening his records and house to us last night was like live TV. In a Hullabaloo ad that played often on a Vegas AM radio station, Omar Smith, with an exaggerated accent, struggled to pronounce his name. The gag went on for maybe twelve seconds, right to the edge of being too long, and then cut to a smooth, crystal-clear voice saying, "This is the Turk and this is Vegas. Parties should never be hard in Vegas."

Then came the Hullabaloo pitch for his party-rental business. Hullabaloo vans were sherbet tricolors. In Vegas you saw them enough to conclude the business was successful, but already investigative reporters were turning up griping vendors and unpaid bills and the shadow of lurking bankruptcy. That was news this morning, and we had agents questioning those same vendors. We also had agents in conversation with Turkish police in Istanbul, where Smith was from.

I heard footsteps, turned, and was surprised to see Venuti. Maybe because of how emotional I felt in the restaurant, seeing him unsettled me. Dan looked tall and gaunt, his face hawklike and gray, shoulder bones sliding under a thin, dark blue suit coat. But everyone looked beat this morning.

"Didn't hear you come in."

"I need your help clearing out Jane's condo before the family gets there. I picked up food for lunch. You probably haven't eaten since it happened, have you?"

I hadn't.

"You've got to eat. How long are you going to be in here?"

"Not much longer."

"I'll be in my car making calls. We need two agents present if we remove anything. We also just got test results back on the explosive used here. We can talk about that. You were right. It was C-4."

We left my car parked near the LVPD patrol that was watching the lot, and I ate the turkey tortilla Venuti handed me as he drove.

I was grateful for it. I hadn't thought much about food, and, despite everything, it felt good to eat. I was hungry.

"The C-4 in the Alagara bomb and in the pickup bomb came from a batch made for the army in 2009," Venuti said.

"That's coming from the manufacturer?"

"Yes."

"That was fast."

"They're more ready nowadays." Venuti added softly, "They have to be. All of that batch shipped to Afghanistan."

"And some of it disappeared and didn't turn up."

Venuti nodded.

"You got it. It made it to Kandahar Airfield where 311 pounds disappeared. The CIA is saying they tracked the C-4 through the Haqqani network to Al Qaeda in the Arabian Peninsula. At some point ISIS got involved too."

"A joint operation? Is that believable?"

"They say it is."

"Then what?"

"Then by boat from Africa to South America, where operatives working for the Sinaloa cartel moved it north. We'll get more on that today, but not hard details. The CIA made that clear this morning. Either they don't want to share all of it yet, or they don't have the full path it tracked north on. But you could say they administered delivering it to a Phoenix warehouse. It then disappeared from that warehouse. Apparently we were helping watch over it when it vanished."

"Why were we there?"

"We got briefed once it was obvious that it was coming here. It got here and we took over and had surveillance teams rotating at the storage facility in Phoenix."

I nodded. That made sense.

"So we were waiting to see who would pick it up and where they were taking it," I said.

"Yeah."

"What happened?"

"It's not clear."

"What do you mean by that?"

"I mean that the briefing I was in only went so far. Our guys are saying we had it under surveillance the whole time. A batch match had already been made with an earlier sample, so we knew when the C-4 was made and where. Our agents went into the Phoenix warehouse at 3:30 a.m. this morning and didn't find any C-4."

I thought about that and said, "Okay, but we do know C-4 shipped to our army in Afghanistan and 311 pounds were stolen, sold, and made their way into the hands of AQAP and ISIS and then were brought all the way back across the world. Same batch."

"Yes, so now it's a very high probability that it was a terrorist attack involving Mideast actors and recruits here."

"Are they speculating homegrown recruits here?"

He nodded, and I asked, "Why would they move this C-4 halfway around the world?"

"Lot of debate over that too. The going theory is the symbolism of getting it from an American military base and using it to attack America made it worth shipping. I don't see that, but that's what I heard this morning." He added, "The army wants to control how it goes public."

"I thought AQAP and ISIS were at each other's throats."

"They mostly are."

I wiped my hands on the greasy napkin and crumpled the paper bag as we pulled into the garage beneath the condo complex. Venuti used a swipe card to get into the elevator room, holding it against the reader then showing it to me before slipping it into his wallet.

"Jane gave this to me. We sometimes met here. It's on the way from my house, and it was a good place to talk."

"Her condo was a good place?"

Venuti glanced at me.

"It was convenient."

Venuti hit the fourth floor button and the elevator rose. He unlocked her door as if he'd done it a thousand times. In the main room I looked through the windows to the deck and at the desert beyond the city. The city of Las Vegas looked like an overnight guest in this view of the desert. Jane had made a good buy when the market was down in '09. She got it very cheap, but it was like her to be unafraid when others were fearful. I knew she liked to sit on the deck with a glass of wine and unwind.

Venuti cleared his throat.

"I was here with Jane when the first bomb went off. Louise thought I was at work on a minor emergency and wouldn't be home for another couple of hours, and then we would celebrate the Fourth of July. I was here having a drink with Jane first. That's how I've treated the mother of my three children, the woman I've been with since I was twenty. Sometimes I don't even recognize myself anymore."

It took me a beat to register what he was communicating, but I wanted no part of it. I didn't want to hear a confession.

"When the bombing happened and the DOD called, I realized you couldn't be the lead on-site. Jane didn't feel qualified to run the crime scene after the bombing, but I talked her into it. She'd be alive otherwise."

"You thought it would help her career."

"That's not why."

The fuck it wasn't.

"It's because she was ready, and I knew I had to pull you," he said.

"She was a good choice, but you didn't need to pull me. It may as well get said now. You didn't need to. There was no reason to."

He ignored that and said, "I talked her into it, and it got her killed."

"You didn't get her killed."

Jane once told me she liked unraveling the frauds, the money launderers, and cybercriminals. She loved sophisticated criminal types in twenty-thousand-dollar suits who were confident they were smarter than everyone else. She didn't want a career dealing with the psychopaths, murderers, righteous zealots, and nihilistic bomb-building freaks.

She'd said, "The bombers and stone-cold killers are all yours, Grale. You can hold hands with them and stare into the abyss together. I'll move off the DT squad in a couple of years. I don't want anything to do with bombers. I want the guys who dream of cleaning out J.P. Morgan in under sixty seconds."

"Jane and I talked about letting the bomb squad clear the vehicles first," I said. "It wasn't your fault."

"If you'd been there, no one would have gone near those vehicles."

"Jane knew to stay back. It was just bad luck she was crossing the lot. I'm sure she had a reason and it was a calculated gamble."

"You wouldn't have forgotten there could be somebody holding a cell phone and watching."

"She didn't forget either."

"But for that bastard washed-out drone pilot, you would have been there. You would have kept everyone back."

"You didn't get her killed." I came a breath from launching into him for pulling me from the Alagara, but decided not to. Couldn't tell you why, maybe because it wasn't going to get us anywhere. But neither did I want to hear him talk about himself. "How do you want to do this?" I asked.

"Check her computer and look for flash drives."

Jane carried flash drives like some people carry gum, and there was also a pretty good chance her computer had case files. Not bringing home a case file was a regulation she had exempted herself from, another thing I liked about her.

"She used the second bedroom as an office. Her computer is in there. There might be things on it you would recognize and I wouldn't, so start in there, Grale."

I walked into her office, pulled her chair back, and sat at the desk. Jane and I worked together a lot. Technically, I wasn't supposed to, but I had the four-digit security number she used on her laptop. She had mine. I typed in hers and found various work files; the most recent concerned Denny Mondari, an FBI informant. Mondari, or Mondi, as Jane whimsically called him, had provided a casino-bombing extortion tip in June. I didn't see anything new there but copied the file onto a stick. I copied others and looked up to see Venuti standing in the doorway.

"Anything?" Venuti asked.

"A few files and the hard drive will need to be wiped. It'll have to come with us."

We didn't find anything else in this room or her bedroom. But just before leaving, Venuti found a red-and-black memory stick, a SanDisk Cruzer Glide USB 16G in a coat pocket in the front closet. He acted as if it were significant when he handed it to me. The gesture felt fake and theatrical. It was as clumsy as his explanation for having the elevator swipe card, and it left me uncomfortable as we drove away.

"What do you know about this memory stick?" Something hard crept into my voice as I asked.

"Only that I recognize it."

"From where?"

"She had it with her a lot lately."

"And you were with her a lot lately, so you saw it and knew it was important."

"I saw her every day, same as I see you."

"You knew to look for it in a coat in a closet in the middle of summer, but you have no idea what's on it? What did she tell you was on it?"

"She was as bad as you about not talking until she was ready."

"You know something more about this memory stick."

"Watch yourself, Grale."

"Watch myself?"

When Venuti dropped me at my car, I asked again. I held the memory stick between two fingers and said, "Are you really telling me that you have no idea what's on this?"

"I don't know what's on it."

"I'm going to hold you to that."

"That's what makes you good at what you do. See you at the office."

13

At dusk as I skimmed files uploaded to the Joint Terrorism site, the Islamic State and Al Qaeda in the Arabian Peninsula—ISIS and AQAP—both claimed the bombing. I stopped to watch the TV news on that. The media was hard at work. On two of the major cable stations, expert panels were already analyzing the Middle Eastern groups' joining forces, though it wasn't even necessarily true that ISIS and AQAP were collaborating. When speaking to infidels, you're allowed to lie.

An older file with a year-old tip we'd investigated from here about radicalized Islamic recruiting in Las Vegas looked relevant again. Jane Stone worked that but hadn't gotten anywhere with it. She'd also chased Denny Mondari's bomb-maker rumor. Mondari had been my confidential informant before she took over. I called and left a message for him. I also tried his apartment manager, who stonewalled me, saying Mondari was on vacation.

"When is he coming back?"

"No idea," the manager said.

"He communicates with you. You need to tell him to call me. Here's my number. If I don't hear from him, I'll come see you in the morning."

I wouldn't, but I might as well warm up the conversation. I made another call before leaving the office, this one an inquiry to the Royal Australian Air Force about a drone pilot named Philip Ramer. An officer politely took down the message that I'd like to talk to Ramer. He asked why, but I didn't say.

Near midnight I left the office and drove home for a shower, clean clothes, and maybe four hours' sleep. Home was a beige stucco house at the edge of the desert, with a two-car garage, a brown concrete-tile roof, oak plank floors, and a lap pool installed two years ago to help strengthen the muscles of my lower back. When my wife, Carrie, died in a car accident a decade ago, domestic life ended. Other than the lap pool, I'd done nothing with the house since. The first two years after her death, I had avoided coming home altogether. When I did, I avoided our bedroom. In those days of billowing sorrow, I'd slept outside on the lawn furniture or on the couch in the front room.

Even today, I live mostly in the kitchen or on the terrace in back. That's where I like the light and air most. Sitting outside in the night, looking up at the stars and the black lines of desert mountains calms me. I understood what Beatty meant when he said he lived in the trailer park because from the back of his trailer he had open sky. I take comfort in knowing it will all still be here long after me.

A sensor light at the porch kicked on as I limped to the front door. The limp arrives when I get tired. The lap pool helps keep it at bay. In the kitchen I pulled a bottle of rum off a cabinet shelf and tapped a baguette, bought on a whim a few days ago, against the countertop. The bread was brick hard, but I sawed through and made a sandwich before pouring a short glass of rum. I showered with the water as hot as I could take and directed it at the lower left side of my back. The shower is part of my drill.

When I returned to the kitchen, the rear patio lights were on. Their motion sensors were hair trigger. Most likely it was the coyote that had been around lately. I liked the craftiness of the coyote and how it was building on what it had learned, but it was after a neighboring cat and I was going to have to run it off soon.

Not tonight, though, nothing tonight. The rum tasted right. *Now get sleep. Get back to the office. Try not to let grief take away what you need to do.* I opened the slider to let air in and rummaged once more for food. When muscles in my lower back spasmed, I debated getting in the pool for fifteen minutes. Often that helped.

After returning from the hospital in Germany and when I was still learning to walk with a rhythm rather than jerking, halting steps, I'd started jogging on the track at the local high school. I ran in the cool early light or later in the dusk-to-dark hour. I ran when I was least likely to be seen, being too proud to do it any other way. Even with yoga and Pilates classes and orthopedic massage and all the rest, I pitched to the left with each stride.

That first summer it didn't take long for a couple of bored kids to figure out that the freak sometimes showed at sunset. The boys were maybe twelve and thirteen. One would get out in front of me and the other behind, and they'd circle the track half-tipped over. The mockery didn't really bother me, and they didn't run many laps. It's not easy to run and giggle when you're bent over. I was a smart-ass kid myself once, and their unsentimental judgment was better than the somber visits I got from agent friends who felt compelled to give me career advice.

Running helped my mind as much as my body, and that first summer I worked my way up to sixteen laps, and somewhere along the way the two kids figured out it wasn't funny anymore. I tore the same adhesions loose, day after day after day, hurt all the time, and took painkillers until they made me stupid. I stopped those, connected with the bomb techs in Washington, and started forward again.

I took another swallow of rum as my phone vibrated with a text. It read, I'm out back. I walked out and saw her.

"Jo, what are you doing here?"

"I came to see you. I'm so sorry. I was thinking about you being alone after what's happened. I came in the garage side. I hope that's still okay."

"It'll always be okay."

"I'm—"

She paused and I put an arm around her shoulders. Our breakup didn't need to happen, or maybe it wasn't a breakup. Another doctor, a guy a couple of years off a divorce and close in age to her, was the catalyst. I never looked him up or learned anything more about him than what she told me. He was a brilliant surgeon, great athlete, piloted his own plane, owned a vineyard, and so forth. The surgeon was just living his life, and Jo and I had reached a place where she needed more commitment and wasn't getting it from me.

One Friday morning I had to go to Chicago on a case, so I canceled out on our weekend plans. Jo was on her rounds. I couldn't reach her and left a message with a promise to call back. By three o'clock that afternoon, we were closing in on a suspect. That carried on into the night, and I never got a call off to Jo. I didn't apologize until Monday. When she answered, she was angry and said, "No problem. I went with Dr. Gravure and had a great time. We're going out again Friday night."

I left it there. She called and texted a number of times a few weeks later, but I didn't return any of them. Too much pride—one of my many flaws—though I didn't stop thinking about her. That was six months ago. Melissa said I was acting like a teenage boy and was a fool to let her go, but it was more complicated than Melissa knew. Jo was forty-three and fit. She was looking for someone to love and grow old with, and I wasn't a good bet for that.

In Germany when I was just getting over the worst, a doctor there, who prided himself on candor, told me I'd age out sooner than normal because of internal organ damage. He told me this like I'd won a contest. His guess was I had fifteen to twenty years more. He urged me to heal and get out and make the most of it. Jo could do better than me, although tonight I was very touched that she was here, and it was great to see her. It was more than great. It was emotional just to touch each other again. She wept as I told her I was first into the Alagara and found Melissa.

"How can you even work?" she asked.

"How can I not?"

I moved the conversation to Julia, and Jo said, "I came to tell you. I checked on Julia before I left and talked to the surgeon. He said he'd spoken to you."

"Yeah, we talked early this morning and again this afternoon."

"There's new swelling from the surgery, but it's still looking hopeful tonight. Did he tell you that?"

"Not quite like that, no."

"He's being careful with you."

Jo sat down on the edge of a lounge chair.

"I didn't know if you'd be home, but thought I'd try."

"I'm home for a few hours, and I'm glad you're here."

I sat down next to her. She reached a hand out. I took it.

"You have a lot to figure out," Jo said.

"I do."

Neither Jo nor I have kids, and I wasn't really sure what it meant to see my niece through high school into college, or how to make it work if it turned out that Julia was paralyzed. Jo squeezed my hand.

"I think she'll be okay," Jo said.

"Do you really believe that or just hope for it?"

I saw her hesitate and heard her choose her words.

"Swelling after injury varies in all of us. Julia may be on the low end of the curve."

"I thought this was about bruising."

"It's about both, and the early signs are good. Latik is the best we have. He heard about the bombings last night and drove straight to the hospital." She squeezed my hand. "This is terrible timing, but I have to say this. I've been thinking a lot about us. When I heard about the bombings and your family, I decided I wouldn't wait any longer. We made a mistake. We belong together. That's not for tonight, but I want you to know that."

I had similar thoughts most days.

"I'm here for you," she said. "I'll call you if I learn anything. About us, I'm going to leave it there for you to think about when you're ready."

She kissed me, then walked out the back gate. I heard her car start and pull away as I sat thinking about her. Then alone in the night by the pool, I let go and wept for everything: for Melissa, whom I'd never hear laugh again; for my closest friend, Jim Kern; and for Nate, so full of life and forward-looking. Melissa used to tell me in a regular way and only half-jokingly, that I was so, so lucky she and Jim and their family were in Vegas. I had a standard retort, but I knew her point was true. I was always a workaholic cop, and after Carrie died, that only got worse. Melissa's family was my family, my link to seeing children grow up and a lot of other things. I was so lucky. I knew that and never forgot it. I'd have to change and be more than I have been to truly help Julia cope and move on.

I sat there by the pool and talked to Melissa and promised her what I would do. I don't even remember what time it was when I got up and walked inside. I slept an hour, maybe an hour and a half, and headed back in.

14

In December 1988 a bomb brought down Pan Am Flight 103. That was nine years before I joined the FBI, but I still kept a file titled *Lockerbie*. In it were scanned copies of satellite imagery, helicopter surveys, and an accounting of the path leading to the Swiss-made part, a Mebo MST-13 timer used to make the bomb. Early in the morning on the sixth of July, I scanned the file as a kind of touchstone. At 7:00 a.m., I sat down with Lacey Shah, the young agent Venuti had assigned to work with me.

I drank black coffee, my habit, and Shah drank tea while she thumbnailed her background. This was her first year with the Bureau, first six months, really. Started in January and arrived here yesterday. Headquarters was beefing up staff in the area for the duration of this investigation. Venuti had said he didn't know if she was aware yet that I'd lost family. He left it to me to sort that out, and from the easy way she was talking, I knew she didn't. I liked the calm, confident way she expressed herself and I didn't want to interrupt that with my sadness. It could wait.

"You rate yourself highly computer literate?" I asked.

"I am and I believe the computer is the greatest investigative tool ever."

Venuti loved to say the same thing, but were we solving more cases now that everyone camped out in front of a screen? That conversation could also wait. We moved on. Lacey had never written a FISA request nor done a Title III, but was confident she could, along with anything else we needed.

"I need coaching, but I'm resourceful."

"That's a good trait around here."

"When I was six years old, my mom would go to work and leave me to take care of my baby brother and sister."

"How old were they?"

"Three-and-a-half and five."

"Which one was easiest?"

"My brother. He was the five-year-old, so he understood that if he gave me trouble I'd beat the shit out of him."

"You left this out of your FBI interview."

"I don't tell many people."

I liked her right away, dead serious but with a strong dark sense of humor.

"How are you with sleep deprivation?" I asked.

"It sucks, but I can fake it."

"How about on the phone?"

"I can talk to anybody."

"Bring in some extra clothes and stick them in a gym locker. If we get onto something, we're going to stay on it. We're working local leads. How did they place the bombs? Who helped them? Where did they stay? What did they eat? Anything, everything. Everyone leaves a footprint."

I smelled the strong black tea as she lifted the mug and took another swallow. My feeling about her was good, but chasing local leads while the drumbeat to bomb somewhere in the Middle East intensified would take concentration. I took the conversation back to the C-4.

"The CIA says 311 pounds of C-4 made it home to America. Maybe half of that was used in the Alagara bombings," I said.

She nodded. She knew that already.

"Our primary focus is finding the bomb maker. Most of all, we're looking for him."

"You say him."

"It's far more likely."

"Okay, if you say so, but I didn't know we made assumptions."

"We don't, but we have to filter. It could be a woman, but if you go through the known database you're going to see men."

"Will I get out in the field with you, or am I going to be in front of a computer all the time? I don't want to just fill out forms."

"You don't want to be anybody's girl Friday."

"I don't know what that means. Is that like some old-school thing?"

"You want to do it all."

"Yes."

"Then let's get started."

She logged into my list of bomb makers, and I drove to the leased airplane hangar where debris from the bombings had gone. I wasn't a bomb geek, but I knew the techs and talked their language. I had a good head for science and therefore they figured I was, underneath, one of them.

The hangar was near the airport. Before I got there, a call came from the FBI yard where the Hullabaloo van Juan Menderes was driving had been towed.

"Grale?"

"Yeah."

"Come take a look at this."

"We're working the bomb maker. What have you got?"

"A hidden compartment that's too small to hold a big-ass cake. This van was modified."

"Did you call for a drug dog?"

"Dog is on the way. Where are you?"

I changed lanes and made a hard right, though I was unsure now where I fit into the search for Menderes. We'd put out a fugitive warrant on him. Half of Las Vegas PD was searching for him.

"Heading toward you, maybe ten minutes out. But I won't be there long."

I arrived with the drug dog and her handler. It didn't take long to determine that the compartment in the interior of the van had held cocaine. Nor was it hard to deduce that the Hullabaloo van delivered more than cake. Which brought to mind the cake in the van with the address tag still on it, despite the people at the delivery address having claimed they had received it.

We all got in the van and looked at the clever compartment with its sliding steel cover. You park the Hullabaloo van and carry the cake box up, and inside is cocaine instead of cake. You make the delivery, then dump the cake that was ordered. Or like Juan, maybe you give it to your girlfriend.

The night of the bombings, Menderes made all his deliveries and texted they were done. One answer to that was he didn't know about the Bar Alagara bombing and continued work. Another scenario was he'd detonated the bar bomb and making three more deliveries was his cover. The first one was simpler and rang closer to the truth, I thought. *He delivered the coke, abandoned the van, and ran because he was nobody's fool.* He heard about the bombing and knew we'd want to talk to him and look at his van. I thought through that as I drove to the airplane hangar.

There I surveyed the debris and remembered the parallel investigation the FBI had conducted with the National Transportation Safety Board after TWA Flight 800 went down. I was there for that one. I had interviewed witnesses who claimed they saw a streak of light move toward the airliner. That put me right at the heart of the accidental-missile-launch controversy. Several witnesses I walked the beach with were certain they saw a missile arc toward the plane, though we couldn't find any evidence of that in the wreckage, and the conclusion was that there was a spark in a gas tank. Remembering that was a reminder to let small details accumulate and to believe that when you have enough, the truth will reveal itself.

I turned as a bomb tech walked up to me. Ted Darza. He fist-bumped me.

"What's up, Grale?"

"I'm looking for Special Agent Stone's Apple Mac laptop."

"There's a half a Mac here, but it's pretty trashed."

It took Darza several minutes to sort out labels on plastic bags holding debris. Then he pulled out a Mac without a screen and with its keyboard half-scraped away. It was dented but not burned. He showed me a map of where the damaged laptop was found. I turned the laptop in my hands and said, "I need a copy of everything on it—today, if possible."

He shook his head.

"Is that too fast?" I asked.

"Well, yeah, because I work for the Bureau not you. But the other problem is everything is going through headquarters first."

"First?"

"Yep."

"Not this. This is about something Jane Stone and I worked on that Washington doesn't know anything about. They wouldn't know what they were looking at. It's important here and lost there, and it could matter. So I've got to see it first."

"They said no exceptions."

"They always say that."

Headquarters wanted to control the investigation, no surprise there. A rumor making the rounds this morning was that a cell phone found inside the Alagara had a video of a candlelit cake and small children at a table in front of the bar. According to the rumor, the video had a time stamp, and headquarters knew the exact moment of detonation. That fed a suspicion Washington was seeing evidence ahead of us, and Darza had just confirmed it. I looked down the line of tables with plastic bags of bomb debris lined up and numbered.

"If that laptop is going to Washington, I have to get a look at what's on it first. Can you at least do that for me? Text me. I'll come here and read what's on it."

"It's tight around here. They're down on us and very clear about the protocol."

"Are we being videotaped?"

"Yes."

"You and me talking?"

"Yes."

"What I'm looking for predates the bombings. It's something Jane and I were working on in early June. She took the lead, and I don't have her most up-to-date notes. I've got to follow up on it, and you've got to help me with her laptop."

That wasn't reaching him, so I took another tack. I pulled a twisted aluminum fragment from my pocket.

"How much of this have you found?"

"Plenty. Where did you get that one?"

"A surgeon removed it from my niece's hamstring. I think it's an aluminum fragment from a wine refrigerator that was behind the bar. Does that make sense to you?"

Darza shrugged, not even willing to answer that, though it was already accepted that the bomb had been in a wine refrigerator.

"I was the first person inside. These fragments were everywhere. Under the bar the concrete was scarified by the blast. Where are you storing these fragments?"

"They shipped to DC."

"When?"

"This morning."

"Okay, so we'll see a report posted soon."

"I don't know about that. That's above me."

I handed Darza the aluminum fragment again, and I said, "I hear there's a cell phone video. I'm looking for the driver who delivered the cake in that video. He might be in it because he helped carry the cake in. He's missing."

"The guy everyone is looking for?"

"Yeah, him, and I'm working him, so the cake delivery timing matters to me. Part of the rumor I heard this morning is there's a stamp on the video that reads '8:03 p.m.' If that's true, hand me back the aluminum fragment I just gave you."

Darza handed me the fragment, and I calculated as I slowly slid it into my pocket. My three-minute, forty-two-second conversation with Jim Kern had ended at 7:48. Lake Mead Boulevard is a long road, and I was on it for a while after talking to Jim. I'd hit a string of red lights, the last at the stoplight where I had looked across and seen the Hullabaloo van headed in the other direction, driven by Juan Menderes.

My call with Jim ended at 7:48. The blast was at 8:03, so there was a fifteen-minute gap between my hanging up with Jim and the bomb going off. How long did it take for Jim and Menderes to walk the cake to the table? Not too long, I guessed. Maybe a few minutes, and the cake was already paid for. All Menderes had to do was set it down and go. His text that delivery was made arrived at Hullabaloo's office at 7:53. That left ten minutes for Menderes to cover the mile to where I saw him. That was too much time, and it troubled me.

There was another thing. When Menderes left the van, he left his phone under the passenger seat, most likely out of fear of being tracked with it. Its last activity showed a happy-face emoticon in a text to Hullabaloo and nothing more. So when I saw him on the phone in the intersection, he must have been on a different phone.

"Grale?" Darza said.

"Yeah."

"I've got to go back to work now, but we'll get to the laptop today. Are you going to be around?"

"I'll make sure I am."

"I'll call you."

15

Beatty called after I left Darza. He said he'd seen his face on a TV in a mini-mart. He'd kept his head down, paid, and went from there to the insurance office of a friend in Tonopah he rented garage space from to pick up the garage key and retrieve a couple of things.

"With what's happened I shouldn't be bothering you," Beatty said. "I'm sorry, Grale."

"It's okay."

"When I asked my friend for the garage key, she said she was supposed to call the FBI if I showed up. I said, 'Call them while I'm here.' She did, and I talked to the agent."

"Was it one of the agents who interviewed you yesterday?"

"No, someone else, a guy named Patterson."

"How did it go yesterday?"

"Not that well. This Patterson told me to wait at the insurance office and two agents would come get me and bring me back—the FBI has more questions. I told him, 'Not today, not after yesterday.' He got fired up and told me to stay right there and agents would come get me. I don't know what I said after that, but it wasn't nice. My insurance broker friend told me the FBI took all my stuff out of her garage early this morning. We're talking camping gear, the gun my dad gave me when I turned twelve, that kind of thing."

"You'll get them back."

"On TV they're turning me into a psycho. Where are they getting that from?"

"Not from us. Why don't you answer their follow-up questions and then be on your way?"

"Did that yesterday, and there's nothing happening at the airfield today. Besides, they're just fishing. I think I'm going to take a ride and go see a friend. I'm just letting you know."

"You don't need to let me know. You're making your own decisions. I'll talk to you later."

July 6th, late morning

Beatty got on his bike and rode south then west across the desert toward California. As he clipped through at ninety miles an hour he flashed back to a colonel pointing at him in a flight trailer, saying "Trigger puller," meaning that as a high compliment, the one who takes it to the enemy. Back then it felt righteous.

He thought of Dr. Frederic lecturing him on post-traumatic stress disorder, telling him what to expect and how to manage it. He'd waited nine months after his discharge for an appointment through the VA with Frederic, and after all that, Dr. Fred turned out to be an asshole. But Frederic was right about his guilt.

He pushed the bike to 130 mph and screamed past a Nevada Highway Patrol officer sitting on the shoulder. The trooper threw on his lights and sirens but never had a chance. He was into California before the cop got anywhere close. He rode fast along the White Mountains and didn't slow until Bishop and didn't stop until he was south to Independence, where he took the turn out to Laura's ranch.

Her truck and her old Jeep were there, but as he got off his bike he lost his nerve and for a long moment debated leaving. If she hadn't opened the front door, he would have.

Laura came down the creaky porch steps, asking, "Why is the FBI getting serious about you?"

"I test-flew some drones in Taiwan and accidentally got into a Department of Defense investigation."

"Is that the truth?"

"As best I know."

"Do you want me to help?"

"I don't want to pull you into this. I just wanted to see you. I don't think there's anything anyone can do. The FBI is looking at me for the Vegas bombings."

"On TV they're saying after your discharge you expressed extreme hostility toward the air force. Did you write any more letters to the air force like the one you did for Dr. Fred?"

"None like the one you read."

"But you wrote more?"

"You can read them. There's nothing wrong with them."

"Is Paul Grale still helping you?"

"He's telling me to suck it up and ride it out."

"I've seen that trailer at Wunderland on TV. What are you doing living there still? You promised me you'd move out of there as soon as you had enough money. And why is plastic over the windows?"

"My computer is right there. The plastic blocks the sun. There's too much glare without it."

She had hated the trailer, hated the whole idea of him living in it. She called it hiding and only slept one night there.

"You look really good, Laura. I hope you're doing great. I'm not here to freak you out."

She came down off the steps.

"Why don't you call one of these TV reporters and tell them what the plastic over the windows is for?"

"I told the FBI yesterday."

"Dude, sometimes I wonder how you got this far. They're not against you. They're trying to figure out what happened with those bombings, and they don't know who you are yet. Park your bike in the barn and come on in. I'll be in the kitchen."

He rode the bike to the barn and rolled it in. The smell of horse urine lingered, but the horses were long gone, the barn floor dry as sand. Two fluorescent lights hung from roof trusses and looked new, so maybe she was going to stay for a while. This ranch used to be in her mother's family and they had once talked about living here after they were married.

In the kitchen, he looked at her and wondered how he'd screwed up so bad that he lost her. She reached across the table and took his hand as they talked about the Kerns getting killed. Laura cried and they ate and talked and took a walk before he left. Laura believed in him, or maybe he just needed to believe that. Either way, on the ride back to Nevada and the airfield, Beatty felt calmer. It wasn't until later when he checked news stories online that the feeling went away. When it did, it went a long way away and he came down hard.

16

At 12:01 p.m. Vegas time, Al Qaeda in the Arabian Peninsula uploaded a video to their website with an English speaker talking about a corrupt American army officer at Kandahar Airfield in Afghanistan who had sold them the C-4 they'd used to strike against the devil. They outed an army warrant officer named Lansing Guthrie. The spokesman ranted about how easy it was to bribe an American soldier, as if that proved the West was corrupt—this from a culture where bribes were the norm. The rest of it was the usual crap, but I listened to all of it.

In an early afternoon briefing, we learned details of the sale of C-4 to the Haqqani network. The CIA had obtained the information about this and the secondary sale to AQAP from its sources. No real details were divulged of how they tracked it from that point. They never informed the army, but via a separate theft the army picked up on Guthrie and a second warrant officer, as yet unnamed, who was now cooperating.

There was additional information uploaded to the JTTF site on how the C-4 crossed into the United States. According to a still heavily redacted report, it came in a routine shipment of household-cleaning products from the manufacturing plant of a well-known US corporation. At the border an intentional spill of chemicals in the cargo area blunted border dogs' ability to detect explosives. Many salient details were missing, including how the C-4 left a Phoenix warehouse without being detected. I reread this information and was still skeptical about the Phoenix disappearing act. I leaned back in my chair mulling that over.

"Get what you wanted from the briefings?" Venuti asked me.

"Not really."

"Talk to me."

"How did the C-4 leave the Phoenix warehouse if the warehouse was under constant surveillance?"

"A mistake got made somewhere. That happens. What else?"

"How do we know they weren't watching boxes of detergent, and the C-4 crossed the border a different way?"

"How do we know anything? How do we know the earth is round? We know because a CIA team tracked it from Afghanistan to Phoenix. Why do you do this? Why can't you take things at face value?"

"How did they confirm the poundage of what was actually delivered? Did they just assume that what was stolen got delivered?"

"Okay, that's a good question." Venuti wrote a note to himself and said, "There's another shorter briefing this afternoon. I'll find out what I can. What else?"

"Beatty. How did the interview with him go?"

"He answered all questions. He was alternately combative and contrite. People who know about these things say he exhibited paranoid tendencies."

"But he answered all questions?"

"Yes, and you can watch the tape and draw your own conclusions."

"We owe him a public response if we're satisfied he had no direct involvement in the bombings."

"He's still under investigation, and we have follow-up questions he's evading."

"But so far, nothing ties him to the bombings other than the imagination of the DOD investigators."

Venuti lifted a hand to stop me.

"I don't want to sound condescending, especially with what you're going through, but I doubt you can keep an open mind about Beatty's motives." He tapped his desk. "And he's not your problem to solve. Just let him go for now, Paul. I mean that."

"Are we leaving him dangling because we don't have anything else? We're going to let the media feed on him to buy us time to come up with better leads? Is that the plan?"

"Listen to yourself. Twenty-nine died inside the Alagara, including your sister, brother-in-law, and nephew. Including Jane, eight law enforcement officers were killed in the secondary explosion, and a Las Vegas Metro deputy commander was left paraplegic, but you're indignant about a guy who sat in a blacked-out trailer with the US Capitol on his target screen. If we didn't look hard at him, we wouldn't be doing our jobs."

"I've read everything that came from the Air Force Office of Special Investigations and the DOD. There's nothing there."

"We're done here."

Venuti pointed a finger at my chest.

"Beatty washed out after sitting in a lounge chair, flying drones for seven years. He should have gotten back on his feet a long time ago. The reason he didn't is he has psychological issues, including extreme animosity toward his former employer, which happens to be the United States. I can't do this with you, Grale. I don't mean to cut you off, and I can't imagine what you're feeling today, but I can't do this right now. With everything else, I just can't."

Throughout the afternoon, the story evolved on the Kandahar Warrant Officer Lansing Guthrie. Guthrie stoked the press by communicating through his lawyer that he had sold the explosives to an Afghan warlord to battle the Taliban after Obama pulled the troops out of Afghanistan. He did it for America. Some of the media loved that angle, one major TV station in particular, and, of course, various wing nut radio hosts in the desert.

At 2:30 p.m., I drove to the hospital and at the nurse's station was told, "Julia's grandmother is with her right now, sir."

"It must be somebody else. Her grandparents are dead."

The nurse hovered while I went in to resolve who the "grandmother" was. I was very grateful that a couple who were neighbors of the Kerns had sat with Julia yesterday. That's who was there. Patricia Hunt, the neighbor, was in a chair reading a magazine. Near her were pound cake, pretzels, and a cup of coffee. It looked like she'd been there awhile. I couldn't remember her husband's name until I shook her hand. I thanked her for all she and Charlie, her husband, had done.

"We've been here as much as we can. Charlie has gone home to get some sleep, but he'll be back tonight. We haven't seen you at all."

"I'm doing what I can."

She looked long-faced and disapproving, and then just laid it out there as I moved to Julia's bedside.

"What is it you're doing that's more important?"

"I'm working on things I can't leave alone right now. Let me spend some time with my niece, if that's all right."

Julia was weaker than I'd expected, but she'd passed strength and motor tests on both sides of her body earlier in the day, so that was good. A doctor stopped in soon after and communicated that she wanted to talk outside in the corridor.

"She's withdrawn," the doctor said, "but she also has painkillers in her that could exacerbate those feelings. The back of her legs, her ear, and her back are very sore today, not so much from surgery as tissue trauma from the initial injury. And we need to talk about her ear.

There'll be a decision this afternoon about whether she needs another surgery. We'll need to be able to reach you. Or would you rather her grandparents make the decision?"

"Her grandparents are dead. These are neighbors. Call me regarding anything to do with her health."

"I must have misunderstood." She paused on that, then said, "Try to be here as much as you can."

"What about her spinal cord?"

"So far, so good, but we're still waiting."

I sat with Julia, and while I was there she texted several of her friends about coming to see her. I also realized as she scrolled through her phone that she didn't have my number. I gave her all the ways to reach me, and she entered those in her phone. But I couldn't do anything for her grief and was disturbed by the encounter with the neighbor. I told Julia I'd try to get back by tonight.

In the hallway I ran into Patricia again, who told me the Kerns' dog, Coal, was now at their house. "He's very happy there. Charlie moved him over today."

"Thank you. Are you okay having him with you for several days?"

"We think ours should be his new home."

"He's going to keep on being Julia's dog."

"We have lots to talk about," she said with peculiar brightness. "We had a number of very good conversations with Jim and Melissa. We were very close to them, and in these hard times we have to rise to do the Lord's work. What is it you do, Mr. Grale?"

"I work for the government."

"My father worked for the government. He was a postman, but he would have found the time to be here in this moment of need. God calls us. We have to answer when we're called. Are you married?"

"Not anymore."

"You're divorced?"

"No."

We did this for several minutes, during which I took a longer look at her. Sturdy chin, a rock-solid certainty in her blue-gray eyes, hair long and braided as though she were a young girl.

I said, "Thank you for everything you've done, Patricia, but I'm her only remaining family. Do you understand?"

"Melissa came to me last night."

I had no answer for that and left her in the hallway.

17

"Beatty rode his bike a long way to see his former fiancée, Laura Cotter," Venuti said. "Why would he do that?"

"He's looking for someone he can trust."

"She left him. Why would she help him now?"

"Why wouldn't she?"

"Oh, I don't know, maybe because she was his fiancée, and when he imploded she had to give up on her dreams after burning through most of her youth with him. Sometimes people get an attitude after that."

"Are you sending agents to talk to her?"

"Read this first, and then we'll talk."

Venuti slid a piece of paper toward me.

"A Dr. Bernard Frederic sent that to us. I talked to him today. He works for the VA and treated Beatty for PTSD. He felt compelled to contact us."

The letter was addressed to an air force general, handwritten on the kind of lined paper you used to see in a schoolroom. It was written in bold blue ink. You could tell that even with this scanned copy. I read slowly. Beatty called the air force's actions evil and said he would "take action on my own, if I have to." Nothing was specific about the action, but the language was colored by grandiosity and anger in a way I'd never heard him speak.

"Just your basic letter to an air force general, right?' Venuti asked.

I laid it down on his desk.

"If he sent this, how did the doctor get it?"

"It was never sent."

"Laura, the fiancée you just asked about, mentioned a letter once that was written as a therapy a doctor had proposed. If this is that letter, I don't think it was ever intended to be sent."

"He wrote it."

I read the letter again. He started by arguing that it was not only the right thing to do, but it was inherent in the air force code of honor to acknowledge the wrongful killing of an American citizen. I skipped down to a particularly inflammatory paragraph near the end.

"If the air force command fails to do this, then those who know the truth must defend it at whatever cost, in whatever circumstances. It is unacceptable to me to take the coward's course and forget or deny what we did. If the air force fails to take action and acknowledge this wrong, then I will do whatever is necessary."

"Grale."

I laid the letter back down.

"What else do you know about Laura Cotter?"

"That it was very hard for her to leave him. She's a great human being. The manager in the trailer park where Beatty lives is already giving tours of Beatty's trailer to TV crews. Don't bring the media down on her."

I saw I wasn't getting through and had another thought.

"Laura has an older brother in Denver. Why don't we give him a call? He might be able to give you a better sense of Beatty than I can. Google the name 'Van Cotter.' He's in the oil business in Denver."

In an online photo taken at his Denver office, Cotter wore cowboy boots, jeans, and a light coat. He looked tanned and healthy and a bit like a throwback to an earlier era. Venuti found a phone number and, though he seemed to think it was a waste of time, he went along with it. He put the call on speakerphone as I pulled a chair over.

Cotter's first words after I said hello were, "You calling about Jeremy?"

"My supervisor and I are."

"I hear you're looking for him."

"He spent all day yesterday at our office," I said.

"Then I must listen to the wrong news stations. I heard he escaped capture earlier this morning and is wanted for questioning about Al Qaeda connections. Al Qaeda connections, hell, he's killed more of them than damn near anyone in the country."

"He was with Laura today," I said. "Has Laura talked to you about Jeremy recently?"

"To tell the truth, she never talks about him. When he hurt her the way he did, he lost me, and Laura knows that."

I saw Venuti's tight smile. Just what he wanted to hear, but Van Cotter continued.

"Time has gone by, and I don't really hold it against him anymore. We don't give those drone pilots enough respect. Do you remember the book *All Quiet on the Western Front*? When I was growing up, it was required reading. I've forgotten the author's name, but I've never forgotten his note at the beginning. I remember it word for word.

"'This book is to be neither an accusation nor a confession, and least of all an adventure, for death is not an adventure for those who stand face to face with it. It will try simply to tell of a generation of men who, even though they may have escaped its shells, were destroyed by the war.'

"That's stayed with me, Paul. I think some of the morally ambiguous things we do now with such impunity have consequences that fall hard on our soldiers, and we don't acknowledge them the way we should. Drone pilots live in that arena. I can understand what happened to Jeremy. If he went to see Laura, it was probably just to be near her. Hell, when I feel blue, I'll call her. I'll call her now. If I learn anything, I'll let you know."

"We'd appreciate it."

"I've still got your card. Good to hear your voice again."

"Likewise. Talk to you soon."

18

I was deep into bomb makers but wanted to double back on Menderes's roommate, Enrique Vasco. Now looked like the right time for that and to let Lacey work at locating Denny Mondari. We'd scratched off two other local leads, but Mondari was still on the plate. I'd be off Menderes soon, but I was sure Vasco had held back the night of the bombing, so both Lacey and I had been digging into him. I got what I needed from a Metro vice cop I knew and drove over and knocked on his door.

Vasco shook his head when he saw me. He squinted at the bright sunlight in the street. He looked tired.

"I've got nothing left to say, dude, and I've got to go to work."

"You'll be late today."

Lacey had learned that Enrique Vasco grew up in Houston in an upscale neighborhood. Both parents and two sisters still lived there. One sister was an attorney, the other in politics. When Vasco graduated from high school, he moved to Vegas and had been here since, working his way up through casino jobs to his current gig, bartending at a hip pool bar. He was well liked and no doubt saw great tip money. Bartenders at the right place could make $50–$60,000 a year in tips. He was good-looking and smart and probably led a good life, but he was also questioned after a sting operation busted a cocaine ring five years ago.

He'd sold coke from behind the bar where he was working. He was never charged, though others were. In exchange for talking, his testimony was sealed. The Las Vegas PD vice officer who stopped by the office and talked outside with me this morning stressed that. Only six went to prison. Vasco skated in exchange for testimony.

But here's the kicker. Juan Menderes was also questioned in the same investigation. The sealed compartment in the van made complete sense to the LVPD vice officer, as did the fake-cake delivery scheme. He'd seen the same technique with pizza deliveries.

I glanced at Vasco's bare feet, shorts, and T-shirt.

"Throw your sandals on and walk out back with me, but not to look at the fence."

He shook his head, said, "Naw, dude, I gotta get going."

"Let's talk about when you and Juan got busted. But let's go around back. I want to show you what's coming."

That stopped him, but not for long.

"Any testimony I gave back then is sealed, so you just fucked up."

"Yeah, it could be, but it won't change anything. Grab your sandals."

As we walked, I cut to the chase.

"We know Juan made coke deliveries from the Hullabaloo van, and you made the decision not to tell us."

"I didn't know he was doing that."

"How could you not know?"

"We don't talk drugs. I don't deal anymore. I don't touch drugs. I don't go near cocaine. I don't use it. I don't sell it."

We turned the corner, and the stucco wall of the house radiated heat like a barbecue. Dry weeds crunched underfoot.

"Watch over there across the subdivision," I said, but didn't have to. Vasco saw the line of Las Vegas Metro Police vehicles with their flashers come into view.

"They're headed here," I said. "We probably have less than three minutes. They've got a drug dog with them and a warrant to get into your house. Are they going to find drugs?"

Vasco didn't say anything. It was as if he'd shut off a switch and gone inside. The seconds ticked down. As part of the theater, an LVPD officer let out a little whoop of his siren when they neared.

"This is it, Enrique. Start talking or don't say a word."

Vasco could do the same calculation I was doing. If the dogs found salable amounts of cocaine anywhere in the house, he could be arrested. He was a loyal guy, but if he wasn't part of the drug dealing, then it was time to cut loose from Juan.

"I don't know where he is. I really don't," Vasco said. "Juan bought someone else's papers or his sister did. That's why he took off. She lives near here. I'm not even sure if she's his fucking sister, but she lives near here."

"You remember her full name now and can show me where she lives?"

"Yeah."

"That the Rosamar you were talking about the night of the bombing?"

"Yeah, that's her. She found out about a Juan Menderes in prison in Mexico who was a US citizen and bought his ID for Juan. Social security number, birth certificate—Juan became that dude. I don't know if she's mixed up in drugs or works for the same people, but she doesn't ever need money. She tells people she was a blackjack dealer and quit when she married a rich guy, but I've never seen the husband and the chica sure doesn't act married."

"What's her full name?"

"Rosamar Largo. She's tough, man."

"Why didn't you tell us this the night of the bombing?"

"Because I didn't want anything to do with any shit she and Juan were into. That's the truth."

It sounded like truth, but you never really know. The drug dog was out of the vehicle and getting ready when we walked back around front. Two of the officers started toward us as Vasco talked to me in a fast, low voice.

"You know about the case I talked on. It was supposed to be fucking sealed forever, so it's bullshit, you know, but that was it for me. I haven't gone anywhere near drugs since. When cartel soldiers come to my bar and tell me I have to sell, I quit and find another bartending job. I don't move coke. I don't know what Juan does now. I know he wanted that driver job real bad, and Rosamar slept with the dude that owns the company so he could get it. Omar, Homer, whatever his name is, she did him at a party at his house."

"How do you know that?"

"Juan told me."

"Did you know he was making coke deliveries in the Hullabaloo van?"

He shook his head and explained. "He doesn't talk to me. He knows I'm out and never coming back."

"Did he know you testified?"

"He knows. He also knows I protected him. I'm not lying, you find any drugs in there, it's not me. It's him and his fucking made-up sister."

"What are we going to find in your room?"

"A gun."

"Why?"

"In case they ever come for me."

"No drugs."

"None."

"Nothing you were holding for Juan."

"Nada."

"Where did he run to?"

"Got to be Mexico. He worked for a coyote. He knows some bad dudes, and they'll get him back across the other way."

"Why did he come home first?"

"You were right on before. ID, money, like you were saying that night."

"Are you sure the drug dog isn't going to find anything in your bedroom?"

"Not unless they plant it."

"That won't happen. Okay, if it's a gun only, we'll float along together awhile longer, but if it looks like you're holding back and have lied again, then you go down with the ship."

"Get the dog there."

The coke dog scented cocaine in Juan's room and was all over it when the mattress was flipped and a zippered slit found in the middle of it. When it was unzipped, there was no coke, but there was a cell phone. The phone got bagged and I took it with me. The pouch in the mattress had held cocaine at some point. The dog made that clear. Maybe it had once held money and a different ID as well.

The coke dog ran through the rest of the house. There was residue in the bathroom nearest Menderes's room but nothing in Vasco's room or anywhere else. Vasco's gun, wherever it was hidden, wasn't found and I let that be. When it was over, I told Vasco to get in my car and that I'd talk with the vice officers who were ready to take him in and question him. I briefed them on what Vasco had told me, and then, with Vasco in my car, drove to Rosamar Largo's house.

"That red Mustang is her car," he said. "And everything I told you is true."

"Don't leave Vegas."

Minutes after dropping him back at his house, I was on the phone with Venuti telling him what we found.

"How do you want to do this?" I asked. "Do you want another agent to take it from here?"

"Do you have any kind of rapport with this Enrique Vasco?"

"Not really, but he is talking to me. This Rosamar Largo I haven't met or had any contact with."

He was quiet, then asked, "What do you think, Grale?"

"She knows Vasco. I have the Vasco connection, and that'll carry weight with her. I think I'll stick with the Menderes search another day, maybe two, but no more than that. I'll brief whoever you put on it."

"I agree with that. Call her. Talk to her, set up a meeting, but don't meet with her yourself. I'll send agents. Where are you now?"

"I dropped Vasco at his house and headed back to hers."

"Why go back there when you can call from where you are?"

"I want to see how she handles it."

"I'm not following you."

"She could panic. She could take off."

"Okay, but you don't intercept her."

"That's fine."

I eased over down the street from Rosamar Largo's house and called her cell phone. When she answered, I identified myself. Moments later, her front door opened.

"I'm looking for your brother, Juan," I said.

"I am too. I'm looking everywhere for him."

"We need to meet with you."

"Okay, let's do it."

She came out the front door carrying her purse and rolling a carry-on bag while telling me, "I'm out shopping, but I'm about to get in my car and drive home. If they want to talk to me, they can come to my house. I'll be there in thirty minutes."

"There'll be two agents," I said.

She was Anglo-Hispanic, dark-haired, and no doubt once striking-looking. I told her the agents would call first.

"Good," she said. "I'm about to load some groceries and then am heading home."

She loaded her suitcase in the trunk and put her purse on the passenger seat as she got in. I thanked her for cooperating, then ended the call and followed at a distance after she pulled out of the driveway and sped away.

Three miles later and across town, heading toward Henderson, she pulled into the small lot of a law office I recognized. Harold G. Agnew, crusty, unrelenting, and very capable. Summer or winter, he dressed in corduroy pants, white shirts, and what used to be called a sports coat. He referred to FBI agents as "look-alikes." He didn't have any partners. None would have lasted anyway, and he was too cheap for anything more than a part-time secretary. But for some unexplained reason, he liked me. In the office they teased me about it. Today, it was good luck. I called him before she got in the door.

"When did a fugitive warrant go out on Juan Menderes?" Agnew asked.

"Somewhere around three a.m., July 5."

"If she aided her brother prior to that, she wouldn't have known he was a fugitive."

"That's possible."

"No, it has to be true for her to come in now and talk."

"Then it depends what she did."

"She may have dropped him at a freeway on-ramp. I don't know that she did, but she may have."

"And who picked him up?"

"She doesn't know."

"Does she know where he is now?"

"No, but she's willing to talk if there's a guarantee of immunity."

"You know that can't come from me, and she'll have to tell us what she knows first."

"I'll bring her in. The Bureau needs someone available who can make a decision."

Agnew brought her in forty minutes later. He'd figured out that she knew nothing about a terrorist plot and was negotiating the immunity demand to protect herself should drug charges arise from our investigating her and Menderes. Some compromise would get reached but not until we were satisfied that she'd told us everything she knew about her alleged half brother. There was a lot of back and forth with the lawyer, Agnew, and then they got her into an interview room. I watched the interview on the video feed.

Rosamar was very nervous. She fidgeted and shifted in her chair as she recounted dropping Juan at a West Cheyenne southbound ramp on 95 at 11:10 the night of the Fourth. She knew because she'd looked at her car clock. Juan wouldn't tell her where he was going. He'd gone over his back fence and crossed the open space between the subdivisions, climbed her fence, dropped down into her backyard, and knocked on her kitchen window. He asked her to drop him at a freeway on-ramp and lay across the backseat with a blanket covering him as she drove.

"What was he wearing?"

"Jeans, a baseball cap, new Nike sneakers, a T-shirt, sunglasses, and a backpack. He looked like a dork waiting to be robbed."

"Who was his ride? Who was going to pick him up?"

"I don't know."

"Where was he going?"

"Why do you keep asking that?"

The interviewing agents turned to Juan's drug trafficking. They embellished. They created witnesses and a confession that might implicate her, then showed her photos of the secret compartment in Juan's Hullabaloo van.

She blurted, "He messed up."

"Who messed up?"

"Juan did."

"How?"

I saw Agnew shake his head, as in "Don't answer," but she was frightened. An agent asked quietly, "What do you mean he messed up?"

She stumbled to her feet, saying, "I need a bathroom."

Before she reached the door, she vomited. An agent led her to a restroom. Everybody else stepped out into the hallway. I looked at Agnew dabbing a dampened Kleenex on his white corduroy pants, trying to clean vomit splashes off, before informing everyone the interview was over for now. My phone rang as he said that, but I didn't answer. I didn't listen to the voice mail a Las Vegas Metro homicide detective named Donna Perth left until after Agnew made it clear that everything to do with his client was on hold until an agreement was in writing.

Detective Perth's message said, "I'm working a homicide you might be able to help me with. Adult Hispanic male, young, and possibly killed the night of the Alagara bombing outside of Jean. Please call me."

Probably smiling when she hung up. She knew she'd get a quick call back.

19

I didn't check in with Venuti and went out the back way to my car, though that was more habit than dodge. Thirty miles south of Vegas, hot crosswinds swept I-15, and gray dust clouded the valley east of the interstate. I exited at Jean, turned into a Shell station off to the right, and pulled up alongside Detective Perth, who was parked beneath an American flag whipping hard in the wind.

"Thanks for coming," she said.

She drove, and I looked at photos on her iPad as we made the gradual five-and-a-half-mile climb up to the Goodsprings Bypass Gravel Haul Route.

"Gruesome, aren't they," she said. "An old boy that lives out this way got curious about the vultures and went out for a look yesterday, but he didn't tell anyone until dawn this morning. Maybe what he saw got into his sleep and he had a change of heart."

"What did he say?"

"Oh, some mumble-bumble bullshit that didn't make any sense." She glanced over again. "He didn't want to get mixed up in it, or he owes on a ticket, or, I hate to say it, he may have found a watch, a wallet, something out here and took it home."

I couldn't tell much about the victim's identity from the crime-scene photos, but I gave her what she was waiting to hear.

"If there's any possibility it's Juan Menderes, we'll expedite DNA testing. If it's Menderes, there's a woman named Rosamar Largo who claims he's her half brother."

"Is he?"

"Probably not."

"If it turns out he is, I want to talk to her."

"Sure."

She slowed to a stop. "Here we are. Lovely, isn't it?"

Despite bright sunlight, I pulled off my sunglasses for a better read of the ground. It was a flat gray-white spot facing desert hills, littered with beer cans, trash, and bullet casings. Tire tracks crisscrossed the sandy soil. It looked like a regular place for target practice. Taking it in I had an obvious, quick early thought: whoever killed the victim wasn't worried about him being found.

"Busy place," I said.

"Yep, civilization," she answered. "People come out here and drink and target shoot. It's far enough out to not bother anybody and close enough to the road not to be inconvenient. The dark spot there is where he died. What I don't understand is why he was disfigured the way he was. I can't get my head around them cutting off his hands and doing what they did to his face. Makes me think they had something personal with him."

Perth was a big-boned woman, sturdy not overweight, in jeans, cowboy boots, a solid leather belt, and white shirt, probably freshly ironed this morning but sweat-wrinkled now in back. Her hands were big, her face strong-featured. I heard sadness in her voice that caused me to look at her more closely.

She pointed at two knee prints in the gray-white soil.

"I think he tried to stand after being shot. See the second knee print and the toe dug in? See there and then there, where his left foot landed as he stumbled to his feet."

She pointed out dots of black blood sprayed and dried hard on mesquite.

"Shotgun," she said. "The coroner thinks the first barrel took away his lower jaw, so he wasn't going far when he stood up again. He was bleeding out and struggling for air. Look here, though, the footprints that come in from the side after he's up on his feet again."

I saw them, but it was a hard read so I asked her, "Are you used to tracking game?"

"All my life and in desert country."

"What made you think the victim here could be Juan Menderes?"

"Body type, and I thought maybe that might explain the violence done to him." She added, "I needed something that could explain it."

"This isn't public yet, but it's looking like Juan Menderes delivered drugs in addition to Hullabaloo party cakes. The Hullabaloo drivers use the same van every day. They're responsible for keeping them clean and cared for. Looks like he had his modified. We found a hidden compartment welded in the floor of the van. The Rosamar Largo that I was telling you about says she dropped him at a southbound 95 on-ramp a little after 11:00 p.m. the night of July 4. A ride was set up."

"He's her brother, but he doesn't tell her where he's going? That's a little bit hard to believe."

"He's not her brother."

"Is that opinion or fact?"

"A little of both. I don't think she's worried about him. She's worried about herself. It's in everything she says."

My opinion was just more hearsay to Perth. She pointed at mesquite thirty yards away.

"Part of his jaw was over there. If we come up with dental records, there won't be any way to match them. The shotgun took away his nose, cheekbones, and eye sockets. Took away any easy way to visually ID him."

That was probably the goal, I thought. Perth turned to me.

"I saw a dismembered body once. A man butchered his wife after a fight. He gutted her and pieced her like he would an elk, then wrapped the pieces in butcher paper and put them in his garage freezer. He doubled up two garbage bags and ran her guts out into the desert in his pickup and dumped them. Told us he aimed to dispose of the rest slowly. That's as close as I've been to something like this. The victim here, even his ears and genitals are gone. They aimed to erase his identity. Is there any reason you can think of to take it that far with Juan Menderes?"

When I didn't answer quick enough, she pointed at the dark stain then a boot print, a heel dug in, the shooter trying to balance between what he was trying to achieve and keeping blowback off himself and the shotgun.

"I think the shotgunner is a little bit of an artist or thinks he is," she said. "He's got a way of doing things. This wasn't his first time. He's too good with the gun. He's got a feel for the spread rate of the pellets. That's not easy, and I know. I grew up with a shotgun in my hands." She paused then said, "I may have heard the name Rosamar Largo before. What does she say about who picked him up?"

"She says she doesn't know who he was getting the ride from."

"Do you believe her?"

"No."

"A sister would ask." She thought about that another several seconds, then repeated. "A sister would ask unless she already knew what was going down. Is she claiming they were close?"

"She said they were coming from different places, but he was her only sibling."

Which made me think of Melissa. I pushed that away to get back to this conversation.

"Rosamar Largo said she grew up in LA, Juan in Mexico. They had the same father," I said.

"And you don't believe her?"

"I need to see proof."

"We found a cap the wind had carried. Don't know if it was the victim's. It was new, not even sweat-stained on the brow. A new cap doesn't wander out here by itself. Blue jeans and a T-shirt that was white at some point."

"Shoes?"

"Black Nike sneakers, also new. Nothing else. No wallet, nothing."

"The sneakers fit. Describe the cap."

"It's a blue baseball-style cap with a black Nike emblem."

"That fits. What about a small black backpack?"

"No other clothes, nothing else." She turned. "A blue baseball-style cap with a black Nike emblem fits?"

"It does."

I took in the sandy white, the mesquite, and hills once more before we left. When we reached the paved road, Perth pushed the air-conditioning fan up but left her window down and we were both quiet on the drive. I looked down the valley and out at the bright, hot, windy day and couldn't stand it that Melissa, Jim, and Nate were gone.

"Let's start by finding out if it was Juan Menderes," I said after we pulled into the Shell station. "Get a DNA test sample together, and I'll get it out today."

"Get it out today?" She smiled at that and said, "I liked your voice as soon as I heard it. Now I know why."

20

Julia looked younger and frailer and withdrawn into grief tonight. A stack of used Kleenex was on the nightstand near her. I pulled a chair over and was talking to her when hospital administrator Dr. Lena Schechter stopped by.

"You're her uncle?"

"Yes. Paul Grale."

"Can I have a few minutes of your time?" Outside the room and down the wide corridor, she asked, "Are you close to Julia?"

"We're good friends. I'm very fond of her. I've watched her grow up. Why do you ask?"

"There's a couple who are neighbors of the Kern family who have told me they'd like to adopt her. They've spent much of the last several days here. Do you know them?"

"I've met them. Julia will live with me unless she wants to do something different."

"Do you live alone?"

"I do."

"Is your lifestyle compatible with raising a teenage girl?"

"Not really, I'll have to make changes."

I reached slowly for my wallet to give her my card. I didn't doubt the responsibility I was taking on, to see Julia through high school and college and the years it would take to get over the loss of her family, if ever.

"Again, I have to apologize for invasive questions, and you don't have to answer if you don't want to."

"It's not a problem. I have a house. There's a bedroom for Julia. My wife died in a car accident a decade ago, and I live alone. I know I haven't been at the hospital enough and people are wondering. I understand."

I pulled one of my cards out and handed it to her. She read it and looked puzzled.

"FBI?"

"Almost nineteen years. I'm on the Domestic Terrorism Squad in the Vegas field office. It's why you haven't seen more of me in here."

"I had no idea. The neighbors . . ."

I stayed another hour with Julia, then drove to the Alagara on my way home. I didn't get out but did stop and lower the passenger window. There were many more flowers, many roses. I'd heard someone had tweeted something about roses that went viral. But for me, it was knowing they were out there and that they cared. I sat parked there several minutes. At home, Jo was waiting with Chinese to go and a bottle of red that felt out of place tonight, but it was grand of her to get anything.

Some agents hadn't been home since the bombings. They showered in the gym and slept on chairs, but that didn't work well for me. Sometimes answers come when you take a step back. I used to joke that my brain worked best when I didn't think. We ate and I checked in with the office. When I walked back out, Jo was in the lap pool, her clothes draped neatly over a pool chair. She swam a slow crawl and her body looked lovely. When she stopped, she waded toward me and said, "I want to see you swim."

"You want to see me swim?"

"Yeah, I want to see if you've kept working on stretching out those lower back muscles. Show me."

Water beaded on her skin as she climbed out into the warm night. It wasn't about my back or torn muscles or disfigurement. She was putting herself out there at a hard time, but it felt right to heal the hurt between us and move somewhere new. A fence blocked the view of the only neighbors, and the other side looked out on the desert. I stripped off my clothes and swam, and maybe for the first time since I was wounded, I gave myself up to what I'd become.

Many got hurt in Iraq and Afghanistan. What were my wounds next to what soldiers had done and endured? Mine were nothing. They were bad luck, a failed mission. The way I had looked and felt before was gone forever, so let it go. Let it just be that I'm lucky to hold Jo again. Let it just be that and nothing else. Let it be without questions. Later, we made love in a slow way in the bed where I'd once slept with my wife, and then lay with the sliding door open and moonlight falling across the floor.

Early the next morning I wrote Jo a note before slipping out at first light. I like the gentle quiet and beauty of dawn. The early morning drive to the office is also when I sometimes do my best thinking about cases.

This morning I felt particularly down. I felt terrible sadness, yet tried to think through the pieces of what Lacey and I had: Mondari, Menderes, Rosamar Largo, the unknown bomb maker who I thought had to be here. I thought about C-4 magically disappearing from a Phoenix warehouse. My head also swirled with dark thoughts and images from the Alagara. I needed to think about cremating the bodies of Jim, Melissa, and Nate and what to do about a memorial service. Should Julia see them once more, or would that be traumatizing? She wanted to see them, and no one had significant facial injuries. Maybe she needed that finality, but I shuddered to think of a trip to the morgue with her. I was there in my head when my phone rang.

A soft-spoken southern voice identified herself as with Alcohol, Tobacco, Firearms and Explosives. She then conferenced me into an ongoing call with a DC-based ATF unit working the Vegas bombings. I heard static, a piercing electronic squeal, and then without introduction, an ATF agent, a male voice, maybe midcareer, hard-edged, and not a voice I recognized. But I could guess why he was calling.

"Good morning, Special Agent Grale, we're calling about your request."

"I've been patched into a conference call?"

"You have. We got your request yesterday and are wondering what you're after."

"It wasn't clear enough?"

"Whatever partial DNA came off the bomb detonators and the casings has already been run through the terrorism database. You must know that, so why do you want to run it through the ATF database?"

"ATF has the best database on domestic bombers, and the lists haven't always matched in the past."

"It might have been that way once a long, long time ago, but it's not anymore. We'll do the run for you, but it's not going to turn up anybody new. Are you looking at a domestic bomber?"

"I'm leaning toward a freelancer."

There was a pause that I knew I was supposed to fill but didn't.

"Can you tell us what you're working on?"

"My first cup of coffee."

Somebody chuckled, and something about that chuckle was familiar. Couldn't quite place it yet, but it was familiar.

"Look, I'm not working any headline stuff. My role here is to chase the orphan leads along the edges of the main investigation. I'm like a guy in the basement with a flashlight and stacks of files in moldy cardboard boxes, which would fit, right, for an old-school guy not up to speed."

"I'm not sure what all that meant. Do you have a bomb maker you're specifically looking at?"

"I'm working a list of known bomb makers."

"Your request made it sound like you have someone in mind."

"Can I get it run if I change the wording a little?"

A deeper voice broke in. "We'll get it run for you, Grale."

"Carl Brady?"

"It's me, Paul, and it's been way too long. What's going on with you? Why aren't you a supervisor by now?"

"I'd rather solve cases."

Brady laughed and I smiled, and the brutality of the bombings and all the darkness I'd carried into the dawn receded just a little. Maybe it was Brady's laugh calling up better times. He was a big guy with a deep laugh and a head as bald as a bone. I'd been ready to jump down their throats for this pimp phone call to get whatever lead I had, but Brady's voice reminded me that we were in it together.

"I'm looking for a freelancer we may have been tipped about in early June, but not in the context of what happened. The tip came from a confidential informant we've worked with before. I'm not clear where he got it. I can't even find him right now. Our agent killed in the secondary bombing was working with him, and I've been going through her notes. It could be he was hustling us as he's done before, but he's missing and there are other things unexplained. I'm looking for the bomb maker, Carl. That's my focus."

"We'll get it run for you today."

"Thanks, and somewhere out there, we'll catch up."

Maybe we would. Most likely we'd never get the chance, but it was good to know Brady was still there.

Midmorning, Venuti asked me to sit in on a meeting with Dr. Frederic, the psychologist for the VA who had treated Beatty for PTSD. Frederic chose a seat at the end of the table and pulled two files from a briefcase. He consulted notes as he recalled Beatty as a paranoid, angry patient suffering from alcohol dependency. He talked about the letter he'd copied Venuti, and then told us he'd agreed to this meeting because of what he called "the very real possibility that Jeremy Beatty was capable of violence." His notes included the Hakim Salter drone strike, which he termed the *precipitating incident* and Beatty's account of it as *delusional,* so I had to ask.

"Did you ever talk to an Australian drone pilot named Phil Ramer?"

"There is no Phil Ramer. There never was. He existed only in Jeremy's mind. Stress can create events that have the quality of reality. We can carry them as memories." He tapped the file in front of him and said, "I have notes on this."

He read aloud from notes he'd made after a conversation with an air force officer at Creech Air Force Base who had told Frederic that he didn't know of a pilot named Philip Ramer. The officer hadn't denied Ramer's existence, but Frederic heard it that way. I could tell him I was trading calls with Ramer but didn't see the point, and Frederic had already moved on.

"Let's talk about the present," he said. "Jeremy Beatty lives in a remote corner of a trailer park. He has covered the windows of his trailer in heavy black plastic and gutted the interior to reshape it to a militaristic fantasy. This is classic withdrawal from society, provoked by an anger catalyst. It's a foretelling, a kind of preconfession, if you will. View the events through that prism, and the timing makes sense. Getting from here to a confession is what you're wrestling with."

He was authoritative and certain, and when it was clear he wasn't finished with his lecture, I made a show of checking my phone, and then shook my head as if time had slipped by and I was late. I gathered my things and stood. As I went out the door, an agent apologized for not quite grasping the prism concept. The last thing I heard was Dr. Frederic say, "Perfectly understandable. Let me put it in simpler terms." No doubt he did.

21

At noon my phone rang. The front desk said a Laura Cotter was holding and asking to talk to me. I said, "Put her through." I hadn't talked with Laura for a year and a half, but her heartfelt sympathy for my loss reconnected us. The compassion in her stood out. Some have to work at it, but a few like Laura are born with generosity wired in. I'd forgotten how much I liked the timbre of her voice.

"Two FBI agents came to see me," she said, "and I'm not going to draw you into it, but they want dirt on Jeremy. They asked about the letter Dr. Frederic asked Jeremy to write when he was being treated for PTSD. They shouldn't even know about that. It wasn't supposed to be mailed anywhere. It was part of his treatment. He was supposed to express all of his anger toward the air force. How did the FBI get a copy?"

"It'll end, Laura. We're looking in a thousand directions right now."

"But Jeremy of all people—"

"I know."

"The agents were after any incident I can remember where Jeremy was unstable. There's only one, and I didn't tell them. Is that bad? That was when he burned his uniforms. He said, 'Let's go see the sunset in the desert.' We stopped at a Chevron for gas on the way out of town. I thought it was for his pickup, but it was to fill up a two-and-a-half-gallon gas container. Did he ever tell you about this?"

"No."

"We went out on this dirt road to the base of some mountains, and he dug a pit. He had a crazy look in his eyes. He told me it was a celebration. He had ice in a cooler and a bottle of tequila and had packed everything else into a duffel bag of his father's. In it were his air force uniforms, his letter of acceptance into flight school, commendations for performance as an RPA pilot, photos with friends who flew remotely piloted aircraft, and other things. He emptied everything into that pit and poured all the gas on it. It made a huge ball of flame. He was crying and laughing and drank most of the bottle of tequila alone. I drove us home. Before he passed out, he said some things that were way out there. Way beyond that letter. Should I have told the agents who came to see me?"

"What did he say?"

"Crazy, drunk things. Have you seen what the media is doing to him?"

"It's hard to miss."

"But you're not doing anything about it."

"There's nothing I can do. He's getting looked at, and then the investigation will move on."

"Really, you're just watching too?"

The line clicked as she hung up, disappointed in me. I couldn't get the conversation out of my head all afternoon, and didn't lose it until trolling through Jane Stone's computer files downloaded from the flash drive. I opened one labeled *Vacation Ideas.*

Some were vacation spots—Tulum, Mexico; the Fiji Islands; touring the fjords of Norway; a spa in France; skiing at Val Gardena. I went from one to the next. Most predated Jane's February transfer to the DT squad, but not the last four. The first of those was titled *Hong Kong.* I scrolled through typical tourist stuff, Victoria Heights, Kowloon.

I opened *Argentina* next and looked through the photos and places to stay. Jane made notes on where to eat in Mendoza and hike in Patagonia. I read a restaurant menu, then backed out and opened the second-to-last travel file, *New Zealand*. In New Zealand were trout streams to fish, hiking routes on the South Island, mountain-biking tours, and after the cycling tours came a file with snippets of conversation captured in a chat room by the NSA and forwarded to the FBI.

What the fuck? What's this, Jane?

I backtracked through the previous files, then returned and read transcripts between a Lebanese businessman with ties to Hamas bomb makers and another as-yet-unidentified man within the United States, intercepted in Mexico City in mid-May. A transcript excerpt read:

> *"Is it on?"*
>
> *"Yes."*
>
> *"Are you certain?"*
>
> *"Yes, we helped with things."*
>
> *"And they are safe?"*
>
> *"Everything is waiting. If everyone does their part the events will be spectacular."*
>
> *"Good."*
>
> *"If this is successful, this will be the new way we do business."*
>
> *"I will pray that I do my part."*

Jane had moved this into her *Vacation Ideas* file under *New Zealand*. I didn't know what to make of that. She had a labyrinthine, borderline paranoid way of coding information when she worked a case. She tucked investigative pieces away in places seemingly with no connection. Maybe the key here was travel or route of travel or something else she heard that tied an aspect of this to New Zealand. But I couldn't get there by guessing. All I knew was that the intercepted conversation mattered to her and that New Zealand tied in somehow.

I took a late afternoon sip of cold coffee and made a call to Metro detective Perth and left another message for Philip Ramer as I turned the NSA intercept in my head. The word *events* was used, not *event*. When I hung up, Venuti was standing in front of me looking haggard.

"Hey," I said, "I just found something in Jane's files. Do you know anything about an NSA intercept of a Lebanese businessman in Mexico?"

"She mentioned something. She said the date of it fit with a comment your informant made."

"Mondari wasn't mine anymore. He was Mondi by then and Jane's and had been for months. Do you remember exactly what she said?"

"No."

"I don't know how you could forget if you knew what was on the transcripts."

"I track a lot of things, Grale. I see a lot of transcripts from the NSA with suspicious conversations. You made a run at supervisor and you went back to being a GS-13, and you'll probably retire a 13, but you were there long enough to know you can't read and absorb everything."

"I'm not holding your feet to the fire. I'm just trying to get my head around Jane's notes. She thought that transcript was important."

Most agents retired at the higher pay level of a GS-14, and Venuti was right in saying I wouldn't. It was typical of Dan to get defensive then aggressive if challenged. Yet I needed to know what Jane had told him. Instinctively, I knew it tied with taking me to her condo to find the memory stick. He'd set me up to discover these files.

"Look, if I missed it or dropped the ball, I'm sorry," Venuti said. "Jane never said what was on the memory stick. That's where you're going with this, right?"

"Yes, and she must have said something."

"If she did, it wasn't definitive, but I'll try to remember. The reason I'm here, though, is that ISIS has posted a new video. Bring it up on your screen. Let's have a look."

The video started with an American ISIS spokesman. Venuti said softly, "This kid is from Minneapolis. Disappeared a year and a half ago. He's barely nineteen."

The young recruit said, "Unbelievers, who shower us with bombs and kill our innocents, be fearful. Prepare to lose many more of your own. We are only beginning. We will strike again soon in your desert city."

"It's time we take out all of these people," Venuti said. "They couldn't invent a pair of pliers on their own. They use our technology to proselytize and attack us. How about we show them another higher level of technology and take them back to the Stone Age?"

22

Late in the day I watched the reinterview of the plumber who'd worked on the Alagara men's room urinal and a bar-sink leak on the Fourth of July. Every time he answered a repeat question from the first interview, he sounded annoyed. An agent standing next to me said quietly, "What a prick." The plumber was hard to like, but a surprise was coming his way. The two agents interviewing him were nearing that point.

"I got there at 10:50 a.m.," the plumber said. "I was supposed to be there at 11:00, but I always get to a job ten minutes early. That's just the way I work. I left at 4:20 that afternoon."

"Are you certain it was 4:20?"

"Same time I gave you last time. You should take notes."

He was there when the wine refrigerator was swapped out. Video cameras at the bar area filmed that. Total elapsed time for the change-out was seven minutes, thirty-two seconds. Two weeks prior, Omar Smith had requested a new refrigerator be installed in the first few days of July. E-mails between Smith and the sub supplying the new wine refrigerator put the install date at July 3.

That changed. Late afternoon on July 2, the install date got pushed to July 5. The supplier notified the installer and Omar Smith that they wouldn't have the refrigerator in stock until the morning of the fifth due to a combination of a shipping problem and the holiday. On the same e-mail thread multiple exchanges followed between Smith, the refrigerator supplier, and the installer. Smith pushed the supplier to find another way to get it there and installed on the Fourth, when other repairs were occurring. Other refrigerator manufacturers were discussed. The size of the new refrigerator got reconfirmed. Smith made it seem urgent to get the new one installed on the Fourth, though it wasn't clear why. Smith's e-mails verged on angry, and the supplier stopped responding by midday on the third.

The installer's last e-mail affirmed that if it reached Vegas on the third, he would pick it up and install it the next day. Installing meant delivering, unwrapping, sliding it in behind the bar, then plugging it in. Maybe twenty minutes max. Smith in his last e-mail said he did not want the plastic wrapping removed. He wanted it slid into the slot and left there. He would cut the wrapping off and plug it in himself, when he was satisfied with it.

That and Smith's insistence it be installed on the Fourth made him suspect. It was what the agents interviewing the plumber were circling. This because Smith had also e-mailed the plumber's boss asking that he have his plumber help get the refrigerator into its slot if Smith was able to find a different refrigerator rather than the delayed one. When asked about this, Smith said it was exactly what it sounded like. Told he couldn't have the wine refrigerator he'd ordered installed on time, he'd tried to find a replacement. Alagara had another rental scheduled for the night of the fifth where the client wanted to chill white wines ahead of the party. Smith said he tried hard but wasn't able to find another refrigerator, and yet, the plumbing company had received a follow-up e-mail from Smith late the night of the third saying he'd found one after all. It would be delivered during the afternoon of July 4.

Agents had interviewed the client who wanted to chill wines for her party on the July 5, and she backed Smith's story, but none of that lessened suspicion of Smith—in part because Smith had wanted the plumber's help only as far as getting it into the cabinet slot and texting him that it had arrived. He would personally do the rest of the install, cut away the wrapping, and plug it in. That was too unusual a request to pass over. Then there was this: the final e-mail to the plumbing company owner from Smith, saying that he'd found one after all and it would be delivered on July 4, was an e-mail Smith claimed he didn't send. Yet he was very happy to walk in on the holiday and find a new wine refrigerator installed.

Our computer techs backed Smith's claim that someone had access to his computer. They didn't say he was hacked but agreed it was possible someone with access to his computer sent the final e-mail confirming delivery and installation of a new wine refrigerator the afternoon of the Fourth. That's where it got spooky. All of the refrigerator talk had started less than three weeks prior to the Fourth. Notice of the delay was just a few days before. If Smith was telling the truth, the bombers conceived and executed the wine-refrigerator-bomb concept in a very short time. That implied a high level of sophistication and coordination. It supported the theory of a capable sleeper cell in the Vegas area. It was also hard to believe the bomber didn't have prior knowledge of the refrigerator's size.

A complicated story, I know, and after all the questioning we probably now had three or four agents who could install wine refrigerators in their sleep. But this recalcitrant plumber in for a reinterview could have information that mattered. While I watched, the plumber, Rick Alpert, changed his story.

"I talked to the guy who brought it in and told him I would help him if he needed it."

"In the last interview you said you didn't talk with him," an agent of ours named Korb answered.

"Well, yeah, because he didn't say anything to me when I said that. I offered and he just sort of fucking nodded."

"Did you try to talk to him again?"

"Naw, I went back to work."

"Why didn't you tell us that last time?"

"Because it doesn't matter."

"Why don't you just tell us exactly what happened, and we'll decide what matters. Since we last talked, we recovered videotape we're going to show you. We'd like you to tell us what you were doing. These are short takes. Here's the first one."

In the first one, he squatted down in front of the refrigerator after the installer left. One of the agents interviewing asked, "What are you doing there?"

"I was trying to look inside."

"Why, if it was wrapped in plastic?"

"My wife wants a wine refrigerator. I was thinking about cutting the wrapping off."

They had him pictured from another angle, and that did seem to be all he was doing. He'd jerked on the door several times.

Korb, the agent questioning, had a face and head like a Marine sergeant and didn't cut him any slack.

"How do we know you weren't arming a bomb?"

"Ask my wife."

"Did you just say, ask your wife? I'm asking you. Here's the next clip. What are you doing in this one?"

What he was doing was fixing himself a drink behind the bar. He rejected ice cubes for the drink until he found three he liked, and that had gotten some needed laughs in the office. He also chose the most expensive bourbon. When the plumber didn't respond, Korb asked, "Were you testing bourbons for your wife?"

Outside the room that got laughs. Inside, the plumber's brow knotted up.

"I was working the holiday. I figured the owner would be okay with me having a drink."

"Rick, are you saying you stole liquor from the bar and thought the owner would approve of that?"

"I'll pay for it."

"You have a problem with the truth?"

"None."

"Did you steal liquor from the bar?"

"I had one drink."

"Why don't you just say, 'I stole a drink of high-end bourbon'?"

The plumber didn't answer.

"We need to know that we can trust your testimony. Can't you just call it what it is?"

"I have."

"'I stole a drink of high-end bourbon from Bar Alagara.' Is that so hard?"

"I don't steal."

The agent alongside Korb shifted in her chair. This was making her nervous. The plumber was a piece of work, but so what? We didn't view him as a suspect, and we needed him as we put our case together. Still, I knew Korb wasn't doing this for entertainment or to humiliate. He was calling him on his bullshit as a kind of reality check to bring him around.

"If you didn't pay for it, you stole it."

"The owner was supposed to have met me. He didn't show up and I figured it was a trade."

Korb rolled with that.

"What were you going to talk about with the owner? And don't give me any shit about having already told us."

"The work I was doing. But honestly, I don't fucking know why. It's not like we were going to talk about the valve for the urinal. But he made it sound like it was important."

"How did he contact you?"

"He got my phone number from the office and texted me."

"Are you saying you didn't see any real reason to meet with him?"

"That's about right."

We'd already read the text messages the plumber received during the month prior, but Korb kept working it. He worked it, and the plumber was effusive about how unfair it was to be held there on the holiday by the owner for no good reason.

"What do you think now?" Korb asked.

"Well, the dude is Muslim right?"

"What do you mean?"

"He just wanted to say he met with me."

Korb nodded as if that made sense, but steered the interview to the white panel van that had delivered the wine refrigerator. He went slowly with the plumber through his recollection of the man wearing a hoodie who had installed it. The man had walked funny. From behind, the plumber saw him walk away wheeling a green dolly. His left foot was possibly pigeon-toed or injured. It made his gait awkward. That and clean fingernails that looked manicured to the plumber. The guy had said something when he came in. He might have had an accent. All were new details.

Smith had wanted an ENERGY STAR–rated appliance—a 30" wide × 32" tall × 29" deep wine refrigerator made by LG. He included the model number in his first e-mail to his supplier. The bomb was in an LG, a different, more available model, less efficient, but one that fit the size requirement.

Now came questions about the man in a suit who'd shown up just minutes before the plumber left. He was still there when the plumber drove away. Korb went after the plumber on that.

"Your boss thinks you were the last one there. You were supposed to lock up. Last time you told us you did."

"I didn't want to get fired. I can't get fired right now. I've got another kid on the way."

"Correct the record."

"What do you mean?"

"In the last interview, did you lie to us about locking up the building?"

Korb made it sound very serious, although we'd figured it out two days ago. When the plumber was slow answering, Korb unloaded. We watched the plumber's face turn white as Korb told him the criminal implications of lying in a terrorism investigation. His face paled, but his stubborn streak was unfazed. Instead of confessing that he'd lied, he said, "I told that guy I was leaving and was supposed to lock up. He said he was meeting the owner about wineglasses. He showed me a text. What was I supposed to do?"

"When you left, was that man still there?"

The plumber nodded.

"I need audio," Korb said. "I need you to talk."

"He was still there when I left."

"You told your boss you locked up."

"I don't remember saying that."

"You told him that and lied to us. You're flirting with danger here. I want you to set the record straight and explain on tape why you lied. Then you'll sit with a sketch artist again."

As the interview ended, I returned to my desk. As agents were doing with the main investigation, Lacey and I were tracking any local leads that might take us to the sleeper cell suspected of being in the general Vegas area. At my desk I read transcripts from an Omar Smith interview I'd missed.

Smith flew back to Vegas from Houston in the afternoon of July 4. He'd gone to Houston to convince a new investor to buy two of his properties, but that went badly and he didn't have the energy to go by the Alagara and deal with the plumbing repairs, so he'd gone straight home. At home he ate, showered, changed clothes, and then went to Bar Alagara, ostensibly to make sure everything was ready and so he could be there when Melissa Kern arrived. It was clear he had some attraction to Melissa or was chatting her up to get information about the drone pilots. The strong feeling in here was most likely the latter.

Where Smith had stayed, who he saw, where he ate, his flight home—everything was examined in the first twenty-four hours. Agents were deep into his text messages, e-mails, voice mails, everything. But there were still unaccounted hours and gaps in Smith's compulsive texting and the tweeting he did to promote Hullabaloo. He was also very active on Facebook. All of the feed came from Smith. That he was so active made his electronic fingerprints easy to track, but activity doesn't translate to answers.

Sorrow reached deep into me as I sat there with disparate pieces. I lost my focus, as I had many times since the bombings. I stood. I drank some cold water and took a couple of aspirin, and checked the time: 3:30 and no call yet from the surveillance team. As of this afternoon, Omar Smith was cleared to go back into his building. I wanted to be there or show up while he was there, but I didn't want to clear that with Venuti. I'd end up with five agents there with me. Any element of surprise would be lost. So I was quietly communicating with the surveillance team watching Smith's house. I checked in with them again.

"I'm headed there now," I said.

I brought along the blast report from TEDAC, the Terrorist Explosive Device Analytical Center, which is the FBI center at Quantico that analyzes terrorist explosive devices. The report was preliminary, but the detonator had been reviewed in detail. An ion mobility spectrometer had confirmed C-4, and earlier I talked with a TEDAC analyst about that. They were all but saying a cell phone was the likely trigger device. I also got the runback from the ATF Arson and Explosives National Repository. Nothing new there.

The reinterview of the plumber, the TEDAC report, and the somewhat varying accounts of Omar Smith's Fourth of July visit to the Alagara ahead of the party provided more of a timeline. Also, there were more details about the alleged salesman Smith met with at the Alagara just ahead of the party. That individual was yet to be located, a fact that further heightened suspicion of Smith.

At the Alagara I stood out on the patio rereading the TEDAC report, and then moved out into the lot. I read about the overlap from the secondary explosion and the conclusion that the bombs were well designed. I checked out the flowers. Many had wilted and browned in the heat. I was back in the building when my phone rang.

"Grale here."

"Grale, it's Dietrich."

"What's up?"

"He's on the move. Are you at the Alagara?"

Dietrich was the agent in charge of the surveillance teams watching Smith. He was no-nonsense but also very intuitive. I trusted him.

"Yeah, I'm here," I said.

"He's backing out of his garage in a red Audi A8. Looks like he's got a place in mind. Maybe he's coming your way."

Another call from Dietrich came five minutes later.

"Drifting your way."

I walked out, moved my car, and Dietrich called again.

"Less than a mile from you and speeding up."

"I'll be here."

"You won't have to wait long."

23

Hard-soled shoes clicked on the concrete floor of the bar and echoed in the restroom, where I waited in darkness. They stopped, and Smith let out a low, eerie wail, perhaps shocked at how much damage there was. A rush of Turkish words flowed from him, and then a long silence followed by footsteps. His shadow passed by in the corridor. Minutes later and after I had eased out of the restroom, I heard what sounded like a cordless drill start and stop and start again. I walked quietly toward the sound.

Smith's back was to me as he removed trim and wainscoting to reveal a wall safe. He had spun the dial and opened the safe before he felt my presence near the office door. I saw him react then continue removing bundles of one hundred dollar bills from the safe. He glanced up but wouldn't look at me as he talked. It was as if he were talking to the bundles of cash he fed into a backpack.

"This is my money. This is my building again as of today, and this is my money. I have proof of this. I must make a payment today. This is why I take it out now."

He finally looked at me. "The men who loan to me rob me with high interest."

"Where are these men?"

"In Istanbul. Businessmen."

"How much do you owe?"

"More than I have. But how much is it your business to know what I owe?"

"Why didn't you tell us about the wall safe?"

"Why would I? I opened my home and my office to the FBI. Do I owe you everything about my life because of these terrorists?"

"The money could have been removed and taken to a bank."

"With all the police, it was safer here."

"What do you mean?"

"Look at it. It's cash."

It was a lot of cash. If these bundles were all C-notes, it was hundreds of thousands and we'd want to get the Secret Service or Treasury to run the serial numbers. I told him that.

"You cannot do that to me. You must not do that. I mean this. I cannot explain, but it is very important I make a payment."

"What's the payment?"

"I can't explain."

"That's not going to work, Omar."

"My lawyer said wait until the building is returned to you. It's mine again and everything here is mine as it was before the bombs."

"It's not going to work that way with this money."

"It has to."

He continued loading bundles into a dark blue backpack, and then in a gesture both impetuous and condescending, tossed a bundle of one hundred dollar bills at me, as if that should buy my cooperation. I caught it and laid it on the desk.

"I have to make this payment. It is an imperative. You must allow this." He dropped the remaining bricks of money into the pack and pulled his phone. "I'll call my lawyer."

He didn't reach the lawyer. He tried twice more as his face reddened and sweat glistened on his forehead and the sides of his nose.

"If it's clean, we'll return it in a few days," I said.

"Please don't do this. This payment is late. I couldn't get to the money."

"You could have asked us at any time. Where did you get so many one hundred dollar bills? What's the payment about?"

"Please!"

"I'm sorry."

He was shaking when he left the backpack on the desk and walked out the door.

24

"You're going to like this French pilot, man. She's hot. The drone pilots are following me. They're right behind me, and we're not that far away," Eddie said. "Hey, your shitstorm is spilling into my life. The FBI came to see me. They're looking into my business because of you. That's not good for you or me. You need to call your FBI friend and ask for a favor."

"Doesn't work like that, Eddie."

"Everything works like that. You call him before I get there, okay? Don't fuck with me on this. You figure out what to tell him."

"Not going to happen."

"Who else is going to get you work when the company you're working for, Strata Data Mining, cuts you loose? Who's going to hire you?"

"I'll flip burgers, Eddie."

"You'll flip burgers? You flip burgers and I'll come eat there. The fuck you'll flip burgers."

Beatty broke the connection and looked at the cleft in the mountain rock where the wind funneled from the west and swept over the airfield. No one thought enough about these bony-ass mountains when this land was leased for the training airfield. He watched the neon orange windsock trying to rip itself off the pole. Then his phone rang again. Had to be Eddie, but it wasn't. Turned out to be a vice president from the Strata Data Mining Houston office named Anna Lee Peale.

"I hope you don't mind me calling you directly. I didn't tell Edward Bahn I would be calling you, but I think it's right. Are you okay with talking directly to me?"

"Sure, I work for you."

"Mr. Bahn has told us you want everything to go through him."

"He didn't get that from me."

It did surprise him she was going to do this herself, but maybe it was Eddie's idea of how to handle it.

"How do you like the airfield we built?"

"I like it."

"We hope to use it year round. We're converting to drones and we'll train pilots from all over the world where you are. This will sound crazy, but I wish I was out there with you. You're on the edge of the new world and I'm in an office in Houston."

"Come on out."

She laughed. It wasn't a bad laugh, but neither was it real. *Here it comes*, he thought, *and Eddie didn't have the balls to say.* Or he wanted the call made to Grale first. More likely that; what an asshole.

"You can appreciate it's a difficult situation we're all in," she said, "and we believe you've taken appropriate steps to exonerate yourself. But we also have to pay attention to public perception. We're pursuing mineral rights leases of US government land, and we don't want a politician grandstanding and accusing us of anything that we can't defend ourselves against. Polling data that we're using says 44 percent of the public believes you had a role in the bombings, 17 percent says no role whatsoever, and the other 39 percent are undecided. It may be morally reprehensible, but we have to pay attention to this."

"Forty-four percent think I had a role?"

"I'm sorry, but that's the data I have. Of course, that can change fast. If the FBI clears you, I'm sure that number will be cut in half overnight."

"If the FBI clears me? There's nothing to clear me of."

"We're moving on a secondary strategy to speed up the training there. This will involve another instructor as well as you. That instructor is on the way. He'll arrive within the next forty-eight hours."

"You're trying to get my replacement here as fast as you can."

"That's not how I would phrase it, and I want to propose higher pay for you in return for longer teaching hours in the near term. Would you be open to that idea?"

"Work harder so I can be fired sooner?"

"You could be fired today, but we're trying to avoid that."

After she hung up, he looked down the black asphalt of the runway and into the desert dusk. He looked at the darkening mountains and thought, *Come on, dude, you knew this call was coming. Don't let it get to you. Concentrate on the drones you'll fly with these pilots tomorrow. Best time to fly will be very early morning before thermals start kicking off these baked mountains.* Strata had done a really smart thing that was going to help. They'd approached the FAA years ago and wound through the bureaucratic process to get special dispensation to fly above the regulation ceiling of four hundred feet. That would get them longer, safer hours in the air. *You're a pilot, dude. It's what you are and they can't take that away. So, longer hours, fly early, teach them faster, and then get fired. Hurry up and get fucked. Could it get any worse? Laugh about it, dude. You'll get cleared on this bullshit, and you've got enough money to get some gear and disappear for a while. Life will go on.*

Bahn's pickup led the others in. A white Jeep Cherokee followed. Headlights washed the two-inch-deep white gravel in front of the flight trailer, then the Jeep crunched through it and parked. The pilots climbed out of the jeep and evaluated Beatty as hard as he did them.

He got a cold stare from the one Bahn said was from Eastern Europe, Balkans, Ukraine, or someplace. Eddie didn't know, but he was a big guy. Hard grip. Then a Saudi pilot who'd been in the Saudi Air Force, or his father had—Eddie couldn't get his story straight. The last was a French woman. She got her own trailer. Lights came on in it and then the other trailer.

An hour later a new black Land Cruiser with two soldier types in it showed up and said they were the security team—all smiles, dead eyes, and news to Beatty. He didn't know what they were going to secure. There was nothing out here but trailers, drones, and a runway. One of the men was short and made up for it by lifting weights. His name was Tak. He did the talking. The other one was quiet, tall, and huge. His name was Big John. Comic book names, but definitely former soldiers, mercenary types, and watching him like he was a problem. Beatty pulled two beers out of the flight-trailer refrigerator, then went out to find Eddie.

"Come on, Eddie, let's go talk."

They walked out to the temp drone hangar and sat on rocks nearby. The rocks still radiated heat. He handed a beer to Eddie and took a long pull of his.

"It's Nevada, home of the drone pilot, Eddie. How come you didn't find pilots here? She's from France. The big guy is from somewhere, you don't know where, but you got a cut for his hiring. How much did you make for that? The last one is a former Saudi Air Force pilot or his dad was. Which is it? How much did you get paid to say they're trained drone pilots?"

"Did you make that call to your FBI friend?"

"I don't have friends, Eddie, and I don't make those kinds of calls. I'm done with everything, Eddie. The old ways are over. You and I are done."

"I've got money for you. It's your piece for vetting these pilots."

"Say what? Vetting pilots? No fucking chance. You hired them. I just met them twenty minutes ago."

Eddie laid an envelope on the rock. The dude was just a hustler. Money was a fix-all for hustlers. They were all the same that way. *Fuck me*, he thought. *How did I ever sign up with this guy? What happened to my life? How did I ever get this low?*

"Keep your money. I'll get the drones up tomorrow. I'll teach these pilots until the replacement shows up. We'll finish this clean, but we're totally done, as in forever, Eddie."

"Man, that's alcohol talking. I've got a job in Hawaii you could take. You talk to your friend in the FBI, and if everything works out and they stop looking at you, you go to Hawaii."

Beatty looked away at the horizon, but felt Bahn studying him.

"You think I got you fired?" Bahn asked.

"No, you're a loyal guy. You wouldn't do a thing like that unless it was going to make you some money. But, congratulations, you found a replacement for me on short notice. Good for you, Eddie. It probably was a fucking scramble to find somebody. Don't forget your money when you leave. I'm calling it a night."

As Beatty walked away, Bahn said, "You're making a big mistake."

"Good to know. Now, fuck off."

25

"Grale, it's Mike Staley. We found him. He's in a hotel room with a young woman about a hundred yards from us. How do you want to do this? We could bring him to you. Do you want us to bring him into the office?"

"I'll come to you and I'm walking out the door right now. Don't let him leave."

"Leaving isn't what's on his mind right now. We're almost to the Hoover Dam. Sure you want to make the drive?"

"I've got to be the first to talk to him."

Staley was at the gas station below the hotel. The agent with him was parked farther up the slope, keeping watch from a dirt lot, where drivers staying at the hotel left their big rigs parked for the night. We sat in Staley's SUV and looked upslope at the hotel's dimly lit backside while we talked. The two upper floors had decks on this side. The bottom level had the same sliding doors but concrete patios and white plastic chairs. A rental car was parked just this side of the patio of the unit Mondari and the woman were in. We needed to watch both sides. Hardly a big deal, but really, I didn't want to lose him.

José Chou, the other agent, stayed on this side, and Staley and I went around to the front and knocked on room 113. The shades were drawn. I heard bedsprings rocking slow and steady inside, not loud but familiar. Staley's hard smile said he heard it, too, and that he carried disdain for Mondari. Many in our office viewed the CI, the confidential informant, Denny Mondari, as a mathematically gifted pathogen.

I rapped on the door again and it quieted. A few seconds later, a gruff Mondari yelled, "Wrong room."

"FBI. Paul Grale. Open up, Denny."

No response, then whispers and footsteps, and I heard the worn-out sliding door to the patio dragged open. Staley was on the phone with José, and Chou pulled up to the patio of the unit with his brights on.

"Patio door just shut again," Staley said.

As far as I knew, Mondari didn't own a weapon or know how to fire a gun, but we stood to the side as the lock snicked open and closed several times before the door opened a crack.

"FBI," I said, and held my creds up.

"Pleased to meet you," and the door opened wide enough to show a young naked woman. She was long-legged and well built. Behind her, Mondari tripped pulling on his underwear. I saw a mole that looked like a tarantula on his lower back.

She asked, "Can't it wait five minutes?"

"Not this time. We've been looking for your friend here."

"Wouldn't you rather look at me?"

"Anyone would, but I've got to talk with Denny. I'm sorry, but the party is over." Then to Mondari, "I've been leaving messages for you."

The young woman swung the door wide open and walked over to the lone chair in the room and picked up her clothes. She pointed a finger at Mondari and said, "Get your wallet out," before walking into the bathroom and shutting the door.

"I'll wait for you outside, Mondi," I said. "Make it fast."

I left the door ajar. Mondari was a bright guy. Buy him a mixed drink, a Manhattan is his preference, and he'll tell you how high his IQ is. Not that you asked, but as a reward for buying him a drink. We know he's into cybercrime, and if we looked hard we'd find something, but for a decade he's fed us tips on his competitors. It's not a healthy relationship, but he's delivered other information as well. His mother died violently, and any casino rumor of a hit man or killer in Vegas he'll pass on. At least two of his tips netted arrests. One was a hit man we'd been after for years.

He refuses to be paid for tips. The Bureau pays little anyway, so we go for drinks with him. We take him to dinner. I ran him for a number of years before Jane Stone took over. Basically, we quit fighting the tape. Mondari likes women more than men. He once told me they're more sophisticated. That might be true. It was Jane who nicknamed him "Mondi," for no other reason than she liked the sound of it. She put a droll spin on it. Jane had had a wicked sense of humor.

Staley tapped me on the shoulder.

"Once he's in your car, are you good? We'll follow if you want."

"No need. I've got to take him somewhere to talk. I'll Uber him back here when we're done."

The young woman left first. She looked me in the eye as she walked past. Mondari came out talking.

"Sorry Jane got killed. I should send flowers." He mulled that over in less than half a second. "I gave her bad information. I would have followed up otherwise. The casino-extortion plot turned out to be bullshit. There was no bomb maker. I got taken for a ride on that one, and you just fucked up my night, Grale. Donna, the girl I was just with, would eat you alive. You wouldn't even know what to do with her."

This from a pudgy guy close to my age, with a bleached-blond, rock-star haircut. Wearing his Brioni or Canali suits with high-polished Gravati shoes, he threaded casino crowds dressed in T-shirts and shorts. Safe to say, Mondari was watching a different movie than the rest of us. He was a five-foot-seven James Bond leaning over a craps table and living proof we make our own reality. But he was brilliant with computer systems and uses, brilliant and inventive.

He made another semipolite run at dismissing the bomb-maker tip he had given Jane, then got pissy when I said we'd come back for his car later. I drove to a new steakhouse a couple miles up the road, but it wasn't until we were inside in a red leather booth and he had a drink in his hand that he started talking again. Across the room, a woman played old jazz on a piano by the bar. Mondari kept his eyes on the woman playing as he talked with me.

"I can't help the Bureau this time."

"I'm not looking for you to solve anything. I want what you told Jane Stone. Start at the beginning. Tell me the story you heard."

"I think I'm going to introduce myself to the piano player and get another drink first."

He did that, and I checked my messages. I've learned to let him feel like he's in control. He returned and started chatting about how the piano player found him very attractive.

"I can feel it," he said. "You can leave me here. I'll talk with her. I don't have anything to say to you."

"What did you tell Jane about a bomb maker?"

"That I'd heard one was hired and brought to Vegas to set off several small bombs, glass breakers that wouldn't kill anybody but would scare the public away from the tables. After those would come the threat of a much bigger one and a ten-million-dollar demand."

"Why would anyone give you this information?"

"Someone who heard about it and didn't want it to happen, because her kid works at the casino."

"She heard about it how?"

"I don't know."

"I need her name."

"I can't do that."

"You told Jane you saw the bomb maker."

"I did, but from across the room, and I don't have a description. Three guys were with him, supposedly taking him up to a meeting. I never got a good look and he was gone. He left."

"How do you know he left?"

Mondari shrugged. Jane could do a killer imitation of that shrug. What a sad, terrible thing to lose her.

"Was he there to scout the Bellagio?" I asked.

"Oh, yeah, that's right I told Jane the Bellagio. Forgot all about that. I lied. Had to. I was going to tell her at the right time that it was the Wynn."

"Finish your drink. We'll eat at the Wynn after you show me. I'll put you in a cab or Uber to get you back to your car later."

When we got to the Wynn, Mondari claimed he'd looked across the pits toward the elevators. He saw the bomb maker accompanied by three men turn into the corridor toward the elevators. He turned and pointed at an older Asian gentleman in a cream-colored suit at a blackjack table.

"He was about that tall and kind of that build."

"The bomb maker looked like that guy over there, and the bodyguards were Hispanic. You're making this up on the fly, aren't you? I have Jane's notes. I know from reading them you told her something different."

"What I told Julie was wrong."

"Julie?"

"Right, Jane, what I told Jane was wrong. I got burned with that story. I think someone was checking to see if I'm feeding information to the FBI. Fed it to me, I fed it to her, and someone inside the Bureau fed it back to the source."

"No."

We crossed the casino and took seats along an open stretch of bar, and Mondari got very specific with the bartender about how he wanted his vodka. His precision with the drink order was similar to the accuracy that showed in some of his tips. Sometimes he was worth the effort. I watched him sip his drink, testing it, his lips extending almost sexually to the rim of the glass. I was disappointed and borderline angry, but then realized that whatever Mondari had told Jane and wouldn't repeat to me worried him. I pushed him harder and the vodka loosened him. I listened, watched his body language, and there it was again. Mondari was scared and wasn't going to say anything tonight. It wasn't just spite for ruining his good time, though that would be like him.

I paid the bill, leaned in and said, "We're picking this up again in the morning. If I have to look for you, I'll ask for a warrant. You clear?"

He nodded, and I walked out and drove to the hospital.

26

That night at the hospital I stayed late, sitting in a chair in Julia's room. At 3:30 a.m., the first of several calls from Beatty that I didn't take came. I'd also had a string of texts from him that were confusing and hard to follow. I answered an e-mail from a bomb tech in DC before dozing and dreaming of Melissa and me as kids, hiking through the woods behind our house. At dawn, I called the ASAC. Thorpe was an early riser. From years of watching him arrive at the office, I knew we had that in common. I also knew he arrived most mornings with a full agenda and wouldn't want to be sandbagged with an issue that should fall to my supervisor to solve.

"I'm getting calls from Beatty," I said. "He thinks I should take a look at the drone pilots he's teaching and the whole setup at the airfield. He's talking like something is wrong about it all, and I don't know how to evaluate that without taking a look. The three drone pilots he's training are all foreign nationals, which he thinks is odd, though the company says it's exactly what they're building, an international multilingual team of drone pilots."

"Is he saying these things to deflect our interest in him?"

"Not to me."

"You're talking about an out and back for a look around?"

"Well, to get a look at the pilots and a feel for where Beatty's at."

"How's your niece?"

"Devastated. All she knows right now is what she lost."

"And you?"

I didn't want to talk about myself this morning. "I'm working."

"Does nursing Beatty's psychological problems or seeing the pilots-in-training get us closer to the bomb maker?"

"No."

"But he's reaching out to you, and you think it's a worthwhile trip?"

"I do."

"Make the trip and I'll talk to Dan, but make it a quick trip. By the way, I did look into Beatty's military record. You were right. He was top drawer at Creech before he went out. I also looked at what the DOD has and agree there's not much there."

I was 2.2 miles past the Mercury exit when across the highway I spotted the sun-bleached 6 × 6 post marking the unpaved road to the airfield. It cut straight as a knife into the desert. I made a U-turn and picked it up. After 1.7 miles, the road crossed a rocky wash, then skirted low barren hills. It was a place of implacable, relentless heat. If I saw one of NASA's Mars rovers climbing a rocky slope out here, it wouldn't surprise me. Another mile in at a narrow valley, there was a fence. I used the combination Beatty gave me to open the gate and rose over a rocky crest of dry hills and saw the black strip of airfield in the hot, flat valley below. A wide graded road ran down to it. It did look like they were thinking long term here.

Ten minutes later I parked on gravel and climbed steel stairs and knocked on the door of what had to be the flight trailer. A young guy who couldn't be more than twenty, but must have been one of the pilots in training, opened it. He was broad shouldered and tall, olive skinned and green eyed, wearing a thin leather jacket and black pants, as if the heat outside meant nothing. He waited for me to explain myself, before Beatty waved from a table and stood up. He got the pilots working on something, pulled the door shut, and we walked out onto the airfield.

"What were you trying to communicate about the drone pilots last night?" I asked. "What I got was that you were worried about how legit they are. Today you seem okay with them."

"They're real. They can fly these things. They're not going to need much instruction. They're experienced."

"Is that bad?"

"No, it's good."

"Then what is it?"

"Maybe they don't fit with what I'm used to, but I'm pretty spun out right now. Did you see where the manager at Wunderland is giving tours of my trailer?"

"I saw that. What else about these drone pilots?"

"They're all from different places and supposedly they don't know each other that well, but I'd say they're tight. They stick together."

"How can you know that already? You just met them."

"I don't know. Maybe I'm wrong, but they look at each other and seem to communicate." He looked at me and shook his head. "Who knows? Maybe it's me. They've heard all the stories and know I'm getting fired, so they don't want to get too close."

"They cut you loose?"

"Yeah, my replacement is on the way."

"I'm sorry to hear that."

"It pretty much had to happen, didn't it? Just a matter of when, right?"

"What are you going to do next?"

"What am I going to do? Good question. I've got some strange ideas running through my head."

"Like what?"

"Like you don't want to hear about them."

He moved on to Eddie Bahn. I remembered Bahn as a talkative sales guy with ten to fifteen jokes he played like cards. Same deck every time, but with the cards reshuffled and fun at first, then tiring like a tape played over and over. Beatty had introduced us in a Vegas bar last fall. Bahn was dressed that night in a rose-colored silk shirt, elk-skin boots, jeans with a sharp crease, and a belt buckle probably worth ten grand. His talk was all about the money to be made in drones. He'd been a Navy recruiter, then worked other sales jobs, and as the Bakken shale took off, got into finding engineers for the fracking industry. When fracking slowed down, he slipped out the side door. Now it was drones that were going to change the world, and he was an instant expert.

It sounded that night like he'd found another sweet spot, and until we started digging deeper into him, it probably felt pretty good riding along in his big new pickup on his way to the next pitch. From the agents looking into him, I'd heard he had both IRS and Canada Revenue Agency problems. He had too much money in the bank for what he'd reported in earnings for the last decade. Bahn was a little careless, but he wasn't stupid. He had a Panamanian shell company with bank accounts we might never find.

Beatty showed me the drones, shiny and silver, in a temporary hangar. He said the mechanics worked on them every night and made modifications based on sensor data the drones gathered while flying. These were prototypes. He pointed at dry, gray mountains behind as he described the survey routes they were flying.

"It looks like Strata has put some money into this airfield," I said. "At their Houston office, they're telling our agents they have long-term plans for drones. Looks like that's what you've got here."

I nodded toward a drone pilot who'd come out of the flight trailer and was standing on the landing looking at us. "What do you know about him?"

"Next to nothing. Eddie claims he vetted them, but he didn't. He got a good fee to hire from a consultant that approached him. He's tried to pay me to say I vetted them."

"When did he do that?"

"He's been doing it. That guy over there you're looking at, there'll be a hundred thousand pilots like him in a few years, and all they'll need for skills is to be good gamers. Then what will you do to check them out?"

"Good question." But the least of my problems this morning.

"When I started flying, we flew like we were in a cockpit. We literally flew the drone. We moved the flaps. We landed and took off. If you're military, you've got to know the communications and how to talk to people on the ground, but these dudes will just move the paddles." He paused. "I need to get back to the flight trailer."

"I want to sit in there and listen for a little while before I leave."

I sat behind the pilots for twenty minutes, then slipped out and had just climbed over the first low range of rocky hills when Venuti called.

"Another bombing," he said. "A car bomb at rush hour, just north of the Sahara on-ramp. It killed two men inside and left four others dead in adjacent cars. Do you know the name Raj Nasik?"

"I do. He's an aeronautical engineer, big in the drone program."

"That's right. The car was a Hertz rental and in his name. Based on videotape, as he and the other man left a casino garage this morning, he was the driver. Both were due at Creech this morning. Casino garage videotape shows them getting into a white Kia that matches the bombed vehicle. The man with him was an engineer named Mark Statham, who may be an even bigger deal than Nasik in drone technology. Most likely, the bomb was planted yesterday after Nasik picked up the car. I want your thoughts on the bomb maker when you get back here. No more airfield trips. Nothing but the bomb maker from here on, Grale, nothing else."

27

I was in the office when AQAP and ISIS both claimed the car bombing. They posted within minutes of each other, ISIS from an encrypted phone app that then populated other sites, and AQAP with their website. Nobody reacted. Shah got up to go retrieve a list she had left on her desk. Venuti used the moment to say, "The ASAC is a big believer in you, Grale."

"Even bigger than you?"

"I know you better."

"You're a cold bastard when you get crossed. It was a short trip to the airfield just for a look."

"Was it worth four hours?"

"Couldn't tell you yet."

"But you could tell me that you haven't put any time into Mondari this morning. Yesterday, he was urgent. You rousted him out of a hotel and got zip. Does that mean we're done with him as a lead?"

"We still want what he told Jane. He had a bomb maker tip she believed in. It's in her notes. I need what Mondari didn't tell her."

"Why would a casino rat have any information relevant to this investigation? I'm sure you've wondered if he strung Jane along and is dodging you because he lied to her. Here's what we'll do. I'll give you forty-eight hours to come up with something credible. After that, we'll sit down again with the ASAC and talk about moving you onto one of the teams."

Venuti left, and when Shah returned I told her we had two days. It was melodramatic, but I figured she may as well know. I also showed her a new report analyzing the build of the man videotaped switching out the wine refrigerator in Bar Alagara. It put his height at six foot two. He wore overalls that covered his arms and legs. He wore steel-toed boots—we'd identified their maker. He wore reflective sunglasses and Beats headphones over a bandanna and under a billed cap. Not much of his skin showed, but some people wear sweaters in summer and don't get hot. He was Anglo. Little could be said about hair color. A computer program had read his body as if he were unclothed and put his weight at 185 pounds.

We talked through that and as Lacey turned to her computer screen, I called Detective Perth and left the message, "We've got a match. It is Menderes's body. I just forwarded you the e-mail and am mailing a paper copy. Let's talk."

Then I hurried downstairs to watch the latest Omar Smith interview, though as it turned out there was no rush. Smith's lawyer was on his feet making a statement and a threat. Treasury and the Secret Service had yet to respond on the impounded cash. If Smith lost his business due to inability to make the payment, they would sue.

The agents ready to interview Smith commiserated. They were just as interested in the money as Smith and his lawyer, though for different reasons. One got up to ostensibly make a call to check with the Secret Service. He probably used the bathroom then checked his messages instead. He came back with no new news. The interview started with Smith frustrated and angry.

"Mr. Smith, we want to revisit the Fourth of July. With as much detail as you can give us, take us from when you awakened on July 4 in Houston until our agents arrived at your house after the bombing."

"With as much detail as I can give you?"

"Yes."

"Everything I remember?"

"Yes."

"Is this not a waste of everyone's time?"

"Please proceed."

As he did, his anger crystalized. He recalled waking, yawning, using a toilet, shaving, brushing his teeth, showering, choosing the clothes he would wear, then dressing and eating breakfast of yogurt, tea, and fruit. So it went, item by item. He talked about checking out of the hotel, gave details of the cab and the black mole on the cab driver's right temple, and the number of stoplights on the way to the airport as he left Houston. He detailed people in the airport security line and names on the badges of the TSA security officers. He described the sink with the faulty handle in the restroom and where he sat to wait for the plane. He demonstrated a remarkable memory, and did it aggressively.

A half hour passed and his plane wasn't even in the air yet. He continued with even greater detail, pausing occasionally to let them interrupt him and end the interview. Agents watching the feed got restless, but in the interview room they rode him out. They waited. The more detail, the better. When he was done, Omar Smith would own the timeline.

He grew hoarse as he told how he took a seat in 3A on the flight home. The plane was twenty-two minutes late taking off. He declined alcohol and drank water, and now started into the people who had sat next to him on the plane. He described a chicken salad lunch and the color and taste of the things he ate and drank. The agent next to me tapped my arm and said, "The guy's making me hungry. I've got to go get something. Think you could text me when his plane lands?"

"Sure, but maybe you want to wait until he picks up his luggage."

Finally the plane landed, and he retrieved his luggage. He hadn't been able to carry anything on, so we were off to carousel 7B, where he described each piece that came up on the conveyor belt ahead of his bag, and then wheeled his luggage out of McCarran Airport.

Then came the late afternoon and his stop at the Alagara. Videotape from an adjacent camera put him in the area of the Alagara at 5:13 p.m. on the Fourth of July. Smith said the Alagara stop happened at 5:27 and lasted less than ten minutes. But no one interrupted as he detailed his drive to the Alagara and his brief stop there. Only after Smith's recounting moved on did the agents interrupt to bring him back.

"What else did you do inside the Alagara?"

"I looked in the restrooms at the repairs. I wanted to see everything was clean and ready for the party."

"Describe the tile repairs."

He described the seventeen pieces of tile installed and his issues with the grouting. He described flaws in the caulking around the urinal.

"Were you alone there?"

"Yes."

"When you entered the Alagara what door did you enter through?"

"The back door."

He started to say something more and stopped. He stared at the agents.

"I am tired of this," he said. "I am finished."

"We're all tired," an agent responded. "Bear with us. When you came in through the rear door, did you lock it behind you?"

"It shuts on its own. I am nearly through speaking with you today."

"Did the surveillance camera record you entering?"

"I don't think it was on."

He stopped again, and the agent asked, "Why wouldn't the camera be working?"

"There was an electrician doing work on July 3. The alarm goes off if they're not careful how they shut it down, so usually it gets disarmed. I wasn't home to rearm it, so it was probably off. Do you know if it was off?"

"We don't. It's why we're asking."

"Please describe in as much detail as you can why you're lying to me."

"We're not lying, Mr. Smith."

Smith's response to that was a very detailed accounting of what he did in his office once inside the Alagara, starting with sorting the mail that had arrived while he was gone. Junk mail, everything, a remarkable memory for each piece, if accurate. He ticked through everything that had to do with the party, which was scheduled to start in less than half an hour. He checked the back bar and recounted the bottles on it row by row. He recalled the new wine refrigerator and described the face of it, plastic not yet removed, and the deal he made with Melissa Kern allowing the pilots to bring their own alcohol.

Hearing Melissa's name was like a hot stone dropped in my gut, but I listened as he described the children's party table with a red, white, and blue paper tablecloth. He had checked the air conditioning and lowered it one degree, then readied to leave.

"I wanted to see Melissa Kern. I liked her very much. I assumed she would come early with her family."

"Why did you assume that?"

He stared in disbelief at the agent who was asking why Melissa would arrive before guests to her party.

"When you were in your office, did you open your safe?"

"I don't remember."

"Surely, Mr. Smith, after all the detail you have remembered . . ."

"I don't trust you. Is that better? I have no reason to trust the FBI and many reasons not to."

Smith turned to his lawyer who lifted a briefcase onto the table, opened it, removed a file, shut the briefcase, and set it back down on the floor. The lawyer looked to Smith for approval before sliding the thin file across the table. In it was a list of scheduled repair work, including the wine refrigerator.

"Here is another copy of the work done. Most of it was in June. There was only a little left, and it was not the time to check everything. I was tired from traveling and only there to make sure the building was ready, and to make sure the children were not forgotten and the table was ready for them."

"Did you turn the alarm on when you left?"

"No, it was too close to the time of the party."

"Could somebody have come in after you?"

"They would need a key."

"There was a man waiting for you earlier. Did you meet with him when you were there?"

"He was a salesman peddling trash. I sent him away and forgot about him."

The agents didn't answer that. Instead, one asked, "Would you mind sharing the code to the alarm with us?"

"With your prejudices, that is a bad idea," Smith said. "The code will frighten you. It will frighten you, and you'll keep holding my money."

"Why would an alarm code frighten us?"

"Through your prejudices."

"Giving us your alarm code won't affect the release of the money."

"You think not?" Smith looked from one interrogator to the other. "The code is a very simple code. The code is 'God is great.'"

He tapped with his right index finger into his left palm as if tapping on the alarm keypad.

"All capitals. G-O-D-I-S-G-R-E-A-T. God is great. I say this to myself many, many times every day so I always remember. It is short and I never forget. On our money it says 'In God We Trust,' but that is not the same. Even as you ask questions here, I say inside, 'God is great.'"

To the left of me, an agent said, "There you go. Right in our face, this is our guy. He just told us. Come on! Get it out of him! He's on the edge. Get him to talk."

The agent was still coaching the interrogators when I concluded nothing was going to happen here today and walked out.

28

After leaving a message for Mondari, I opened a file on Umar Patek, the bomb maker in the 2002 Bali bombing that killed 202 people. Patek's file included his apprehension in the town of Abbottabad, Pakistan, on January 25, 2011. Other arrests in northwest Pakistan occurred close to the same time. Four months later, a raid in Abbottabad killed Osama bin Laden. Did Patek give up bin Laden's location? I've pinged different intelligence officers I know who might be aware of the truth, but I've never gotten a definitive answer.

When the name Abbottabad faded from the news, the gathering of bomb makers there stuck with me. Perhaps subconsciously I was trying to connect the chatter about a Lebanese financier's successful Mexico meeting to the C-4 allegedly tracked as far as a warehouse in Phoenix and the rumor passed by Denny Mondari of a bomb maker smuggled into the country.

Somewhere near Las Vegas was a bomb maker. Right or wrong, that was my conviction. If the target is the drone program, what's next? More than enough agents had been and still were looking at Strata Data Mining. I had called one of them earlier and she downplayed any worry about the pilots in training. *Find the bomb maker,* I thought. *Find the C-4 and we'll shut them down.* But nothing is as simple as that, and what began as a nagging worry was morphing into the very real possibility that with the help of a trained sleeper cell, the goal might be to wage a much longer campaign.

"Special Agent Grale, I'd like to introduce you to Special Agent Jane Stone's parents."

I looked up and saw Jane in her dad's face. Same clean cheekbones, strong jaw, and light in the eyes that even grief couldn't extinguish. I saw where Jane got her easy rapport.

"We loved her," I said. "I've been with the Bureau nineteen years and have never met anyone I liked and respected more than Jane. I'm very, very sorry for your loss." As they started to move on, I said, "If you want to talk more, I'll be here."

Jane's father did return. He was agitated and watching to make sure his wife didn't follow.

"I'm hearing on TV that Jane made a mistake that got her killed. Is that true?"

I saw the agony the question brought him. The truest thing to say was, "Yes, Jane should have waited until the bomb squad cleared the vehicles," but I couldn't do that.

"Knowing her, I'm sure she had a very good reason to be where she was when it detonated."

To me that sounded hollow, but it seemed to help him. He gripped my hand.

"Jane told me you never quit. Find them."

"We will."

I said it so easily, yet Venuti was right. So far I had nothing but disconnected facts, fragments, hunches, shadows of patterns, and news today of a June 17 plane crash of a four-seater Cessna hijacked from an American couple who'd been murdered on the airstrip of a ranch they owned in Mexico. A second look at the plane's wreckage in the dry mountains at the edge of the Imperial Valley pointed to a bomb in contrast to the engine failure the FAA preliminarily cited. Lacey had found that out this morning and was awaiting a transcript of radio communication between the pilot and an air traffic controller as the plane had crossed into US airspace. No cargo and no other bodies were found in the plane. The pilot had radioed in an oil pressure problem, made an emergency landing, took off again, then crashed, all the same day the plane was stolen. According to the DEA, this pilot did occasional work for the Sinaloa cartel. Did he ferry someone from Mexico?

I left a message with the FAA and fielded a call from the DOD investigator Sarah Warner, who said, "Let's meet and talk. I want to confess and repent, and we've got an overlap going you need to know about. Name a place for coffee."

"Gaudi Café. Repent?"

"I'm serious."

At Gaudi's I bought two iced coffees and carried them outside to a table in the shade. It was pushing 105 degrees, but dry heat. Warner smiled and I leaned back against a smooth shaded concrete wall with the cold cup in my hand. I was tired and thinking about Julia and the memorial on the drive here, but trying to focus on Warner's urgency. I took another swallow. Good coffee and much needed. Cold brewed forty-eight hours, I'd read inside.

She exhaled and sighed. "You're not going to like this," she said.

"What happened to repenting?"

"I'll get there. Denny Mondari approached us in June about working as an informant. He told us about his relationship with the FBI and we made an inquiry, but we didn't say anything about his offer to us. It was my responsibility to tell your office we were starting a relationship with him, and I held off because you were a question mark."

"And now you're over that, so that's not why we're meeting. Did Mondari call you today?"

"He did and asked me to find out through your supervisor if there's someone else at the FBI he can work with other than you."

"He asked that today?"

"Yes."

"Let him know I was in tears when you told me." Warner smiled her crooked smile. "What's the Department of Defense's interest in Denny Mondari?"

"He claims he's tied in with some hackers we'd like to talk to."

"Hackers are his tribe, so that might be true. But you need to be careful with him. He's helped us, so we haven't looked hard enough at his other activities. That's changing."

"Activities? Like what?"

"Like you check into a casino and you're up in your room on the twelfth floor and you want to go online and check out restaurants for tonight. You find out your room didn't come with free Wi-Fi, but you don't want to go down the elevator and wait in line again, so you boot up your computer and check for other strong signals in the area. You click on the one just below the hotel Wi-Fi. It gets you online and everything looks good, until a little box pops up and says you've got to pay. Good news is, it's less than half the hotel rate. Bad news is, you're giving your credit card numbers to the wrong people. That's the kind of operation Mondari would have a piece of. He would never be one of the guys to get busted, but he's in the background."

"You're saying he's a scumbag."

"He's nuanced. Think of him as the venture capital guy who funds the little, dirt poor, garage-start-up cybercriminals. On the good side, he's not violent and he's bright. He's a gamer, a schemer. He knows his casinos. His type probably didn't exist before them. He reminds me of the guys who used to hang around horse racing when I was a kid. For some, it was their whole life and they were part of the juice and energy of the track. They knew every inch of it. Denny is that way about casinos and computers. Where are you meeting him?"

"The Bellagio, for dinner."

"The Bellagio is one of his favorites. We're talking about a guy who shops for just the right cologne, and shaves and dresses carefully before going out at night. He'll be dressed when you meet him tonight. When he's lucky, a younger woman goes back to his love pad with him."

"Yuck."

"Think period piece. It's worth seeing."

"If you can tell all that from being around him, I'd like to know some things about my life." She leaned toward me. "Will I ever find true love?"

Right there at that moment, I started liking Sarah Warner. I smiled and drank and said, "I think it's inevitable for you. Look, I've studied Denny. Sometimes he comes up big, so I've learned to pay attention. That's why we took his casino-extortion bomb plot seriously."

"But that tip doesn't really fit with anything, does it?"

"So far, it doesn't. Are you buying dinner tonight, or is the DOD?"

"The Criminal Investigative Division will pick up the tab if I get enough from him."

"Don't leave the table before everything is ordered, or you'll end up in your supervisor's office a month from now explaining the bill."

"Okay, I'll remember that."

"He'll order, but he won't eat. He just drinks and he doesn't get drunk, and he doesn't go all the way on the first date. He'll give you something but not everything. He knows how to tease, and he knows how to find out what's valuable to you. You're law enforcement so you're untrustworthy, but that doesn't mean you're not fun to dance with. You can be worked and if you work him in return, he'll respect you. I know this is probably too much information."

"Actually, after everything, I can't believe you're even talking to me."

But she could. She was proud and determined and not afraid to put herself out there. She might not believe it right now, but my guess was, she'd become a top investigator at the Department of Defense.

"I can't either," I said, "but I'll be waiting for your text tonight. I'll be close to the Bellagio. I need to catch him when he leaves you."

I stood and picked up my coffee, then saw she had something else she wanted to say.

"Can we start over?" she asked. "You and me, I mean."

"Want to do it right now?"

"This second."

"I'm good with that."

We shook hands, then tapped our plastic coffee cups together in a quick toast, and you know, that would never have happened with a younger me. The younger me would still be offended that DOD had suspected me. But if you live long enough, you learn we all make mistakes. Then you learn how to let them go. That's the hard part, letting them go.

29

At the morgue in the midafternoon, an assistant slid open the drawer holding Jim Kern. I unzipped the body bag and looked at my old close friend and brother-in-law with a five-inch gash in his scalp. Maybe the gash could be hidden, maybe not. I wasn't up on their techniques, but white bone showed and Julia didn't need to see it. When the bag was unzipped farther, I saw his left arm detached and lying in the bag, his right shattered and flayed. I slowly rezipped the bag and slid the drawer back in, and then had to take a few minutes before looking at Melissa.

Her face was nearly unmarred. For that, I was thankful. I knew when I found her the night of the bombings that she'd bled out rapidly, but that night I hadn't registered the full extent of her wounds. The ripping tear through her abdomen brought bile to my mouth, even as I told myself she couldn't have felt much, if anything. She lost consciousness in the initial blast. She didn't suffer, did she?

I looked at Nate last. He'd lived long enough to bruise on one side of his face. Maybe if Julia looked at him from only the other side, or if the bruising was masked, it would be okay. But if it was my choice, I'd tell Julia to remember them as they were, not as they are.

Outside I was glad for the bright hot sunlight and made one more stop and a drive-by before visiting Julia. The stop was to see the car from the freeway bombing. It was in the airplane hangar with the Alagara bomb debris. I stood with a couple of techs and looked at the twisted-and-burned shell, glass and doors gone, roof deformed. It smelled heavily of melted plastic. Early analysis said only a small amount of C-4 was used, but incendiaries were with it. In the intense heat, the car interior ignited. Neither man had a chance. It underscored the skill of the bomb maker and to me was another indication of a pro.

When I left the hangar, I drove past the Alagara to see the flowers. I didn't linger and wouldn't have told anyone, but it helped me to see that people were moved enough to leave flowers. I still didn't know what the rose thing was about, but there were more and more of them. They spilled over the sidewalk into the bar lot and, though wilting in the summer heat, they were quite beautiful.

Driving to the hospital I scrolled cell numbers until I reached the name Peter Henley. For a long time Henley was in CIRG, the Bureau's Critical Incident Response Group at FBI headquarters. Retired now, he lived in Vermont but still had limited clearance and was a resource for certain bomb investigations. Some combination of the morgue visit and fatigue had left me shaken, so I waited a few minutes before calling him.

Henley picked up on the second ring and said, "Good to hear your voice, let me get to a chair."

An armchair squeaked: a big man getting older. When Henley was FBI he was overweight by Bureau standards, and they periodically got on him about it. Chemist that he was, he brewed great beer. He reworked a shed he had and figured out how to make an IPA with a distinct bite, but a good one. When I tried it I wanted more.

Beer put weight on Peter. Now that he was retired, he'd gained another thirty pounds. I was out east in April and had driven to his house in Vermont to see him. Physically, he was struggling. Diabetes was a problem.

I heard him clear his throat, then his deep voice with the familiar question, "What have you got, Paul?"

"A detonator of a type I haven't seen before. We found bits of tubing on the Alagara lot and again today on the freeway."

"Could be an igniter," Henley said.

"With C-4, why go to the trouble?"

"I'd guess it's what you already probably suspect. He's changing his signature. I don't see any advantage in terms of detonating the bomb."

"I don't either. It's why I'm calling."

"I would look for a known bomb maker."

"I have been, and the CIA is telling us AQAP has much deeper pockets now. They're getting Saudi oil money through several charities and can afford an expensive freelancer. At the same time, ISIS and AQAP have better bomb makers and more of them now, so who knows?"

"I think you're right about a pro."

The chair squeaked and I knew that was Peter leaning forward. After so many years working around him, I could easily visualize him. Henley cleared his throat again.

"You're guessing he's using a different igniter to throw you off from recognizing his signature because he's aware he's in our database, Interpol's, or the Russians'."

"I am guessing that, and whoever they have on the ground here is getting very good information. We're struggling with that. The car was rented less than twenty-four hours before, and it's a different type than Nasik, the engineer, usually rents. Yet the charge was shaped for the car. They found out what type of car, got the information to the bomb maker, and got the bomb planted, all inside twenty-four hours."

"This bomb maker may be getting in your head, Paul."

"No, I'm okay."

"How much C-4 is left?"

"Roughly half."

"It's not a one-off-then-run-away operation."

No need to respond to that. That was Peter thinking aloud. The freeway bombing was the third. Henley was headed to the same conclusion I was debating.

"The bomb maker is being careful," Henley said, then paused. "But there are more and more law officers concentrated there. If a sleeper cell is in Las Vegas, it's just a matter of time before it's uncovered."

"I agree that the risk of being found increases for them with every passing day. At some point, economizing with C-4 doesn't make sense. We'll have so many law enforcement officers here, we'll find them sooner or later. They know that."

"They could take the bombings to another city."

"Drone pilots. Drone engineers. AQAP. This is about the drone program," I said.

"You're looking at all the C-4 left and thinking they'll go big if they're not caught before."

"That's part of why I'm calling."

"Can you send me photos of the igniter pieces?"

"I've got to get it approved, but you've still got your clearance, right?"

"For this, yes."

"I'll get them to you. Thank you, Peter. I miss working with you."

I clicked off and called Jo, who had texted she'd just been with Julia.

"How is she?" I asked and heard the catch in her throat as she answered.

"The swelling is diminishing. She'll be on her feet soon."

"I'm headed there. That's such good news."

"That's the good news. The bad news is her state of mind."

I brought a present with me, a new iPhone for Julia. I knew from Melissa that she wanted an iPhone. She tried to smile when she saw it, but her heart wasn't in it. She placed the phone on the bedside table as tears came.

"I just really miss Mom and Dad and Nate."

"I know you do, Julia."

You always will.

"I thought more about it like you asked, Uncle Paul, and I want to see them. I have to see them. I know what you said, but I have to."

"Then we'll do it."

"Are their faces all—"

She couldn't finish the sentence. Her chest heaved as she wept, and I felt a great rush of sadness and a desire to protect her from what I couldn't.

"Their faces are the faces you know, but they aren't there anymore. The light in our eyes is how we know each other and that's gone. I stopped at the morgue today. It's going to be hard and you won't ever forget the change."

"I want to hold my dad's hand just once more."

I couldn't bring myself to answer that and continued on in my clumsy way.

"You saw your grandmother at her funeral. How old were you?"

"Four, but I remember her."

I nodded.

"A lot of energy gets released very fast when a bomb detonates. There's a rapid, almost immediate, expansion that rips things in its way apart. I don't know any other way but to tell you the truth. If we do this, you only get to see their faces."

Through her sobs she said, "I want to know everything. I want to see. I have to see."

"We'll go and after that they'll be cremated and we'll need urns for their ashes. I think we should look at urns together and find ones that are beautiful." *Or they come home in cardboard boxes with gray ash and fragments of bones and teeth. Urns were a way to start. We could find urns and talk about a memorial and a place for their ashes. And I'll hunt the people who did this and when I find them . . .*

"I brought your laptop and headphones too. They say you're healing so fast you'll get out of here soon. You know this already, of course—your friends Krissy and Elysa and Natalie are coming this evening and bringing dinner. I was thinking music might help, so I got you the phone."

She said nothing to that and went quiet and back into herself. Later, she dozed and I answered e-mails. When Julia woke, she said, "I thought I felt Mom today."

"Maybe you did."

"It was like she was in this room."

"Could be."

Two nurses came in and I kissed her forehead and left. Sarah Warner called as I got in my car. For a moment, I was afraid Mondari had canceled out on her.

"Just calling to let you know we're on. He moved the dinner to nine o'clock, but we're a go. I'll text you."

"I'll be waiting."

30

Near midnight, the text came. It read, **Almost done. Waiting for the check. Mondari in restroom.**

Which restroom?

I didn't wait for her response. The restaurant faced the arcade. The nearest restrooms were a short walk to the left. At the line of urinals I spotted Mondari and ducked back out. Less than a minute later, Mondari came out. He looked toward the restaurant then walked the opposite way.

I texted Warner, **He's leaving. I'm following.**

No way!

I didn't answer her next text or the one after as I trailed Mondari outside onto the midnight street. She called a moment later.

"He'll call you," I said. "Something will have come up, an emergency, a friend who needs help, but he'll call you. How did it go with him?"

"I thought it went well. Now I don't know."

Up ahead, Mondari slowed, lit a cigarette, and pulled out his phone.

"Here comes your call from him. Talk to you later."

"You're right. It's him."

I slid my phone into a pocket and watched Mondari talk with Warner. I saw him smile and stroke the tuft of upright hair on his head. Probably just promised to cook for her at his place next time. She had long legs he wouldn't have missed. He crossed the road and started toward a casino lot. I cut him off.

"Time to talk, Denny."

He started to step around me.

"Here or in the field office. Your call."

"You'll have to arrest me."

"Okay."

Mondari looked back toward the Bellagio. Must be thinking Warner burned him.

"Here or in an interview room, what do you want to do?" I asked. "Why did you lie to Jane?"

Not sure why, but I was centered on that question still. He'd still balk at answering but I could read his face, and I'd be back with the question again. Then he surprised me; that was the thing about Mondari, he had that trait.

"I was scared," he said.

"Of what?"

"If I tell you and it goes anywhere, I'm fucked."

"You'll be an unnamed confidential informant."

"I need a guarantee."

"Start talking first."

"No really, Grale, I'm serious. If it goes anywhere, I'm dead."

"It won't leak out of our office." I saw he didn't believe me, so I added, "I don't have to name my source."

What followed was a silence. There were all kinds of people on the sidewalks and neon lights glaring and traffic up and down the strip, but between us a silence I could almost touch, me waiting, Mondari weighing risk.

"Okay," he said.

"Okay, what?"

"There's a mid-level Sinaloa cartel manager who stays in the same room every time he comes through Vegas. He's a gambler, so the casino treats him well. They loan him a laptop when he's here, and he logs into a dark site. Some guys I know figured out a way to see his e-mails while he's reading or responding. They take screenshots. They've made some money with what they learned."

"Some guys you know steal the e-mails of a mid-level Sinaloa cartel manager?"

"Yes."

"And this cartel manager always stays in the same room?"

"Once a month."

"What's his name?"

"The name he uses is Miguel Catalangelo."

I couldn't match anybody with that name and asked, "What happened?"

"The guys fucked up. They left a trail and the cartel followed it."

"Your computer-thief geeks?"

"They're not mine. I know them, but I don't have anything to do with whatever they're up to."

"Right. Where are they now?"

"They're missing."

"When did they go missing?"

"Mid-June. That's why I've been hiding."

"How do you know they didn't just take off?"

"They fucked up, they got found out, and now they're missing. What's that sound like to you?"

"What was in the e-mails they read?"

"A confirmation of a delivery and a wire transfer of money."

"A drug sale?"

"No, it's what I was starting to tell Jane."

"You told Jane or were starting to tell her?"

"I told her part of it. I told her the guys read an e-mail that mentioned a bomb maker."

"Do you still have the screenshot with that e-mail?"

"I never had it."

I didn't believe that, but we could come back to that later.

"The e-mail said the cartel delivered a *fabricante de bombas*."

"Delivered?"

"Catalangelo's e-mail was a confirmation of delivery. That's what it was about."

"The cartel delivered a bomb maker? And you're certain this Catalangelo works for the Sinaloa cartel?"

"Yes."

"How long had your guys been reading his e-mails?"

"Three months."

"Give me their names."

"Uri Pylori. John Edelman. Catalangelo's e-mail said they were paid in full for the delivery of the fabricante de bombas, so now they would move the product."

"The product?"

"Yes."

Maybe it was true that a bomb maker was delivered like a shipment. Smuggled over the border in the drug pipeline. I turned the phrase *fabricante de bombas* in my head. There were no other meanings. *Bomb maker*. It translated as *bomb maker*. This Catalangelo oversaw delivery of a bomb maker, and the cartel got a big fee. Then delivered what product? C-4?

"We're going to the field office."

"I knew you'd fuck me."

"Not doing that, but we've got to take it there."

At the office Mondari repeated the same things he'd said under the lamp in the lot. He didn't know where his guys or Miguel Catalangelo were. He didn't know where the fabricante de bombas was delivered. He couldn't help us find anybody, but he showed us his phone texts and e-mails from the guys when it was going great.

I could place Uri Pylori and Edelman now. Edelman was late twenties, gaunt and pale. His eyes danced around like he was looking for his next fix. Pylori had bad teeth and had worn the same short-sleeve black T-shirt for a decade, but he was good with numbers. It was best to keep a step back from his breath.

Mondari showed us a worried text from Pylori. **Screenshots not working anymore. Hang up calls last night. Two guys in a car outside on the street. Freaking out!**

At three a.m. Mondari asked, "Can I go home?"

"We may need to move you someplace safer."

"I'm okay tonight."

I should have listened to my instincts. I should have known.

31

Before dawn, Beatty sat on the cool steel of the metal flight-trailer steps and watched mechanics disassemble the last drone. Lights strung from the aluminum struts of the drone hangar illuminated enough for him to see their progress. The wings came off and were strapped to side brackets inside the truck. The fuselage was hoisted and slid into a custom cradle. All three drones the same way, one truck for each. When the trucks left, he watched their lights make the sweeping climb up and over the rock hills.

Then it was quiet and there were still stars back over the mountains behind. To the east the sky lightened. To his left he saw the headlights of Eddie's pickup, two pinpricks of light way out there but coming this way. Funny how he'd worried that if he were out here for months he'd go stir-crazy. It turned out so different. Now he wanted to stay out in the open desert and not have to hear his name on TV or have a waitress refuse to seat him, like yesterday.

When he checked again, Eddie's headlights were much closer. *Eddie liked fresh coffee, so what the fuck, let's make Eddie some coffee.* Beatty stood. He stretched, then went up the remaining stairs into the flight trailer. As the coffee brewed he slid onto his chair in front of the computer. He checked the audio file. Ready to go. A few minutes later Eddie rolled up, parked, and came through the door ready to fight.

"Did you talk to your FBI friend like I told you to?"

"Not yet. Want coffee? I just made it for you."

"You're going down if you don't back me on this. I told the FBI you looked at the drone pilot résumés and said which ones to hire. It'll be your word against mine."

"You didn't answer me."

"Fuck your coffee."

"You sure?"

"You listen to me."

Beatty listened as he poured the coffee down the sink. Eddie said, "The only reason the Feds are on me is you. They're in my bank accounts, everything. You and your problems are fucking up my life, so you're going to do what I say or I tell them all kinds of shit. I'll make it up as I go. You made threats against the air force. Maybe it was drunk talk or you were high, but what you said scared me. They're looking for anything on you. They keep pushing with questions, and I'm keeping them hungry, okay. They know I want to deal. But what I really want is to make a deal with you. Everything about the drone pilots, anything to do with drones, that's you. I've got papers you signed that you vetted them."

"What's wrong with the drone pilots, Eddie?"

"Nothing is wrong. They're all good, but I need the FBI off my back. I need everything to do with you out of my life. I'm going to give you money. Ten thousand dollars and until noon today to give me an answer."

"And what happens when I don't?"

"You don't want to know. It'll be bad. It'll be really bad. It'll be all the things you talked about doing to get even with the air force. I will fuck you up for life. Or you do the smart thing and take some money and do what I say. You're going to need the money. You call me before noon or—"

"Shut the door on your way out, Eddie."

Eddie shut it hard, and Beatty closed the audio file. He e-mailed the recording to Grale, then just sat there.

32

When I stopped by the hospital, Julia was asleep. I left her a note and drove to the office. I had access to all terrorism databases but also kept my own list of bomb makers. On my list you needed to be active within the past five years.

Some built bombs in primitive mud-walled buildings high in remote mountains. One had holed up for years on the twenty-seventh floor of a Bangkok high-rise. Another worked from an abandoned warehouse in Spain. Some were hermitic. Some had relatives who helped assemble the parts. A few visited the scene of their work to try to figure out how to do it better. Many dealt through third parties or through a friend or family member. Most didn't travel, or if they did, didn't go far, and those who traveled to another country were usually pros.

We could be looking for someone homegrown, such as a disgruntled former armed service member who knew C-4 and was recruited. Aspects of that profile are what made Beatty a person of interest. If AQAP could recruit and train a sleeper cell, then why not a homegrown bomb maker trained by our military? That was possible, but I doubted it.

I divided bomb makers into two basic categories: Religious zealots and the ideologically driven were filed under *Righteous*. This included the Timothy McVeigh and Osama bin Laden types. It didn't matter to me what religion or political belief they killed for, so long as they were true believers and were willing to murder for their particular religion or political persuasion. They were always right. Their bombs were always just. The dead were always infidels or labeled with some dehumanizing word.

The second group I called *Trolls*. Trolls had zero interest in doing God's or Allah's work, or engaging in politics. They built bombs for money, the thrill, power, or all three. They had no more or less morality or lack of it than the religious true believers, but they had key differences. They weren't driven by a sense of outrage or purpose. They weren't seeking retribution, validation, or a prestamped ticket to the afterlife.

Some trolls made a lifestyle out of bomb making. They lived well from job to job and were shrewd about what projects they took on. A few were adept travelers and dangerous anywhere. That's what I thought we were looking for here. A traveling troll. Mondari's claim of a cartel delivering a fabricante de bombas fit the traveler group. On my list there were twenty-three who met that criteria. That didn't rule out a new bomb maker, but I felt odds were, we were looking for somebody known.

I scrutinized that list and was at my desk when an audio file came from Beatty. I listened, saved it, and forwarded the e-mail to Venuti just before Jo called.

"I'm at the hospital," she said. "They're telling me Julia had another very hard night. I think she needs grief counseling to start now. I know a retired nurse who isn't a counselor but who would be really good. She's seen it all and has a huge heart. Should I send you her phone number? What do you think?"

"Send it. I'll call her."

"There's something else. One of Julia's friends thinks Julia isn't going to see them very much anymore. She thinks that when she lives with you, she'll have to go to a different high school and will lose all her friends."

"If I can't get it approved for her to attend the same high school, then I'll lease my house to someone and move to her school district."

"I know and I'm sure she wouldn't think of saying anything. I'm not even sure she said anything to her friend. It may just be that her friend thinks that."

"It's legit. I'll figure it out."

An hour later I took a call from Rosamar Largo, who wanted to meet for lunch. I was on the fence about that and threw it out for Venuti to decide.

Venuti said, "We've found no evidence that Menderes was her brother, and she's not exactly grief stricken. We talked to her ex yesterday. He says their marriage ended because she was sleeping with a drug dealer boyfriend. He also said cocaine cost her a good casino job. Go ahead and have lunch with her, but make it clear that if she holds back anything more, she's dealing herself in. She met with two agents yesterday. Why call you?"

"Juan Menderes's murder. When the homicide detectives questioned her, they used me as the bad guy. They told her I believe she knew what would happen to Juan."

"Do you believe that?"

I nodded.

"Do you want to do this lunch with her?"

"I'll do the lunch and then I'm out."

"Meaning what? Meaning you think Largo and Menderes are about drugs only and everything to do with them is unrelated to the bombings. They killed him, so he couldn't talk about the drug deliveries."

"Probably. He's got a history of moving drugs. He worked for a coyote. Under his former name he's got enemies in the drug world, and she's got money she can't explain."

"Why does she want to have lunch with you?"

"Good question."

"I'll send a couple of agents in ahead of you, so look for them when you get there. What's the coyote work Menderes did?"

"The roommate Enrique Vasco told me Juan ran a crew for a coyote who led border crossers to their deaths from dehydration and heat exhaustion. Juan's crew followed and stripped the bodies of anything valuable, including gold fillings. I think there's something there that ties to the cocaine peddling, and it worries her."

"I can't even follow that."

"Never mind, I'll go do the lunch."

The restaurant was large, cool, and quiet inside. I was ten minutes early, but Rosamar was already at a table with a margarita. Two agents sat at a table behind her. She ordered sparkling water and an appetizer. I ordered a chicken sandwich and iced tea. Before the waiter left, she changed her sparkling water to another margarita then stared at my hands.

"You don't have a ring."

I took it off a decade ago after the memorial service for Carrie. Rosamar took a generous sip and looked at me with a glint in her eye, something humorous occurring to her. I doubted it was my left hand.

"I once slept with an FBI agent who was married. This is when I was dealing blackjack and before I was married the first time. He wasn't from your office, but honestly you all look alike."

"People say that. It makes them feel better, I guess. How many agents do you see in the room?"

She looked around.

"Just you.

"The agent I slept with was working on an interstate fraud thing and would come to my table every night and wait for my shift to finish. I knew he was married and it wasn't going anywhere long term with him. While I was undressing, he would call his wife and talk to her in a low voice about the surveillance he was on. When he got tired of me, he told me about his moral compass. He said all FBI agents have one. How's yours?"

"How about the drug business and who you and Juan worked with? Who wanted him killed? Did you get a call after the Alagara bombing and get told where to drop him? He phoned somebody else first. Did they phone you with instructions?"

"Why are you saying that?"

"We know where Juan got his new name and ID. Juan Gutierrez needed a new last name when he came out of prison. He'd made some serious enemies, but luckily the real Juan Menderes was willing to sell his identity to keep his family alive. So Juan Gutierrez became Juan Menderes. Of course a new name doesn't mean people don't recognize you, so after crossing the border, he went to work for the Sinaloa cartel. Probably figured that would protect him. He's not your half brother. So if you want to make this a working lunch, let's talk drug dealing. I think you need us, Rosamar. What happened to Juan could happen to you. You know too much, so let's talk. Let's figure something out."

"I'm unemployed and looking for work. I did a tryout to deal cards again and I'm still good with them, but they won't hire me because I look too old. These lines at my eyes and around my mouth, they're a no-go. They said it was my card handling, but it wasn't."

"Try another casino."

"I've tried them all."

"I think you're in danger. I think you should come clean with us. You do that, and I'm sure we can help you. Did Juan have any connection to the bombing?"

She answered that by reaching across the table and gripping my hand, and then pretending to jerk hers free just as the waiter approached with food.

She said loudly, "I just can't do this with you. I can't be in a relationship right now."

She grabbed her purse and left. The waiter paraded a bemused smile as he returned with the check.

Midafternoon I sat down with Venuti and Thorpe.

"A lawyer called, not what's-his-name, she's got someone new. She intends to file a complaint against you for telling her that if she had sex with you, you'd make all the FBI questions go away. We talked to the lawyer and told him we had other agents there and the entire conversation is on tape, so no issue, but that's it with you and her."

"Works for me, and I've got a question for both of you. If Omar Smith knew about the Alagara bomb plot, then he knew the building could be destroyed or burned down. Would he risk letting the money get burned up or blown apart?"

Venuti shrugged. Thorpe said, "Maybe it's his cover."

"Hundreds of thousands of dollars? I don't see that," I said. "He likes having money."

"He knew something," Venuti said.

"You mean he's not telling us everything? I agree, he knows more, but I don't think he thought a bomb would detonate inside the Alagara."

We left it there.

33

It was inevitable someone would post a YouTube video after a tour of Beatty's trailer. When it happened, it went viral. The video was shot to make the trailer look like a creepy place, cracked wood at the deck steps, dead cactus in a planter, sliced-open garbage bags taped over the windows from the inside, dead flies on the floor, a door creaking open, and twilight gloom inside. A flashlight beam swept the tabletop and lingered on duct-tape repairs to the Barcalounger and Styrofoam trash no longer stacked neatly on the floor. A voice-over talked about confiscated computers targeting US cities.

The camera panned across stripped walls. It moved behind the tacked-up sheets to the bed and small bathroom still cluttered with clothes. The flashlight beam circled a vomit-caked bathroom sink. The video ended on the table and the open door. Eerie and nothing like the Jeremy Beatty I knew.

I walked into Venuti's office soon after. He was in a clean suit and had a new haircut. Must have gone home. Good. He needed to.

"Shut the door, Grale, and let's have that talk again."

"What happened to forty-eight hours?"

"The Bureau will announce tomorrow evidence is conclusive that Al Qaeda in the Arabian Peninsula supplied the C-4 for the three attacks and that ISIS aided in its transport and built the cell here."

"Are we going to provide any evidence of that?"

"We're not going to reveal too much but will ask the public for tips."

"Whose idea is this?"

"There's consensus. To be blunt, we need people looking hard at their neighbors."

I didn't say anything to that. I looked past Venuti, and Venuti said, "You're thinking this may push them to act sooner with the remaining C-4."

"It could and we're not really giving the public anything to work with."

"We are. We're giving probabilities."

Venuti ticked them off as if that would convince me. The sleeper cell most likely was predominantly male with an age range between twenty-one and forty-five. He went right down his list, but he had many of the same doubts as me.

"If the analysts are right, there's a sleeper cell of seven to ten individuals," he said.

"Where are they getting these numbers?"

"Through hours required for tasks performed, coordination, phone analysis they're not talking much about, and an algorithm drawing from the variables. So do we adjust what you're doing? Do we still put hours into Mondari?"

"How did we jump from this to Mondari?"

"We're going to see a flood of tips, and we're going to need everyone. We're going to account for every house, every apartment, trailers, hotels, everything in southern Nevada."

Another computer-driven idea, I thought, someone's metadata fantasy. Before he could explain the grand plan, I said, "Mondari told me a much different and more credible story last night of a bomb maker moved north via a cartel pipeline and brought across by them."

"And how would he know?"

"By chance, through a scam his tech thieves had going. They were remotely stealing information from a Sinaloa cartel manager."

"There's a bright idea. Where are they now?"

"Missing."

Venuti laughed.

"The cartel operative they targeted is enough of a high roller to stay in the same casino suite every month when he comes through here. From the room he logs into a dark site to retrieve his e-mails. Mondari's geeks were reading his e-mails right along with him, and they were able to take screenshots. Don't ask me how it works, but one e-mail screenshot they caught talked about the delivery of a fabricante de bombas and payment for delivery. He says he told Jane part of this but not all."

"Bullshit. She would have told me. She would have been all over it."

"No kidding, she would have. Mondari's two tech guys disappeared about two weeks ago. That's right about when Mondari started moving around."

"He got scared."

"Yeah, he put it together, though he swears he had nothing to do with stealing information from the cartel."

"Sure, he had nothing to do with it, but, okay, let's stretch our imaginations. Let's say Mondari is telling the truth. What do we do?"

"We look hard for Mondari's tech guys and put agents on finding the Sinaloa manager. If we find him and put it to him the right way, it might be worth it to him to give us the information. We can let him know that otherwise, it'll get whispered that he's working with us. That could lead to a real job-promotion setback for him. He might talk, and he's the one who can verify what Mondari claims his guys saw on the screenshot."

"And that's the problem—it's according to Mondari."

"Hear me out, Dan. The fabricante des bombas, the bomb maker I think we're looking for is a traveler and experienced. He may have arrived ready to blend in and go to work. He may not be with the sleeper cell. A pro bomber is going to want to do it his own way, in his own space. He could have ID, credit cards, everything he needs to get set up. The e-mail said a fabricante des bombas was delivered. The Sinaloa cartel delivered him. They're capable. It fits. It's a smart way to bring a traveler in."

I expected Dan to brush that aside, but he heard me. He knew I was serious.

"You're saying one of his tech criminals worked for the hotel and knew about this cartel mid-level guy who stayed there monthly."

"Yes."

"Targeting a cartel manager is stupid but also believable. How hard have you looked for these missing tech guys?"

"Not very hard. I've reached out to contacts, and Lacey is working it different ways. We do know their phones were canceled within minutes of each other on June 21 and that they were last seen approximately forty-eight hours before that. The girlfriend of one called the North Las Vegas police, but she's not quite enough of a girlfriend to fill out a missing-persons report. She told Lacey she'd have to take off from work to do that."

"It feels real to you."

"It does."

"You went out with a BOLO on Mondari and his car this afternoon. What's that about?"

"I can't find Mondari today after all but tucking him into bed last night. He's missing again, and I'm asking for help finding him, so yeah, I went out with a be-on-the-lookout-for."

"Most likely he just took off again."

"Probably," I said, but I knew Dan had heard me.

"You're saying Mondari saw 'fabricante des bombas' in the e-mail?"

"That's what he says."

"So why is he reversing himself and telling us now? It's not because you've been chasing him around."

"He's scared. Remember, I worked with him a long time. I know him in some ways. He's scared enough to need our help. That's why he gave it to me."

Venuti shook his head and said, "He didn't give Jane anything that specific. All right, Grale, I'll stop fighting you on this. Let's move Mondari to a priority and get him in here."

34

"I need to do more for her."

The charge nurse neither agreed nor disagreed. She said, "Your niece needs somebody to guide her through the worst."

When I walked into the hospital room, Julia's eyes were open but listless. She gave little sign of recognition and had nothing to say about the visit from her friends. I pulled a chair over and took her hand.

"Bad day?"

"Real bad, Uncle Paul."

"Maybe it's time to get out of here."

"What will it be like if I live with you?"

"Hard at first, but we'll make it into something good. I don't know how yet, but we will. We'll give you your mom's car, and as soon as you get your driver's license that'll give you mobility and some freedom. I'll always be there for you, but you'll also have to become pretty independent."

"Can I have friends over if you're not there?"

"Sure, of course, and I'll do everything I can, Julia. It'll just be you and me, but do you like Jo?"

"I like her a lot. Mom said you broke up with her."

"Jo and I made a mistake."

"That's what Mom said."

"She was right."

I felt a surge of emotion.

"I'll tell you a story about your mom. When our mother died, your mom was fourteen, I was twelve. Melissa tried to become a mother to me. That didn't work because nothing was the same anymore, and I didn't want a substitute mother. Your mom figured that out and that we needed to start new lives. You can't start life over, but she realized we'd reached the end of what we'd had and needed to make something different that would make our mom proud of us. I know it sounds sappy, but it was pretty real. Your mom brought us back into life again."

"Mom did?"

"That's right, my older sister, Melissa, showed me a way. That was the biggest gift anyone ever gave me. Ever. She was my North Star when it mattered. I think we take a page from her book and make something new and good. I see that part of your mom in you. I always have."

I didn't know if I'd reached her or not, but thought I might have. As I was leaving she asked, "Do you have any stories about Dad?"

"I have a million stories about your dad, maybe more."

"I want to hear all of them."

"You got it. See you tomorrow."

Late that night I climbed out of the lap pool and was sitting in a lawn chair talking on my cell with Jo when I received a text from the office alerting me to expect a call from the Nevada Highway Patrol Southern Command. It came twenty seconds later.

"A vehicle with a VIN matching the one you're looking for was found out on an old desert road running toward Potosi Mountain. That's the good news. Bad news is, it was on fire."

"White Mercedes registered to a Denny Mondari?"

"It wasn't white when we got there, but yeah, and we have an officer on-site. If you're going out, he'll wait."

"Tell him I'm on my way."

I missed the cutoff road on the first pass and turned around at the break for Highway 159, then retraced slowly until I found the dirt track. It crossed an old military tank road, but it wasn't until a fire vehicle passed by heading out that I knew for sure. A mile later, I saw the lights of the Nevada Highway Patrol officer and smelled the burned car in the wind.

The highway patrol officer on-site perked up and got cheerful when I said I'd take responsibility for the car. After he left and I was waiting for FBI ERT, I walked a wide area with a flashlight searching for anything that could explain this.

An hour and a half later, ERT arrived with a canine unit not far behind. The car held no human remains, and a cadaver dog working a broad area around the vehicle didn't scent on anything. At dawn I drove the dusty road back out to the highway. I had various ideas about why Mondari's car was out here, but nothing quite explained it. In a café up the highway, I ate scrambled eggs and toast and drank enough coffee to carry me into midmorning, then drove back to Vegas and met Lacey at Denny Mondari's apartment.

The manager unlocked the door for us and we looked for signs of violence, but didn't see any. A tuna sandwich had dried on a plate in the kitchen. Next to it sat a glass of warm flat beer. The eyeglasses Mondari often wore were alongside the plate. In a bedroom was a half-packed suitcase. In the bathroom in the big master suite, I saw blond hair dye in the shower and condoms stacked four high on a counter next to an unzipped Dopp kit with an electric razor lying next to it.

"What do you think?" Shah asked.

"That it looks staged. It's as if he saw us coming and put some props out and left."

"Doesn't the torched car worry you?"

"Neither the dogs nor ERT found anything."

"Did Mondari burn his own car?"

"No, but he might sacrifice it to make it look like something else happened to him. I mean, torch the car, disappear, and leave us guessing."

"Do you really think Denny Mondari did this on purpose?"

"Not really, but I can't rule it out. It would be like him. It's his way." I gestured around at the room and knew I was just talking. "He knew we'd be in here if he disappeared again. The sandwich, beer, and glasses are just a little too neat."

I glanced over at her.

"I have a bad feeling, Lacey, but I can't go there yet. If Mondari believes the cartel came for his tech geeks, he has to assume the geeks gave up his name. Let's widen our search for Catalangelo again. We're missing something."

"I've tried everything."

"I know an undercover DEA agent who might be able to help us. Maybe he's heard the name." I pulled out my phone. "I'll call him."

35

The Neptune Society phoned later that morning. I told the polite woman that I'd sign and scan the papers today, but that my niece wanted to see the bodies so cremation would be delayed.

"I don't think that's a good idea, sir."

I didn't either and sat thinking about it for several minutes after hanging up. I missed Venuti's approach behind me. He pulled a chair over and sat across from me.

"How are you feeling?" He asked. "I saw you limping when you came in."

The limp was harder to control when I was tired. Sometimes I worried it would cost me my job, or they'd finally box me into limited duty. I'd get a "we don't want to lose you" speech, and then no more badge or gun and I'd become a back-of-the-room guy with clean clothes and glasses, who spent his days in front of a computer or in meetings. Not for me.

But the FBI wasn't about wheelchairs, grab bars, or handicapped agents. The Bureau was about reinforced gates and steel bollards planted in 7,000 psi concrete, deep enough to where a bomb-laden truck couldn't ram through. It was about agents who fit an image. Venuti never let me forget that I'd volunteered as an SABT and gone to Iraq. A career choice, he called it, and maybe he saw it that way, but at the time the army was overwhelmed with bombings in Baghdad and asking for help.

After volunteering for bomb-tech training at Quantico and becoming a special agent bomb tech, I made three trips to Iraq during the period when the army was asking for help. On my third tour, and after all the worry about IED Alley and Route Irish, a booby-trapped motorcycle had caught us on foot in a market in Baghdad. Three of my team and seventeen Iraqis in the market died.

In Frankfurt a lacerated lobe of my liver was removed, along with my spleen. Then came multiple reconstruction surgeries, skin grafts, healing, adhesions, and more surgery. The scars on my lower back aren't something you flash at a public beach, and the initial FBI response was to offer me limited duty, meaning no badge or gun in the field. Or option two, take early retirement and try to find a new job to cover the hole left by the smaller pension. I could have dealt with the money, but not losing my career. I leaned on connections and spent my limited duty with the best bomb techs in the FBI. I commuted between here and headquarters, and I learned the bomb makers' craft. When I qualified for active duty here, I landed on the Domestic Terrorism Squad.

Problem was, I didn't fit the FBI image anymore. I had passed the physical but walked with a limp when tired. Rumor was, other agents avoided being paired with me because it was dangerous. Maybe that was true. Maybe it wasn't. But this much was true: I worked alone a lot. The autonomy Thorpe gave me for this investigation I took routinely.

I knew in some ways Venuti and perhaps others were waiting on my career to wind down. Venuti may outlast me. He might see my retirement as a victory for the Bureau way of doing things, but Beatty had nailed me. He'd been right on when he said at Willie McCool that I'm a Fed to the core. I am, and I'm after the bomb makers of the world. That's my mission.

"You and I are the old men around here," Venuti said.

"Lay off the limp."

"Take it easy, I'm here about Mondari. What happened to his car?"

"It was torched. ERT didn't find anything and neither did a cadaver dog. ERT is in his apartment, but so far the only blood is in a bathroom and probably from a shaving cut."

When Venuti didn't respond, I added, "They're not going to find anything."

"How much longer will they be in there?"

"No more than an hour."

"Let me know what you learn."

My undercover DEA friend Bruce Ortega hadn't called back. Maybe we weren't going to hear from him at all. He worked deep undercover at times, so I reached out in another direction, calling a retired Las Vegas Metro homicide detective I trusted. Mike Sulliver retired, then started a private investigation business with one employee, himself. His cop friends joked about it, but Sulliver wasn't a golfer and, as in my situation, his wife died too young. He liked having a reason to get up in the morning, and in his own words, he was "permanently restless." He was pushing sixty-five, silver-haired, and in some combination of the same clothes every day—jeans, a leather belt with a buckle he was proud of, a button-down shirt, and a Stetson, as if he had a horse out front instead of a blue SUV.

He also carried a steady, quiet certainty about right and wrong, and though he and I differed politically in every way, we saw eye to eye about justice. We stopped to pick up coffees at a little restaurant where, as Sulliver said, "The coffee sucks, but I know the owner." That was Mike. We sat outside in his SUV with the air conditioning running.

"The rumor I heard is that Mondo boy and his two twerps were into somebody's business and got caught," Sulliver said.

"That's pretty much what Mondari told me. Now he's missing too."

"Missing or hiding?"

"Could be either."

"And now you're reaching out every which way because you don't know where to look."

"Yeah, pretty much."

"I know where one of his tech geeks lives."

"Which one?"

"Pylori."

"I've been by his place," I said. "I went by after I got the story from Mondari, and no one was home." I paused. "The apartment manager stalled me and I haven't been back yet. We're getting a warrant signed today."

"You don't need it. I can get you in. An ex-Metro cop manages that complex and a half dozen other buildings. He doesn't like Feds. That was your problem."

"But he'll open the door for you?"

"Sure."

He did open the door to the apartment, and none of us said anything for several seconds. The place was ransacked, torn apart, everything cut open or emptied, yet I didn't see any blood. Sulliver and I stepped in with Marty the manager behind us, saying it was now completely legitimate for us to look around. When the look didn't turn up anything, I thanked Sulliver and headed back to the office thinking we'd gotten more from their phones.

Lacey called before I got there.

"The casino gave up Catalangelo. They asked that we refer to them as an anonymous source."

"We can do that for a little while. What have we got?"

"A contact e-mail, cell number, credit card, and a Nevada driver's license for a Catalangelo Garcia, not Miguel Catalangelo."

Half an hour later I sat down alongside a triumphant Lacey, who waved an invisible banner for the new FBI where you got more from a computer than you could ever get knocking on doors. She'd made calls and done the rest via computer and access to databases. I could have reminded her that this all started forward when I'd confronted Mondari late in the night after his drinking dinner with DOD Warner, but why interrupt her when she was on a roll.

Later that morning we got copies of the phone records on Pylori and the other missing man, John Edelman. The most recent group text from Denny Mondari to them was yesterday, so Mondari still had hope. But that text, like all in the prior weeks, was never received.

I was still with Lacey when my undercover DEA friend, Ortega, called. I put Ortega on speakerphone and introduced Lacey.

"I know some things about Catalangelo," Ortega said, "but I've never dealt with him. He has a rep as tough. Make a mistake and you're hurting. He watches over a dozen managers in the southwest and oversees shipments from Mexico into California. They'll cut open empty plastic bottles, line them up, and put glow sticks in them to make a runway. Sometimes they'll leave a plane behind. They're using drones more and more now."

I'd heard that, but everyone was using them more or planning to. It wasn't surprising.

"What else?" I asked.

"Catalangelo likes flying product and people in. He's big on flight. In my office we call him Cat Airlines, so, yes, the guy you're looking for could have been flown in. Everything that crosses our border gets seen, but that doesn't stop them. You know that as well as anyone, Grale. If it was their cartel and they brought your bomb maker in that way, Catalangelo would know about it."

"That's an answer we've needed," I said. "Do you know where to look for him?"

"I don't, but I can ask, and I'll give you a number to call. I'm only calling back now because it's you. Anyone else and I wouldn't have."

He gave me the number and said, "Take care, G-man."

"You too."

36

In the afternoon we got deeper into Denny Mondari's bank records, credit cards, e-mail, phone messages, mail, everything we could reach. But it was a routine run for any outstanding traffic tickets in Nevada and the surrounding states—Utah, California, and Arizona—that turned things. The traffic ticket was for speeding and a burned-out taillight. A CHP patrolman on Highway 62 south of the Mojave National Preserve issued it on June 27. We also had Visa purchases on Mondari's card made in the same general area. He'd bought gas in Borrego Springs a day after getting ticketed by the CHP. A few days prior, Mondari was in Scottsdale, Arizona, where the same Visa had also been used for gas.

And it wasn't his first trip along this route. We mapped another that more or less followed the same path as recently as a few days ago.

"Look at this," Lacey said. "Same hotel. He's done this a couple of times. Why didn't Agent Stone get into his credit cards?"

"There wasn't a reason to. He was giving her information."

The California Highway Patrol officer who'd ticketed Mondari on Highway 62 returned my call. We talked as I read an e-mailed copy of the citation.

"You're lucky because I happen to remember the stop and the driver. Just something about the guy, I guess. He was jumpy and surprised to get pulled over. He told me he was moving to San Diego and had mistakenly gotten off I-15. He talked like a human road atlas for five minutes, then asked for directions like he didn't know how to use his phone."

"That's our guy."

"I get people regularly going twenty to thirty miles over the limit, and they still argue with me. He was barely ten over and apologizing. I don't usually ticket for ten over, but he had a taillight out, and to be honest I'd had a slow night."

"Can you remember anything about his face?"

"Only that it matched the driver's license. He told me he hadn't had a ticket in twenty years. He was surprised about the taillight, so surprised he didn't believe me and got out and looked."

"Any idea where he went after you gave him the ticket?"

"None. I watched him drive away, and then he was gone."

"Any chance anyone was following him?"

"Funny you say that, there was a pickup I'd seen earlier that I'd tailed. It came by again right after he pulled out. The pickup should have been miles away by then. I remember wondering about it."

"Do you remember the make?"

"Not really. It might have been a Ford F-150, but I'm not sure."

I thanked him for calling back, and he asked if my questions had anything to do with the bomb investigation. "They do," I said.

"Could these be pleasure trips?" Lacey asked. "Or going to visit somebody in the area. Girlfriend? Boyfriend? Going back there twice, it could be something like that. I mean, he's not hiding where he's been. He's using the same Visa. You say he's always after the next new woman. Maybe he went to Arizona, picked up the new girlfriend, and they drove to the Anza-Borrego. How much do you really know about him? He wasn't paying cash and hiding his tracks. Walks like a duck, talks like a duck, and all that. Maybe it is what it looks like."

"Why would he go to the Anza-Borrego Desert when he already lives in the desert and prefers living in casinos? Mondari likes a roof over his head and air conditioning."

"You think you know him, but maybe he likes wildflowers."

I tried to get my head around Mondari hiking out into the desert to look at flowers and said, "Wildflowers are in February."

"Well, hiking or wildlife then."

"Hiking for Mondari is crossing the street to another casino. Wildlife is two-legged with a short skirt."

I worked the Arizona end of Mondari's trip and confirmed the hotel in Scottsdale, which led to more calls to confirm wherever possible that it was Mondari who had come through, not someone else. On each trip he did a lot of driving, and with both he made no effort to cover his tracks, which raised Shah's question again. Were we investigating a vacation?

I switched focus when an update on Omar Smith's financial situation was posted in a JTTF report. Smith was in arrears on a high-interest loan made by private investors in Istanbul three years ago and was being sued in Turkish court. Smith had told me about a loan payment but said nothing about a lawsuit. The loan in arrears was 2.3 million American dollars and it was not news in Istanbul. The lawsuit was filed a year and a half ago. Maybe there had been some form of settlement, and this was the urgent payment he'd needed to make.

Lacey made a late afternoon run for sandwiches. I kept making calls and the feeling grew stronger we were onto something with Mondari. As she returned with the food, Beatty called.

"Hey, Grale, I'm up on Spring Mountain where the road ends at the ski resort."

"The lookout."

"Yeah, it's too gusty today for the drones, and the new flight instructor clocks in tomorrow, so I got out of there for a few hours."

I looked at my computer screen while I listened. We'd been on Mondari for hours. I could take a break.

"Hang out there for a little while and I'll come on up and talk."

I talked to Venuti first. I got the gear for the wire I'd wear today and had to laugh when he suggested testing the equipment during the meeting with Beatty. No way would I do that.

"When you come off Spring Mountain, we'll get the van rolling toward Smith's house," Venuti said. "I agree it's worth a try."

I left the highway and started climbing with two agents in a black Suburban a third of a mile back and keeping pace with me. Venuti didn't want me alone with Beatty. The road went right up and the air got cooler. I killed the air conditioning, lowered a window, and took in the clean cool air. Thousands of feet higher, just beyond the ski resort where the road ends and there's parking near a trailhead, I spotted Beatty's pickup with his motorcycle tied down in back. A few minutes later the agents crept into a slot down the slope.

"Tell them in your office, I lost my job," Beatty said. "Tell them mission accomplished."

"The Bureau was never targeting you."

"No, they're friendlies." He laughed at that. "This radio dude I used to listen to has me running a sleeper cell for ISIS and Al Qaeda. This is going to chase me the rest of my life; you know it will. Is that black SUV down there with you?"

"It is. Talk to me about the airfield. You said they modify the drones at night. I've been thinking about that. Where do they do that work?"

"Sometimes at the airfield, but they've also trucked them out to a warehouse. I don't know where the warehouse is. Ask Strata."

"We did."

"And?"

"Almost all modifications are done on-site, and the drones have only left the site once."

"Not true, G-man. They've left twice. I've watched them hauled away and brought back in the morning. Strata is out of touch."

"Where do they go?"

"I don't know, but it wouldn't be too far away. You know, Bahn signed off on the pilots without knowing shit about them. What's that tell you about how Strata operates?"

We lingered a little longer looking down and out over the desert. Standing there he looked thinner and older. He turned to me.

"Julia used to love ice cream. Does she still?"

"She does."

"I know where to buy the good stuff. I'll bring her some. I'll call you tomorrow."

37

From the first night, it was clear Omar Smith ran two economies, one with cash, the other a more normal business standard. He owned liquor stores, gas stations, various properties in the valley, and had done well with short sales and flipping houses as the real estate market recovered from the recession. He used his buildings as collateral for short-term, high-interest bridge loans, as the money sharks call them. Paying them off depended on cash flow. With the terrorism investigation, a lot of Smith's cash flow had ground to a halt. Hullabaloo cancellations were over 90 percent, according to Smith's lawyer. This morning an aspiring local politician proposed a public boycott of everything Smith owned.

I called Venuti as I came down Spring Mountain. "I'm five minutes from 95, then headed to Smith's house. Are we ready?"

"We're ready on this end. Are you ready?"

"I've got the wire on, everything is working."

"Why didn't you test it when you were talking with Beatty?"

"I wanted to talk alone with him."

"What did he say?"

"Congratulations to the Bureau for getting him fired, and Strata is out of touch with their operations. He's seen the drones leave the site twice."

"So he says."

"Yeah, so he says. All right, Dan, let's hope this works."

I knocked on the tall oak door to Smith's big house in Summerlin. The housekeeper frowned but took my card. Minutes passed and then Smith padded down the long tiled hallway dressed in loose pants, a sport coat, and slippers, looking defeated and withdrawn, yet offered his hand before leading me to the open room with the TV. He gestured at a couch. The housekeeper brought a tea tray and set it down between us.

When she left, Smith poured, looked at me, and said, "I have some serious problems, Agent Grale. Are you here about the money in my safe?"

"In a way I am."

"What the FBI did was very unfair. You knew the building was released to me that afternoon. You knew I would go there, and you hid like a criminal to watch me. You took money that was very important. You don't understand what you did."

"You'll get it back any day now."

"You don't understand."

"Well, then tell me. Where was the money going?"

He shook his head, gave a rueful smile.

"Where did the money come from?" I asked.

"From different loans. I borrowed from everyone who had money they could lend me. Now they see what's happening and want the money back. The FBI is destroying everything I built. The FBI is good at catching a businessman who does not run and opens his home and businesses to them, but not so good at catching terrorists."

"I'm not here about money," I said. "And I wish I had news for you on it, but I don't. I have a photo I want to show you."

From an envelope I pulled the photo the Mex Feds had sent of Juan Gutierrez and handed it to him.

"It's Juan Menderes," he said. "What is this?"

"When this photo was taken, he was Juan Gutierrez, who'd been arrested in a drug raid and would go to prison. In prison he bought

Juan Menderes's ID and became him. Did he ever talk with you about any of this?"

"No, I am shocked. He was a good driver. He had all the required papers in the name of Menderes. I did not understand why he ran."

"He was making drug deliveries in the Hullabaloo van."

"That is not possible."

"For some customers he would deliver a cake with a side order of cocaine. The van had a secret compartment."

"I didn't know that."

"We don't understand how you wouldn't know."

I thought I'd said that without being confrontational, but from his reaction I saw he was debating whether to end the conversation. He stared at me as he debated.

"I look in the vans only to see they are clean. They are serviced twice a year. I can ask the shop where they are serviced if they saw the compartment. I can call them now if you want."

"We've already talked to them. The question to you is whether you were aware of the compartment."

"I wasn't."

"Are you certain?"

"Do my other vans have this compartment?"

"No."

He shrugged and said, "I am very surprised about Juan."

He poured more tea for both of us, then took a delicate sip. I waited until he cradled the cup in his hands before changing up on him.

"I'm sorry for the delay in getting the money back to you," I said. The true delay was that we intended to track the bills returned to him, and it took a few days to get that set up. "I'm sorry I had to take it from you. You have to understand that I had no choice."

He said nothing to that. His eyes narrowed as he sipped again. The tea was quite fragrant and perfumed the air of the room.

"Did you supply phones to your drivers?"

231

"Yes, I buy phones on the secondhand market and have a good price with the carrier. It is for security and for a record of calls and to collect the phone number of clients for the database."

"Are the drivers allowed personal calls?"

"This has already been asked, and the FBI has seen the phone records. Only if the calls are local and short can they use the company phone. I tell the drivers this. I am very stern on this point."

"Do they keep the same phone?"

"As long as they are drivers."

"If they need a replacement, how is that done?"

"They tell me and I give them a new phone. When they get dropped and lost or broken, they tell me and I give them a new phone. It is a cost of doing business."

"Did Juan get a replacement phone on July 3?"

"This was asked the first night."

"And you answered you were in Houston July 3, and no one else is authorized to activate a phone. But you knew Juan would be delivering cakes on the Fourth."

"He used his personal phone. He texted as he was supposed to that the cake was delivered. I told the agents on July 4 that he'd called from his phone. This is not a secret."

"He didn't use his phone. Did you supply him another phone?"

"No, as I said, I was in Houston."

"Could somebody working for you have done that?"

"Only me."

"And you were in Houston."

"Correct." He gave me a quizzical look and said, "You are repeating yourself, you are asking the same things again."

In the long interview our agents had with him that I'd watched, he'd demonstrated a remarkable memory. We'd confirmed a number of things he'd recounted. He didn't make them up. I unfolded a piece of paper and handed it to him.

"Do you recognize these numbers?"

He could say no, but that could get tricky. He could say yes and remember that Juan made a call to him on July 4 from the phone that was supposed to be broken. We hadn't told anyone, but that phone was found in the pouch cut in the underside of Juan Menderes's mattress. The drug dog found it, and I brought it to the office in an evidence bag. It was very unlikely he knew that. Why did Juan leave it there? Was he protecting himself in some way? Was it insurance?

"I don't recognize them," he said. "I don't have the memory for phone numbers I have for other things."

"Okay, thank you, that's all. Thank you for the tea."

I took the paper back and refolded it and let myself out the front door.

Late afternoon, I sat alone with Venuti and talked through my interview with Smith. Venuti, of course, had already heard the tape.

"What do you think, Grale? Did he recognize the number?"

"I think he did, and I think he's always known we'd get there. It was just a matter of time before we reconciled the different phone numbers and matched that July 4 call to the allegedly broken driver phone. He was ready."

"If he recognized it, then he recognized it was Menderes calling him and had a reason to answer. Do you believe he's not good remembering phone numbers?"

"I don't believe that. I'd guess he's good."

"I would too."

The bigger question was why Menderes hid the phone. It had meaning, but whether it had bearing on the investigation, we couldn't say yet. But safe to say, it was another thread needing chasing. We weren't going to solve that sitting here guessing, and I moved the conversation on to the road trips Mondari made to Arizona then California. Before starting in on the next thing I wanted to talk about, I reached out and shut his office door.

"Mondari's trips might tie in with a folder called 'Vacation Ideas' that Jane kept," I said. "Inside that was a file called 'Short Trips.' This morning I looked at 'Short Trips' again. I couldn't figure out what the 'Vacation Ideas' was doing with all these other work files, but I think you figure in."

"What are you talking about?"

"You tell me, but here's what I've got so far. In May, Jane was at a four-day conference in San Diego. So were you. It was joint with ICE and DEA. You flew back here from San Diego, but she drove back to Vegas and made an overnight stop in Borrego Springs. That might tie to the bomb-maker tip. She mentions DV in her notes, which sound to me like the initials of Dan Venuti. Were you with her, and do you know where she went?"

Venuti nodded and looked like he'd just taken a blow and was trying to get his breath back.

"I was with her in Borrego Springs for a night. She would remember the hotel. I don't remember the name of it. There should be a room in her name and one in mine."

"There's one in her name, but I'm not asking about that. I want to know why else she was there. We believe Mondari was in Borrego Springs as recently as a few days ago. We're trying to figure out what he was doing there."

"It could be about the airport. Mondari had said something to her. I don't know what he said, some gobbledygook that made her want to go to the Borrego Valley Airport. She didn't get anything from the airport staff and never said anything more about it. I'd forgotten about the airport visit. She did that on her own. I got there later that day and drove back to San Diego the next morning."

"Mondari went from Vegas to the Phoenix area and then into California and possibly to the Anza-Borrego. We have a credit card trail and a traffic ticket from the CHP for a late June trip, and it looks like he went again. What was he doing there? Why would he make two trips to the area within two weeks?"

Venuti shook his head. "I don't think her going by the airport had anything to do with the bomb tip."

"I think it did. I think Mondari said something more to her."

Venuti shook his head and said, "Jane concluded it was a waste of time. She was like you, she was close to giving up on him."

"I'm going there. I know a San Diego County deputy in Anza-Borrego. I'll connect with him so I'm not alone. Lacey is very good but for this to work, she needs to be in the office. It's going to fall on you to find Mondari while I'm gone. We need him. I'm heading there today, inside of an hour if I can do it."

Venuti didn't argue. I was at my desk, getting ready to leave when the front desk transferred a phone call. I picked up and a deep male voice said, "G'day, mate, this is Captain Phil Ramer."

38

RAAF Captain Philip Ramer had read everything he could find online. He'd seen the video of Beatty's trailer. As he talked, I opened a computer file with a headshot of Ramer in uniform, stocky, solid chest, firm chin, straight-ahead look.

"I knew some of the pilots killed in the bombing. They were all good guys, and smart. They're playing up the sleeper cell bit here, putting Jeremy in it. They don't know him. He'd be the last one to help AQAP or the other bastards. Can't believe you're even looking at him."

"He's not a suspect."

"You wouldn't know, mate."

"You wouldn't know it here either."

Ramer was quiet, yet had to know what I wanted. He threw it back at me.

"You called me. I'm calling you back."

"I called about the Hakim Salter drone strike."

"The American schoolteacher, yeah?"

"That's right."

"He got taken out with some Taliban."

"Was it just bad luck for Salter?"

"I'm not allowed to talk about it."

"You can talk to an FBI agent."

"My commanding officer wouldn't agree."

"Give me his number and I'll call him. I'm not reporting this conversation to anyone."

"Recording it though, yeah?"

"I am, but you're talking to someone who knows Jeremy personally."

Ramer considered that a moment, then said, "Wouldn't much matter anyway, the truth is gone on that one."

"What do you remember?"

"If I talk to you, where else does it go?"

"Depends on what you have to say."

"If it shows up in Yank media that I don't agree with the official version, then I'm in a mess here."

"That won't happen. I can promise that."

"Can you now?"

"It stays inside the Bureau."

"I'll tell you more if you keep my name out of it."

"I can make you an unnamed source."

"All right, mate, I'll go with that. You're giving me your word?"

"Yes."

"What happened is, we were ready to launch a missile on the Taliban targets and they had us wait. The Taliban were there and we circled and circled. Jeremy is asking but getting no answers back about the wait, and then out comes the schoolteacher and the order comes to launch. Jeremy is at them, saying he's looking at the American lad who teaches. The order comes again. So you just do it. You don't think on it too hard. It's not yours to identify the target when it's the CIA sitting on your shoulder looking down with you. You fly the bird. But they knew what they were doing. They waited for the Salter fellow to come back out. Whatever they say, there was no question about it then. Straight up, we took him out."

"Did Jeremy say anything that day?"

"He said a lot. Surprised his mates and the captain. He was stone-cold calm otherwise, but not that day. He said it there and plenty loud, 'I didn't sign up to kill Americans.' Said it and walked out. That was the start of things going wrong for him."

"There was an investigation. You were questioned. I've read your transcript. It doesn't have any of this in it."

"They told me it all happened a different way, and Jeremy and I misunderstood. They put it to me and gave me a choice." His voice quieted. "I went the coward's way. It was to keep my career, you know?"

"I know the feeling."

"I'm not proud of it."

"Did they really ship you home the next day?"

"Nothing like that. Orders were to cooperate with the Yanks and talk to no one except the questioners. What they did was send me home to where I was living in Las Vegas. I was told to have no contact of any kind with Jeremy. We didn't talk again until after he was discharged. I told him what I did and he understood. We talked a bit. He needed to know what I remembered. He was questioning himself until I said I remembered it the same way."

I got an address on him and more contact numbers and sat for a few minutes at my desk before moving on. I called the pilot who flew the FBI Cessna.

"What's up, Grale?"

"I need a ride."

"They're cracking down on us. You'll need a good reason."

"I've got one."

"Where do you want to go?"

"Borrego Springs."

"When?"

"Now."

"Seriously?"

"Yeah."

"Okay, well, we did some minor repairs yesterday, and I'm thinking I need to take a test flight. Meet me at the field in an hour."

"See you there."

39

July 10th, midafternoon

Beatty met the guy who had called about his motorcycle and sold it to him for $17,000 cash in a Target parking lot. Then he bought a good little gas stove, a sleeping bag, and a box of ammunition and replaced the camping gear the FBI had impounded. He bought a cooler and ice and some fresh food, four one-gallon jugs of water, and enough MREs to last for a while. He gassed the pickup, checked the tires and oil, and stopped at a pharmacy for another list of things before buying more groceries, ice, and water. He bought three more throwaway phones and packed everything into the king cab of his pickup, and then called Grale to say he'd get another bike someday and he'd be staying a few days with Laura. He also talked to Bahn, Eddie threatening to go to the FBI.

I told Beatty, "I've got the file you sent me. You're okay."

But he couldn't seem to get that into his head. Later, he left me a message that he'd met up with Laura in Big Pine and gone up to the Bristlecones. They took her jeep and rode up the alluvial plain and into the winding canyon on the eastern slope of the Whites. Once, long ago, they'd made a game of finding the Methuselah tree. It was all there in a long message that rambled near the end about everything coming apart, but that he was fighting it.

"I'm pretty down," he said. I picked that message up when we landed in Borrego Springs. When I called him back, he said he was with Laura on the highway running through the Owens. That was good to hear.

"What is it about these drone pilots, Jeremy? What's your problem with them?"

"They don't care."

"What do you mean?"

"You know how I like Willie McCool and flying remote-controlled aircraft?"

"Sure."

"That's about flying. It's the same with the drones, you have that or you don't. The three pilots I was training, even in those few days, I could tell it wasn't in them. They don't have flying in them. It's just a job. If it was just one of them, then okay, I'd get that, or even two of them just looking at it as a good opportunity in a new market. But all three? That's hard to believe. You know what I mean?"

I did. That resonated. I thought about it for a long time after hanging up with Beatty.

40

A San Diego County Sheriff's Department deputy named Pete Nogales was waiting in the Borrego Valley Airport. He was chatting with the staff inside. They all seemed to know him. Two women were laughing at some joke he'd just told.

"Seven years since I've seen you," Nogales said and took in the changes in me as I did with him.

Nogales was moving into middle age, hair thinning on top, face fuller, a little more around his middle than he probably wanted. But he seemed much more confident and at ease. I could tell that the women he'd just told the joke to liked him and were waiting for another laugh.

Years ago he wanted to join the FBI. He'd filled out an application and been interviewed, but it didn't happen and I'd barely talked with him since. I'd done everything I could for him and called several times after he was rejected. The disappointment hit his pride hard. It stripped away a dream.

"Are you acting on a specific tip?" Nogales asked.

"All I have are grainy photos from the terrorism database and some correlating info."

"Correlating info?"

"I'll go over it with you."

"What do you want to do with the photos?"

"Come up with a cover story, drive around with you, and talk to people."

Anza-Borrego was desert country. A wide swath was state park. In winter and sometimes into early spring, people came for the wildflower bloom, but even in the summer heat like today, there were hikers and off-roaders. The café we'd just passed was packed. In the sheriff's office, I shook hands with Nogales's captain, Tim Albrecht, and as Nogales had predicted, Albrecht wanted something solid before Nogales toured with me.

"I'm looking for the bomb maker," I said. "I don't have evidence, but I have things that say it's possible he could be in the Anza-Borrego area."

"Where are you getting that from?"

"Some of it from a tip through a CI."

"Where did your confidential informant come up with that?"

"From a cartel manager's laptop."

"Is that right?"

"It is." We looked at each other as I opened the manila envelope with the grainy photos, slid them across, and said, "I can tell you more if it stays in this room."

Nothing ever stays in the room, but I needed the San Diego Sheriff's Department to be completely onboard and could feel the clock running. Nineteen years of doing this had taught me that if you want local support, you never talk down. You don't hold back unless you have to.

"Some on the Joint Terrorism Task Force think AQAP and ISIS each trained their own teams and sent them separately over time. Some think it's a combination of a sleeper cell in the Vegas area and more crew smuggled in over the Mexican border. My focus is the bomb maker. I think we're looking for a tested pro hired for this who has a place to build bombs far enough away from Vegas to be outside the main law enforcement search. That's part conjecture, part what I've seen in my career, and what we're putting together with the little we've gotten so far. This area could fit."

"What about the guy you've been questioning, the ex–drone pilot?"

"Not a shred of anything connects him to the bombings. Air Force OSI and a DOD criminal investigative unit were tapped into his communications for six months and came up with zero."

"We're three bombs in," Captain Albrecht said, "and the estimate I hear is that's only half of the C-4."

"That's right."

Albrecht circled back and asked, "Why Anza-Borrego?"

I felt impatient circling back to that question, but knew I couldn't be.

"For the same reasons the drug traffickers and fugitives like it—the access to the border and it's close enough to Vegas."

"How long do you expect to be here?"

"Depends."

The captain registered that with a noncommittal nod.

"Well, Deputy Nogales knows everybody. He's the right guy to take you out. But he's got another job to do as well, so I can only give him to you for a couple of days, unless you're onto somebody."

"If that happens there'll be an army here." I paused. "Captain, I want to ask you about something else before Pete and I get out there. There was a small plane, a Cessna four-seater that may have been brought down by a bomb. It was definitely brought down by an unusual explosion. Score and burn marks show that. There was the Alagara bar bomb, the pickup bomb, and a car bomb, all made with the same C-4. The plane debris is scattered, but pieces have been retrieved and it's getting looked at. Are you aware of that plane crash?"

"Sure."

"I figured you would be. The plane crossed from Mexico and landed and took off again from an airstrip in the Imperial Valley. Do you know anything about that airstrip?"

"Sure, I've heard stories."

"What kind?"

"Drugs. Smugglers. You know how it is down here."

"Does that airstrip have a rep?"

"Yeah, a little bit of a rep."

"Thanks."

We toured Borrego Springs first and then outback places, where everyone living there was off the grid. Nogales knew a cadre of eclectics, antigovernment wackos, retirees, survivalists, parole violators, drug dealers, sportsmen, desert rats, rock collectors, painters, sculptors, and others just drawn to the stark beauty. Nogales networked, and he went to his people now. After the first couple of stops, I felt like a ride along. Nogales was also a natural at asking questions without revealing much. Too bad the Bureau passed on him.

I checked in with Lacey, who was looking at rentals in the area, recent property-sale closings, Craigslist, and everything she could find where an individual looking for a short-term rental would go. Then we made a stop at a bar in Ocotillo Wells. It was alongside the highway, just before a road running out to a gypsum mine. The bar's windows were coated in gray-white road dust from massive trucks carrying loads from the mine. Even the cool air inside the bar was dust-laden and carried a faint tang of diesel fumes.

The bartender looked at the artist's sketches Nogales laid down, then a photo of Mondari's white Mercedes.

"Who are you looking for?" the bartender asked Nogales.

"A stone-cold killer."

"A stone-cold killer driving a car like that?" The bartender chuckled and asked, "Are you sure you've got your story right? Go ask Nora or Crazy Pete or the owners of the general store."

"The car was stolen from a victim. Do you recognize any of these faces?"

"Not offhand."

"I'm not interested in offhand," Nogales said. "Look again. This guy is truly bad."

"I'd tell you if I recognized anybody."

"Just take another look at the photos, okay?"

"If he's a killer, what did he do?"

Nogales nodded toward me, then said, "There was a dismembering here that looks like one of his. Six states have unsolved murders done in the same way. Nevada, California, Oregon, Wyoming, Louisiana, and Missouri." Nogales rattled them off. "That's why the FBI is here. We do not want this guy among us."

"Who says he is?"

I fielded that, saying, "We were tipped. That's why I'm here."

The bartender picked up the photos. This time he sifted more slowly but still handed everything back to Nogales and shook his head. We tried the small handful of store owners along the highway, then drove out the dusty gypsum road and made a number of stops before returning to the general store to cobble together some sort of meal.

"Let's try Nora the Dawn Artist," Nogales said.

"Nora the what?"

"Dawn Artist. Her family was killed some years ago, and she moved here from LA. She was crazy for a while, then started painting."

He turned and looked at me.

"It's different out here, but you know that. Nora lives up here on the left in that building that looks like a little water tower."

"How was her family killed?"

Nogales told me as we drove to her house.

"A truck ran a red light. The driver was texting his boss. Nora's husband and two kids died in the car, and she came apart. Now she paints the morning. That's what her name is about. A week after she got here, I found her fifteen miles out on a desert road, dehydrated and with no water, and brought her back home. She's never forgotten and we're pals. Every dawn she paints the sky and the land so that no day is lost. That's her thing. No day lost."

"I like that," I said. "No day lost."

Nora the Dawn Artist was in her late forties, with skin tanned and dried by the desert. Her eyes were a crystal bottomless blue. I showed her a photo of Denny Mondari's white Mercedes, first thinking she might have seen it pass by on the road to the mine. The whole theory hung on Mondari driving here, so I had hope.

She said, "Well, maybe," then shook her head and said, "No, I'm sure I haven't seen that car."

I prodded.

"Seemed like you might have had something there for a moment."

She shook her head no, and I showed her six photos of known bombers. Several were poor shots, grainy rail- and bus-station photos, crappy airport video, and partial views later given a percentage of probability by some analyst in DC. They weren't much to look at. The car was the best hope, though Shah was trying for better resolution images on four of them.

Nora sifted from one photo to the next, then studied my face before looking out across the desert. She was watchful and trying to be helpful but in truth was just waiting for us to leave. I got it and thanked her.

After the dawn-artist visit, we slow-drifted the gypsum road. Desert dirt roads branched off on either side, and most had some housing before ending in rocky desert hills or flattening out in the scrub. Plenty of it was unconventional housing, and where we were headed was even more so, a place nicknamed Cargoland.

Once years ago, Nogales and I were in Cargoland together, but that was an investigation I didn't like to think about. It was how we first met. I was working human trafficking. A lead took me to Sacramento to track down a motorcycle gang leader named Mikel Richter. Richter was able to shake me, but not a series of spotter planes that tracked two motorcycles and a blue van to Ocotillo Wells. I arrived an hour behind, then checked in with the sheriff's office and teamed up with a young Pete Nogales to check out a bar in Cargoland.

That was on November 10, almost eight years ago and just after sunset. A cold wind was blowing and a full-on party was underway in a bar built from cut-open used shipping containers. Two girls, one fourteen, one seventeen, were chained naked to bolts welded to a steel wall of the bar. They weren't for sale that night, instead were being rented, and I pushed through the crowd bidding on them. One bar patron was just pulling up his pants when I pulled my badge and gun.

"You there?" Nogales asked.

"Yeah, just thinking about last time."

"Do you want to turn in to Cargoland?"

"Not yet, I'm changing my mind. I don't think we're ready with the right questions yet. Let's go out toward the gyp mine and work our way back."

We drove an hour of unpaved desert roads and past cobbled-together housing, and then on out toward the mine before returning to the sheriff's office in Borrego Springs. There I logged into the terrorism database and printed more photos and sketches, including one of another bomb maker who was believed dead, but as far as I knew had never been confirmed dead. That was reaching for straws. I felt the early hope fading. Probably another dead end.

Julia and I talked for a while. I called Jo, but she was with a patient.

When Nogales returned, we ate burritos outside at a table in the night air, then nursed beers in four different bars as we showed sketches and photos. We reshaped the story. The dismembering murderer now stalked at night and favored bars. He was alone and would keep to himself and might have a barn or other outbuilding he lived in. He was friendly, outgoing, and good-looking. You wouldn't have a clue how bad he was.

At midnight Nogales dropped me back at the motel and at five thirty the next morning picked me up again, and we returned to Nora the Dawn Artist's house. Nogales looked over and grinned as he said, "At least we know she'll be awake."

I had an additional motive for wanting to see Nora again, other than to show her the new photos. I was drawn to how she had tried to cope with the devastating deaths of her family. Nogales said she was considered half-crazy for the painting of the dawn each day, but that wasn't crazy to me. Far from it. It was an affirmation of life. I admired her will to turn pain into beauty.

She showed us today's painting, which caught the sky burning in crimson streaks and caught the first sliver of sunlight on the gray desert rock. It moved me and strangely brought tears that I hid and wiped away. She offered coffee. I took her up on it and used the moment to show her a better image of the Mercedes but got nothing but a shake of her head. I showed her the three new photos of the bombers I'd printed in the sheriff's office late yesterday afternoon, and she picked up the grainy black-and-white of the man who was rumored dead and said, "That's him."

"Him?"

"Yes, this man I've seen here."

"Recently?"

"Just a few days ago."

The photo was of poor quality and taken by a bus station security camera in Austria eight years ago. He was last seen alive at an Obama rally in Chicago in 2008, and he was a probable suspect in a bombing in France four years ago, but after that, nothing but quiet.

"He's one of those who look older than they are," she said. She pushed her hair back and looked at me. "From the side he has a stoop."

I nodded but inside leapt. That was in the bio on Garod Hurin, and you couldn't know it from the photo.

"And a wispy kind of goatee."

"Could you draw him and tell us where you saw him?"

Without answering, she sketched him quickly in profile—drew him tall, thin, and stooped as he walked from the entrance of the general store facing the highway. She drew sideburns and goatee and ponytail and a loose, dirty linen shirt flowing over jeans. Her eyes twinkled at me.

"I love linen," she said. "I always notice linen."

She drew worn boots with heels ground down on the outside, another detail that was accurate. She didn't know where he lived, but it was somewhere around here. She didn't know what he drove. She drew his long-fingered hands.

"He's new here," she said.

I looked at her drawing again, the posture, the stoop, height, chin and head, the worn boot heels. She touched the photo gently and said, "I saw him in the morning outside the market here."

"When?"

"I'm not sure but recently."

"Are you sure it was this man?"

"Yes, I am. I'm very sure."

I stared at the drawing and compared it to the photo and felt a rush that wiped away all my fatigue. I called in and asked for both the ASAC and Venuti and that they be interrupted from whatever they were doing. Then I stood in the sun and waited, thinking, *He's here.* She was so sure, and her drawing was right on. *He's here. Garod Hurin is here.*

41

I texted a photo of Nora the Dawn Artist's sketch to Venuti and Thorpe, along with the most recent Hurin photo in the terrorism database. The more I compared features, the more the tension built inside me. It was hard to stand here and wait. Ten minutes later, my phone rang.

"We're comparing the sketch with the photo, and they're running it in Washington," Thorpe said. "What do you see as the next step?"

"We push the CIA. We get ready. We figure out where here he is. If it's a go, we'll need the enhanced SWAT squad out of the LA Field Office. I'll call an analyst I know at the CIA, but if that goes nowhere, I'll need help."

"Make your call and I'll get a back channel going," Thorpe said. "We'll talk to LA SWAT from here. Let's get back on the phone in half an hour, but first give me a quick bio on Hurin."

"Ukrainian. Into the military at eighteen and trained in explosives but had discipline issues. Went AWOL and may have lived with a Swiss relative for two years while studying chemistry. First known bombing was in Lebanon in 2003. Mossad got onto him. Fled Lebanon. Worked with Iranian elements in and around Baghdad, building IEDs during the war, then disappeared into Asia and started freelancing. Speaks five or six languages. Tied to two Africa bombings in 2012 and 2013."

"Okay, that'll do it for now. Make your call to the CIA."

When I did and my call transferred to CIA analyst Sally Sassari, she sounded exasperated.

"We've already had this conversation or one like it too many times, and I have a lot going on today. I'd think you'd be busy too."

"This isn't one of my nagging calls, Sally."

"They're never that. I didn't mean that. I'm just busy. I don't mean to be short with you, Paul. I've got a deadline."

"I have some reason to think Garod Hurin is alive."

"Well, you're in Las Vegas looking for a bomb maker, so let's not play games. What have you got?"

"A possible sighting in Ocotillo Wells, California." I let that sink in for a moment. "Does the CIA know whether he's alive or dead?"

"We would need whatever information you have to answer that."

"To answer whether the CIA believes he's alive or dead?"

"Yes."

"Okay, just so we're clear, I'm not asking for an evaluation. I'm asking if you know whether he's alive. If he's confirmed dead, then we're done with this lead, in which case I'll leave Ocotillo Wells within an hour."

"Where are you, again?"

"Ocotillo Wells, California."

I heard her fingers on a keyboard and knew she was looking down at Ocotillo Wells. I also knew that what she'd see wouldn't get her anywhere.

"Let me call you back," she said. "Half an hour."

"I've got a conference call over this in twenty-two minutes. Call me back within ten."

She called seven minutes later and said that prior to giving an answer the agency would still need to evaluate what the FBI had before responding. She gave me an e-mail to send the sketch to and added, "That's the way it's going to have to be. It's not up for debate. When can I expect to see the sketch?"

"I'm not sure. If it's comes from me, it won't be until I get back to the Vegas office."

"I thought this was urgent. Get someone to send it."

"You're missing the point."

I hung up with Sally, called Thorpe, and said, "It's up to you. They want to analyze what we have before they'll say anything."

"I'll call them, but if I need you where are you?"

"Borrego Springs, about to get on a plane to fly back to Vegas. I'll see you at the office. We're taking off in a few minutes."

When I walked into our Vegas field office, I was intercepted and directed to a conference room filled with analysts and agents. On-screen was an aerial view of Ocotillo Wells and the surrounding areas of the Anza-Borrego, including Borrego Springs. In LA, the SWAT commander watched remotely. The San Diego County Sheriff's Department SWAT team was also available and watching, though because procedures were different, the two SWAT teams wouldn't operate near each other. All of this presumed Hurin was alive and there.

I zoomed in on an aerial view of Cargoland so those in the room could get an idea of what a village in the desert built of used cargo containers looks like. I left the image up until I reached the Denny Mondari link, and then switched to the map Lacey had created of Mondari's two road trips. Trip one was in yellow. Trip two was in blue. I traced the credit card trails.

"Follow the most recent trip," I said. "You can see he was in the Phoenix area on this day, and here on the next."

The laser pointer followed the road. I stopped the pointer and drew a little circle with it.

"He got tagged for speeding and a burned-out taillight on the twenty-seventh of June. The highway patrol officer said the driver's license matched Mondari. He doesn't remember his face, but he's a veteran and his drill is to always compare license photo to face. He remembers the man as nervous and apologetic. The bottom line is, we can put him in Arizona within two miles of the warehouse where the C-4 was allegedly stored, and we can follow him from there to the Anza-Borrego. We've got a second, almost identical, trip that just happened."

Somebody interrupted and asked, "What did you mean when you said 'allegedly stored'?"

"I'm not sure it was ever there, but that's me. Forget that for now."

I stopped and looked around the conference room. I didn't want to lose them with my personal theories about how the C-4 entered the US. Nine people in here, and they all had to be thinking, *There's no evidence connecting Mondari to Hurin.* I turned the PowerPoint back to the Arizona-to-Anza road map.

"If you're wondering whether we're wasting our time charting some pleasure trip Denny Mondari took, I'm wondering too."

Somebody laughed, but nobody thought it was funny.

"The CHP officer remembered Mondari because he sensed something was off. Those are his words. After he was ticketed, Mondari continued on to the Anza-Borrego. We can follow that movement with credit card charges. With this most recent trip, we're talking about just a few days ago, and with that one, there are no credit charges of any kind on the return trip."

"So he's still there," someone said. "Why don't we go out with a warrant, find him, and answer this?"

"We're already looking for him." I paused. I gave it a beat. "We're not looking for his car anymore. The car was found torched on a dirt desert road beneath Potosi Mountain late on the night of the tenth. ERT went out. So did a cadaver dog early the next morning, and there was no sign of foul play. Either Mondari drove the car to the Anza-Borrego or someone impersonating him and able to forge his signature near perfectly drove the car. We're pretty sure it was Mondari."

John Munoz, an agent on the DT squad, interrupted.

"I want to make sure I'm getting this right. You're proposing Mondari as a courier, possibly unaware of what he was delivering. He thinks he's delivering a drug shipment, but he's carrying C-4 in the trunk of his car. He delivers to Hurin."

"More likely to a drop point."

"Why would he do that?"

"Because he's on the hook for his guys hacking into a Sinaloa cartel manager's computer. I'll explain, but let me go on a little further here first. Here's why we're meeting. In the Anza-Borrego in Ocotillo Wells, we have a sighting of a known freelance bomb maker who—"

"Who may or may not be dead already," Munoz said.

"That's right."

I looked over the group again. I like skeptics. I like a hard sale. I wouldn't be any different listening to this than they were.

"We may get a call any minute from the CIA where they tell us they've 100 percent confirmed Garod Hurin's death, and for reasons they can't discuss, et cetera, it's been left for the rest of law enforcement to guess about. That would end this, but we'd still be looking for Mondari and still have reason to look at the Anza-Borrego. Look, I know it's sketchy. I know we're short on hard facts, but we're arguing there's enough here that it can't be ignored, and if the CIA says the face the Ocotillo artist drew is Hurin's and he's alive, well, in that case, I think we know where to look for our bomb maker."

An analyst smiled at me. She heard drama and conjecture.

"Okay," Munoz said. "I get that, but what if it's as simple as Mondari and his guys burned a cartel manager then got scared when they realized they were found out. The guys take off. Mondari thinks he's insulated, so he sticks. But his guys don't contact him, so he gets worried they were kidnapped by the cartel, and if that happened, they probably got interrogated. So he's thinking that as his guys were tortured to death, they put it all on him. He decides to disappear and do some special effects because you're all over him for something he said to Agent Stone. Have you checked to see he didn't fly away somewhere?"

"We've checked, and he's also afraid of planes."

"Maybe having a cartel hit man on him made him more open to flying the friendly skies."

I nodded, said, "I might have agreed with you until the artist flipped through bomb-maker photos this morning, then sketched Hurin down to his linen shirt and worn boot heels. I think we've got our bomb maker."

I brought up the two images of Garod Hurin I'd sent to Venuti and the ASAC. Then I did something else. I brought up the enhanced image of the wine-refrigerator installer and put it up alongside the other images. They could draw their own conclusions.

"The photo on the left is from the terrorism database. That's the artist's sketch on the right. We're asking the CIA for confirmation, and we may get it today, but either way, we know the driver of Mondari's car gassed up in Phoenix not far from the warehouse the CIA identified. The same day, though much later, the car was gassed up again in Borrego Springs. Is it just coincidence that the car of the guy who gave us a bomb-maker tip shows up in the same area where a known freelance bomb maker was spotted?"

Agents shifted in their chairs. The two analysts looked at each other, and after a few moments I looked at Munoz before repeating myself.

"In our scenario, Mondari is following orders to save himself by making a delivery. He believes it's drugs, but we're using drugs because it's a drug cartel his guys were trying to rip off. Let's say he's been told, 'You deliver, you get to live.'"

Munoz jumped in. "Why would they use him? Seems like an unnecessary risk."

I was ready for that.

"No cartel wants to be tied in any way to explosives used to attack the United States. They're not stupid. So they insulated themselves. They used a known guy, who owed them, and they were probably ahead of him and behind him as he drove. That's the guess Lacey and I are making."

I brought up a photo of the Mercedes, its wheel rims sitting on desert sand, the tires burned away and the paint blistered to raw metal, the interior down to blackened metal.

"And here's a look in the trunk where the fire was hottest. There were no human remains in there, so what was all that heat about? I'm going to say they were burning away any trace of C-4." I left the image up but brought the conversation back to Nora the Dawn Artist. "I watched her pick out Hurin's face. She did it in a blink, then drew from memory in a few minutes without looking again at the photo. I pulled the photo away."

I looked at Munoz and said, "I hear you, but we can't ignore this."

Munoz made a little circle with his hand that included himself and the agents around him, as in they were ready to go to work, and Thorpe, who had been looking at his phone and was quiet through all of this, looked up and said, "We just got our answer from the CIA. It's Hurin. He's alive. They knew he was alive. They've worried he was ready to turn active again. Let's go find him."

42

July 12th, 4:30 a.m.

A Nevada Highway Patrol officer rapped on the side of the pickup bed with his flashlight, then shined the flashlight beam in Beatty's eyes, blinding him. Beatty showed both hands as he blocked the light with one and sat up. His gun was under a shirt near the clothes he'd used as a pillow. He slid his sleeping bag back over the top of it as he climbed out.

"You need to move now."

"Can I stay here if I sleep in the cab?"

"No."

The flashlight beam was on his face again.

"Sir, I'd like to see some ID."

"No problem. My wallet is under the driver's side floor mat. I'll have to get it out." The officer kept the light on his face, though there was no reason for that. "I was just sleeping for a few hours. Can I move to another turnout? There must be a dozen along this road."

"They're scenic overlooks, they're not for sleeping."

"I tried the campsites. I was too late."

"Keep your hands visible as you remove your wallet, sir."

"Sure, but take it easy, I was just sleeping." Beatty turned and reached down. "Can you see my hand?"

The flashlight beam was on his hands, but the officer didn't answer. Beatty slid the black rubber mat back and the flashlight beam fell on his wallet.

"Do you see my wallet?"

"Pick it up."

He picked it up and moved slowly as he pulled out his driver's license and handed it to the officer.

"Sir, I'd like you to stand over here," the officer said, then got on his radio and ran the license. His voice was loud enough to carry, saying, "Is this the Jeremy Beatty questioned about the bombings? I thought he was being held."

Beatty couldn't hear the response but pulled his phone and brought up Grale's number. He tapped it before the officer looked back at him.

"He's up here in Red Rock Canyon at a scenic overlook, sleeping in the back of a pickup bed."

The officer made that sound as if Beatty had just robbed a bank. He stood outside his patrol car with the radio mic in his left hand and his right close to his holster as he waited for further instructions.

Now the officer looked over and saw Beatty with the phone to his ear. It rang once, twice, and on the third ring Grale picked up.

"Sir, get off that phone immediately."

The holster opened. The gun started to slide out.

"A cop just rousted me. He's got a—"

"Drop the phone! Drop it!"

Beatty dropped his cell and saw it go dark. The officer backed him away from it at gunpoint.

"I called an FBI agent named Paul Grale."

"Do not talk. Do not speak!"

Beatty looked out across the wide valley at the eastern sky lightening with the coming dawn. The officer picked up the phone and returned to his radio mic. He asked for backup and was told it was on the way.

With his gun still out but not pointing, he asked "What are you doing up here?"

"Sleeping."

"I asked why you were here."

"I don't have a place to go to."

"Are you the drone pilot who was questioned about the attacks?"

"Yes."

"When I tell you to, I want you to turn around and face your truck. Spread your legs and arms and put your hands on the roof of the vehicle and do not move. Do you understand me?"

"Yes."

When Beatty started to turn toward the truck, the officer yelled, "Freeze! Do not move until I tell you to move! Turn now. Slowly! Put your hands on the roof of your vehicle."

Beatty exaggerated the slowness, and the officer handcuffed him and led him to the back of his patrol car. Fifteen minutes later, two Nevada Highway Patrol cars arrived, and though he could turn his head and look at them, he didn't. He watched the sunrise and heard them talking, though not their words. Then his door opened and the officer who'd handcuffed him told him to get out. They removed his handcuffs and watched him put his sleeping bag in the pickup cab and rearrange the gear in the back.

"Can I have my phone back?"

"You can pick it up at the station."

Beatty started his engine and backed up slowly. When he was ready to drive away, one of the two officers who'd arrived after he was handcuffed rapped on his passenger window. Beatty lowered it.

The officer said, "I want you to know I did three tours in Iraq. If it was up to me you wouldn't be walking around. Now, get out of here."

Beatty kept his foot on the brake. He left the window down. The engine idled.

"I just told you to leave."

"I'm leaving. You did three tours. Okay, and I flew drones for the US Air Force for eight years, and I lost pilot friends in the bombing, and whatever you've heard about me is wrong."

"Is that right?"

"You don't believe me? Okay, I'm out of here, but just so we're clear. Fuck you!"

Beatty took his foot off the brake and rolled. He expected lights and sirens and to be handcuffed again and hauled in, but nothing happened. In his rearview mirror he saw the three officers watching as he rounded the curve. But where should he go?

He reached under his seat for another of the burner phones and powered it up. He punched in Grale's number but didn't have a signal. He dropped the phone on the seat and made the long drop back down to the highway and went north on 95. Grale had said don't run. He remembered Laura's skin against his and her saying, "Do not forget who you are."

He swept past Creech Air Force Base and Indian Wells. A senator from Utah had told Fox News that Beatty should be held until there was more information. Jailed until there was evidence. Maybe that's what the cop back up there in Red Rock was thinking. Was this even America anymore?

When he'd joined the United States Air Force, it was easily the proudest moment of his life. He loved flying drones and learned everything he could about remote split operations. He learned on the MQ-1 Predator and flew the RQ-1, which was about the size of a small plane. Press the button and it went and stayed up, cruising near dry mountains in Afghanistan for twenty-four hours, reading everything through the ball, one camera for day, one for night. It read through smoke and dust with synthetic aperture radar, and targeted with lasers, and dropped Hellfire missiles. He made good friends among the pilots in the flight trailers and everyone kept track of their kills.

But they didn't talk about the collateral dead very often. There were fewer civilian deaths using drones, so it was better than before. But there were times when you watched a house long enough, and you knew who lived there. You saw the kids run around and play. He had started to envy the old-school pilots with the bomb bays and drive-by bombings. They never saw what they did.

Up the highway he doubled back and took the road to the airfield, crossed through the wash, and climbed into the narrowing valley. He tried the gate combination and when it still worked, he drove through, relocked it, and climbed the rock hills. He was sure the security dudes would come charging, but no one did and he continued down and took the old prospector track, breaking right toward the Ghost Mountains.

He had plenty of water. He had food, beer, and a bottle of whiskey. Maybe this was a good place to hole up and think for a few days. If the security dudes intercepted him, he'd turn around and find another place to disappear. No one stopped him, and from this distance it didn't look like anything was happening at the airfield. Even if they saw him, who was going to follow him up this forgotten road? Soon he disappeared into the dry mountains.

He switched into four-wheel drive as the road climbed, and he recognized the big band of red iron ore across the gray rock as the road rose along a rock face. Another quarter mile up brought him to a cave-like overhang of rock. He parked and checked it out. It looked really good, then not that great, pretty small and hard to back into. But it had shade and a view of the airfield in the valley below. He spent ten minutes backing the truck into the cave, during which the left front tire came dangerously close to the edge.

Now he was under a rock roof where no sunlight would reflect off the truck and give him away. He had food and water. He could deal with the heat, and no state troopers would ever be up this mountain. He doubted anyone ever came out here. He got out one of the little coolers with food and sat on a flat rock.

He opened the cooler and checked the sandwiches and beer. Both were still cool, not cold anymore, but still pretty good. He pulled out one of the beers and, even though it was morning, twisted off the top and drank and thought about the cop rousting him and what the other cop said. He thought about Laura and how he lost her, the hard things he'd said to her way back then. He never wanted to hurt anyone that way ever again, and in some way couldn't even understand her reaching out to him the way she had.

He checked his phone, saw he had a signal and called Grale. When it rolled to voice mail, he left a message that he was where he could watch the airfield. A drone was on the runway. With binoculars he saw two people standing nearby. He couldn't make out their faces, but one stood like the Saudi who'd trained on fighter jets. The first question the Saudi had asked him was what he flew before drones. What he'd flown was a PlayStation 4, but he didn't tell the Saudi pilot that. Instead, he'd ignored the question.

He shifted the binoculars again and watched a guy who must be the new flight instructor turn and look this way.

"Weird that," Beatty said. "But you're right on, buddy, I'm out here and I'm watching you."

His phone rang, and when he saw it was Grale he put the binos down and reached for the phone. But something stopped him. He let it ring. He let it go to voice mail. *No one knows where you are*, he thought. *For now, leave it that way.*

43

Beatty left me a disjointed message I couldn't deal with yet. I looked over at the San Diego County deputy who'd ride into Cargoland with me, a young guy who looked at home on a mountain bike, so at least that part was right.

"Ready to roll?" I asked.

"Whenever you are."

We bounced down the washboarded dirt desert road, playing the part of two tourists. It was an awkward cover, half-assed, really. Within minutes, we were in the village, if you could call it that. More like a postindustrial-age apocalyptic vision. The bar made from a cut-open steel cargo container was still here, though it looked bigger. I saw a bartender and rode toward him, and per plan, the deputy continued forward into the rows of rusting, sun-faded, blue and red containers. Stacked two and three high, they formed a village like the drunken dream of an ex-maritime officer run aground. The deputy would scout out the village, then circle back and meet me at the bar.

The bar was changed, different than what I remembered. The steel rings welded to the wall that had held the girls' chains were gone. Nothing left there but the weld scars. A large segment from the side of a steel container provided shade now for a handful of rusted tables and chairs that sat out front. The bar top, also made of steel and fabricated from scraps welded together, was longer and had a row of metal bar stools. I saw a lot of new steelwork and welds. Maybe an alcoholic welder had traded work for whiskey.

I leaned my bike against a rusted post as Ace Marks, the bartender, tried to place me. It didn't take him long, and it was bad luck to get made so fast, but I'd known it was a possibility.

Marks was a big guy with prison muscles and still lifting, from the look of him. He wore sideburns from another century and a T-shirt that read *Bastard Bar*. He had the same tattoos but no new ones. He looked at my biking shorts and cleated shoes and closer at my face as the helmet came off.

"We're not open yet," he said.

"I'm here to talk to you, Ace."

"I know you are, but I haven't broken any laws since I last saw you. I don't do drugs and I don't trade them. I don't drink. I don't even have a girlfriend, though you look cute in your shorts."

"Back at you—love those Civil War sideburns. I thought you went home."

That seemed to reach him. His voice was slower when he spoke again.

"I did, I went home for a while, for a couple of years, but things had changed and it's just too fucking cold in Minnesota."

"You were complaining about the heat here."

"Well, I didn't know anybody at home anymore. They've all moved or gone back to prison. Can't get a straight job once you've got the record."

"Well, good to see you again. I'm not here to bother you. I'm looking for a guy."

I reached around to the back middle pocket of my biking shirt, then started to unfold Nora's sketch but stopped when Marks preempted me, saying, "Don't bother, I don't recognize him."

"I haven't showed him to you yet."

"People come and go around here," Marks said, but was focused on the helicopter floating above pale desert mountains to the southwest. "That helicopter with you?"

"It depends."

"On what?"

"On whether we can do this another way."

"The drug fucks stick people in here every now and then, but I don't listen to the talk, and so far I've avoided the money they push in my face. I'm living clean."

"I wouldn't be here over drugs."

"Whatever you're here for is bad news. That's all I know."

I let that be, but then because I'm always curious about people, said, "I can understand you not wanting to go back home, but I'm surprised you're here."

"I lost some weight and the heat doesn't bother me the same way anymore. You want to chat me up with that thing flying around up there? Who is it you're looking for?"

"Someone who might be hiding here. Does Coffina still own this bar?"

"This bar and about half of everything here. He only did about two years of his sentence and must have gotten to the money. I don't know what he's thinking. The first one of those dudes who gets out of prison will kill him."

I had checked on all of them before coming here. The other three guys got thirty-year sentences, so Coffina didn't have to worry for a while.

"Where is Coffina?"

"Don't know."

"He needs to be here if this is going to go well. This is what I suggest. Call him. Tell him it's not about drugs or anybody other than one guy who has probably only been here four to six weeks. Tell him we'll have to search container to container if he can't help. You know how that can go. Things get found, people get arrested, there's a lot of shouting and sirens. It would be a lot better for Coffina if he talked to me first."

"Describe this guy you're looking for."

He said that in a command voice that annoyed me. I unfolded the sketch and slid it across the bar.

"He's in his midthirties. He'll be friendly but will mind his own business and won't want anything from anybody. Maybe he'll have a beer here occasionally, but he won't talk about himself, and if he does, he won't brag in any way. If he rented a place here, it's a quiet spot on the outskirts where no one will bother him. He will have paid cash up front. He'd want air conditioning. He's not American, but you wouldn't necessarily know that." I gave it a beat and added, "You might pick up a little accent."

Marks flipped the sketch back like he was tossing down a bar napkin.

"I heard about him, a serial killer we're all supposed to be afraid of. One of the Diego cops was pushing the story yesterday. A bartender friend told me about it, but fuck, everyone knows it's drugs."

"That's the cover story we're using in town," I said. "This guy is actually a lot worse than that. You don't want him here. I mean that. You really don't, and it's not about drugs."

I let Marks think about that before adding, "He could be a poet or a painter this time. You won't have seen him much and he's not selling you anything and doesn't want anything from you. If he bought a beer, he probably left a good tip and didn't sit at the bar. He doesn't bother anyone's girlfriend. He's not really here. He's a ghost moving among you."

"How tall would he be?"

"About my height, maybe a little taller but with a little bit of a stoop."

"He's got a beard?"

"Look at the fucking drawing, okay?"

Marks smoothed the edges of the sketch and surprised me. "That artist who lives here drew this," he said. "I know her. I like her."

"Nora?"

"Yeah."

"She did draw it."

I glanced at the tats that wrapped his biceps, then looked at his face.

"I know your boss Coffina doesn't like to lose tenants and you don't want to fuck up with him by leading us to his doorstep, but this time the alternative is far worse. We're not leaving here without searching everywhere here. I really wouldn't fuck with me too much longer."

"You've got warrants?"

"Everything we need."

"If I help you and he's a major with a Baja cartel, they might cross for me."

"Last time I say this—we're not here about drugs."

"So what are you going to do if you find drugs?"

"If we're forced to search every unit and drugs are found, people will get arrested. People in jail can't pay rent. Coffina will want to keep the rent coming. He'll cooperate. Call him. Quit stalling, we're running out of time."

The San Diego officer, Pentane, came around the corner and rode up. He smiled at Marks and showed me a text: Ready to go.

I nodded then showed the text to Marks.

"They need an answer from us, Ace."

"One man, this guy in the picture, that's all?"

"Just him."

"Who is he?"

"If we get him, I'll tell you."

Marks held my gaze.

"He was here. I don't know if he is still, and I don't know where he lives. He comes from that direction and drives a '98 Honda Civic."

"Ever see a white Mercedes in here?"

"No."

"Tell Coffina he gets thirty seconds."

"Why are you always so fired up? Chill. I'll call him right now."

44

Marks knocked hard on a steel door and the sound reverberated. Nothing happened for thirty seconds, then footsteps thudded toward us and the door swung open. The red-bearded, thick-shouldered Coffina looked like he'd walked off the set of *Game of Thrones*. He said, "Shit, not you again."

"Good to see you too. Look at this and tell me where this guy lives."

Coffina stared at the sketch as he debated how to avoid dealing with us. He squinted at the helicopter shadowing the mountains to the west, so Marks must have brought him up to speed.

"I rent to him but he's not here right now, and I don't know where he is. He left yesterday or the day before."

"What does he drive?"

"An old beat-to-shit gray Honda Civic."

"Okay, so knowing you, you've got the plates and his driver's license number."

"I've got the plates. They're California. His license I don't have. He said it got stolen. He was getting a new one. I never followed up because he paid for everything ahead."

"How far ahead?"

"Three months and in cash."

"Show us where he lives."

I checked it out with binoculars before approaching. The house, if you could call it that, sat in desert scrub on the western outskirts of Cargoland and was built from two shipping cargo containers welded together. A dirt track crossed a dry gully and climbed through sand to it. Two clouded Plexiglas windows faced this way. The only door in was locked with a hardened link chain looped through the steel door and wall and held tight with a heavy padlock. Behind the makeshift house was a dusty area with a propane tank and a wood-framed storage building on concrete pads.

"Door hinges are welded on," Coffina said, like a realtor noting a selling point, which out here translated to "no one is going to kick that door in and steal your shit while you're gone."

Solar panels were on the roof. So was an air-conditioning unit. There was Internet and cell coverage. Of course there was. After all, this was the States.

"Did he tell you what he's doing here?"

"Said he was hiding from his ex-wife's lawyers."

"Did you believe him?"

"Naw, but until you showed, I didn't care why he was here or who was after him. He's paid up. I've got a big deposit and he keeps to himself. Lights are on at night. He's up then and sleeps in the day. He looks like he's from around here, but he's not." Coffina touched his left ear. "I got hit and this ear doesn't work well, so I'm not good on accents anymore and can't tell you anything about where he's from. But like I said, his license plates were California."

"You used to be more careful."

"I'm getting older, Grale."

"How big a deposit did he give you?"

"Five grand."

"Hope it's enough."

"It's three times the rent." Then he got what I meant and said, "If you want in, I'll cut off the lock he put on. I've got the tools to get through anything, so don't do any damage."

"What about friends, other people here he associates with?"

"Keeps to himself."

"You talk to him?"

"Some."

"So what has he said?"

"Not much. The ex-wife is trying to take all his money. He's thinking about moving to Mexico. He's got a kid he misses."

"A kid?"

"Yeah, like four years old or something."

"How old does he look?"

"Late thirties, maybe older."

That fit.

The SWAT helicopter landed in a clearing to the side of the village as armored SWAT vehicles rolled down the washboarded road and emptied out. They were disciplined and fast surrounding Hurin's place, guns ready, the road sealed. A bullhorn was used to call him out before charges were set, and with a short hard pop, the lock holding the door closed was blown off. The chain slithered to the ground. White smoke drifted away. The door swung open just like in the movies. We watched video feed from the first of the SWAT squad inside, a guy named Olsen. The SWAT commander wouldn't let me go in with him.

"I'm looking at an open room," Olsen said, "with nothing on the metal floor except a throw rug, maybe twelve feet long by eight wide. On the east side there's a workbench running almost the whole length. That looks like his shop. Here, I'll give you a view of that. There are tools and a couple of shelves, along with an open laptop."

I nodded and said, "That's what we're looking for."

Olsen again. "To my left is an L-shaped kitchen with wood countertops, drawers, a sink, a small refrigerator, a microwave, and dishes drying in a rack. To my right are a metal-framed cot and two steel shelves welded to the side wall for clothes."

"Any personal effects?" I asked.

"Looks cleaned out, like he's gone."

"Don't step on the rug or move anything." I turned to the SWAT commander. "I need to go in."

"When I tell you that you can, you will," the SWAT commander said. "Just hang on a little longer."

Olsen tested for explosive residue on the workbench. He wiped and then radioed.

"I've got residue."

The SWAT commander turned to me and nodded. I put on a suit, joined Olsen, and two other SWAT agents scoured the exterior and shined flashlights underneath. The steel building had been jacked up on one end to level it and there was some room underneath.

In front of the workbench along the wall, I squatted down and swept a flashlight beam along the underside of the bench and over the wiring and cords. A power cord was plugged into the laptop but nothing else. I straightened and, without moving, worked along the ceiling with the light, then moved into the kitchen and took inventory. The cooking area was small: a stove with a propane hookup, a small stainless sink, four or five feet of countertop and open shelving with a handful of glasses and plates. We weren't going to open the refrigerator yet.

My flashlight beam caught spiderwebs in a wall-hung furnace, and I felt disappointment that we'd missed him, and not by much. The bed was a folding cot stripped to the mattress. No covers or pillow, no clothes, no toothbrush, shoes, anything. We missed him and needed to find him and fast.

"He's gone, but he left us a laptop," I said. "Why would he do that?"

Steel L-bar welded to the side of the container held up the back of the desk and the long workbench. Chains at the corners held up the front. Where they'd been wiped for residue, the color was bright. C-4, Semtex, another plastic explosive, or dynamite had been here. In front of where the laptop sat on the bench was a wooden chair with long legs. I saw Garod Hurin in the late night in here, sitting on this chair as he built a bomb. Fluorescent tube lighting hung above the desk, everything neat and clean, tools oiled and lined up, things in their place.

The scene brought back a memory of a government-research cabin in the Wind River Range where a neo-Nazi bomb maker had holed up for months. Same as that guy, Hurin knew we'd get here. He knew enough about our approach to the situation to anticipate us. The open laptop drew my eyes, drew Olsen's too. But if you want an open laptop as a trap, why not make it look like you're still here? Leave some clothes hanging off a chair and dirty dishes in the sink. Otherwise, what the hell?

"What do you think?" Olsen asked.

"What I think is we gather touch DNA, then go out and check the storage box before we do anything more in here. We think first. We don't do anything yet. We're missing something. He left the laptop for us, and we don't want to do what he's hoping for."

"Okay, if you've got a vibe, let's back out."

Ten minutes later, SWAT blew the door off the storage hut. Inside was gear that Coffina identified as belonging to a former tenant: a suitcase of old clothes, three cardboard boxes of dusty yellowing books, and two assault rifles and six boxes of ammunition wrapped in a blanket. The weapons looked cared for and Coffina explained another man had used them to train for the coming war, when the government would suspend the Constitution and join with the UN to confiscate all guns and make Americans slaves to the New World Order.

"No shit?" I asked.

"Swear to God."

Olsen and I went back inside. A SWAT agent who had looked beneath the house poked his head in and said, "There might be something in the area under the throw rug. Could just be rocks or debris. We can't get a good enough angle to tell what it is. It's more or less in the center so it could be a support for the floor."

"Let's treat it as dangerous," I said.

I skirted the rug, moved back to the cooking area, and picked up on a faint solvent smell as I leaned over the sink. It was there on the dishes in the rack too. We'd tested for DNA in a dozen places in the kitchen and found nothing here. Hurin must have worked slowly and carefully in the kitchen, wearing gloves, wiping and re-wiping the counter and cabinet faces, the sink and every dish and glass with a diluted solution. He'd scoured away DNA, though not bomb residue. He left the laptop and guessed we'd focus on it, but not touch it. We were looking at a stage set created for us, and designed to lead us somewhere.

"Let's check the laptop again for wires," I said to Olsen. "Only this time you do it. Maybe I keep staring at the same thing and am missing what's important."

Olsen was younger, more agile than I was, so he got down lower. He balanced. He rocked on his heels and got on a knee and didn't see anything.

"There's no wire coming off the laptop to anything underneath. There's only the plug into the wall. If we hit a key, it's not going to detonate anything."

"Yeah, but don't touch a key yet."

I pointed at the exposed wiring that ran from the four-plug outlet the laptop was plugged into. The wire ran up and across to the kitchen ceiling and a junction box there. Other wires along the ceiling fed lights.

"That's where the electrical power for this place comes in. If that landlord walked in, as he would have done sometime soon, he would have seen it and seen the guy was gone. What's he going to do?"

"Take the laptop, lock the door, and keep the huge deposit."

I laughed. So did Olsen.

"And what does Hurin think we'll do once we figure out it had no leads running to explosives?"

Olsen didn't answer. He didn't want to be set up.

The other SWAT officer was at the door again. He didn't step in but said, "They're ready to cut power to the building."

When I heard that, it hit me. "Tell them no! Do not cut the power until we're a hundred yards away. Relay that as fast as you can."

"Fuck, man, you're scaring me," Olsen said, and I felt sweat start as I listened to the SWAT officer radio and wait for the response.

"There's nothing we'd like more than his laptop," I said. "So I'm guessing it's a bomb. There's no hard drive in there. I'm betting if we pull the plug out, it blows up. And when that happens, the power will short out, and if there's another bomb in here, that's when it goes off. Go ahead and unplug it. Let's see if I'm right."

That got a big grin and we left the laptop and backed out. We crossed down through the little dry creek and climbed the slope toward the armored SWAT vehicles. We were only fifty yards away when the stubborn son of a bitch SWAT commander cut the power. The first blast was a hard sharp bang that had to be the laptop. If you were standing in front of it you were dead. The second blast tumbled us into mesquite. Neither of us was hurt, though something big landed nearby.

Olsen started laughing then said, "Dude, I owe you a drink. I would have unplugged it, for sure."

Or I think that's what he said. My ears were ringing as we laughed with giddy post-adrenaline relief. We walked toward the officers running our way, and I looked past here at my fear at how far ahead of us the bomb maker was. Garod Hurin saw us coming and was ready. He was on the move again. We wouldn't have much time.

45

The sound was small and faraway, a rapid pop, pop, pop. Beatty capped a gallon jug of water and set it down on the flat rock. He picked up binoculars and stood in the shade of the overhang scanning the airfield and trailers first, and then working his way out, pausing and lowering the binos as he heard more assault-weapon fire. From the echo off the mountains, they could be anywhere down there.

He widened his scan and on a spidery gray desert track running south of the airfield along a rocky plain, he spotted the security dudes' black Land Cruiser. A different vehicle raised a ribbon of dust as it drove away from the Land Cruiser and back toward the airfield. He focused in on the moving vehicle. At this distance it was difficult, but it looked like Bahn's pickup. He followed its progress for several minutes before bringing the glasses back to the Land Cruiser.

An hour later the black Land Cruiser was still sitting in the heat in the same spot, so he unpacked his spotting scope tripod and extended the legs. They were sturdy and tall enough so that he didn't have to bend over much once he'd screwed on the scope. The scope was so sensitive that the trick was getting the legs set so they wouldn't move at all. When the scope was ready, he started with the airfield, looking for Eddie's truck and finding it parked near the trailers where the pilots lived, and then adjusting the scope to view the runway where the drones were lined up.

A silver drone rose through his field of vision. He kept the scope there and a second drone rose through his view thirty-three seconds later. He timed the third as well, thirty-three seconds again, so not much room for error if there were a problem with the drone ahead. But enough time if you were experienced. Not many reasons to launch so quickly, though.

He thought about that, then reached for his phone. He brought up Grale's number, but didn't call yet and adjusted back to the spidery thread of road and followed it to the small white rocks bright in the hot sunlight and to the black Land Cruiser still sitting there. He focused on the passenger window and with maximum magnification could make out a shape in the passenger seat. Large enough to be Big John but hard to tell with the tinted glass, and hard to tell what he was doing. His head lay against the window like he was sleeping, or maybe leaning that way and talking. Hard to tell.

Beatty straightened. Without the spotting scope, the Land Cruiser was just a black dot and barely that. When he leaned over again, he brought the scope over to the driver's side and slowly crawled up the vehicle until he reached the driver's mirror. Tricky. Small movements jumped the scope. He moved the lens in tiny increments and still overshot the first time.

He straightened again, feeling a little bit frustrated at overshooting, and rubbed a sore spot on his lower back and cleared his vision by looking out into the desert. He used to be really good with a scope. He leaned over again and got the lens on the driver's side mirror and realized from the reflection that the driver's window was down. That was lucky. He upped the magnification and adjusted the scope hoping the side mirror would give him a view of the driver.

"Fuck."

He'd overshot again. He worked his way back and very slowly down the mirror. Now he was getting there. *Just chill and do this calmly,* he thought. Another tiny turn and there was the top of the driver's seat. Don't knock the scope. Come slowly down the seat. He came down from the headrest and still no driver, but another small turn and black hair showed and a scalp and forehead. He took his hand away from the lens adjustment when he reached the eyes.

"Tak, what's going on out there? That's Big John in the passenger seat, isn't?"

Beatty leaned over again and moved down to Tak's open mouth, chin, and neck. That was as far down as the side mirror reflection gave him. He worked his way back up to the dilated pupils. A fly landed on Tak's left eye. He watched it crawl around until it made his stomach turn.

He straightened and looked down over the desert valley at the airfield, trying to make sense of it. When he looked again, the fly was still there and another was at the edge of Tak's mouth. He left the spotting scope and found an old gray blanket he kept behind the truck seats. He draped it over the front of his truck and checked the clip in his gun before laying it down nearby. Then he picked up his cell and called Grale.

46

Desert dust and smoke drifted away from the container house. Debris from the blast glinted in hot sunlight. My ears rang. All I heard was a humming. Behind me the SWAT commander gave orders in a hard, sharp voice that I couldn't bring into focus as I stumbled then walked back to the destroyed house.

A weld that had joined the two cargo containers at the roof was peeled open by the blast. Sunlight streamed in. Smoke wafted out. I looked at blue sky, then at fragmented debris around me and out the windows where blast spray spewed into mesquite and scrub. Burn marks scored the metal wall behind where the laptop had exploded. The air smelled of C-4 and was acrid from scorched paint and burned bedding. In the tiny kitchen a severed water line bled into holes in the floor. I turned to the burned and shredded mattress and the smoking strips of rug. White porcelain fragments from a toilet or sink pocked a wall. The design of the primary bomb had spread a blast wave evenly across the space. A now-deformed steel box cut in and welded to the floor had held the bomb. No one in here, nothing in here would have survived.

Yesterday, if I hadn't told Nogales to drive past, we might have come here and found Coffina then Garod Hurin. I faulted myself for that and was thinking about where to go next as I walked out. Nogales hurried toward me as I stripped off the SWAT suit.

"We got a call from a hiker about a gray Honda parked up a canyon out beyond the gypsum mine. Don't know yet if it's a Civic, but it sounds like it. I'm headed there. Do you want to come with me?"

"I do, but let's get lined up with everyone here first, just in case we find something. Ask your bomb squad to keep their dog here. If it's his car, we'll need a bomb dog first."

We drove rough desert roads out past the gypsum mine, me watching ahead, not talking much, Nogales filling the gap. I listened but was thinking about Hurin. Did he move because he was worried or because it was time? He could have left quietly rather than booby-trap the building. He didn't do that to kill Coffina, so he knew we were close. That thought chilled me and I was silent as Nogales drove. The dirt road hugged bone-colored mountains. We were two miles along it when we rounded a bend, and I spotted a car up a narrow canyon ahead and to our right.

"There. Between the rocks," I said. "That's a Honda Civic."

"Got it."

I turned and looked back. Agents following had fallen back as they navigated rocks an old flash flood left in the road. But probably for the best, since we'd kicked up a rooster tail of dust with Nogales driving hard. We lost them but they couldn't miss us. We parked short of the tire tracks turning into the narrow canyon. The car was well up there. With the rocks strewn along the canyon's floor and its narrowness, it must have been hard to get the car in there.

"I'll walk up and call the license plates down to you," I said, and did that as the other agents arrived. I smelled decomp as I got close but didn't see a body when looking through the windows. Seats were empty. The smell came from the trunk. Could it be Hurin? I circled the car and saw where it was dented and paint was scraped off getting it up here. The driver was motivated.

When the bomb dog arrived with her handler, she worked her way around the car and didn't scent on anything in the engine compartment or underneath. The officer handling her dog was patient. She let the dog run, then worked her back over each area of the car at least three times before saying she thought it was safe to open a door.

Inside, the bomb dog scented explosive residue on the driver's seat and floor mat but most likely that came from clothes. The dog didn't scent on anything near the trunk and her handler was confident decomp odors wouldn't fool the bomb dog. Nonetheless, everyone gave the car some room as I popped the trunk lid. It rose and a heavy wave of gases escaped. We let that drift away, then got a long look at a body, its back to us, knees drawn up, shoulders turned and the head facedown. Not a big man. Two entry wounds were clearly visible in dyed-blond hair at the back of the victim's head.

"Adult male Caucasian," somebody said.

More Bu-cars—Bureau cars—and San Diego County Sheriff's Department vehicles arrived. Our evidence recovery team did their initial survey as I searched upslope for an answer to why the driver banged off boulders and dug the wheels deep into sand trying to get higher. Several silvered timbers covering an old mineshaft had been pulled away, and looking down into the darkness of the mineshaft I guessed this was the goal. Dump the body down the shaft, maybe even the car. There was never a plan to get the Honda back out of the canyon. Another thought occurred: it wasn't Hurin who had shot him and there must be other vehicle tracks, though there weren't any in the canyon.

Radio responses from a San Diego County Sheriff's Department unmarked carried into the canyon. I could hear as a dispatcher reported the Honda Civic was registered to a twenty-seven-year-old San Diego male named John Carl Delbo. In San Diego, police officers were already knocking on Delbo's apartment door. Ten minutes later we heard Delbo's account. He'd sold the car to a man named John Marco six weeks ago. Marco hadn't haggled over the price, paid cash, and promised to register the car right away. Delbo had just assumed the buyer had followed through on the registration and hadn't bothered to fill out the form DMV requires of the seller.

None of that was particularly surprising, but we needed the seller, Delbo, to look at photos, as soon as possible. Did Hurin buy the car? Was he operating independently with a contract to produce the bombs but on his own to find a place? It was possible. We knew his predilection was to work alone.

An hour and a half later, ERT was ready to move the body. It was quite hot now in the narrow canyon. The bomb dog was panting when they brought her back one more time. Then ERT moved the body. The smell was awful as more fluids leaked out. One of the bullets had exited the right eye on an upward slant and taken out a good-sized piece of bone at the brow, but there was no doubt.

"I know him," I said. I'd already figured out it was him and was debating how he got here and why. "His name is Denny Mondari. He's from Vegas. He's worked as a CI for us for a decade."

"What's he doing here?"

"Don't know yet."

It was a sad ending for anyone, but honestly, I didn't feel as much for Mondari. Somehow he'd earned his way here. An hour and a half later I caught a ride back from Nogales and called Venuti as we reached an area with better cell reception. A plane left Vegas soon after to retrieve me. Nogales drove me to the Borrego Valley Airport. We shook hands and he left. I was on the phone with Venuti and the ASAC when the FBI plane landed.

"Make your best guess," Thorpe told me.

"Mondari didn't know he was delivering explosives. He thought he was trading his way out of his computer-hacking problem by delivering drugs, and the cartel wanted a disposable deliveryman to bring in the C-4, so they used him. They probably trailed him to keep an eye on the delivery then executed him after. After his cyberthieves broke into their manager's computer and they got tracked down and kidnapped, you can bet they gave up Mondari's name. Mondari was walking dead. They just put him to work first. That's what fits for me."

"And Garod Hurin?"

"He built the next bomb or bombs, got warned or picked up on us, and then closed down the shop and left."

"Meaning he guessed we'd find it."

"Sure. We were already in his neighborhood."

"Call as soon as you land," Thorpe said. "Stay with your bomb maker. He knows you're coming for him. Figure him out. You just found where he worked. As the media gets this he'll know you're right behind him. Stay with him. Where would he go now, Grale?"

47

From the plane, the Anza-Borrego looked sere, stark, and cathedral. It was beautiful country in its own way. Sometimes I couldn't help thinking about the beauty on earth in contrast to the life's work I'd chosen. But I wasn't going there today.

What could motivate a freelancer like Hurin to work for Al Qaeda or ISIS? The answer could only be the old one. Money. He wouldn't care about their religious zeal or vain certainty their interpretations were the only true ones. Those would be abstracts to him. Maybe there was a thrill in striking at the country whose law enforcement had hunted him for a decade, but most likely it was a big payoff that brought him here. Hurin, if we could find him, would have a lot of information we needed. We definitely wanted him alive.

At the office I walked into another conference room meeting, only this time with more buzz and excitement and Washington brass piped in to listen. We started without any delay. Like me, a CIA analyst conferenced in doubted Hurin had shot Mondari. Their profile showed him as reclusive, careful, and physically withdrawn.

An hour-long debate began about what else might be in play here. Into that mix someone threw Beatty's name. Beatty had bought yet more throwaway phones and his whereabouts were unknown. Also, the phone Juan Menderes used to confirm his coke deliveries was on the short list for the cell phone that detonated the Bar Alagara bomb.

I hadn't been briefed on that yet, but it offered another explanation for his murder.

An agent summarized Beatty's confrontation with police officers at a scenic overlook northwest of Vegas, saying a patrol officer found him sleeping in the back of his pickup and Beatty was hostile, so he'd called for backup. He was not charged or held but was aggressive on leaving.

"He tried to call me from there," I said. "What did he do that was aggressive?"

"Lowered his passenger window to flip off an officer. You can read their report. The GPS tracker attached to the underside of his pickup was found in a rest-stop trash can. He must have suspected he was being tracked."

Of course he did. The agent must have read my face. He stared before continuing.

"There's been no credit card activity. Why is he still calling you?"

"Maybe because I believe in him."

"And why is that?"

"A better question is why not."

Venuti cut it off and we moved back to Garod Hurin. One of those conferenced in from headquarters, a heavyweight in domestic terrorism investigation, John Saran, asked me, "Do you have anything resembling hard evidence that Garod Hurin has returned to the Vegas area?"

"None."

"So some good guessing, good tracking, but really nothing."

"Correct."

"And Mondari's cybercriminal crew is still missing?"

"They are. They could be sitting on a beach somewhere."

"Do you believe that?"

"No."

"Why haven't we found them?"

"We haven't put much effort into finding them."

"You haven't or we haven't?"

"We work for the same agency, sir."

I got a few smiles at the table for that. Saran was a ball-breaker with the nickname "Sarin," for the nerve gas.

"Tell me why we should find them, Agent Grale, and we'll do it. All I've heard so far is they were scamming a cartel and got discovered. How do they tie in?"

"This will be speculation on my part."

"Well, you're on a streak. Let's hear it."

"Mondari's cybergeeks are dead. Sinaloa soldiers kidnapped and interrogated them. They're lying in shallow graves in the desert. Before they died they gave up Mondari's name and everything else they knew."

"That's believable."

"But if they're not dead, they can validate what Mondari told me and they may know more. We need to look for them."

"Okay, but get on with what you think has happened."

"Cartel operatives sat down with Mondari next and laid out their terms. Maybe he made a large restitution payment and agreed to do cyberwork for them, something like that. Something that made him believe there was a way out. But another piece was doing deliveries, some finite number, two of which were C-4. Why use Mondari for that? The reason is, he was disposable. They wouldn't want any kind of trail tying them to a terrorist bomber. The Sinaloa cartel is who the CIA says moved the C-4 up from southern Mexico. As long as I'm speculating, I'm going to say it never delivered to the warehouse where it allegedly disappeared from."

"Really?"

"Yes, sir."

"Okay, now I'm all ears."

"It's too improbable that it was stolen out from underneath us. I read the report. There was backup on the backup surveillance. I think the cartel picked up on CIA surveillance. Then they thought about it and decided it had just gotten more expensive to deliver. They told whoever was communicating with ISIS or AQAP that they had a problem and it was going to cost more money. They did have a problem and came up with a more profitable way to deal with it. I'm going to say they faked the delivery the CIA was tracking and brought it in through another route. Maybe they split the delivery in half."

"Why split it?"

"So they wouldn't lose it all if the courier got busted crossing the border, as well as it got the size down to where it could easily be moved with two car trips. Maybe Mondari thought it was drugs he was ferrying. You know what, I take that back. I don't know what he thought, but I'm sure he thought he was squaring the books with the cartel over the theft of data his cybergeeks pulled off."

"You're saying this Denny Mondari drove the C-4 to the bomber's shop?"

"No, I'd guess a neutral point is where it was off-loaded. Mondari went home after the first load. After the second he wasn't needed anymore, so they took him out in the desert and put him down. They would have lost the body and the car carrying him, but the car got wedged between rocks and stuck in sand in a desert canyon. Mondari was killed for leading his cybercrooks into the Sinaloa manager's e-mail. He was walking dead as soon as that was discovered. They just found a use for him first and let him think he was trading his way out. He came to us with the bomb-maker story because he was scared, but he couldn't tell us the truth. He probably figured we were his only hope, or let's say he knew that by the time he told me about seeing the fabricante de bombas e-mail."

"You don't think he was part of the plot?"

"No."

"Do you have any proof?"

"I have little pieces. Do you know Mike Sulliver, a former detective here in Vegas?"

"I know of him. We worked with him on several cases. He was damned good."

"He's got a private investigative business now. He'd also heard rumors that the Sinaloa cartel had some talk with Mondari. Mondari talked to a casino-bartender friend when he was drunk and Sulliver got it from him."

"You first said we should look at Mondari's crew and then you said they're likely dead."

"My guess is dead, but what if they're alive? If they're alive, we need them."

"All right, point taken, we'll look for them. Now tell me why this drug cartel or any cartel would want to have anything to do with an attack on the US government? Last time it led to a whole lot of smoking coca fields. The CIA maintains the C-4 crossed the border in an 18-wheeler carrying cleaning products. Why don't you believe that?"

"Because I read the report where the drug dogs got fooled and the C-4 was stolen out from under joint CIA-FBI surveillance. But I think the CIA got fooled."

Saran chuckled and said, "Keep going."

"The C-4 was never in that truck and when twenty-four-hour surveillance was set up on the warehouse, the teams were watching detergent. Meanwhile Sinaloa is telling AQAP and ISIS or a Lebanese businessman the NSA tapped into in Mexico City that they needed more money. They had spotted CIA spies and were going to bring it in a different way. But they also knew if the C-4 was used for terrorism, it would ultimately get traced back to them, so they took very careful steps. They made the CIA agents believe it had been delivered with the semitruck full of detergent."

"We believed," Saran said.

"There you go. We believed, and meanwhile it came in a different way and got used while we were still watching the warehouse. The cartel worried about what they should worry about, the US government tracing a delivery of explosives used for terrorism here back to their smuggling pipeline. They still made good, but at a much, much higher price. That's my guess. Maybe some hard-core Wahhabi Saudi prince paid the difference."

"Do you think the final delivery has been made?"

Had to think a moment about what I wanted to say there, then said, "I guess this is how I see it. Hurin may have gotten wind of a search under way and left. A San Diego County deputy and I were making rounds with a story of a serial murderer allegedly working from the Anza-Borrego. Deputy Nogales is someone we ought to be working more, by the way. He's very good. It's possible Hurin put it together and closed up shop. More likely, he knew we were closing in and hoped to kill us. He finished the bomb making and set the booby trap."

That was about all the speculation in one sitting that several in the room could take. I saw people shift in their chairs. The agent who'd sparred with me about Beatty leaned back and folded his arms. But John Saran on the conference call couldn't see that.

"Is all of this about the drone program or is it bigger?" Saran asked.

"You're asking my opinion."

"I am because you're getting results. If you weren't, we wouldn't be having this conversation. I want to know how you're seeing this."

"I see an enemy testing the viability of asymmetrical warfare inside the US."

"Testing bringing the war to us?"

"Testing the viability."

"And where do you think that probing goes next?"

"If the CIA is right, they still have enough C-4 for numerous smaller attacks, but we're bringing more and more pressure to bear, and that's got to figure into their thinking. They've shown us they're sophisticated and have people here. They got the bomb into the rental car. Someone was ready when Nasik's name showed up in the Hertz system. Maybe through a hacker. It suggests long-range planning. I've come around to believing in a sleeper cell and think that's what we're seeing."

"So do I. Go on."

"We've identified their bomb maker and asked the public to help find him. That intensifies the pressure. They know the clock is running down and I think they'll go big. A grand finale followed by a promise to be back later with more."

"That's what I think too. They've got enough left to do that. I'd be emboldened if I were them. I'm with you on this and we'll keep talking, Agent Grale. I don't agree with everything you've said but I want to keep a conversation going. You've done some very good work. Anything else, anybody?"

Nobody said anything. They were just waiting for Saran to finish. The meeting broke up as soon as Saran signed off.

48

When I arrived at the hospital, a nurse flagged me down and said Julia was now down a floor in a shared room. Number 323. First thing I saw was that Julia was off the drips. The tubes were gone. The young woman who was her roommate was asleep, so I drew the curtain and carried a chair over. We talked quietly.

"Dr. Segovia stopped by," she said. "I really like her. Mom liked her."

"Yeah, and remember when I said Jo and I made a mistake? We're not going to make the same one again."

"Was it your fault?"

"Usually is."

I saw the faintest glint of humor in her eyes.

"Your mom always nailed it."

That brought her close to tears.

"I'm very glad you like Jo. You may get out of here tomorrow, Julia. It's not certain yet. We'll know later today. Have more of your friends come to see you?"

"Kylie and Cara came yesterday."

I didn't know any of her friends. I couldn't put names to faces. That would have to change.

"One way or another we'll keep you in the same school," I said.

"How?"

"I don't know yet, but we will."

I'd toyed more with the leasing-my-house idea and then renting a condo, but given the circumstances, maybe the school district would make an exception for her two remaining years. After she had a driver's license, the logistics would get easier. Logistics were the easy part. I looked at black stitches on her right forearm and her bandaged left ear and the brace on her neck, and thought that all the worst is what no one could see.

Her dinner arrived as we were talking. She picked at the plate without eating. She needed someone she trusted deeply to hold her and tell her life would go on. I wanted to be that person, but that person should have been her dad. I was the uncle who worked all the time and joked and talked to her at family barbecues. I needed to step it up and be there always.

"We'll figure it out, Julia. That's what I can promise. There'll be some hard days, but each time we'll find a way through."

She nodded and murmured something about the vacation her family would have gone on next week. Melissa had talked it up, Glacier National Park, Waterton, then Banff. No more family vacations. No brother teasing her or mother who loved her enormously and dad who would have done anything to protect her. All I could do was be there for her in a different way, but we talked about the planned vacation because it seemed to help her. She talked and cried and then smiled at a good memory.

"Julia, if you can, eat a little. You need it."

She ate a few bites then I made her laugh with a story about her dad. She cut into the chicken and I told another, this one about Jim bringing a B-52 home on two engines and landing cleanly in a heavy storm. My phone buzzed several times and I looked at the number and guessed who it was but kept my focus on Julia.

Half an hour later as I walked out, I called Beatty back.

"What happened at Red Rock with the police officers?"

"I couldn't find a campsite and needed to sleep. I figured it wouldn't be any big deal, but the cop who rousted me wanted to try me on terrorism charges."

"Where are you now?"

"In the mountains behind the airfield."

"The Strata airfield?"

"Yeah."

"Doing what?"

"I couldn't think of a place to go, so I'm camping out for a few days. But it's bad news out here. I'm seeing this through a spotting scope, but it looks like the two security dudes are dead in their Land Cruiser about a third of a mile south of the airfield. Eddie's truck is at the airfield, but I haven't seen him. I tried to call you last night."

"How do you know they're dead?"

"With my spotting scope I could see a reflection of Tak's face. His pupils were dilated and I saw a fly crawling over his left eyeball with no reaction from him. He's dead."

"Did you call 911?"

"I figured after what happened at Red Rock I couldn't call 911 or the sheriff. They'd just come for me. I called you."

"There's nothing about this in the message you left me earlier."

"I'm on a watch list. I don't know who listens in on your voice mails. I only wanted to talk to you."

Get the information first, I thought, *and then check it out.* The rest we could deal with after, but I didn't know why Beatty was out there. If I didn't, no one else would either and I could hear the questions already. Sometimes it's the murderer who calls in the killing.

"You'll have to come down and meet whatever officers or agents come out. Are you clear on that?"

"It's not going to be you?"

"It's going to be whoever can respond fastest. I'm caught up in the bomb investigation. We caught a break."

My phone beeped and I said, "Hang tight for a minute. I've got a call coming I've got to take. I'll be right back to you."

"I'll switch phones. I'll call you back."

"Jeremy, just hang on, it's not going to be long and no one is trying to get your location. I've been with Julia and just walked out of the hospital. Stay on the line. Don't go away. I'll be right back."

I took the other call. It was the front desk and they transferred me to Venuti.

"Come to the office as fast as you can. Omar Smith and his lawyer just arrived and Smith is asking for Special Agent Paul Grale. What is it with you two? He says he's got a confession to make but wants you here."

"Okay, but I'm twenty minutes out and I've got Beatty on hold. Let me tell you what he just told me."

I did and asked, "Can we get agents out there?"

"How good a shot is he?"

"Very good."

"Then I could be sending agents to their deaths. We need to be careful here. I'll call Strata. Get here. Get into the room with Smith and then we'll deal with the rest of this. I'll make some calls before you get here, but Smith is ready to talk. You need to focus on that. Do you have any ideas about what he's going to say?"

"It'll be something about money. Let's stick on Beatty for a minute. Let's say he's right."

"No, let's say he's dangerous. We know he had a beef with these security guys and we know he has no reason to be there. Based on what you've told me, we have to treat Jeremy Beatty as a possible murder suspect. If it's sheriff's deputies that go there first, we have an obligation to warn them."

"If you frame it that way, you'll get him killed."

"Get here and we'll talk. I've got to go."

He hung up. He was exasperated and questioned my judgment. Truth was, I wavered for a moment as well and when I switched back to Jeremy, he was gone.

49

Despite air conditioning, Smith's forehead and scalp glistened with sweat. His gaze held mine for a moment then moved to the wall behind me. The tall, thin lawyer to his left looked worried and nervous. He'd probably advised against this meeting.

"On May twentieth, my sister's three daughters were kidnapped in Istanbul. They were pulled into two cars and the kidnappers told my brother-in-law they would kill my nieces or sell them into Syria to ISIS or for prostitution in Turkey if he did not pay $300,000 for each of them. So almost a million dollars, and my brother-in-law has no money. He doesn't even work. The kidnappers must know this. Everyone knows this, so I am wondering, 'Who is behind the kidnapping?'"

He answered his question a moment later.

"I am thinking the men I am in court with in Istanbul are the ones. It is a way to pressure me. Perhaps the ransom goes to them and the kidnappers get a cut. Thoughts like these are in my head, but my sister is nearly without words when she calls me. She is crazy with worry."

"Did you contact the police in Istanbul?"

Smith looked at me like I was a fool and said, "It was a condition of the ransom we make no contact with the police."

"It always is."

"The police, I don't trust them. The men I owe are speaking to me and they are very angry. They want money I owe and they want it now. This is what I am thinking. I do not expect them to hurt the girls, and they know Ozan, my brother-in-law, has no money. Why take the children of a man who has no wealth? It was obvious, it was to reach me."

The lawyer scowled and twisted a pen between his fingers as if this was difficult for him to hear, though I didn't grasp why. Maybe he knew what was coming next.

"I told my brother-in-law $300,000 for each girl is more than I can pay. There is nothing I can do with numbers like that. But I love my family and I am not a coldhearted man. I am thinking every second how to get them back. Through Ozan, I tell the kidnappers we must negotiate. When my sister hears that, she collapses. She believes I am very, very, very rich, and that negotiating means I do not love my nieces. Nothing could be more false. One week later I offered $150,000 for all three."

"On May 27?"

"Yes."

"You offered a fraction of what they had demanded?"

"This is normal for the purpose of starting a negotiation. For them to know I am a serious man, I must start low. Ozan is shocked by this. He is very angry and goes to the kidnappers without telling me."

I jotted down *May 20* and *$300,000 each* on a pad, and *May 27, give or take,* and *$50,000 per girl as a first offer.*

"How much were you willing to pay?"

"Perhaps $100,000 each."

I wrote *$100,000* as he continued with his brother-in-law.

"They put a hood on Ozan's head and took him to see the girls. The girls are in cages beneath a house, one cage for each girl. There is not much light and they are frightened and weeping and Ozan is shocked, but of course this is what the kidnappers want. Ozan tells them I am not as rich as they believe and in the name of Allah they must release his children. They say they know about the lawsuit for $2,000,000 against me, therefore I must have money. They repeat the demand for $300,000 each and make a deadline of tomorrow. When Ozan calls me, he's crying. He is apologizing for going to them and frightened at what he has seen. He is a very weak man."

A quick but strong emotion crossed his face and made me think what he was about to say disturbed him deeply.

"The next day the kidnappers sent a video of the body of my youngest niece lying in a gutter. She was the most beautiful girl and the favorite of my sister. When they did that, I canceled the wire transfer I was trying to arrange. I called a friend in Istanbul and asked him to hire people who could find and kill them."

His lawyer interrupted. "You did not do that."

"I did."

He said that and stopped and, for almost a minute, stared through me. When he spoke again his voice broke.

"My brother-in-law blamed me. He told my sister I played games with the kidnappers and she went crazy with anger and sorrow. She stopped eating or sleeping. She refused my calls. She talks to herself, and the kidnappers no longer take Ozan's phone calls."

"This was what day?"

"May thirtieth. There was no need to kill my niece."

"How do we contact your brother-in-law and what's his last name?"

"Yildiz. Ozan Yildiz. He is gone into Syria to join with ISIS."

The lawyer wrote down the name of the brother-in-law and slid it across the table. I pretended to focus on it, though we already knew Ozan Yildiz's name. The Bureau was in contact with the Turkish National Police regarding Omar Smith and his family and all other known connections.

"I'm sorry I have to ask for this," I said. "Can you forward me the video they sent of your niece's body?"

The lawyer forwarded it to my e-mail, and Omar Smith looked away as I watched it. It was forty-three seconds and long enough to capture a tragic truth about all of us. A young girl who couldn't be more than eight or nine was lying on her side in a gutter amid trash and filth. Whether she was Omar Smith's niece or not, her throat was cut.

When Smith spoke again it was in a slower and quieter voice.

"They asked for proof that I didn't have the ransom money. They wanted to see business records including bank statements."

"Your computer records are in English. Did the people you were negotiating with speak English?"

"Yes."

"Did that mean anything to you?"

"Not much. Many speak English."

I thought about what was coming next and my heart skipped a beat as he worked through the mechanics of giving them remote access to his computer. A computer expert was consulted. Things were done to limit what they could see.

The lawyer slid me a business card with the consultant's name. Smith's banks were fed a story about ferreting out a hacker. The banks cooperated. I listened and took notes but inwardly urged Smith to just say it. Say what they focused on after they got in remotely.

"I gave them access on June 5 and they went through everything. The computer expert said they already know how to do this. He said this was not the first time for them. They asked me about future business, about what was already booked."

Smith stared at me. He wanted my reaction, and though I was sickened I wasn't going to show him.

"This is how they found the party for the drone pilots," he said. "It's how Ozan came to know also. In the schedule of signed contracts, it was called 'Air Force Drone Pilot Party.'"

Smith said something to himself that I couldn't hear but the lawyer did. The lawyer put an arm around him as Smith bowed his head. When he lifted his head again, he nodded at me.

"I am very deeply sorry that the drone pilots' party is what they wanted to talk about. When I said no to that, they began working through Ozan. Ozan begins to speak around me."

"What does that mean?"

"It means they are making a deal with Ozan, and I am remembering when he was at university how much he hated America. Like the Iranians, for him the United States was the great Satan. He is not a man who can think for himself."

"Were you afraid Ozan would try to sell information about the drone pilot party as a way to save his remaining daughters?"

"For that and for more money and to strike at America. I think it was all these things. He found other people who were not the kidnappers who said they would pay for the information and pay the kidnappers too."

"Did Ozan tell you that?"

"No."

"How do you know that?"

The lawyer cut in. "He doesn't know that."

Smith's fingers worked at the left cuff of his shirt.

"I wired money on June 12 as an act of good faith to save the two girls."

"How much?"

"Fifty thousand dollars. The kidnappers got the money and told us that was good but not enough. Yet there was no hurry. Now they were willing to negotiate. I could feel Ozan was not as worried. So I became frightened that something was working in the background. We were very close to agreeing on a final price. Then for more than a week I heard nothing before something incredible. They would send someone to America and collect the money in person. Can you imagine?"

"Did you believe them?"

"Of course not."

I looked hard at him, at his calculated decisions, at what he knew and held back. I felt a cold anger.

"You'd figured out they were waiting for the Fourth of July."

"No, I did not."

But he had.

"You are wrong," he said. "It was arranged in this way. A man would come to the Alagara. I would pay him and he would call the kidnappers from my office. The money for this was in the safe."

The lawyer's chair scraped back. He stood and said, "I need to talk to my client."

Smith shook his head. He waved his lawyer off.

"I insist," the lawyer said.

"I was to meet this man on July 4 at 10:00 p.m. at the Alagara."

"The night of the party."

"Yes, the night of the party. The party rental ended at 9:30. They knew this from my computer files, and I thought it was 10:00 so that it was after the party. Now I know this was to keep me quiet until the bombs went off." He gave a small shrug. "But I was relieved we were making a deal."

"What is the name of the man you were to meet?"

"Mansur, only one word. I would know him by that name and he would come at 10:00 the night of the Fourth, but I was to call him earlier in the day."

"Did you?"

"I have the phone number I called. You will have no record of it." He turned to the lawyer. "Give it to them."

The lawyer stalled finding the number. Smith checked it before it was slid across.

"You were going to be at the Alagara at 10:00 the night of July 4 to pay the ransom to a man named Mansur?"

"Three hundred thousand dollars. I called that phone number from Houston and he said the meeting time had changed and to call him as soon as I returned to Las Vegas. When he said that, I became frightened. I didn't know why it frightened me, but it did."

I took it the next step. The drone party information got sold and the kidnappers got more than they were going to get haggling with Smith. I asked Smith, "When did you find out the girls were dead?"

That caught him off-balance. I may have seen fear in his eyes.

"This afternoon. How did you know they are dead?"

I looked at him, remembering Melissa saying she liked Smith so much that they'd become Facebook friends. On her Facebook page she wrote about the upcoming party.

"We're going to be here awhile," I said. "I need a few minutes before we continue. Do you want tea or something to eat?"

"I wish only to die."

"Agent Ruiz and I are going to step out a few minutes and then we'll be back."

I walked out with Carlo Ruiz, the other agent in the room with me. I needed to sit alone for a few minutes. Ruiz went to find Venuti and Thorpe.

50

Near dawn Omar Smith asked to pray and rest. His expression said, *Read nothing into my prayers. They are not because of or for you.* When I left him I left the office and drove to the Alagara and walked around as Smith prayed and rested. I looked at the building where so many had died and thought about things Smith had said in the night, reliving the decisions he'd made. It wasn't religion. It was survival. It was money. It was thinking he was smarter than the bombers, but he wasn't. A hollowed sadness flooded me as I looked at the ruined building. Then some voice inside, and I would like to think it was Melissa, said, *Walk away, walk toward the sunrise and the first light on the fields of flowers draping and laid with notes and cards on the Alagara lot.* I knew I was looking at what connects us, what joins us. I needed that this morning.

An hour later, Smith was brought back to the interview room. He picked up the sketch of Garod Hurin I placed in front of him before asking him, "When did you last speak with Ozan?"

"July 4, the day he left for Syria. The men he respects so much will put him in a truck with a bomb and tell him he's honored and lucky."

"He never made it. The Turkish police have him. They stopped him at the border. He told them you advised him to cross into Syria. Why did you suggest that?"

"Yes, why would I? I wouldn't, of course, and you, with what you've suffered, why would you want to play games? Ozan is dead."

"How do you know?"

"Someone I pay inside the Istanbul police informed me."

"Your friend was fed misinformation. He's alive. He told Turkish police you didn't want to pay a ransom, so you came up with the idea of selling the information on the drone pilot party."

"Nothing could be more untrue."

"Through people he knew of, Ozan made contact with a man who set up a meeting. In the meeting he was told there was great interest."

Smith smiled at that, but his expression was disdainful. "Ozan said this."

"That's what I've been told."

"I see. But you haven't talked to him."

"Others have."

"So they are saying I allowed my building that is uninsured for terrorist acts to have a bomb planted in it to kill the pilots and their families and end my business and life here. And why would I do this? Am I crazy with a religious fever? Is that what you believe?"

"Ozan is willing to testify you discussed selling the information several times before he went looking for the men who would buy it. You pushed him."

"I pushed him?"

"That's what he says."

"I am sure he's not saying that and you are telling me that because the FBI wishes to frame me."

"We're not trying to frame you."

"That's another lie."

Smith grew agitated and when his lawyer reached and touched him again, he turned on the man and said, "Leave the room. Go. I don't want you here anymore."

He folded his arms over his chest and scowled until his lawyer was out of the room.

"My brother-in-law has no credibility. Whenever he talks he is lying. Anytime he speaks it's that way. The two things cannot be separated."

I leaned back in my chair and flipped through my notes.

"Let's talk about your businesses, the juggling of cash flow, the pressure you've been under. Were you offered money for access to the Alagara?"

"You accuse me of such a thing?"

"I'm asking a very direct question. Were you offered money to allow access to the Alagara?"

There was no return from this path, but I was okay with that.

"Ozan said this?" he asked, and in his eyes this time I saw him mocking me. So he knew about Ozan. He saw a texted photo or some other proof. He was letting me know.

"Ozan believed his daughters would be released after the attack," I said. "But you saw something else. What is the phrase they use in chess? 'Think deep'? I believe that's it, think deep. You think about the other side's move, then your move, and the next and the next and beyond. You knew the girls were dead. You'd figured it out."

"I found out today."

"It was confirmed today. That's different. You were aware the kidnapping-ransom negotiation wasn't proceeding in a normal way."

"I know nothing about kidnappings."

"Ozan had met with people who agreed to pay, but of course he couldn't make the deal himself. It wasn't his building. Perhaps you only encouraged Ozan to find out what was possible. You couldn't know that Ozan would actually come up with people who were funded and interested. Is that how it started?"

"You are a fool to try to trick me."

"Here's what I'm guessing. Tell me if I'm wrong. You were told there would be no bomb inside the building. Maybe no bombs at all, maybe just some drone pilots shot in the lot outside the building."

He shook his head at the absurdity of that, yet his face changed. When I saw that, I knew the lawyer was right not to want this interview. Smith had real regrets. He was struggling with himself. I couldn't tell what I had gotten right, but something. I felt a rush of energy.

"Your brother-in-law is under arrest on terrorism charges. He's confessed to providing Al Qaeda in the Arabian Peninsula with the information on the party, and he has testified about conversations he had with you."

He allowed a small smile and the quiet pleasure of saying, "I am very surprised he is talking. The whole world should be shown, though children should not see."

I heard his sarcasm but didn't respond though it confirmed again he knew what we knew. His brother-in-law was dead. The badly decomposed body of Ozan Yildiz was found two days ago. Wild dogs had fed on the body.

"Ozan told you he had a very good offer and that it was time for you to get involved. Maybe with his history of lying, you didn't believe that. You dismissed it as more talk."

"You are circling the same over and over. That you keep saying it does not make it true."

A long silence followed with Smith staring at me. Outside, watching the video feed, they must see it too. He was debating, weighing options, gauging what we had learned, what we would learn, and then made some internal decision. He wore his face like a mask when he spoke again.

"Ozan talked always in ways to provoke me. For years and years he is like this, so I do not take him seriously. I didn't believe he would know how to find the people and sell the information. He always talked about jihad, but all fools talk in a loose way about life and death. It is a characteristic of fools, and what they say doesn't mean anything. All people know this."

"We want to know what you did when Ozan brought the offer to negotiate back to you."

"You're not getting this from him. I want you to say this."

"We're not getting it from Ozan," I said, then paused before trying a different lie. One I thought was plausible.

"Ozan didn't like you any more than you liked him. He didn't trust you. He was afraid of you and what you might do, so who do you think he told? He told someone he knew you wouldn't kill. Your sister is who he told. She went to the Turkish police."

"That is another lie. She despised her husband."

"Yes, she has said so, but he did tell her because he didn't trust you. There's no way out of this, Omar. The cards are falling. It's all coming down around you. This Mansur coming to the Alagara is you wanting to be paid in person. You made it a condition. You wanted to be paid in person if a deal was made. You were surprised they agreed. You gave them access during the day when the building repairs were under way. You were told they wanted to learn the layout. You didn't know they were planting a bomb. You were right to be worried when Mansur moved the meeting time from 10:00 p.m. to just before the party. And you couldn't know he'd leave behind the pickup he'd arrived in."

He didn't acknowledge or answer any of that. He said, "I was trying to save the girls."

"What do you mean?"

"The deal was made and the girls would be released, but not until July 5. I was warned they would be killed if I said anything about the kidnapping to the police. Today, I find out they're dead, so I came here."

"Okay," I said, as if that made sense, but was asking myself again, *What is the real reason he came in today?* A *New York Times* reporter covering the bombings had followed our tracks and gone business-to-business along Lake Mead and wrote that sources said the FBI knew when the pickup carrying the secondary bomb arrived at the Alagara lot. That article ran this morning. It was true. Was he reacting to that? I nodded, then went there.

"From various external video cameras at businesses along Lake Mead Boulevard and from interviews of neighbors, including a neighbor with a third-floor condo on the other side of Mead, we know when the pickup with the bomb arrived. We know the driver pulled into the lot, parked in a slot left for him, and then came inside and met with you. We believe that man, Mansur, is part of a sleeper cell here."

We had a screen in the room and I pointed at it.

"Let me show you some video."

I played the video. There were two short segments of footage of the pickup with the bomb driving along Lake Mead. The first was at 5:40, the next, 101 seconds later. Both caught the driver's head, but all efforts to enhance the face and make the driver identifiable had failed. Working with facial recognition software, we'd tried to match the driver to the man Smith had met with. The probability was 83 percent, but who knows with these software programs. And 83 percent wasn't going to get us anywhere in court. Yet Smith must have met with the man who had delivered the pickup bomb. He would likely claim not to have known what the man calling himself Mansur was driving, but that didn't really matter.

If this Mansur delivered the pickup and then met with Smith, we had a link from him to terrorists. If I were given that foothold, I could get there.

With some drama, I opened a manila folder and removed one of the copies I got from the facial-recognition guys. It was one where they had just overlaid the profile of the man Smith met with on the profile of the driver of the truck. The truck and the profile of the man were easy to read.

"I'm going to let you see what we have. I'm not supposed to, so it's going to be a quick look."

I showed him the images the facial-recognition team overlaid, but I didn't hand it to him. I held it in my left hand out toward the middle of the table. He got a clean five-second view. Long enough to recognize Mansur. Not long enough to see this was facial-recognition techs' experimenting. I slid it back into the file folder and looked at him.

"That's where we're at. Mansur, who you met with, delivered the pickup bomb. He parked on your lot, went inside, and met with you."

"I'm an American the same as you, Agent Grale. I wasn't part of any plot to kill the pilots."

"How did a negotiation for your sister's daughters come to this? How did they get to you?"

"They didn't get to me."

"You needed money to pay the ransom and money to keep your businesses going. Bankruptcy was starting to look very real. Did you go along because you were desperate for money?"

When he didn't answer, I felt I had to acknowledge a different truth.

"You didn't know about the bombs."

I said that and he looked at me and nodded.

"I didn't know."

"But you knew something would happen at the party."

He couldn't bring himself to go there yet, and I didn't make him. I knew he'd broken and it would all come out. It might come in pieces, but he would tell us. He made an odd request.

"Please bring me paper and a pencil."

We got him that and he drew a face in profile. He wasn't an artist and drew and erased the nose several times before he was satisfied. The nose was average in size and with a slight hook, forehead tall, lips full, and chin ordinary. The skin was smooth, so a young man. He slid the sketch over to me. Not a great drawing, but it was a face and he had a point to make.

"This is Mansur," he said. "He looks very different than the one in the photo you showed me."

"How long have you known him?"

"I don't know him."

"Do you know where we should look for him?"

He shook his head then said, "I don't know anything more about him."

I touched the sketch he made and asked, "Did this man introduce himself as Mansur?"

"Yes."

"Had you ever seen him before?"

"No."

"Have you seen him since?"

"No."

"Did he make a payment to you that night?"

"Yes, in my office."

"The money in the safe?"

"Yes."

"Did he say anything about where he lives or where he was going?"

"No, it was only business."

"I believed you when you said a few days ago that you would never leave hundreds of thousands of dollars in a safe if you knew a bombing was about to occur. Maybe you thought some pilots would get shot and that would be it."

He shook his head and tears came. He shut down and wouldn't say any more. He bowed his head. I tried for another ten minutes, then left the room.

51

Two Nye County deputies went out to the airfield the day before to look for the bodies Beatty had reported. In truth, they were looking for Beatty. They didn't find him and left me three messages last night. It was pretty clear they thought I knew where he was. I went looking for Venuti. I found him in a conference room with his laptop and morning coffee.

"You did a good job in there with Smith," Venuti said. "You didn't quite bring it home, but he'll give up the rest. He's done. The question is, will he help us anymore?"

"I'd guess no."

"I agree. Why did he come in today?"

"I've been wondering."

"And what do you think, Grale?"

"Not sure yet. For him it's been about money and keeping his enterprise going. He didn't know his building would get blown apart the way it was. He bargained for something else."

I saw Venuti was waiting for more, but I switched subjects on him.

"I've got three messages from the Nye County deputies. They didn't find anything and it sounded like they were out there looking for Beatty, not bodies. I thought we were getting agents out."

"We don't have anyone available and you're right, the Nye deputies didn't find anything. Strata told us the security pair was fired after what may have been an attempted rape of the French drone pilot. The French pilot doesn't want to talk about it, so I don't know where it's going. The Nye deputies want directions to wherever Beatty is camping. They want a statement on these alleged bodies."

"Beatty told me he's in the mountains behind the airfield."

"They say there are a lot of mountains."

"It's all I've got."

"Why don't you try to reach him and get him to come in?"

Instead, I called the Nye County sheriff's deputy who'd left the message. He described the search they'd made for the black Land Cruiser with bodies in it and made clear he didn't think it was out there.

"We need to interview Beatty. Where do we find him?"

"Check the mountains behind the airfield."

"There's a whole range. What about a phone number?"

"I'll give you the last number that worked. Are you ready?"

"Go ahead, and can I ask you something?"

"Sure."

"Everyone knows this guy should be in custody, so why isn't he?"

"I can't speak for the Bureau, but I think the main reason he's not under arrest is that nothing connects him to the terrorist bombings. That makes it hard to hold him. We're pretty good at working around that, but in this case there doesn't seem to be a good reason yet. If Beatty calls me, I'll tell him he needs to give you a call."

"I'd appreciate that."

Less than an hour later, Beatty called. "Eddie's pickup is still hanging at the flight trailer. It's the only vehicle left there. Everybody else moved out in the night. I saw the lights. I'm going to put you on speakerphone so I can use the binos and scope while we're talking. Can you hear me okay?"

"I hear you fine."

"I could sure use some coffee. Have you got coffee, G-man?"

"I'll bring you some."

"You wouldn't be able to get up this mountain in that car. A sheriff's car was out here yesterday, but they'd already moved the Land Cruiser."

"Two Nye County officers want to get a statement from you about what you saw. Is there a phone number they can call?"

"No."

"Okay, I'll give you their number. Are you ready?"

I read it off and Beatty recited it back to me, but I was sure he hadn't written it down and would never call them.

"Want to read the number back to me?" I asked.

"No, I'm good."

I sat on that a moment. "Did you see the Land Cruiser get moved?"

"Didn't see it, and I'm moving on. I'm out of here today."

"And going where?"

"A long way from here. Hang for a minute, okay? I'm lining up the scope."

Beatty went quiet and I thought about Smith making the decision to take the money and let it happen.

"Okay, I'm looking at the runway and looking into the hangar. The drones are gone."

"Maybe they took them off-site to work on them and they'll bring them back later today."

"They're not bringing them back. It's empty down there."

"If they're working on them, maybe everybody took a break and went into Vegas."

"Eddie's truck is there. He wouldn't leave it there. He loves that truck. He'd sleep with it if he could."

"Nye County sheriff deputies were told Bahn left his truck there and went with a colleague to look at a project up north. He's coming back tomorrow or the next day."

"He'd never leave it. Do you know what he paid for that tricked-out rig?"

I said no and something in my voice must have communicated I wasn't at all interested this morning. But I was very interested in what else he saw.

"Just to confirm," I said. "You don't see any vehicles other than Eddie's truck."

"Roger that, and hold on, I just about have the spotting scope lined up. Almost there."

I closed my eyes and saw Melissa the night of her high school graduation. I heard her say, "I'm out of here, bro, but I'll always be there for you. Always."

"The deputies were right, Grale. The Land Cruiser is gone. Something is going on."

"Tell me more about the drones. You said they move them in semitrucks."

"That's right, 18-wheelers."

"Okay, I'm looking at a tip right now that came in late last night. We're getting tips about one every twenty seconds. This one is from Pahrump. Three semis driving into a warehouse late at night."

"Could fit."

I typed in my name and took ownership of running down the tip, then read it off to Beatty. The Bureau had gone out to the public with Hurin's photo and a general request to report any unusual activity. This tip was from a sixteen-year-old kid in Pahrump who left his cell as the contact number at 2:47 a.m., last night. Danny Cole. In his message he said his father was a trucker, so he knew trucks. Three 18-wheelers had rolled up to a warehouse on the outskirts of Pahrump and, instead of backing up to loading bays, had driven inside. It wasn't three trucks in the middle of the night that he was calling about. It was that they drove inside the warehouse. He'd never seen that before. *Danny Cole is together,* I thought. Whoever he was. He gave an address and a cross street in Pahrump.

"Could they use a warehouse to do the modifications on the drones?" I asked Jeremy.

"It's about equipment more than workspace. The aircraft skin is thin but strong. You need a way to hold it fixed and steady to cut it cleanly."

"I've got a tip to check out. I'll head north now. If I don't catch you on the way out, I'll catch you on the way back. I'll call you either way. When are you coming down from the mountain?"

"Soon, and I'll go by the airfield on my way out."

"How about you hold off on that until we have agents out with you? Strata doesn't want you near their airfield."

"The deputies punted and the pilots are gone. There's no Strata. There's no one left out here but me."

"Don't go there. Wait until you hear from me."

A meeting that included Venuti, Thorpe, and the district attorney and assistants was under way in a conference room. I caught Venuti's eye as I grabbed gear and walked out. On the highway halfway to Indian Wells, I texted him, Gone to check a tip in Pahrump. Beatty says Strata drones and pilots no longer at the airfield. All vehicles except Bahn's truck are gone. Airfield appears deserted.

I called the young man, the tipster, Danny Cole, and told him I was an FBI agent and on my way. Then I called Strata and learned everything was normal at the airfield. They had just talked to the flight instructor, who forwarded a link from a drone on a survey run over the Ghost Mountains.

"Doesn't seem to be a wind problem this morning," the woman told me. "It looks like all of the drones are up. Why are you calling?"

"We had a report that there's no one at the airfield and the drones are gone."

"That report is incorrect. I'm looking at the video feed right now."

"Thank you."

I called Beatty and got him.

"Are you at the airfield?"

"I am and don't bother coming out. There's nothing to see. The door to the trailer is open. I'm inside. Computers are gone. Bahn's truck was unlocked and looks like it's been rooted through. It's like one of those sci-fi movies where everybody is missing, but the coffee is still warm."

"Back out. Don't touch anything. Any blood?"

"Not yet. I'm going to look for the Land Cruiser, but I can't call you from there. There's no cell reception. I'll call you when I get back to where the phone works. Something bad happened out here."

52

I stood outside my car in a lot three blocks from the warehouse as Danny Cole rode up on a skateboard. He was skinny, with stringy blond hair and acne like war paint, but soft-spoken and poised about what he'd seen.

"How did it happen that you were out here at that hour and on foot?"

"Went to a party and my ride home left without me, the fucker, so I walked." He pointed. "I live that way," then added, "like a mile and a half."

We talked for ten to fifteen minutes and when it looked like I had everything I'd get, I thanked him. As Danny rolled away, I called Lacey, who had also been on the phone with Strata this morning.

"I talked to three people there," she said. "They've got a visual feed and everything is normal at the airfield. They talked to Edward Bahn yesterday afternoon. Maybe Beatty is losing it."

"Or maybe their feed is a loop from some other day."

"Or he's trying to lure you."

"Did you get that from Venuti?"

"Well, he could be, right?"

"While we're thinking about this, let me give you some information on a warehouse in Pahrump. We need to find out who owns it and what it's used for. All I have is an address and I'm going to talk to some of the locals, but call me as soon as you have anything."

I texted Lacey the name of the warehouse owner's daughter, which I got from a nearby business owner who told me the father, the owner, had Alzheimer's. She said the daughter controlled everything, in a tone suggesting that wasn't necessarily a good thing. Lacey called back in under half an hour.

"I talked to the daughter. The building is leased to a trucking firm that distributes snack food. The warehouse is used for storing product."

"So it's probably not a lead."

"Probably not."

"I'll ask around a little more before I head to Beatty. Tell Venuti I'll call when I leave here."

Pahrump was maybe thirty-five, forty thousand people, and this warehouse was toward the outskirts. I went into a café, which seemed to have a strong morning business, and asked the owner if there was anyone she knew who lived close by.

"Half of them do, but it doesn't stop them from driving here."

She pointed out a couple of locals who lived near. One of them, a gray-haired, middle-aged woman, told me she saw four trucks leave early this morning, not three.

"I was out looking for my cat. We lose them to coyotes and I don't want to lose Miss Daisy. They left separately, about one every five minutes, heading west at about five a.m., silver 18-wheelers, unmarked, all male drivers."

"You got all that."

"I used to be a dispatcher and I'm nosy." She added, "But trucks come out of there. It's not that unusual. It's a depot and they load up and go from there, though it has been quiet lately. There are two young men who work there that I see in here in the early morning."

"When did you start seeing them?"

"A couple of weeks ago."

"Anything about them stand out?"

"Not really. They could be from around here."

"I'm going to need a way to get in touch with you."

She gave me a phone number, and I gave it to Lacey when I called her as I left Pahrump.

"There may be somebody else using the building that the owner's daughter doesn't know about. If you can, get the company she leases to."

"She gave it to me."

"Look into them."

I called Beatty and his voice was slowed, but that made sense once he started talking.

"I found their bodies. Eddie is there too. He was shot. They're partially covered, not too far from where the Land Cruiser was yesterday."

"How did you find them?"

"I drove out to the landmark I've been using to sight on the Land Cruiser and then looked around. Eddie was shot there. There's blood in the sand near his head."

"Tell me again how you knew where to look."

"I memorized a rock when I was trying to look into the Land Cruiser with the spotting scope. It's white and looks like a shark's fin."

"Text me a photo of it."

"You don't need it, I've got coordinates. I'll send you those."

"Are you okay waiting with the bodies?"

"No, there's no phone reception out there. I'll take you there."

"Where are you now?"

"On top of the hills on the road out of the airfield."

"You're leaving there?"

"Pretty soon. What did you find in Pahrump?"

"If you leave, you can't go far. You'll need to lead us to the bodies."

"I know."

Beatty was waiting, and I went with my gut and everything I knew about him, despite being troubled that Strata reported everything as fine at the airfield. I flashed on the possibility that Jeremy went back to the airfield and killed the security guards and Eddie Bahn, and then made up a story about the trucks leaving in the night with the drones.

"In Pahrump someone saw trucks like you described leave early this morning."

"They didn't come here."

"I've been listening to you, so I know that. I have to ask you to stay where you are, Jeremy. I'll call you back soon."

I called back fifteen minutes later as I drove south on 95. "Walk me through again how these drones are shipped in trucks and put back together."

"It's easy. They were designed to be shipped anywhere in the world. The wings slide in and get locked in place with screws. The fuselage isn't that heavy. Comes apart in reverse."

"How long to reassemble?"

"A four-man team with the right tools could do it in ten minutes."

"I'm not that far from the turnoff toward you, but there's some big slowdown on the highway up ahead. Cars and trucks are stacking up. Dammit, it's some sort of accident. I may be trapped out here."

"Put the bubble lights on and run up the shoulder."

"Yeah, no wait a minute, something else is going on. Jeremy, could the drones use the highway as a runway?"

"You bet."

"I might be looking at that. I've got to make a quick call then get back to you."

53

"Where are you?" Venuti asked.

"Southbound on 95, looking at an accident or something up ahead. Beatty found the bodies of Eddie Bahn and the two security guards."

"Maybe he found them where he left them."

"Each was shot multiple times. He texted me coordinates. I'll forward those to you. The bodies are a third to a half mile down a dirt track that runs south from the westernmost part of the Strata airfield. He was at the airfield when he called me and says it's empty—no drones, no pilots, nothing. They're gone."

"That contradicts what Strata just told us."

"It does."

"And you believe Beatty?"

"He's there."

"The doctor who treated him for PTSD told us Beatty is delusional and paranoid. You were in the room when he said it. Don't go out to the airfield. Is that clear?"

"It's clear. Hey, Dan, I'm not sure what's going on up ahead, about a third of a mile, but it looks like a semi is parked across the highway blocking the southbound lanes."

"So like you just said, an accident."

"There's another big rig up ahead of it with some sort of activity around it."

"Probably trying to help the one stuck behind it."

"This truck nearest me looks like it's parked to block the southbound lanes. It's not jackknifed. I don't see signs of an accident. This is near the Mercury exit where the highway divides into separated north and southbound lanes. Vehicles are stacking up behind it."

"It's somebody's idea of a protest."

"Could be," I said, though it didn't have that vibe. "I'm going to pull over. I'm where I can still turn around. Listen, I just checked out a tip on trucks in and out of a warehouse in Pahrump last night. Beatty says the drones get disassembled and moved out in semis when they work on them at night. They take them somewhere."

"So what?"

"I'm saying it because Strata says that's not happened."

"Well, Beatty reported the airfield had no drones on it, or whatever the hell he said when they had them up and flying on video feed. I don't know why you've been so—"

"Dan, I think I just heard gunfire. Put me on hold and call the highway patrol. Something is happening here."

Venuti cleared his throat. His tone changed.

"How far are you from Indian Wells?"

I glanced at my GPS.

"Fourteen point seven miles, but I can't get there without getting to the Mercury exit and onto the northbound side."

I looked ahead at the northbound lanes. Where I was, I could do a U-turn and be headed northbound. Up ahead the highway divided and had guardrail where it crossed above the Mercury exit. I reached for binoculars and Venuti asked, "Are you in that daylight testing area where you're supposed to turn your headlights on?"

"Yeah, right at the edge of it, close to the Mercury off-ramp. The trucks are blocking the section that has guardrail. Put me on hold and call the highway patrol."

Highway 95 runs through open desert and can be empty, but not this empty. Not at this time of day. I had yet to see a northbound vehicle.

"Ask the highway patrol if they've got a spotter plane in the area," I said.

"Stay on the line. It's going to take a few minutes."

Venuti put me on hold, and I pulled onto the northbound side and drove slowly along the outside lane, ready to get onto the road shoulder should any northbound traffic appear coming at me. When Venuti came back on, I had a better view.

"They have a plane up, but it's ten to fifteen minutes out," Venuti said.

"That's too long."

"That's what it is."

"Hold on—"

"What?"

"Shooting. I just heard more gunfire."

"What do you see?"

"Activity ahead of the second semi. I see people outside and it looks like they're doing something, but I can't tell yet. I don't have a good enough view. We'd better alert our SWAT guys."

"Whoa, we don't know any—"

"Yeah, I can see more. Hang on."

I accelerated and approached the Mercury overpass fast and dropped down the on-ramp headed the wrong way. Just as I dipped down, I saw a man on the overpass above with an assault rifle trying to line up on me.

I made a hard left turn onto the road to Mercury as bullets battered the trunk. My tires squealed as I swung back and forth on the two-lane road toward Mercury.

"What was that?" Venuti asked.

"That was somebody shooting at me. I'm on the Mercury Highway headed east but am going to cut south on a dirt track that I know is up ahead and try to circle back around. I saw one, maybe two, of the Strata drones on the highway pointed southbound. Call Creech and warn them. If I'm wrong, I'm wrong, but they're not going to have much time."

"Can you verify a drone is on the highway?"

"I just did."

"Protect yourself. No unnecessary risks. I'm putting you on hold."

What I remembered was a lone building out here, just before a government sign warning that no one was allowed beyond that point. Off to the right was a dirt track running south. I overran on the first pass then got on it without knowing how far south it went, but I wasn't far from the highway and there were guns in the trunk. I could cut through the sage on foot.

Venuti came back on and asked, "Where are you?"

"I'm southbound on a dirt track paralleling the highway on the north side. I can see three drones and people assembling them. I count five people and a sniper lying on the roof of the forward truck. Shit, he's turning to me."

"Grale, protect yourself. That's an order. Get out. Get down. Do not engage unless there's no other way."

The sniper would be shooting from behind at a hard cross angle, but he was good. Scared the shit out of me as the windshield took a hit. Big bullet. Loud. Then the back window was gone, glass fragments all over the interior. I slammed on the brakes as I neared a stand of brush and cactus. As best I could, I blocked his view of the car, popped the trunk, and rolled out as another bullet hit. That one punched the engine and steam boiled up. I stayed low, belly-crawled the hot dirt, and reached the trunk as the sniper put two rounds through the trunk lid.

In the trunk were a shotgun, rifle, and ammo. I had only my handgun otherwise. I lay quiet twenty or thirty seconds and could feel the sniper scanning for me. I rose where I didn't think he had an angle and freed the rifle. I grabbed ammo and waited for the sniper to shift away from me.

With my car stopped and a door open, he might swing away to another target. That could give me a window to cover fifty yards to a larger rock outcrop close to the road. I used my binoculars to watch and when he shifted, I scrambled and ran, though there's no way to run fast in desert dirt and sand. He swung back and I dove and belly-crawled the last ten yards.

I was out of breath, heart hammering, as I edged forward and saw a drone with its wings on, and wings being bolted onto the one behind it. One, two, three drones being assembled, pointing south on the highway less than a quarter mile from me.

My phone buzzed. Venuti.

"I'm behind a rock outcrop maybe two-tenths of a mile from the drones. The sniper has me pinned, but I'm safe for now. I'm looking at a drone on the highway with two more lined up behind it. The lead has its wings on. Five guys are working on the other two. Each of the other two has a wing on. Two people are in the cab of the truck. One is female and could be a pilot who was at the Strata field. The truck cab might be where they'll fly the drones from."

"You're pinned down?"

"Yeah, and now I've got another problem. Looks like two guys with guns are heading my way. They're along the highway shoulder."

"Can you get yourself out of there?"

"Not yet, the sniper is on me. How long until the cavalry gets here?"

"At least fifteen minutes, probably more like twenty. Give me more on the location of this sniper who's got you pinned."

I did that as I watched the pair creeping toward me. I also gave him more on the drones.

"These are the three drones from the Strata airfield. I'll video them. Get someone on the phone with Strata. Maybe they know a way to disable them."

I took a stinging graze from a bullet along my left bicep when I held my phone up to get the video. It dripped steady blood and stung as I skirted cactus to get to another rock outcrop with better cover. My bicep burned, and the two guys coming for me looked experienced, but they'd have to cross with almost no cover to reach me. I took another quick look and heard a distant pop, pop, pop of gunfire from where the southbound traffic was trapped. I heard faraway screams.

I saw that the pair coming for me were going to take the risk and do it. One stood at the edge of the road shoulder, gun held above his head, emptying clips and spraying bullets around me as the other ran in a crouch with an AK-47 in his hands. I got a look at his face through the scope, just before centering on his torso. It was the young man, Mansur, whom Smith had sketched. I caught his running pace, led him, and squeezed as gunfire ripped through cactus near me.

My bullets hit, but he was tough. He went first to his knees. The gun fell away and I watched him pick it up again and start a slow crawl toward me. A long string of rounds came from the other gunman, and when I looked back at Mansur he was on his feet again, but I could see he wouldn't get here. His gun sagged as he staggered forward.

The sniper with his big gun chipped rock way too close to me, so I scrambled again, crawling as fast as I could through burning sand littered with cactus spines. I laid the phone down, looked for the second gunman, and caught my breath before talking to Venuti.

"SWAT is on the way," he said. "So is everybody else. Have you backed away?"

"No, and the wings are on the third drone, and no one is working on the first anymore. Can the air force get a fighter up?"

"Trying to get approval right now. What about the two coming for you?"

"I'm down to one, but he's getting close. I've gotta lay the phone down."

The second shooter had gone well up the road, and it looked to me like he was counting on the sniper to protect him as he circled in. A tiny stand of desert trees hid him for a moment, and I sighted along a stretch ahead of him. If he kept going, he'd cross into my line of sight. I stayed focused on a patch where the road shoulder met the edge of dry gray soil and tried to breathe slow and deep. When he came around those small trees, he should see me lying here. I needed to shoot well without thinking and took another breath, and then there he was, tan pants, white shirt, and the gun barrel swinging toward me.

My shot caught him liver-high and he sprayed bullets off to his left as he sat down. But he wasn't quite done. Like the first man, he slowly stood as if making some sort of statement. My next shot puckered his shirt just beneath his sternum. "Try that," I said.

When his legs collapsed, I picked up my phone. Venuti was agitated, high energy, and I was jittery. My hand holding the phone shook.

"There's a blockade like yours, but without drones, stopping northbound traffic. A handheld missile there brought down the Nevada Highway Patrol spotter plane. They're holding all aircraft except our SWAT."

"I got the second shooter. Hold on, Beatty's calling me."

"Assume he's with them. Do not give him anything."

I switched to Beatty's call.

"Jeremy, where are you?"

Beatty's response broke up.

"Say again."

Now his voice was clearer, and I could tell he had me on speakerphone.

"I'm coming hard up the southbound side of 95. Where are you?"

"On the north with a good view of the southbound lanes. Three drones are nose to tail out in front of an 18-wheeler. Two have their wings on, and the last one is almost there. Same drones you were flying."

Beatty asked, "What do you think the target is?"

"Creech."

"We can't let that happen."

"Creech knows. They're taking action. You worked years there. Does Creech have a way to shoot them down?"

Beatty didn't answer right away, and when he did his voice was low and quieter. I could hear him, but it was as if he'd taken a step back.

"They do and they don't," he said. "These will come in low and fast."

"Where are you? There's a sniper on top of the trailer of that semi. Our SWAT squad is airborne and will deal with him, so hang back. Keep your truck away. Tell me how else we can disable these drones. Are they operating them from the truck? I see two people in the truck cab."

"Those are the pilots."

"I'll try to put shots through the truck cab windshield."

"I see it all now," Beatty said.

When I turned and looked down the highway, I saw his truck, small but coming fast.

"Pull over and talk to me about how we disable these."

"Is your SWAT team coming?"

"They're coming. Do they target the truck not the drones? These things may get in the air before they get here."

I lifted the rifle to take a shot at the cab, and the sniper almost got me. The bullet sounded like a loud bumblebee going by. I ducked and told Beatty, "Definitely two in the cab."

"Then that's it."

"What's it?"

There was a pause and I heard Beatty talking as if to Laura and then himself. I kept my head down but twisted and watched his pickup closing. When Beatty spoke again, his voice was even and clear.

"You see the lead drone rolling, right, Grale?"

"I see it and I'm still trying to get a shot at the truck cab without getting killed."

"I can't let this happen," he said, and only then did I understand and yell into my phone, "Pull over! We've called Creech. They know. Our SWAT copters will get here, we'll take out the cab."

"Your SWAT isn't here."

"Creech will shoot them down."

"It's not that easy."

"Jeremy! Jeremy, listen. I need your help!"

"You're going to get it."

Beatty centered on the two highway lanes. His engine roared as he passed by and the first drone lifted off. The second started to roll and I sighted on the sniper whose focus now was the pickup. I heard Beatty say, "Clear my name. Give me your word."

"Hit the brakes. Pull over. Blackhawks are on the way."

After I squeezed the trigger, the second drone lifted off and the roof of Beatty's pickup caught its tail. That made a hard, bright slapping sound and the drone still rose, though its left wing dropped as its shadow swept overhead. A deafening explosion came seconds later when it pinwheeled into the desert south of me.

Jeremy's pickup hit the third drone straight on. The explosion was loud, dense, and sharp. Debris rained and clattered onto the highway and median. A big cactus to my left was cut down. The blazing chassis of Beatty's pickup careened off the highway, flipped, and kept burning. I saw multiple bodies on the highway and the sniper lying on his side, still on the truck roof with his long gun and a pool of blood spreading around his head. I saw the cab of the truck burst into flames.

When I was sure the sniper wouldn't be doing anything very fast, I staggered to my feet and out to the highway, and then walked through smoke with my gun ready. Down the highway I heard a firefight at the other truck. I heard sirens. I walked toward the burning cab of the truck and saw only bodies.

Jeremy was dead. I saw what he did, and yet I looked for him as if somehow he'd be alive. There was nothing left of the pickup except burning tires and chassis. Inside the semi's cab I saw two shapes, both sitting upright and wreathed in fire that roared and was too hot to get close to.

A Blackhawk helicopter passed by fast and low, then swung around and landed. SWAT agents jumped out with guns on me, then ran past, moving on.

I went body to body and found one man alive. He was on his back but bleeding internally, his fingers tracing a distended belly as if exploring something new and interesting. I looked at his other wounds and guessed he had maybe five minutes. I couldn't do anything for him and he just stared when I questioned him. When he lost consciousness, I walked away.

After the fire was extinguished, I looked in the truck cab at the two blackened bodies, one big enough to be the Eastern European pilot, but no way to ID either. The heat off the still-smoldering cab was enough to make you squint and more than enough to have heated the truck's cargo bed, yet I still had hope and waited at the cargo doors as the SWAT guys approached.

"If there's anyone in there alive, we want to keep them alive."

54

No one talked. It was unsaid that the quieter we did this, the safer. A SWAT agent carved insulation off the bottom of the truck's rear door and everybody got to the side or down as a probe slid under the door. Not too far, maybe a foot in, then it sat there reading for infrared but there was just too much heat from the truck cab to know for sure. A video camera with a light and a long cable replaced it. We backed away as the cable spooled out. We hunkered down and I thought about Beatty in the seconds before the light lit up the interior cargo area.

A man lay motionless on the truck's empty bed. There was gear and a backpack that could hold a bomb. The probe slid closer. Close enough for me, yet I hesitated as I tried to make sense of what we were seeing. When it hit me, I said, "That's Garod Hurin, the bomb maker. Looks like they were holding him."

"Got it," somebody said. "What's in the backpack?"

"I can see into it. It's empty, and there's no workspace, not even a chair. They locked him in there. Maybe they wanted to see everything work. Let's open it up. I'll go in. I'll recheck the backpack, so let me go first. But I'm not worried. I can see inside it from here."

The doors were opened and a robot lifted up and in. It checked the backpack before I clambered up with one of the SWAT guys. It was like climbing into an oven. Hard to breathe, and the heat from the metal truck bed came right through my shoes.

Yet Hurin still had a pulse. We pulled him out, lowered him, and two paramedics made a hard run at saving him. A hypodermic needle punched in as a final effort to stimulate his heart. It failed, and the CPR that followed failed.

"All yours," one of the paramedics said. "We've got someone else with a gunshot wound that needs help. This one here is gone, dude."

I knelt. I talked to Hurin, but I was talking to a corpse. Drool and blood had spooled from the sides of his mouth. His bowels had released and he stank. The backpack was empty and one of the SWAT guys and I searched his body, and then the truck bed again. We didn't find anything—no laptop, no secret notebook, no phone with addresses and numbers, nothing, not even ID. When I climbed back down, I leaned over him. His eyes stared up at the sky. He had a thin goatee and artful sideburns. He could have been a thirty-something in a plaid shirt and jeans waiting in line in an upscale coffee shop. Nothing in his look said bomb maker. I wanted it to, but it wasn't there. He could have been anyone. There was something frightening in that, but I didn't linger on it.

We left the body on the pavement. A photographer recorded him from all angles, then stepped over him. I could have covered him before leaving. Someone bigger than me might have, but I didn't. I left him like trash.

Two trucks had blocked the northbound lanes, same as here. Thirteen civilians, five Nevada Highway Patrol officers, including two in the downed spotter plane, and five terrorists died in the firefight there. Seven civilians and thirteen terrorists, including Hurin, died on this side. A trucker was credited with preventing more deaths by exchanging fire with the terrorists, wounding one and giving trapped drivers a chance to escape on foot. A cop told me later that same trucker three weeks ago had threatened his estranged wife with the same gun.

Two wounded terrorists, one from the northbound blockade and the other the man the trucker shot, were at Creech Air Force Base receiving medical care. Neither spoke English. One said he'd crossed from Mexico three days ago. No one had said it publicly yet, but in the Bureau we were shocked by how many terrorist actors there were. ID'ing them would be a priority.

In Pahrump, ten pounds of C-4 was recovered from the warehouse. I wasn't there for that. Venuti and Thorpe wanted me at the office. I passed on a helicopter ride out and didn't leave the highway with a couple of bomb techs I knew until after finding Beatty's remains. I made sure they were covered and marked. I walked one of the ERT over and showed her how I'd identified him.

"He was with them, right?" she asked.

"No, he was one hundred percent with us."

"One hundred?"

"One hundred. He stopped two of the three drones. He gave himself for us."

She looked puzzled by that, and it tipped me to the early narrative. I got more as I talked with Venuti on my phone on the ride back to Vegas.

"The media is making you a hero, Grale."

"But you'll fix that."

Venuti laughed, but it was a laugh of relief. Truth was, Venuti would fix it, no question. But we didn't go there. We moved on to Hurin.

"Are you certain it's him?"

"It's him. They're bagging his body. He died not long after we found him. He took bad shrapnel wounds when Beatty's pickup hit the last drone straight on and everything blew. Shrapnel perforated the side of the truck and he caught a piece in the head. My ears are still ringing from the explosion. There's nothing left of Jeremy's truck but the chassis. He clipped the second drone and it crashed across the highway. He hit the third straight on."

"He switched back to our side in the end?"

"Don't be a jerk, Dan. He was always there. You know he was always there. I was on the phone with him as he came up the highway. I couldn't talk him out of it."

Venuti didn't respond to that, instead asked about my arm wound, which stung but had been cleaned and bandaged. We talked about Creech, where the drone had reached a flight trailer and killed two drone pilots who'd gone back to the trailer to retrieve gear. The explosion had destroyed the trailer and heavily damaged another. I was sorry to hear about the pilots.

"Between you and me, they disobeyed orders to go back in and get their gear," Venuti said.

Okay, I thought, *but that doesn't change anything.*

"Didn't Creech see the drone coming?" I asked.

"It's unclear. We know it came in very low. We have eyewitnesses in Indian Wells who saw it arrive." Venuti paused and I knew what was coming. "Why do you think the targeting was so precise and who is it that knew which trailers were which?"

"With Google Earth and a little bit more information you can get there. It's not that hard."

"Here's another question. Our agents found two middle-aged male bodies in a Dumpster at the warehouse in Pahrump. Any guesses?"

"They may be the mechanics who modified the drones."

"Where's Edward Bahn in all this?"

"You're asking my opinion?"

"We're being asked to put it together tonight."

"He was there for money and didn't know what was going down."

"Where are you getting that?"

"From what Jeremy told me."

"How is that credible?"

"Why wouldn't it be?"

"Okay, what did Beatty the hero tell you?"

"That Bahn was pushing him hard to take ownership of hiring the drone pilots. Bahn threatened to come to us with stories of a drunken Beatty in a bar talking about getting even with the air force. He figured we would lap it up, and he was probably right." I waited a beat and added, "Beatty sent me an audio file. I copied you. Did you listen to it?"

Instead of answering that, he said, "There are times I wonder if you're really one of us. Bahn is dead. A helicopter crew found his body and the security pair. We're out there now. I wish we had Beatty's handgun to compare ballistics."

"If it was in his truck, it can be found. I'd like to find it too, so we can finally end this bullshit talk about him. And you're right. You don't know it, but you're right—he's the only hero in this."

"Call me when you leave the hospital. You get debriefed tonight, so go easy on any painkillers."

"I don't need to go to a hospital."

"You're going."

At the hospital a nurse pulled cactus needles out of my forearms, and they ran me through radiology looking for a bone break before cleaning and redressing the gouge on my arm. It had cut through some muscle and went about a half-inch deep. My arm throbbed. It was tender and didn't want to be moved. After the wound was cleaned and wrapped again, I rode the elevator up to Julia's room.

"Uncle Paul, I'm so glad you're okay."

"I'm okay and I've got to go get debriefed, but I want you to know we're getting you out of here tomorrow morning. We'll go from here to your family's house."

When her tears started, I was sure it was about going to the house, but I was wrong.

"You got them, Uncle Paul."

"Yeah, we got them."

Eighteen terrorists, including the three drone pilots Beatty was training, and Garod Hurin were dead, but more than half were part of a sleeper cell in Las Vegas. A phone one of the terrorists had led to a raid on a house in Henderson and two in Vegas. That was cause for a lot of disquiet in our office, but I could catch up on that later. I went from the hospital to a debriefing that lasted until sundown. By then the media had declared it a tragedy, but an American victory.

America persevered. America fought back. The FBI had cracked the plot and prevented a significant attack that might have crippled the vital drone program. An FBI special agent named Paul Grale, whose sister and family had died in the Bar Alagara attack, was a hero. Former drone pilot Jeremy Beatty also played a role, but his involvement was under investigation. A longtime TV terrorism expert termed Beatty's action a suicidal attempt at redemption, but the media sensed something was off and pushed to interview me. They'd gotten my home number, and Jo screened those calls when I got home.

Then I took a call from Venuti, who told me the FBI director was flying out, and a press conference was scheduled for early afternoon tomorrow.

"You need to be there. We may let the media talk with you. Are you ready for that?"

"I'm fine with it. Are you?"

"Dress for it. It's national TV. It'll probably go global. The SAC and ASAC will stand behind you with the director. It may not be appropriate, but they're asking if your niece can be there."

"It's not appropriate."

"Your call."

"I just made it."

"It might be healing for her."

"It'll be a circus."

"Okay," he said, but he was disappointed and the Bureau wanted the photo op of us standing together, two survivors, the young niece and the career-agent uncle. A storybook ending that I was fucking up. He huffed and stalled a little, then finished with "Paul, from all of us here, thank you. We'll see you tomorrow."

55

Toward midnight Jo and I ate a pizza and drank beer, sitting at the iron table by the lap pool. The night was warm. Not long after eating, Jo waded into the pool, but I just wanted to sit and be. Her hair was cut shorter than six months ago, and as she left the water it dried straight and flat against her head. Her face looked beautiful in the soft yellow light. She wrapped a towel loosely around her body, sat down close to me and gently removed the bandage on my arm. She inspected the wound and added some unneeded ointment. She didn't need to do that, but it calmed me to feel her touch.

"Promise me you'll keep being lucky," she said as she rewrapped it. "How's your head?"

"I'm okay but sorry we didn't put it together before the drone attack."

"You fault yourself?"

"Sure." I paused, then said, "I'm sad about Jeremy. I was talking to him. I tried to stop him."

"Maybe he saw it as the only way."

I tried another slice of anchovy pizza. The taste was sharp and salty and the beer cool and sweet behind it. Death wasn't Jeremy's only way out. In ten years, who knows where he would have been? He was getting there before all this. He would have made it. I laid the pizza slice down.

"All of the drones would have launched if not for Jeremy. In the last seconds I was yelling at him to pull over. I heard him say, 'Clear my name.'"

"The FBI will do that, won't they?"

"Months from now after the investigation is complete, and it'll be muddy. He was a person of interest and he won't be around to defend himself."

Jo reached over and placed her hand on mine.

"Are you going to say something tomorrow? Is that what you're telling me?"

"I'm thinking about it. Even after his hard ending with the air force and the drone strike that killed Hakim Salter, Jeremy still believed the truth would take care of itself. I think that's why he got stuck on Salter's death and couldn't get past it. He was very down about being questioned by us and assaulted by the media. He didn't see a future." My mind tripped forward. "He didn't sound afraid. His voice was clear."

"Where are you going with this?"

"I'm not sure yet."

"You're talking about Jeremy, but you're thinking about Julia too."

"How do you know that?"

"I just know you."

"Crossing the Bureau tomorrow could get me transferred to North Dakota."

"That wouldn't be good for her."

"It would be different."

"No kidding."

I sat on that a minute, then said, "I've got to say something. I've got to speak for Jeremy."

She was quiet. She saw problems with that and asked, "Is tomorrow the right time to do that?"

"If I don't, his story will get written the wrong way."

"You don't know that."

"The media doesn't like to admit mistakes any more than the Bureau does."

We left it there. The next morning Julia wanted to walk out of the hospital, but for legal reasons related to prior lawsuits, they wouldn't let her. They brought her out in a wheelchair and, in defiance, she stepped out of it before it reached the curb. She didn't want anyone's help getting into my car, yet she was trembling as she fumbled with her seat belt.

"Are you sure, Julia?"

"I'm sure."

"If we don't do this, you'll remember them the way they were when they were alive."

"I know, but I have to."

She couldn't know but was still adamant about seeing them. I had called ahead, and they were waiting at the morgue. The smell was as it always was in the morgue, but it was new to her, and I saw her react and shiver in the cold air and cringe at smells she'd never forget.

"My mom, my dad, and then Nate," she said, and the drawers were opened one at a time, the rubber pulled back to show only their faces. Julia registered shock. A voice inside me said, *This is wrong; you shouldn't have let her do this.*

Yet Julia's voice remained strong as she said, "Good-bye, Mom, I love you forever," and that drawer shut. It clicked closed. She said the same thing to her dad, and I got a glimpse of the woman she would grow into. I saw strength. I saw Melissa and Jim in her and felt a surge of grief for everything. Nate was last. She leaned over him and whispered something I didn't hear.

We walked out, back into bright heat and into the too-hot car, and she wept as we drove away, but also thanked me and told me she was glad we had gone. I put an arm around her as we parked and got out at the family house.

As we stood on the driveway, Julia said, "After the bomb I didn't remember anything about the party. I still don't."

I nodded. Investigators were frustrated but hopeful her memory would return. They looked to me to make it happen.

"Uncle Paul, I had to see them. I had to know."

"That they were really dead?"

"Yes."

Though the family always entered through the back gate, Julia wanted to go in the front. She unlocked it with her key. Inside it was cool and dark, and Julia turned toward the kitchen as we stepped in, as if expecting Coal to come running, before remembering we were picking him up next. I moved into the kitchen and let her return to the house in her own way.

She seemed at a loss and sat down on a couch, then rose silently and walked into her brother's room. I heard her break down there. Her wracking sobs brought a great wave of sadness up through me and I opened the door to the backyard. I stepped out, smelling the chlorine in the pool and the dusty heat of a summer morning, another day in Las Vegas. From the corner of my eye through the slider I saw her pass wraithlike, a shadow crossing the living room on her way to her parents' bedroom.

Later, when I checked on her, I saw Jim's air force dress coat and cap lying on the bed and Julia sitting at her mother's makeup station with several photos alongside her. Her fingers traced the face of her dad. She trembled as tears dripped off her cheeks. I wanted to put my arm around her, but backed quietly out of the room instead. An hour later she came out into the backyard with two suitcases and sat down across from me.

"We'll come back until you have everything you want," I said.

"I don't know what to do, Uncle Paul." Through her tears she repeated, "What do I do?"

"You say good-bye and then you carry them forever. Can you remember their voices?"

"Yes."

"Then talk to them."

"Even though they're not here?"

"Yes."

We picked up Coal, who charged Julia and almost knocked her down. Coal hadn't forgotten her at all. He was wondering who'd forgotten him. I made peace with Patricia and Charlie, thanking them for their kindnesses. From news reports they seemed to think I was a kind of hero, which wasn't true at all. We left things in a good place and Coal nuzzled my hand with a sort of "Glad you also showed up, buddy, I guess you're good for something" and then ran back to Julia. She wrapped her arms around him and he rode in the front seat with us as we drove away.

We share in grief and ritualize letting go and moving on, but at heart, all true grief is private. There was only so much I could do for Julia, yet I knew from watching her she'd find her way.

"Uncle Paul, do we have time for one more stop? I saw the flowers on TV."

She didn't have to say any more. I turned at the next corner and backtracked to the Alagara. As we got close, I had to tell her, "We won't have long. There's a press conference I have to be at."

"I just need to see."

I understood. At the Alagara there were people taking photos. I parked down the street and we walked back and caught a moment there when it was just us. There were many different types of flowers and maybe a thousand roses. The air was rich with their scent. Since I was last here, someone had made a peace sign in the lot with white roses. We stood for a little while, then I looked at her.

"Uncle Paul, is it okay if I take some flowers?"

"Take whatever you want, Julia."

She knelt and sorted white roses until she had three she liked and laid them in her palm one on one on one with great tenderness. Then we walked away.

Jo was waiting when we got to my house. She and Julia would pack while I was at the press conference. I wore a dark blue suit and the white shirt the director liked. I stood alongside Venuti, who right down to the buff shine on his shoes looked dressed for an inauguration.

"You've got to do this the right way," Venuti said with the pompousness I've never liked. "This is a Bureau interview, not a Paul Grale interview. Don't fuck it up. Be the humble hero and don't go anywhere you'll regret."

The director spoke first then introduced me. I stood at a temporary podium and faced reporters, some who I recognized from national TV. I picked Kelly Raley first. Her hair was ginned up and her makeup deft. It gave her face gravitas without looking somber.

"Special Agent Grale, I'm speaking as an American when I say we all want to thank you."

"I was just one of many in law enforcement working together."

"You had a special role. How did you know the drone attack was coming?"

"A former air force drone pilot, Lieutenant Jeremy Beatty, alerted me. He saw things at a private airfield that worried him. I've known him for years and trusted him, so I listened and followed up on what he gave us."

"Let me get this straight, you're saying the ex–drone pilot Beatty helped the FBI?"

"Yes. He did."

"We're hearing he was being investigated for espionage and possible collusion with the terrorists."

"He stumbled into a DOD investigation by test-flying drones in Taiwan. I think the Department of Defense will acknowledge that he had no espionage role."

"Could he have been among the plotters here, then changed his mind?"

"I'm not aware of any facts supporting that. Prior to the attack he raised concerns about the pilots and after he was fired from his instructor's job, he continued to pass on information. From a position where he was camping, he observed that the pilots and drones were gone and called me. That proved to be critical, and you know what he did when he found out the drones were on the highway."

"Some have called that a suicidal attempt at redemption."

"Yeah, I heard that, but I was talking with him as he drove toward the drones."

"Why does the Bureau account differ from yours?"

I paused and looked out at the expectant faces. Behind me, the director cleared his throat. When I didn't answer fast enough, Kelly Raley moved on.

"We're hearing from sources that a gun he owned was used to kill the security guards and the job broker Edward Bahn. He then discovered the bodies."

"Your sources don't have that information. They're speculating."

"One of those sources is well up in the Bureau."

"Give me a name and I'll brief that person."

That elicited some nervous laughs, and I knew with that comment, I'd crossed a line. I should back down.

"What about the targeting of cities on the computers in his trailer?"

"That was training software for teaching drone pilots. You can find much worse things in video games your kids play."

"Does your personal connection color your view?"

I nodded.

"Sure, it does. I had known Jeremy for years. He was the real deal and loved the air force but developed a problem with civilian casualties that came to a head with the drone strike that killed the American schoolteacher Hakim Salter. I remember you reporting that story, Kelly, after the family challenged the official version."

She nodded.

"Lieutenant Beatty launched the missile that killed the Taliban in the courtyard and Hakim Salter. He had issues with that. It led to a breakdown and what's called 'kill inhibition.' He struggled, no question Jeremy struggled, and continued to after his discharge, but look at what he did when he thought drones were targeting Creech Air Force Base."

An audible murmur passed through the crowd, and I knew I was out on my own. I pointed at another reporter, though behind me feet shuffled. The signal was there. Cut it off.

"Sir, the Salter drone strike you're referencing has been reviewed and validated," the reporter said.

"I can't comment on the validation process, but the pilot who participated in the strike with Lieutenant Beatty agrees with Beatty's account of events. I've talked to him. But I'm getting off topic here. Any other questions?"

I nodded toward another reporter and took his question.

"Special Agent Grale, you've given us a very different version of Beatty's role yesterday."

"All I can do is tell you what I saw and what I know of the evidence. From what I know, from the leads I worked from, I'd call Jeremy Beatty a hero."

That caused a buzz among the reporters.

"You said you were on the phone with him as he drove toward the drones. Can you tell us what he said?"

"You'll have to wait for the phone transcripts to be released, but I can tell you I tried to get him to stop his truck and protect himself."

"Sir, individuals at various law enforcement agencies, not just the FBI, have implied charges would come and that Jeremy Beatty was a co-conspirator."

"Is that a question?"

"I guess the question is, how can your version be so different?"

"That I can answer. I was there."

I stared out at the room and behind me, Venuti's voice was low and hard. "End it."

On the ride back to the field office, Venuti said, "You're going to get extended leave and you're not to do any interviews. Zero. No reporters. Not the one that calls you from LA or that cute TV reporter here, none of them. Talk to them and you're fired. As it is, you may want to clear out your desk so it isn't done for you. Throw it all in a box and show it to me and I'll walk you to the door."

"So I'm gone?"

Venuti wouldn't answer.

"When does this leave start?"

"It starts when you drive off the lot. Don't show up tomorrow thinking you're needed for something. You're not. You were way over the line there. As a matter of fact, you've always been over the line. You're a street agent who has always had one foot out the door. You flout the rules. You—"

"Out there is where it all happens, Dan."

"We all make choices. You made another today, same as you chose to go to Iraq and defuse bombs. What you can get away with in our office is different than what you get away with in a national press conference. You directly contradicted a Bureau position in an ongoing investigation."

"The Bureau is investigating. It doesn't have a position yet."

"Okay, Grale, whatever you say."

Venuti exhaled hard but said nothing as we pulled into the field office garage. Upstairs, he left me alone at my desk. There were only a few photos, but they mattered. I found a small box and put the photos and an ancient leather-bound notebook and a camera I liked in it. There were other smaller tokens and talismans that I sorted and dropped in. I put the electronic devices the Bureau would want to wipe clean in an upper drawer. Into my box, I put the small wooden plaque my nephew, Nate, had made. It carried the Bureau motto, "Fidelity, Bravery, Integrity." For now, I kept my badge and gun.

Downstairs, Venuti caught me walking toward the door and walked with me. He commented on the box tucked under my left arm.

"That's all you're taking? If I were you I'd clear everything and turn in my badge and gun."

"I'll turn them in after I'm fired."

"Save yourself a trip."

I stopped at the door and Venuti took a step back and put his hands on his hips.

"You're as good an investigator and bomb tech as I've ever met, Grale, but you've never been enough of a team player. If you'd done it right, you could have gotten yourself promoted today."

"And who would have spoken up for Beatty?"

"Beatty was a head case. He had trouble defining reality. Who quits one short of a thousand enemy kills? No one would, but your friend Beatty did."

I tried to understand where he was coming from with that. Why say it? I stood quiet a moment and thought about Jeremy. Among the definitions of a signature wound is moral injury. Grief plays in. Guilt. But not necessarily fear. Maybe I understood Beatty better than Dan. Maybe I shared something with him. Then I had another thought.

"He never really quit," I said.

"That's right, I forgot. He was medically discharged. They got rid of him."

"You still don't get it. He never quit. He crossed over a thousand kills yesterday protecting Creech Air Force Base. See you later, Dan."

That afternoon Julia and I put together her new bedroom and we picked a date for the memorial. Jo called to say her colleagues would cover her rounds for ten days, and the next morning the three of us packed and climbed into my old Jeep with Coal to start the long drive to Colorado and the little cabin Jim and I bought together so many years ago. Julia would get to see and stay in the cabin she'd heard about all her life but never been to.

Melissa wouldn't go there because the cabin needed so much work, but it would be fine for a week in July. It was outside of Ouray, not far from Telluride. It would be new country for Julia but connected to everything before. I watched Jo put on a baseball cap and glasses, and just before pulling away I turned and looked at Julia in the backseat with Coal leaning against her. She knew I was checking on her. She knew I knew how hard it was.

"You ready, Julia?"

"I'm ready."

"Then let's go."

Acknowledgments

Heartfelt thanks to my agent, Philip Spitzer, and to Lukas Ortiz, of the Spitzer Literary Agency. Concentration vanished after the death of my wife, Judy, in 2013. Philip's enthusiasm and confidence that he would sell this novel did much for me when I returned to writing and sent him this story. Thanks as well to former FBI agent and crime writer George Fong, and to John Tanza, also career FBI, now retired from the Las Vegas Field Office. Acquiring editor Jacquelyn Ben-Zekry of Thomas & Mercer hooked into the novel, bought it, and made it better, as did Peggy Hageman's knowing and insightful editing. Thank you Kevin Smith, and a nod to an old friend, fellow writer Tony Broadbent for those conversations long ago.

About the Author

Kirk Russell is the author of numerous thrillers and crime novels, including *Shell Games*, *Redback*, and *One Through the Heart*. His book *Dead Game* was named one of the top ten crime novels of 2005 by the American Library Association. Russell's novels have had numerous starred reviews. Among them, Library Journal referred to his *Counterfeit Road* as "an addictive police procedural on speed." Russell lives in Berkeley, California.